D0048747

PERSECUTION

ALSO BY

ALESSANDRO PIPERNO

The Worst Intentions

Alessandro Piperno

PERSECUTION
THE FRIENDLY FIRE OF MEMORIES

*Translated from the Italian
by Ann Goldstein*

Europa
editions

Europa Editions
214 West 29th Street
New York, N.Y. 10001
www.europaeditions.com
info@europaeditions.com

Copyright © 2010 by Arnoldo Mondadori Editore S.p.A., Milano
First Publication 2012 by Europa Editions

Translation by Ann Goldstein
Original title: *Persecuzione. Il fuoco amico dei ricordi*
Translation copyright © 2012 by Europa Editions

Library of Congress Cataloging in Publication Data is available
ISBN 978-1-60945-074-8

Piperno, Alessandro
Persecution

Book design by Emanuele Ragnisco
www.mekkanografici.com

Illustrations by Werther Dell'Edera

Cover photo © Henk Badenhorst/iStock Photo

Prepress by Grafica Punto Print – Rome

Printed in the USA

For Simona

Is it shamefastness or insensibleness
that makes *thee* silent?
—BOETHIUS, *The Consolation of Philosophy*

CONTENTS

PERSECUTION

PART I

On July 13, 1986, an embarrassing desire never to have been brought into the world took possession of Leo Pontecorvo.

A moment earlier, Filippo, his firstborn son, had been grappling with the pettiest of childhood complaints: protesting the tiny quantity of French fries that his mother had slid onto his plate compared with the unprecedented generosity she had shown his little brother. And now, an instant later, the anchorman on the eight-o'clock TV news was insinuating, before a sizable segment of the nation, that this very Leo Pontecorvo had exchanged depraved letters with the girlfriend of his thirteen-year-old younger son.

That is, that same Samuel, his plate filled with a crunchy gilded treasure that would never be consumed. Presumably unsure whether the sudden celebrity that the television had bestowed on him would be filed by his friends in the compartment of hilarious gossip or in the still empty compartment destined to receive the most unredeemable figure of shit that a boy from his spoiled and lazy tribe had ever run into.

It was pointless to pretend that Samuel's tender age kept him from intuiting what had been immediately clear to the others: someone on TV was suggesting that his father had fucked his girl. And when I say "girl" I mean a kid of twelve and a half with pumpkin-colored hair and a weaselly, freckled face. But when I say "fuck" I mean fuck. And so it was something huge, tremendously serious, too brutal to take in, even for a wife and two sons who, for some time already, had been asking themselves if that husband and father was really the irreproachable citizen whom it had always been natural to feel proud of.

The expression "for some time already" alludes to the first legal troubles that had hit Leo, imprinting with a despicable mark of suspicion the exemplary career of one of the boldest lions of pediatric oncology in the country. One of those doctors who, when the old nurse was filling in the picture for her newly hired colleague, merited comments like "a real gentleman! He never forgets to say 'thank you,' 'you're welcome,' 'please.' Plus, he's such a hunk!" On the other side, in the stifling waiting rooms of the Santa Cristina hospital, where the mothers of the sick children exchanged timid impressions about the nightmare that their offspring's childhood had become, it wasn't unusual to come upon such dialogues as: "He's so available. You can call him at any hour of the day. And also at night . . . "

"I find him reassuring. Always smiling, positive."

"And then he's so good with the children . . . "

While the ringing of the telephone began to give rhythm, expression, frenzy to a shame that until a few seconds earlier would have been inconceivable, Leo, at the height of confusion, felt that the meal just eaten was the last that his loved ones would grant him. Then he considered the thousand other things that from that moment on would be barred to him. And perhaps it was in order not to collapse, not to give way under the weight of panic and sentimentality, not to burst into tears like an infant in front of his children and his wife, that he took refuge in a petulant and hate-filled thought.

Finally she had done it: the girl whom his son had brought home about a year earlier—and whom he and Rachel, the most open and moderate couple in their circle, had welcomed without objections—had succeeded in destroying his life. His and that of the three people he loved most.

So is this how it has to end? Leo caught himself thinking.

Wrong question, old man. What's the sense of talking about the end when we're only at the beginning?

All this happened at a propitious moment.

The moment when Olgiata—that exclusive residential district set in acres of woods, dotted with villas, their gardens perennially in flower, and bounded by massive walls—suddenly emptied out. Like that, like a beach at sunset.

It was like being trapped in an immense amusement park a couple of minutes after closing time. Traces of the athletic energy so abundant during the day were scattered everywhere: the leather Adidas ball stuck in the hedge; the worn-out skateboard overturned on the brick driveway; the orange plastic float bobbing on the oily, sparkling surface of a pool; a pair of maxi rackets, watered by timed sprays set in motion without warning by a click.

Of course, you might also come upon the jogger, in sweat shorts, with a towel over his shoulders, like Rocky Balboa, or the young father returning breathless from the supermarket— a package of diapers in one hand, condoms in the other.

But except for these off-duty loners—these strike-breakers of the evening siesta—all the others had, almost in unison, holed up in their habitations: villas that were a jumble of inconsistent and eclectic architecture, some sober, others garish (the hacienda style had lately been replacing the fashion for alpine chalets). Seeing those houses from the outside, you could imagine the basement playrooms, where everything was as it should be: the fireplace, the baseboards nibbled by green mold, the crocheted doilies, the piles of illustrated magazines, the maple boxes full of lavender leaves, the billiard table tightly covered by a cloth, like a corpse in the morgue, a potbellied television from which the tentacular tangle of wires from the VHS and the Atari console unspooled. You could smell the fake country scent of the logs, of the pinecones, of the bundles of newspapers yellowing like the ping-pong balls hidden in the shadows, wary and motionless as detectives.

It was only an instant. An instant outside the galaxy. An instant of supernatural relaxation. The instant when the epiphany of family life celebrated daily in that district, twenty miles from the center of Rome, reached its apex. A truly touching moment, after which everything would start moving again, on the way to decline.

In a few minutes the inhabitants of Olgiata, orphaned by the Filipino maids, who were off duty on Sunday, would pour into the streets to occupy, in military fashion, with their very clean cars and their shameless vitality, the parking lots of the pizzerias on the outskirts. Because, despite the feeling of satiety inspired by the persistent odor of barbecue hovering in the air, they all intended to end the day with a flourish by gorging on tomato bruschetta and strawberries with cream.

But for now they were all at home. The younger children quarreling with their mothers because they didn't want to have a bath; the older ones being scolded because they'd been spending much too much time in the bathroom lately. As for the parents, some were in boxers and T-shirts relaxing beside the pool with a glass of Chardonnay, their legs crossed. Some couldn't stop teasing the ears of the Lab. Some had trouble abandoning the canasta game. Some were making snacks of olives and miniature hot dogs for the guests. Some were packing suitcases for distant journeys; others getting out their clothes for the next day . . . Everything was a promise, everything was enveloped in romantic expectation. The only anxiety was that produced by the fear of not tasting to the fullest the warm, coppery light of that special moment. Which this time, by sheer chance, coincided with the appearance of a photograph of Leo on television screens all tuned to the same channel (in those years the TV offerings were limited): grainy and pitiless, suspended over the right shoulder of the natty-looking anchorman on the eight-o'clock news.

A photo that did not do justice to our man. A photo that none of the people watching the screen who knew Professor Pontecorvo well would have considered faithful to the original. Part passport photo, part mug shot, it showed Leo looking yellowish and weary. Nothing like the man who, at the age of forty-eight, was traversing that happy period in the life of males where nature seems to have found a balance, as perfect as it is ephemeral, between youthful energy and mature virility. Even though the dorsal spine of that handsome, long-limbed man, after almost half a century of overwork, was curving under the two hundred pounds of a tall and in its way solemn body, it was still straight enough to allow Leo's figure to tower in all its vigorous authority.

Outside Italy the beauty of his face would have been called Italian. In Italy, on the other hand, it would have been dismissed as Middle Eastern. Curly hair similar to that of a walk-on in a film about the life of Moses; olive skin that on contact with sunlight immediately took on toasted tones; eyes of an elongated shape supplied with two precious green pearls; ears as robust as the nose (both paid fervent tribute to Judaism); and those lips—the secret was there, in those lips—voluptuous, ironic, pouting.

Here were the good things that that photo had been unable to take account of. (I knew Leo Pontecorvo well enough to be able to say that for him the tragedy of that appearance on TV was also a tragedy of vanity.)

And yet, all things considered, that unfaithful representation had a meaning. It expressed a threat. A qualitative leap in the bestiality of the aggression whose victim Leo had been for several weeks. And primarily it signified something very precise and extremely disturbing: this time Leo Pontecorvo could not and must not be deceived—he had to give up hope, expect no allowances. They would come as far as this to hunt him down, maybe that very evening. In the middle of a fierce and splendid summer. That was the meaning of that photograph. That was what that photograph—appearing brutally on the TV screen—was promising him.

They would chase him out of domestic intimacy by force, like a mouse from its hole. To let public resentment feed on him just as he was now: barefoot, in khaki Bermuda shorts and wrinkled blue shirt, disastrously perched on a stool in the elegant kitchen that looked out on a garden enjoying in blessed peace, like everything else out there, the last candied scraps of day.

No, they would not be intimidated by the dwelling that he, in due course, had had built in the lush belly of Olgiata, in the likeness of the human being that he wished to appear to be: sober, modern, eclectic, ironic, and above all transparent. The house of a designer rather than of a medical celebrity, whose massive plate-glass windows, especially at night when the lights were on, let you glimpse the comfortable life that was going on inside: a lack of modesty that Rachel—a woman not culturally equipped to live in a shop window—had done all she could to neutralize by means of heavy curtains, whose installation at the start of every autumn was the occasion of one of the most clas-sic conjugal arguments.

On the other hand, when Leo had decided to live there, in a place like that, in a house of that type, he had met with resist-ance far more authoritative than that presented by the curtains of his young and at least for now devoted consort.

"If only you would come with me . . . you'd realize that the place gives you such a sense of protection."

Those were the words that Leo recalled saying to his mother twenty years earlier on that fateful evening when he had communicated to her his intention of selling the apartment in the center of Rome that she had generously if incautiously put in his name, and buying a lot in Olgiata where he would build a "house just for us."

"And from what, exactly, would you need to be protected?"

Leo had perceived in his mother's voice a ripple of disappointment, an expression of that woman's increasing impatience with her only son: the *bechor* who, according to her, the older he got the less able he was to look after himself.

"I suppose it's your wife's idea?" She had laid it on. "Is she the one who put it into your head to go and live in the sticks? Another of her schemes to keep you a safe distance from me? She's the one who's trap-shooting with my money, with my patience, with my feelings?"

"Come on, Mamma. It's my idea. Leave Rachel out of it."

"Only when you can explain to me what sort of name Rachel is! It seems right out of the pages of the Bible . . . "

Was it possible that he, who had been seriously considered by rigorous committees, which had judged him fit for a prestigious post in the hospital; he, whose profession expected him to announce to distraught and incredulous parents that their children were as good as dead; he, who was capable of striking fear in students nearly his age, and whom many, even then, considered the designated heir of the academic domain belonging to the very powerful Professor Meyer—was it really *he*, here, who was still unable to stand up to a mother past sixty?

If he had been able to, of course, he would not have felt the need to communicate to her where he intended to live. If the apartment in the center was his, if she had deeded it to him, why go on and on like that? Why not sell it and be done with it? Why so childishly seek her consent? And why, in spite of knowing that he couldn't obtain it, and now that she had, in fact, refused it, was he incensed?

That woman's capacity to exasperate him. Her talent for driving him into a corner. For making him feel that he was the capricious son he had in fact never been. The charisma of that woman. The stubbornness. Her talent for interfering. Her indestructible, matronly conviction of being right. The whole seasoned with a sarcasm that in recent times—ever since her son had informed her, not without difficulty, that Rachel Spizzichino would soon be her daughter-in-law—had become extremely sharp.

That's how he had gotten caught up in this business of protection and security.

Pressed by his mother, who continued to ask for an account of his crazy idea of going to live "in the sticks," Leo had begun to mumble something pompous about the dangerous time they lived in, all that wretched political antagonism, about his old dream of living in a place that was green, about how he and his young wife already felt a responsibility toward the children they would have, and how that mania for protecting their young had been stimulated by a visit to the neighborhood, which was equipped with checkpoints, security guards, tall fences, green lawns, and sports facilities, all in the most absolute safety . . .

"If it's armed people and tall fences you're looking for, then you might as well go and live in Israel like that fanatical cousin of yours."

"A real earthly paradise, Mamma," Leo insisted, pretending not to have heard his mother's remark.

And the more Leo talked the more he stumbled, and the more he stumbled the more scornful his mother's face grew, hardening into an expression of impatient disgust. An expression full of haughty distrust that said clearly, in block letters:

THERE IS NO PLACE IN THE WORLD
THAT CAN GUARANTEE PROTECTION,
NOT TO YOU OR ANYONE ELSE.

And if Leo—while the news anchor, having launched his dirty bomb into the tidy kitchen of the Pontecorvo household, began talking about the fires that were devastating the Mediterranean scrub in Sardinia—had had the lucidity to think back now on that discussion with his mother of twenty years earlier, well, maybe in retrospect he would have appreciated the tacit and irrefutable way in which that woman, who had been gone for some time now, had tried to put him on his guard. Only now would Leo—with one foot in the grave and the other stuck in an uncertain and threatening terrain—have been able to understand how right his mother had been: there is not a single corner of the universe where a human being, that self-important and ridiculous entity, can call himself safe.

For one thing, the telephone is implacable, and has no intention of stopping. There are a lot of people outside who want to talk to the Pontecorvos about what's happening to the Pontecorvos. Strange, since the only thing that those who are inside can agree on is the desire to cut off all communication with the outside, for eternity. But why—if everything contained in the broad luminous space defined by the large windows of the house, by the hedge that marks the Pontecorvos' property, by the boundary walls of the subdivision is where (and as) it should be—does the rest of the planet seem to have gone mad?

In reality, if there is one thing that has been going mad for a while, well, it's the life of the Pontecorvos. Ever since the hospital unit that Leo had set up was dragged into a scandal involving bribes, inflated bills, beds sold, patients (all young people at the end of their lives) steered into private clinics by deception and for fraudulent reasons, things have been getting steadily worse. Each time taking an unpredictably sinister and increasingly less decent turn. At a certain point there were even insinuations that the success of Leo's university career derived from his Craxian sympathies (or, to be precise, from

Bettino Craxi's sympathy for him).[1] Then it was the turn of an assistant, in due course removed from the university for negligence, who, out of spite, accused Leo of having lent him money at the usurious interest rate of twenty percent.

And yet all those serious charges, which are jeopardizing his career, seem so venial beside this latest infamy. Maybe because there's nothing worse than Leo playing Cyrano de Bergerac with a twelve-year-old. What disgusting letters! Full of "my little one" and "dear child"—expressions of the sort that adults use in addressing consensual partners of the same age, but which here, precisely because they are appropriate to the age and stature of the recipient, seem revolting. The extensive, unseemly excerpts from that dreadful correspondence, which will soon occupy the most high-minded pages of the most important daily papers.

It seems, Leo, that you have violated the only taboo that people can't forgive. A twelve-year-old, good God. Having sex with a twelve-year-old. Seducing the girlfriend of your son. It's not at all a matter of sex. You know very well, no one today is ruined because of a fuck. In fact, if anything a fuck is often at the origin of great fortunes. The trouble is the age of the supposedly deflowered one. Right there is the difference.

At this point every one of your qualities as a sober and civilized man will, in the light of the crime they are sticking you with, be considered a sin or an aggravating cause. Every good thing you've ever done will from now on be considered the bizarre behavior of a pervert. Because no one on the outside will seriously question the plausibility of the charge. Rather, they will choose to believe this story precisely by virtue of its implausibility. That's how things function in our world. And

---

[1] Benedetto (Bettino) Craxi was an Italian politician, head of the Italian Socialist Party from 1976 to 1993, and the first Socialist Prime Minister of Italy, from 1983 to 1987.

just because people ask nothing better than to believe the worst, everything bad that is said about an individual (especially if he has had some lucky throws of the dice in the Monopoly of life) is immediately taken as true. That's how gossip turns homicidal. And the capillaries of the social organism swell almost to the point of bursting.

On the other hand, how could you ask the world to accept the fact that none of the three stricken people who are with you in the kitchen at this moment will ever learn to forgive you?

Samuel's labored breathing. A syncopated panting that has the slightly terrifying effect on Leo that turbulence causes in the passenger with a fear of flying. Leo thinks of the poisoned meatball he has served this boy. An entire nation that, starting tomorrow, will be gossiping about how your father fucked your girl. The kind of thing you don't recover from.

The suspension in which the kitchen hangs in those long seconds is broken by the burbling of the coffeepot, anxious to announce to those present that the coffee is ready, down to the last drop, and if no one decides to turn it off it will be unable to contain itself and will explode.

"Mamma, why don't you turn off the stove? Hey, Mamma, why don't you turn it off? Shouldn't we turn it off, Mamma?"

It's the voice of Filippo. Repulsively whiny. More childish than the person it belongs to. Leo would only like Rachel to make him be quiet. And it's what Rachel does, getting up like an automaton and turning the knob of the burner. Rachel. Holy God, Rachel. It's then that Leo remembers. It's then that he tries to imagine what is whirling around in her head. And it's at this very instant that the airplane plunges down.

Leo feels that he hates her as he has never hated anything else. He blames her for everything: for being there, and for not being there enough, for doing nothing but also for doing everything, for being silent, for breathing, for having set out such an appetizing dinner, for having turned on the TV to that particular channel, for the vice she has of watching ten news shows a day, for not getting up and answering the telephone, for having produced two sons whose presence now is so unbearable to him, for not making Filippo be quiet, for not rushing to help the catatonic Samuel . . .

It was she who instilled in the boys' minds the idea that he is a great man. How can this revered god declare his own fragility? How can he do the only thing he wants to do: break down in sobs? How can he justify himself by resorting to banal excuses, presenting himself in the incongruous guise of the victim of a gigantic mistake?

Because it is a mistake, isn't it? Leo no longer knows. At this moment he is confused. But yes, a mere glance at the letters in question—that he wrote and sent to Camilla (it's true, he can't deny it)—would reveal that they are the opposite of what they seem. No, my little one, your papa did not fuck your girl. If anything it was she who screwed your daddy!

Just as a mere glance at the accusations would be enough to observe that they are not the product of dishonesty but result from a mixture of foolishness and irresponsibility. This, at least, Rachel must know. She's aware of her husband's negligence. She's been complaining about it for a lifetime, often with tenderness, even. And yet she has done it in such a way that Filippo and Samuel could not begin to imagine it. You see? It's her fault. All Rachel's fault.

What is Leo doing? What he knows how to do best: blame others. Shift responsibility. In essence it's the same technique (revised and corrected) that, many years before, he adopted to defend himself against his mother's scolding.

When Signora Pontecorvo annoyed him, little Leo, in response, was offended. He put on a competing scowl. Until finally his mother, worn out by the blackmailing behavior of her little bear cub, gave in. Melting in a smile of reconciliation: "Come on, sweetheart, it's nothing. What do you say we make peace?"

Only then did our strategist give proof of his magnanimity by accepting his mother's apologies. Well, Leo managed to make this scenario a classic of his married life as well.

There must have been many who wondered how a man of the charm and background of Leo Pontecorvo could have married that common little Jewess. Whose reserve might be taken for apathy, and whose desire for invisibility might be confused with insipidness. Someone will ask how that fine, slender figure of a man, romantic as a Slavic pianist (unruly hair and tapering fingers), doctor and professor whom the white jacket suits, as a tuxedo does certain orchestra conductors, could have married the tiny and, at most, pretty Rachel Spizzichino.

From the outside their relationship is so unbalanced . . . their memories (their lives!) speak such different languages. Leo's languish in the solemn spaces of an apartment with high coffered ceilings, filled with heavy inlaid furniture, like mausoleums, and equipped with electrical appliances that no one could afford in those days.

As for Rachel, although a quarter century has passed, the bedroom where she spent the first twenty-five years of her life, studying hard, with the window facing on a narrow alley in the old Ghetto, continues to give off (even in memory) the odor of boiled, refried greens intolerable to her (and even more so in memory).

And yet what divided them then is precisely what unites them today. Because this is the secret of successful marriages, of couples who are happy in spite of everything: they never cease to be charmed by what is exotic in the other.

And then who would have suspected that between them things are not as they seem? That Leo is so afraid of his wife's opinion, and, at the same time, so dependent on her, on both practical and psychological levels, that he had reproduced with her the bond that for so many years ruled his relations with a hypochondriac and overprotective mother? No one on the outside could believe that this new Signora Pontecorvo plays a role in Leo's life not too dissimilar from the one played in her time by the old Signora Pontecorvo. That the new Signora Pontecorvo inherited from the old Signora Pontecorvo (who in fact was hostile to her, hostile as only certain Jewish mothers-in-law know how to be) a type of relationship based on the blackmail practiced by a talented and capriciously fragile boy?

Thus, when Rachel is angry at her husband, he doesn't know what to do except get angry back, with a sulky expression that from year to year grows only a little more ridiculous, until she, irritated by Leo's stubborn pout, which can last indefinitely, even for weeks, puts an end to the quarrel with a remark, a caress, a deliciously diplomatic gesture like offering him a bar of white chocolate, which he loves. In short: the wife gives proof of strength by showing herself yielding, while the husband betrays weakness by remaining faithful to his sulk, leaving her to initiate (only a child could consider it humiliating) a reconciliation.

The crisis set off by the television, besides, was only the latest—though it would turn out to be irremediable and definitive—in a series that had punctuated the past weeks. Ever since Leo, thanks to that fine collection of accusations, had begun to suffer from insomnia and Rachel to watch over him and reassure him like a little mamma. So their life had started to change.

Just that evening, shortly before turning on the TV, Rachel had ended a quarrel begun the night before, after Flavio and Rita Albertazzi—old friends—had left the Pontecorvo house.

It wasn't the first time that something *officially* pleasant like a dinner with the Albertazzis had presented Rachel and Leo with the pretext for a quarrel. But this time the subject of the argument seemed so painful, and had left in the air such a sense of bitterness and hostility, that Rachel had felt the need to bury the hatchet before she normally would.

"I've put something on to warm up in the kitchen. Why don't you come and eat?" So she had said going down to the basement study, where her husband had spent the Sunday listening to old Ray Charles records. Leo had put some time into lining his study-refuge with all those records. The jewel of the collection was, in fact, an assortment of Ray Charles LPs (including the rarest and hardest to find), toward which Leo felt a mystic gratitude. If only because it was a voice that had always been able to comfort him when he felt depressed or when things didn't go right.

"I don't feel like it, I'm not hungry," Leo had answered, lowering the volume of the stereo a couple of notches.

And then that little woman, counting on a sensuality you would not have attributed to her, embraced him tenderly, warmly from behind, and began to laugh and tease him.

"Come on, Pontecorvo, don't be like that, Semi is already there, Filippo is on his way . . . "

At intimate moments she called him by his last name, the way classmates do in school. Or otherwise "professor," a reminder of when he had been her teacher at the university. Yes, in other words, delightfully affectionate ways that for that sentimental fool were irresistible, no less than the nickname Little Bear Cub, which his mother used to call him.

"I'm coming, O.K., I'm putting old Ray to bed, then I'm coming," he had said, pervaded by the sweetness that comes only from forgiving one who has just forgiven you.

This exchange of remarks occurred more or less three-quarters of an hour before zero hour. Neither Rachel nor Leo could know that it would be the last gesture of peacemaking between a man and a woman who many years before had challenged the authority of two such different families in order to be together. The Montagues and Capulets of their generation!

Ah yes, because Leo and Rachel had overcome obstacles and challenges of every sort to consummate their contested conjugal dream, which, over time, and with the acquisition of that fine house, the birth of the children, his success at work and her impeccable household management, had grown increasingly brilliant. Nor could they know that the quarrel that Rachel had just resolved would close forever (and beautifully?) their history of altercations and reconciliations (the secret archeology of every marriage). Even less could they imagine, as they headed toward the kitchen, pushing and shoving each other affectionately like two fellow-soldiers on leave, that what they were about to consume but would not finish consuming was their last meal together, and that the words that they were about to address to each other were the last of their shared life.

In a few minutes everything would fall apart. And although from that day on Rachel chose not to speak to anyone about what happened—burying the story of her marriage in the mental storeroom assigned to clearance and oblivion—very often, after her husband's death, in the dreamlike conversation in which she could never succeed in keeping at bay the protests of that distant phantom, she would ask herself if maybe everything had begun the evening before, during the dinner with the Albertazzis: if the first splatters of slimy mud from the tidal wave that was about to sweep everything away had not reached them then. And if the Albertazzis were not in some way implicated in the calamity.

It couldn't be coincidental if, from that day on, and even more after Leo's death, Rachel no longer answered Rita's phone calls or Flavio's pompous letters, full of self-serving offers of help and friendship when it was too late. It was as if Rachel needed to blame them for what had happened to her. Having borne on her shoulders for such a long time the duties and responsibilities of a marriage that functioned in fits and starts (like every happy marriage), Rachel, now that it had ended wretchedly, moved to the counterattack: identifying in that pair of her husband's friends—who were so emblematic, and whom basically she had always hated—if not exactly the guilty ones then the first, unwelcome witnesses of the grotesque event that had transformed her life as a diligent chatelaine, sweetly lodged in the beautiful villa in Olgiata, into a real battle for survival.

Two witnesses, precisely.

Rita, who at first had done her utmost to make her husband break definitively with the pervert Leo, but who then, after his death, set herself up as the most devoted and fiercest guardian of his memory.

And Flavio, who let himself be dominated by the natural disaster he had married.

Two witnesses to eliminate, along with all the evidence for the prosecution and all the motives of a crime that she no longer wanted anything to do with. And only many years later would she settle accounts with them (from certain things you can't escape). But that's another story.

Flavio Albertazzi had been Leo's deskmate for all five years of high school. And he had quickly learned that the best way of exorcising the sense of inferiority produced in him by the affluence that his classmates wallowed in was to throw his poverty in their faces without holding back. If at the time that strategy had got him out of more than one embarrassment, now that, thanks to determination, self-denial, and powerful intellectual capacities, he had won an important place in society, which made his bank account fat and his social redemption exemplary, it had become a rather unbearable habit. Such, at least, Rachel considered it, having been brought up on the idea that hiding one's situation (whatever its nature) is always better than flaunting it.

The first time Flavio had showed up in class he was in short pants, so Leo, wearing a blue suit with crease and cuffs, felt that he had the right to ask him, "Why do you still wear short pants?," obtaining in response a sort of rhetorical question that had closed the subject for good: "Why don't you mind your own business?"

This exchange had taken place in the early fifties, and in the succeeding decades the two friends continued to recount it with great amusement. It produced in Rachel a series of questions about her husband: why was he so fond of a stupid anecdote that showed what an insufferable little snob he had been, and how his friend had so cleverly put him down? This, for Rachel, was only one of the many mysteries of that friendship of her husband's, which she, like many other wives of her generation, had learned to put up with.

Is it possible that Rachel saw what Leo didn't see? That in spite of all the time that had passed Flavio still treated him like a snotty little rich kid? There was something in her husband's ingenuousness that exasperated her. An exasperation sharpened by the fact that Leo, against all the evidence, saw himself as the shrewdest and most undeluded man in the universe. Whereas to his wife he seemed the most ingenuous.

It should be said that, for his part, Flavio had effortlessly let himself be seduced by his friend's social graces. The first time he set his large dusty shoes on the squeaking parquet of the Pontecorvo apartment he had wanted to believe that the fascination roused in him by his friend had nothing to do with the marble, the boiserie, the upholstery displayed in that dwelling but was provoked by the volumes collected in the bookshelves at the entrance. The conversational polish of which Leo gave precocious evidence, the eloquent language that Flavio so much envied, surely derived from that cultural bedrock, not from living in a world in which the functionality of a piece of furniture was obliged to find a polite compromise with two things as immoral as beauty and elegance.

After so many years Flavio still experienced as a personal victory the fact that his friend had decided to add to his medical profession a career as a scholar and academic that you would not have expected from that handsome, privileged, and indifferent youth.

"It's really incredible that you weren't spoiled by everything you had," he would say, with satisfaction, "and at a time when no one had anything." And Leo was pleased, with the satisfaction of someone who has never tried to be anything other than what, finally, he is.

For his part Leo had followed with equal gratification the route by which Flavio, the sixth and youngest son of a working-class family, had managed to acquire his own little place in the sun. He had been one of the first Italian graduates in information engineering (at the time it was called that), and was now the managing director of a leading-edge company that fine-tuned sophisticated programs for Olivetti.

Flavio, though he claimed to revere scientific progress no less fervently than Leo, nevertheless considered Italian society in those years to be in full *regression*. Affluence. Vulgarity. Lack of engagement. (TV, how he hated TV!) Those were the watchwords that Flavio used to excess and which provided the occasion for long, friendly disputes with Leo. Another thing that Flavio hated was the soccer championship that Italy had won a few years earlier in Spain, in which the Germans had been thrashed in a glorious final at the Santiago Bernabeu stadium, in Madrid. Flavio assigned that sporting event a symbolic power as vast as it was harmful.

"It gave the people of this country the illusion that winning is the important thing. It developed in us a cult of competitiveness and victory. It made us all a little bit American. To see a president of the Republic, a Socialist, someone who took part in the resistance, who risked his life to defeat Nazism, raise that utterly garish gold Cup, the golden fleece . . . An undignified spectacle. It doesn't surprise me that the final in Madrid was one of the most watched events in the history of Italian television. As you see, *tout se tient*."

So Leo, as much a soccer fan as a maniac about the modernization of the country, found himself passionately defending the heroes of Madrid and justifying TV. (How could he know that the latter would repay him so well?)

Flavio, unlike Leo, never raised his voice. He calmly wore you down, taking all the time he needed to complete arguments as rotund as his satisfied face. Faithful to Marxist principles, he was suspicious of everything and attacked his interlocutor with endless rhetorical questions.

But he, too, had a weak point.

Rita, his wife. Whom Flavio loved more than mathematics and more than those political ideas marked by what was in appearance pragmatism and in substance wishful thinking. A tall, curly-haired, angular woman, always on the edge of a nervous breakdown, whose brutal thinness contradicted a voracious gluttony. The slender cigarettes that she always had in her hand were aesthetically suited to her bony, tapering fingers. Sometimes, seeing her against the light, you would have said that it was a skeleton smoking. Other times, in the pitiless neon light of the Pontecorvos' kitchen, she might look like one of those madams painted by Toulouse-Lautrec.

For Rita, marrying Flavio had been a most successful slap in the face of her extremely wealthy parents. Although for years she had had no contact with her family—a dynasty that had turned a vast amount of land it owned on the edge of Rome into building lots and had made a lot of money—she nonetheless seemed to have inherited the arrogance of those speculators and their insupportable lack of tact. Her stinging arguments, unlike those of her husband, were sustained above all by the strength of her prejudices and the ferocity of her shattered nerves. The cunt, Leo sometimes thought. It's the cunt, the most capricious organ created by mother nature, that makes her speak.

Rita's indignation about inequality was a pretext for saying enormously unpleasant things in a strident, superior tone. For her there were no limits, maybe because to resist the family she came from she had had to lose control, or maybe because her family had taught her, by example, to have no boundaries. In her time she had studied literature, but without much direction. And she still boasted with impunity of how she had challenged a professor—a dusty, self-important academic—who inflicted on the students a class in Montale: a bourgeois, decadent, reactionary poet!

Rita recalled those exploits with bitter pleasure . . . the mark of a resentment that had in the end devoured her.

Rachel, less sociological-minded than the narrator of this tale, was sure that the great repressed grief agitating Rita's bony frame was the disappointment of not having had children.

"If she had had children," she said sometimes to her husband, "she wouldn't always be repeating those disgusting little stories."

Yes, children. Children, at least for Rachel, explained everything. This was the reason that, when the Albertazzis came to dinner at their house, Rachel kept Filippo and Samuel from even coming in to say hello, much less from being mentioned. She didn't want to inflict pain on Rita, or see her so-called friend exorcise her own sorrow by making hostile comments about Filippo's slight chubbiness or Samuel's effeminate passion for musicals. It was as if Rachel did her best to feel pity for that woman. Pity was the way she tried to keep at bay the irritation that Rita, in all of her manifestations, provoked. And the way in which she atoned for her unkind thoughts.

It had been difficult for Rachel to get used to these people, after Leo had isolated her from her upbringing. She remained traumatized by their cultural snobbery no less than by their political extremism. Rachel's father, Signor Spizzichino, was too busy getting ahead to cultivate political ideas. For him religion said nearly everything there was to know about what is right and what is not. And she had been brought up to believe that anyone who ran on about certain abstract ideas should be considered a fool. The word "Communist," in the Spizzichino household, was only slightly more acceptable than the word "Fascist," and only because the Communists, at least in Italy, hadn't persecuted the Jews (or, at least as far as the Spizzichinos knew, they hadn't), nor had they had the gall to ally themselves with Hitler.

If Rachel's distrust applied to all her husband's friends, it applied above all to Rita. There were too many self-serving inconsistencies in that woman not to irritate a simple and loyal being like Rachel. And she was often irritated with Leo, too, for his indulgence, his inability to be indignant in the face of certain obvious contradictions in the character and the behavior of his friend.

Rachel remembered the time Rita had made a scene in a restaurant because someone was allowed to bring his dog in. Rita, in those days, anyway, couldn't stand dogs. Or, rather, she was afraid of them. And so she had made a fuss: it was indecent, how could people, and what about respect, then? It had all been very unpleasant, including the no less violent reaction of the man with the dog.

Rachel couldn't bear situations of public embarrassment. She was a timid, reserved woman. If you wronged her, you couldn't expect a strident, or anyway explicit, retaliation. A restaurant manager had treated her discourteously? Well, he wouldn't see her in his restaurant anymore. And she couldn't forgive rudeness. To the point where, if her husband returned with her by mistake to a place that was on her black list, then, yes, she made a scene: but in order not to set foot in the place.

This was her intransigence about certain things. This her memory.

Otherwise she was ready to accept any abuse by a waiter, a client, or the proprietor of a restaurant. She was serenely tolerant of delays or carelessness in service. Of any unjustifiably astronomical bill. Anything was better than reacting. Than arguing. Than putting another human being in the state of feeling himself a reprobate.

She had a stinging memory of her father, who, after finishing a meal in a restaurant, would sit there, with his shopkeeper's glasses, analyzing the bill, item by item. Not to mention the times when, finding some error, he called over the owner and, with ill grace, pointed it out. From then on Rachel had vowed to herself: never again. Never again will I be present at those scenes. Never feel that mortification. Never again will I be humiliated and never again will I humiliate.

A vow that she had been able to keep until Rita entered her life. A kind of troublemaker. Someone who loved to argue. Who adored calling attention to the inadequacies of her neighbor. Just like that time with the man and the dog.

"Does it seem possible?" she had said in a loud voice. "Does it seem to you possible that someone is so rude that he brings a dog into a restaurant? What sort of upbringing is that? I cannot understand what goes through people's minds . . . Is no one going say anything to him?" And, not satisfied, she added, a few seconds later—carefully raising her voice by some decibels—"I would advise everyone here not to set foot in this restaurant ever again!"

The problem was that that time Rita had met her match (there are a lot of them out there), and he had responded angrily: "Instead of making a scene, couldn't you ask me politely to take my dog out?"

"Am I talking to you? I don't think so. I was talking to my friends. But since you have spoken to me, then let me tell you that you are rude. A real boor. Worse than almost anyone I've ever met." In order not to let things degenerate further Flavio and Leo had intervened.

In all this there would basically have been nothing different from the usual.

Except that fate willed that some years after that episode in the restaurant, Rita (now condemned by life not to have children) had received as a gift from her sister an English sheepdog puppy. After her initial bewilderment, and, especially, after a few days of being forced to live with the tender young pup, she had become attached to that creature with all her heart. Her old fear of animals in general and dogs in particular was immediately left behind. From that day on, she and Giorgia (that was the dog's name) were inseparable. Rita was much more preoccupied with Giorgia's food, Giorgia's well-being, Giorgia's health than Rachel was about her boys. The morbidity of her affection led her to take the dog wherever she went. She didn't trust leaving her alone, so she brought her even to restaurants.

Usually people were more understanding of her than she was of them, but once a woman who was allergic had had a waiter ask Rita if she could take Giorgia outside. They were at the club in Olgiata, having dinner in the clubhouse. It was pouring rain. At the request to take Giorgia out, and at the sight of the storm, Rita lost control. And in a dramatic tone of voice she began to intone: "I wonder how people can be so cruel. As for certain people, I would make them stay out in the rain. Ah, the cruelty of people."

Giorgia had already been outside for several minutes, wearily curled up under the restaurant's awning, with her gaze turned to her mistress, who was eating on the other side of the glass, while the mistress wouldn't stop commenting in a loud voice on the arrogance with which the woman had insisted that her Giorgia—the most exceptional being, the best, the sweetest ("the cleanest in this filthy restaurant") she had ever known—be expelled, "like a Jew."

"How can that woman always act like that?" Rachel had burst out that night while Leo, with some vanity, was undressing in front of the mirror in the little dressing room opposite the bedroom. "Until two years ago she couldn't imagine that someone could even conceive of bringing a dog to a restaurant. You remember the scene she made? Now, instead, people who won't let dogs in are cruel. Only because now the dog that has to stay outside is hers. But does it seem to you consistent?"

"Certainly no one makes you as angry as Rita," her temperate husband had commented.

"Yes, her shamelessness makes me angry. Her arrogance. Her failure to remember. The capacity to adapt to any situation at her own convenience. Her way of systematically denying the truth. Her insistence on being always right . . . And that business of the Jews. How can she dare compare the tragedy of the Jews to the most spoiled dog in the galaxy?"

Leo knew that Rachel was right. He had known Rita for so many years! And he knew that she belonged to that rather large portion of humanity that molds its principles to its own conveniences, that lacks the moral force that pushes people like Rachel to do the exact opposite. You had been a pain in the ass to the entire world over the fact that dogs should not be brought to a restaurant? Well, this should have acted as a deterrent to bringing your dog, should you someday have one, to a restaurant for the rest of your life.

But your name wasn't Rita Albertazzi. If that was your name, you did only and exactly what seemed to you easiest at that precise instant. And, convinced that you could boast of a kind of universal credit with the world, you felt you were authorized to judge anyone who placed himself in your way as an enemy, to insult, to push aside, to destroy.

And, speaking of convictions, the more Rita emphasized her own, bestowing on them the sanction of inviolability, the less respect she showed for those of others.

Among all the people (whether Catholic or secular) whom Leo had compelled his wife to be friendly with, and who regarded their Judaism with a feeling somewhere between curiosity, irony, and suspicion, Rita was the one most inclined to allow herself, on the Jewish question, to express value judgments.

One day she called Rachel to ask if she and Leo were free for Tuesday evening. She had invited to dinner some people who would love to meet Leo. In those years he had earned a small reputation that Rita was not at all insensitive to, being attracted by any form of celebrity, even the most obscure. Although she lived under the illusion of having rid herself of every attitude impressed in her by her so volubly hated family, in reality she had inherited both the pleasure in and the talent for gathering at her house those whom she called, emphatically, "serious people." It's irrelevant that the relationships of her detested parents were based on economic convenience, and hers, instead, on political, artistic, and intellectual prestige.

She attached particular importance to that evening. There was a name director. An eminent editorial writer. And in particular the Hungarian ambassador ("a magnificent person, polyglot, a cultivated and tormented Communist, not like our pissants": so she had described him, with the pomposity she always used in discussing "serious people"). In short: Rita wanted to introduce Leo to these personalities and these personalities to Leo. Ever since he had started writing a column in the *Corriere* entitled "Prevention Is the Best Medicine," Leo had been a star among the imaginary sick people of the country.

Rita always called Rachel when she made these invitations. And Rachel had the impression that she was being treated like a sort of press office, whose only function is to throw a wrench in the works of those who wish to become famous. Rachel knew that Rita was at the top of the list of people who, on the subject of the marriage between her and Leo, wondered how a man like that had come to marry a woman like that. If, for example, Leo had showed up at that dinner without Rachel, Rita would not even have noticed, but if the opposite had happened . . . well, if the opposite happened Rita would have had to restrain herself from kicking Rachel out of the house. She would have felt like a head of state who, having invited to his country another head of state, goes to the airport to welcome him and sees descending the steps of the plane only an obscure private secretary.

"Unfortunately Tuesday we can't," Rachel had said that time.

"And why not?" Rita had asked, in the voice of a woman who is about to drown in a lake and begs you to help her and you refuse because you're playing cards.

"It's Yom Kippur."

"So what?"

"So we can't go out, we can't eat, we can't do anything, in other words."

"Yes, but, sorry . . . the invitation is for the evening."

"I know. But Yom Kippur lasts a whole day. For twenty-six hours."

Rachel didn't even know why she was giving so many explanations. Her religion was not something she liked to talk about. Her husband did. Leo always had his mouth full of big fancy words like "the people of the Book," "the marriage between the chosen people and the French Revolution." If only her husband had respected Mosaic law with the conviction with which he spouted off about the importance of Jewish culture, he would have been the most pious man in the world. But Rachel preferred to refrain from talking about it. If there was a lesson she had learned from her family, that her father had instilled in her, it is that certain things are not talked about. Above all with those who don't belong to the "milieu" (this was the euphemistic expression by which Rachel's father referred to the Jews). But this time, who knows why (certainly because of the effect that woman had on her), Rachel was *explaining* more than necessary and this made her irritated with herself. And she was about to be punished for the excess of explanations she had provided.

"Come on, what sort of nonsense is that? For once! It's important. I don't think your Yom Kippur will interest the ambassador. He comes from a Communist country, where they've abolished certain types of nonsense."

"But it's of interest to us."

"To you? You must mean of interest to *you*. Your husband finds such superstitions laughable. At least leave him the right to live his life as he pleases."

"I don't oblige him to do anything."

You see? That woman always forced you to be on the defensive. Her inappropriately inquisitive manner pushed you to give explanations that you didn't want to give and shouldn't have to.

"Doesn't it seem to you crazy, anachronistic, tribal?"

"What are you talking about?"

"This business of Yom Kippur . . . Surely it's time to dispose of certain . . . "

"Listen, Rita . . . " This time her voice trembled. Knowing that she was one of those people who are very slow to get angry but whose anger when they do lose patience takes a strident and inappropriate form, Rachel was doing her utmost not to explode. And yet she felt, just from the trembling in her own voice, that she was at her limit. But even before she could say to Rita what she had wanted to say to her for a long time—and that is that she must not dare to enter into her and Leo's decisions, that she must not allow herself to speak in that contemptuous way about something as fundamental to her as Yom Kippur, that she had to stop being so meddlesome and inappropriate, that she had to stop treating her like a troglodyte—lo and behold, the other, with the intuition typical of women used to total freedom of expression but capable of understanding from the tone of their interlocutor when they have gone too far, backed off. (Like all really arrogant people, Rita was a coward.) Naturally she didn't ask her pardon, but she began to apologize in a way that was even more annoying:

"O.K., don't come. I understand. If for you and Leo it's important . . . But let me say that I'm sorry for you. This was a great opportunity for your husband. I won't tell you that I organized the dinner for him, but practically. You know, it's not enough to have a reputation as a great doctor. It's not enough to have in the papers *certain* columns that are just a bit, at least for my taste, too popular. You have to make connections"—Rita would never have used the word "relationships," or, still less, "friendships." "I think the Hungarian ambassador would have offered him new possibilities. Like doing a round of conferences in Budapest. A big thing. Something that could change a man's career."

Here is Rita's repertoire at its best: rousing in you a sense of guilt. Loading you with her sufferings and her failures. Embarrassing you for your presumed inadequacy. Trying to persuade you (what impudence!) that she's doing you a favor at the moment when you should be doing her one. Putting on the guise of a disinterested benefactor just at the moment when her opportunism is hitting a new record.

And then Rachel couldn't bear all that flaunted distrust. Rita's suspiciousness was wearing. Although Rachel came from a world in which a general distrust of one's neighbor was the rule, she couldn't understand how a woman of Rita's background could be so constantly on her guard. Rita lived in terror that someone wanted to cheat her. Like the time Rachel had gone shopping with her one afternoon: in January, when the sales were on. A nightmare. Not once had Rita left a shop without one of her nasty remarks. "I remember," she had said to a saleswoman, "that these shoes, without a discount, were the exact same price last month."

"It's a matter of principle," she had said, in self-defense, observing Rachel's dismay and irritation after yet another of these conversations. "I can't bear it when people try to put one over on me."

The fact is that she started from the assumption that the country in which she happened to be born and the city in which she lived were the emblem of all that is dirty and crooked. To the point where she could say that matters of principle were for her a sort of standard with which to defend herself from all the violence she had felt besieged by from birth.

This distrust of one's neighbor seemed to Rachel in permanent conflict with the note of sentimentality that warmed Rita's voice when, during her political rants, she talked about "the people." As if the word "people" did not include the abnormal number of people despised and reviled by her, as if those waiters and those shoe salesmen whom she accused of baseness and iniquity did not belong to the "people." For her the "people" were a kind of metaphysical abstraction to idolize, and not something for which there existed an earthly equivalent, which was very often smelly and untrustworthy.

"Why does she always talk with such ecstasy about the people in general and so badly of all people in particular?" Rachel asked her husband, exasperated by the long dinners with the Albertazzis.

"Because she's a Communist," he responded concisely.

In the end Rachel, because of her love for Leo and because of the modesty that led her to love what he loved and desire what he desired, had grown affectionate toward Rita and her pedantic consort. Driven more by tolerance than by regard, more by understanding than by sympathy, she had ended by considering that couple of her husband's friends one of the reassuring habits on which every bourgeois marriage can count. At a certain point, unable to find truly admirable qualities in them, she had become attached to their flaws.

Of course, she continued to control the desire to yawn whenever Flavio ventured into his love-of-humanity digressions, just as she persisted in finding Rita's scenes with restaurant managers and shoe salesmen insufferable, but she accepted these things with the patience with which she tolerated certain flaws in her husband, her children, life, the world. In time she had learned to avoid particular conversations, above all political: no, she would no longer be accused of being reactionary just because she said sensible things.

Whenever the Albertazzis came to dinner she had Telma (guardian at that time of the recipes of the Pontecorvo household) prepare a *torta caprese*, the flourless chocolate cake that Flavio was mad for, and *concia*, the traditional Roman Jewish zucchini dish, and the tomatoes with rice that Rita loved. Yet she prevented this same maid from appearing in the dining room, in order not to hear Rita say, "How can you let yourself be served like this, by another human being? How can you not ask her to sit down with you?" Rachel, knowing that she would never get used to phrases of this type, managed not to provoke them.

Just on the wave of all this, that Saturday, a few hours before the final crash, and maybe precisely because of a kind of foresightedness, Rachel had done her best to keep the Albertazzis from coming to dinner. Not that she was annoyed with them for any reason in particular. Yet she felt a certain embarrassment in having to face the subject of the legal documents that Leo had received, not to mention the newspaper articles that mentioned him. It couldn't be a coincidence if Rita had telephoned more than usual recently. It was clear that she wanted to interfere: the reason she kept her on the telephone for so long, even in silence—after receiving all the confidences she could, except what really interested her—was the hope that Rachel would break her oath of loyalty and vent. It was clear that Rita hoped her friend would give at least a little evidence of her anxiety, and complain a little if not actually cry. A satisfaction that Rachel was naturally very careful not to give her.

But that evening? Lord, that evening loomed as a nightmare. Would she be capable of suppressing her anguish in front of that hyena Rita? Would she keep from falling into a trap? Well, she herself yes, maybe. But Leo? You couldn't rely on him. Let's suppose even that Leo controlled himself and that Flavio (the trusted friend) respected his choice of reserve, how could you expect that Rita would manage to hold back? It was in her livid nature to let a troublesome comment slip out.

Rachel remembered an anecdote that Leo, not without amusement, had told her. Of how, many years before, Rita had invited to a restaurant a select group of friends to celebrate her father's first conviction. "They gave him three years, that son of a bitch," she kept saying, as she got drunker and drunker. Laying it on thicker: "Maybe this country is beginning to understand something. Maybe this country is beginning to redeem itself!" Until, finally, she invited her friends to make a toast: "At last they're starting to realize what sort of criminal they're dealing with."

"And why," Rachel asked every time, "did you all go along with such a disgusting scene?"

"You know, my love, it was that atmosphere, those years. Parents were the enemy. The great oppressors. Apart from your family, which anachronistically loved its old people, and had a lot of pious old Jews you could respect, in the rest of the world it was considered a very serious sin to be old. Paris, Berkeley, Valle Giulia: we were preparing for that, I don't know if you understand . . . Rita had taken that bullshit literally. And of course her parents were easy to demonize."

That story, so entertaining to Leo, had never amused Rachel. She might be a Jewish blockhead, from a family that "loved old people," as Leo said, but she really couldn't understand how someone could celebrate because her father had gone to jail. It might be that Rachel adored her father and had done everything she could to make him happy, but the idea that a daughter who had, after all, been given so many opportunities by her parents could harbor mean and hateful feelings toward them, and display them so brazenly, seemed to her a pathology that she wanted nothing to do with.

That was why, given her record, and considering the avalanche of phone calls in the preceding days, the least she could expect that evening from someone who with her friends had toasted the imprisonment of her own father was that she would ask some impertinent question.

One of the things that Rachel had never got used to—having entered, by her marriage, a higher social milieu than the one she came from—was the nearly complete absence of reserve. These people had no boundaries, no sense of shame. There was nothing they didn't feel authorized to joke about. In the early years of her marriage she had swallowed the tale that such a lack of hypocrisy was a way of declaring one's freedom with respect to certain petty-bourgeois conventions in which she had been trapped by a traditional upbringing. She had gone so far as to ask herself if that tell-all, that don't-hide-anything, was not a refinement that her background didn't allow her to grasp. Very often she had looked at her husband with amazement as he lightheartedly revealed a family secret. Other times she had been openmouthed while he said to whoever he was talking to exactly what was going through his mind.

Until she had finally understood that all this was not for her. That she would not get used to such an attitude. Because she didn't like it. Serious things, by their nature, should be handled with tact and circumspection, not become the subject of yet another amusing little story to share with friends, or to spill in front of strangers, simply because no discretion will ever have the fascination of a witty confession. For Rachel it was better to have many secrets than to have none. On the other hand, that continual confusion between what was serious and what wasn't, that mixture of the sayable and the unsayable, had made these people lose any sense of priorities. Too often their taste for wit meant that they didn't take into account the susceptibilities of others.

Rachel recalled with irritation and regret the occasion when the man who was then her future husband had, without realizing it, humiliated his girlfriend's cousin. Leo and Rachel barely knew each other. He was the arrogant, irresistible assistant of Professor Meyer, and Rachel the lively, passionate student whom Leo, after giving her an exam and awarding her the highest mark, which she well deserved, had asked on a date. A relationship that was opposed, especially at the beginning, by Rachel's father, who, faithful to a practice already quite anachronistic at the time, had demanded that when his daughter and that "professor" went out Sara, Rachel's little cousin, should be present as a silent and embarrassed chaperone. As a result Leo found himself paying for dinner and a movie for his girlfriend and the cousin of his girlfriend. Once, out of either irritation at the situation or a pure taste for fun, Leo, after paying yet another bill at a seaside restaurant, near Fregene, had asked Sara: "Listen, I've noticed that you don't even make a move to pay. Are you just miserly or are you really poor?"

What the trembling and devastated Sara couldn't know was that in the playful vocabulary of the Pontecorvos the word "miserly" designated those persons, very numerous in their world, who, even though they could count on a large inheritance, lived at the edge of indigence out of pure stinginess. Not grasping this lexical shading, Sara began to cry. And for days Rachel wouldn't answer Leo's phone calls. And then asked him, sometime later, having granted the desired pardon, "How could you be so cruel? How can you humiliate someone that way?"

"It was only a joke. Christ, you people from the slums are so sensitive! What's this taking everything seriously? If you want I'll apologize, but I swear to you that insulting her was the last thing I intended."

"You see? That's what I'm saying: you give no weight to words. And so in your view I'm someone from the slums?"

"Come on, sweetie, I was joking."

"Will the day ever come when you stop joking?"

Now, twenty years later, that day had arrived. But Rachel wasn't sure that Leo realized it: she suspected that, over the years, what had at first appeared a simple inclination to playfulness had become a modus operandi that Leo and all his friends used to avoid serious problems, or to speciously minimize them.

There would have been nothing wrong with this if something really serious wasn't happening to him, and if, precisely because of that blowhard spirit, he didn't recognize it as such (or at least pretended not to recognize it).

In fact, although Rachel knew how upset her husband was, literally, by the notifications of criminal proceedings he had received, she knew him too well to be surprised at the fact that he talked about it lightheartedly. That was how he managed anguish in public and in private: by deliberately underestimating its causes. And, if necessary, joking about it. For this reason, although she was aware that at night Leo suffered from insomnia and during the day started at every noise, as if he were afraid of being attacked, Rachel had to pretend to believe her husband's clumsy performance, as he cheerfully professed to be indifferent and hopeful. God only knew how much she would have liked to shake him. Tell him that the situation was serious, yes, but not irreparable. He just had to act like a man, and stop being a wise guy.

Like the morning a few days before, when he had started off during breakfast making fun at Filippo's expense: who, his lips stained with chocolate milk, had asked if it was his father's turn to take him to school. And Leo, the day after receiving yet another notification from the court, had said, "So, little rascal, you feel like driving with a dangerous criminal?"

Well, probably at that point the boys knew, or imagined, especially Filippo. (A few days earlier he had asked Rachel a question. Evidently a classmate had said something to him.) Although Rachel from the beginning had been in favor of keeping them out of the whole revolting mess, it was impossible that they wouldn't hear about it. But what need was there for such remarks? What pleasure could there be in making two boys share his legal troubles, and doing so by means of jokes with excruciating hidden meanings (and not funny, besides) that, just because of the ambiguity, would upset them? But the truth is that, in spite of appearances and his stated intentions, Leo *wanted* to upset them, just as he wanted to upset her. And simply because, being upset himself and unable to admit it, he wished to unload all that anxiety on those closest to him. So when Filippo asked him, worried, "Why did you say that?," he defended himself with one of those remarks that seem made to reassure you but which have the opposite effect: "Nothing, nothing, I'm joking. Everything's fine."

Her husband's bad faith (which irritated her) manifested itself precisely through such performances. Someone who pretends to make light of things at the very moment when that type of behavior makes the situation unbearable. Just as he raises the limit of what's bearable another notch. He pretends to be detached while he's right in the middle. He pretends not to think about it but all he does is brood. He pretends not to be ashamed but he can't sleep at night because of his shame. He pretends not to be afraid and he's pissing in his pants.

In other words, given the circumstances, the only thing missing was Flavio and Rita. An evening with their most dangerous, most unpredictable friends. Which announced itself as pestilential. And Rachel didn't know whether to be more on her guard against Leo or against the two of them: she was sure, however, that someone would make a scene, and this she had to avoid. No, she wasn't ready for that sort of evening. And that was why, that very Saturday morning, when there was still time to cancel the whole thing, she had asked Leo if it wouldn't make sense to put it off. She would take care of it. He wouldn't have to do anything. She would call Rita to—

"Why would you do that?"

"Well, you know, mostly because I'm quite tired, I didn't sleep last night. Then because Telma doesn't feel well today. I don't really want to ask her to cook."

"What's wrong? Fever? Usual sore throat? Want me to take a look at her?," as if Telma were a broken appliance or a horse with tendinitis.

"No, no, she just doesn't feel well . . . female trouble . . . "

"She's a grownup woman, she must be used to it. It's not something that's ever kept her from doing her job."

"Well, this time . . . "

"This time what?"

"She seems more tired than usual."

"Did she say anything to you? Did she complain? Did she say she doesn't feel like cooking?"

"But use your head, do you think she would say something?"

"But you, with your extraordinary intuition . . . "

"I understand certain things. She's exhausted. You know how she suffers in the heat. And then, excuse me, aren't you tired of having people to dinner almost every night? For weeks all you've been doing is inviting people over. If for once . . . "

"And what do you mean by that?"

"What I said. That for weeks all you've done is invite whoever to dinner. It almost seems as if you didn't want to be alone with me and the boys. As if we weren't enough for you."

"And why would I do that?"

"I have no idea. Maybe I'm simply making the observation of a wife who feels neglected . . . Come on, I'm joking. I know you adore having people over. And I like to make you happy. I know that in summer you like to eat outside, white wine, sliced peaches . . . and within the limits of the possible I do my best . . . "

"Please don't start in with the shopping list of things you do for me. What's the matter? Get to the point. Why are our dearest friends, whom we haven't seen for ages, today not right? Why don't you want them here?"

"I don't know what you're talking about."

"You know perfectly well. And you know that the heat has nothing to do with it, any more than the *khaver's* menstrual cycle."

"Don't be vulgar, please. That I can't bear. Anyway, if you want to know what I really think . . . well, the truth is, I think the reason you want to have people for dinner every night is to demonstrate to the world that our recent troubles haven't affected you at all . . . And it's the same reason that, during these dinners, all you do is talk, laugh, joke about it. You've also started to drink more than necessary, and you've never done that. The message is: 'Look, Professor Pontecorvo is fine. He's the same as usual. He's indestructible.' "

"So the *khaver's* menstrual period is merely a pretext invented by a responsible wife to protect her desperate alcoholic husband from himself. A husband who, as I see it, she is somewhat ashamed of."

"Don't be dramatic."

"You're the one who's making up fantastic stories in order not to tell me what you think, and then I'm the dramatist?"

"And if I said that I'm not just thinking of you, I'm also thinking of myself? Tonight I feel like anything but having dinner with that woman who will gloat about what's happening to us."

" 'That woman'? 'Gloat'? So is that what you think of her? Some woman who gloats? I'm amazed that you've agreed to be friends with such a bitch for all these years."

"It wouldn't be a novelty for someone who celebrates her father's three-year jail sentence. Think what a marvelous party she'd have if they gave him life, poor man."

"Apart from the fact that there exists no more inappropriate word for Rita's father than 'poor man,' I assure you that you are mistaken. Rita loves me, Rita loves us. Not to mention Flavio. He's the only friend I totally trust. One who would do anything he could for me. It would be insulting to him if at a moment like this I excluded him."

"Ah, and this is your biggest worry? The offensiveness of excluding a friend?"

"I didn't say *only* for that. I said *also* for that. And then just let Rita try . . . "

"And if she does?"

"I'll make her shape up, God damn it . . . but it won't happen. Flavio and Rita know me too well not to know that there's no basis for any of the things I've been accused of."

"So that's it . . . "

"That's what?"

"If you really think that, if you're so sure you're right—and I am, too, dearest, I swear—why do I have the impression that you aren't doing everything necessary?"

"NECESSARY FOR WHAT?"

"No, listen, if you're going to start shouting let's end the discussion."

"O.K., I'm calm. I won't raise my voice again. Tell me, explain: I haven't done what's necessary for what?"

"You're not taking this seriously, my love. It's the same old story. If you're in this situation it's partly because you've had too much faith in others. And now it strikes me that you haven't learned your lesson. That you continue to put too much trust in others. Which is admirable. It makes you a wonderful man. But it's also dangerous and not practical. You put too much faith in your neighbor. Too much faith in truth. I've told you a thousand times. You're the most optimistic man I know. Your kindness, your good faith are admirable . . . "

"And how do you think the honest man you're describing, that type of good-hearted idiot, could have accomplished all he has accomplished in life?"

"Leo, dearest, what does that have to do with it? I know you have no equal in your work. I understood it from the way you taught when I met you. Passion, intuition, expertise. You unfolded for us the mysteries of human physiology so magically. My friends were all in love with you. I still have a hard time believing that I was chosen by the young, incredibly handsome, unapproachable Professor Pontecorvo . . . And something tells me you chose me just because I was the one who had the least hope. But that doesn't mean you're just as good at managing everything else . . . I really get the impression that for some reason you are underestimating this situation. And that you've left me out of the whole business. Why don't you let me in? Why don't you let me help? What's the matter this time? I've always taken care of you, full time, why this time no? Why did you keep me from going to the lawyer the other day? You don't know how it pains me to be excluded. Not to know."

"Listen, whatever you may think, I'm neither stupid nor

naïve nor irresponsible. The lawyer for Santa Cristina is an excellent lawyer. And he has reassured me in every way."

"That's just what I'm saying! How can you not understand that your interests are in conflict with the hospital's? And that if necessary they'll not only get rid of you but do it so as to pin all the responsibility on you?"

"You see how you are? Same thing. You get so angry at Rita. But now who's being mean, now who's nasty-minded and suspicious? And then what do you know about it? I have the entire hospital on my side. A stack of parents of former patients who have come forward to testify on my behalf. I have the president of the faculty who has publicly defended me, in more than one newspaper . . . not to mention the college of docents, and even the rector . . . It's not my fault if all this keeps me calm. Or if it's a moment when I want my friends around . . . "

Yes, that was him, her Leo, the least malicious man she had ever met. What a strange talent, to have so much faith in others! But was it only a talent? Or also an extremely grave defect? Something to guard against? Her husband's magnanimity (some would have given it a different name, much more trivial). The disadvantage of not knowing what defeat is. Of not having lived as a loser. Exaggerated faith in the benevolence of destiny.

Well, she had been brought up in terror. The reason she had so disliked Rita the first times she met her was that she seemed the extreme version of herself, transported, besides, into higher-class locales. All that distrust, all that circumspection, all that fear. They were things that Rachel knew. Things that had been inculcated from the cradle. To the point where at times she wondered if among the many reasons she loved her husband so intensely was the fact that he seemed a sort of delightful, bracing antidote to all that fear she had grown up in.

It was as if her husband, who by profession joined battle

daily with the irrational, perverse, and usually evil whims of the human body, when it came to grabbing the reins of his own life, gave in to a sort of philanthropic idealism. How was it possible? Had his work taught him nothing? Is there a harsher lesson than the one imparted by a ward where children fight against death? Dirty beds, vomit, blood, all that childish pain and adult despair . . . But evidently this had taught him nothing. Evidently this was not for him proof of anything. Evidently all this had not made him wiser or injected him with the cynicism that aided the majority of his colleagues.

You would say that of the two of them it was he who loved to play the part of the plain man without God: always full of words that to Rachel were pompous and empty of meaning, words like "Laicism," "enlightenment," "agnosticism." And yet, if you looked closely, he was the true religious one in the family. Of the two of them, only he truly believed in a kind of Higher Order, for the most part benign, capable of setting everything right.

"Ultimately, in the end the Nazis lost. The Nazis always lose," he pointed out to her every so often when she told him there were more anti-Semites around than he thought. (And Rachel couldn't help wondering: Really? Did the Nazis lose? But how? Aren't we the ones who lost?)

And now, with respect to the horrible things that had been written about him and the crimes attributed to him, it was as if Leo were content with the certainty that he hadn't committed them. Or at least not deliberately. In his view this was sufficient. Because in the end the truth would emerge without impediments.

More and more often his wife wondered if this unconditional trust in the world had to do with a life that had functioned too well: a fairy tale of dreams realized and promises kept. Ultimately, if there's something that's always in danger it's perfection.

The Pontecorvos were the only Jews she knew who, while Hitler's thugs and their stupid German shepherds were hunting Jews throughout Europe, stayed in Switzerland, in safety, in warmth, without dying of fear like all the others, like Rachel's mother and father. Leo was three at the time. And from that lucky Swiss start in life things had continued to go well. A charmed childhood and adolescence, protected by an idolizing mother and consecrated by a dazzling path of studies that guaranteed him a marvelous career in the family profession, and carried him to a level until then never reached by any Pontecorvo. If you took the Pontecorvos as a sample, life— with its kind and painless passage from one generation to the next—seemed an inexorable ascent toward well-being and happiness.

Was it this? This endless winning that had damaged him? Was it this effortless progress, this resemblance to Gladstone Gander, Donald Duck's cousin, that had made him so weak in the face of adversity? Was it the idea, in essence so virtuous, that in life if you only do things well you'll achieve the best that was now paralyzing him? Was this how her husband, after abolishing from his life the very idea of the unpredictable, reacted to the unimaginably malicious?

On that subject, Rachel would always tell Filippo and Samuel a story that seemed to her emblematic of both Leo's character and her own.

On their honeymoon they had toured Scandinavia by car. Rachel recalled those days with emotion. She was just twenty-five, it was the first time she had set foot outside Italy. And that she was doing so with her twenty-nine-year-old husband, whom she was in love with, whom *all* the women noticed because of his height, his Mediterranean attractiveness, and a certain professorial absent-mindedness . . . well, suddenly that girl's life resembled those stylish Cary Grant movies she was mad about. Finally, even for her, romance had arrived. Now it was her turn. There had been moments, during the honeymoon, when she had felt like Maria Callas, whose vicissitudes she never tired of following in the glossy women's magazines. Leo was so at ease in his unconscious role of Aristotle Onassis—not as rich, of course, but a thousand times thinner—who, faithful to the megalomaniac exhibitionism of his family, had arranged the trip so that everything happened as in a fairy tale: from the dilapidated splendor of the hotels to the tickets for the Stockholm Opera, from the mini-cruise in the fjords to evening clothes that she had found waiting for her in the Second Empire *bergère* in the suite in the Grand Hotel in Oslo. How marvelous!

And yet Rachel recalled that she hadn't completely enjoyed the scene arranged for her by her husband. The idea that Leo had thrown away all that money on things that Rachel had been brought up to consider vain, if not in fact immoral, had spoiled the party for her. She was sure of it: somehow, in the end, all that wastefulness would be punished by a higher authority. And the prophecy had been fulfilled on the way back, when, arriving at the hotel in Monte Carlo, the newlyweds found themselves without a cent.

In those days there were no credit cards, and to send money abroad took time and an endless series of precautions. Leo therefore decided to send a telegram with a request for help to his mother, who was vacationing in Castiglione della Pescaia at the house of her brother, the fatuous Uncle Enea.

When Rachel, alarmed, exclaimed, "Does it really seem right to call your mother? Ask her, like that, all alone, to come and pay the bill? She doesn't even have a license!," Leo hadn't shown the least sign of anxiety.

"You don't know Uncle Enea. He'll offer to drive her. He would never miss a chance for a hand or two of chemin de fer."

Thus, returning to the hotel half an hour later with a copy of the telegram in hand, Leo had said to Rachel, "You see, there was nothing to worry about." And she had looked at him as if he were mad. How was there nothing to worry about? A telegram, that was all he had. The copy of a telegram dictated by him, not a telegram in response. So to speak, a hope. The note in a bottle of the shipwrecked sailor. Who knows how many unexpected events might intervene between that sent telegram and the arrival of the saviors. They might not receive it. They might receive it late. They might have an accident on the journey to Monte Carlo. They might . . . But there was also something else, which Rachel, in the toned-down version of the story intended for her sons, was careful not to confess: it's that she didn't love the idea that it was Leo's mother who was rescuing them—that woman who had opposed her from the start, without pretenses. Rachel felt she couldn't bear her mother-in-law's air of triumph, just as she couldn't tolerate the blame that she would certainly express for her not having dutifully watched over the hedonistic impulses of her wastrel son.

Just as Rachel was grappling with the thought of the imminent arrival of her mother-in-law, no less tormenting than her possible refusal, she had heard herself asked, "What do you say we order dinner in the room, since I don't feel like going out?"

"But if we don't have any money . . . "

"Well, now, no, but the day after tomorrow yes. They won't ask us to pay right away. What are you worried about?"

"It's just that . . . "

"It's just what? Come on, I'll have a shrimp cocktail, a glass of wine, and a wonderful crème brûlée, and you?"

"Nothing, dearest, I'm not hungry . . . well, maybe I'll have a café-au-lait . . . " she had answered, clutching their few remaining coins.

"Not even a brioche? Sure?"

"A café-au-lait is fine, thanks."

To which she added, "I'm not hungry."

She told her sons she had said "I'm not hungry," although she was. And after a few minutes there was her husband, in his white bathrobe with the hotel crest on the pocket, scarfing up shrimp in cocktail sauce, as he kept asking, "You're sure you don't want something? You haven't had a bite since this morning." And she, looking out the window at the famous lights of Monte Carlo (which she romantically associated with *To Catch a Thief*), and suffering sharp pangs of hunger, kept repeating, "Nothing, thanks, really, I don't feel like eating."

That time Leo had been right. Rachel's scruples turned out to be exaggerated. A couple of days later Uncle Enea and his disdainful sister arrived, loaded with money to spend. But that was not to say that things would always go like that. It was not to say that there would always be a genie in the lamp capable of putting everything back in order.

This time, for example, the stakes were a thousand times higher. It wasn't about settling a bill and making a bad impression on some snobbish concierge; it was about their life. And Filippo and Samuel's. That is to say, the whole world! Until this moment such a calamity had never occurred. Which meant nothing. There exist privileged couples who spend decades in the most prudent and carefully calibrated well-being to arrive at old age unharmed. And for some time Rachel had hoped and believed that one day it could be said of them that they belonged to that exclusive club. That their path had been, as the saying goes, "clear" of obstacles.

Things had turned out differently. Those accusations had an alarming specific weight in the life of a family so respectable, and Leo practiced a profession in which respectability is a decisive attribute. That's why the whole business had to be treated with particular care. Well, maybe Leo was right: at least in the first instance everyone had been roused to take his side, to defend him. But how could he be so sure that things wouldn't change? It was clear that the prosecutors working on his case wished to destroy him. Just as it was evident that Leo, like all people who are powerful but not too powerful, could not count on the benevolence of the press, much less of the people.

Certainly if things should take an ugly turn, the intervention of some Uncle Enea (besides, he had been dead for several years) would not be enough to settle the bill. No, this time it was much more complex. A wretchedly dangerous business. Incredible as it might seem, there were employees of the state whose job consisted in demonstrating that Leo was a crook. People paid to haul him in to court. Bloodhounds who couldn't wait to sink their teeth in his neck and never let go. Vampires whose success would consist in putting him down, after bleeding him dry, after incinerating the respectability built up with so much effort over the years—fucking nitpicking bureaucrats, eager to distort the truth to Leo's detriment. Against those treacherous enemies optimism was certainly not a resource, if anything a hindrance.

And if Rachel was wrong? If Leo's problem wasn't an excess of optimism but, rather, the opposite: an excess of pessimism? It certainly could be. She had often observed how behind certain of her husband's blustering attitudes, behind the dazzling scrim of all that trust, lurking like a mole in the guts of a lush garden, was the much darker feeling that is called fear.

Was that what explained everything? Fear? Her husband lived in fear. It could be that, like all people unused to difficulties, like all people spoiled from birth, Leo did not have at his disposal the tools necessary to exorcise fear. Because to do so he would have had to recognize it.

Was it fear that had paralyzed him? Was it fear that prevented him from getting involved in his court case, day and night? Maybe so. A person less frightened would at that point be spending whole days with his nose buried in the documents that concerned him. And instead he did nothing but delay. Delegate. Yes, those were the two things that came easiest to him: putting off the moment when he would have to face a problem and, in the end, placing it carelessly in someone else's hands. All that trust in a lawyer employed by a hospital that had every interest in shifting any responsibility onto a doctor and his team—a hospital that had already circulated several memos in which it stated that it felt itself "the injured party"— was true professional suicide.

But it was also a way to delegate something that he was incapable of facing. Leo increasingly resembled the type of hypochondriac who torments himself endlessly with fantasies of the most disparate and improbable illnesses, and yet is not willing (through a kind of tremendous sloth) to free himself of the vices of smoking and drinking. And who, at the appearance of worrying symptoms, can't find the courage to make an appointment with a specialist or submit to further tests. As if he preferred the anxiety of uncertainty to the despair of truth. That type of more or less imaginary sick person who prefers to live in ignorance.

But of course. What Leo had been struggling with for weeks was a crisis of creeping terror. Rachel recognized the unmistakable signs: lack of appetite interrupted every so often by a fierce hunger. Insomnia suddenly vanquished by long Sunday naps. A tortured alternation of moods.

It's that her Leo was such a sensitive type, so easy to upset! A mere nothing was enough to hurl him into terror.

Rachel recalled the day, a few months earlier, when a letter had arrived, forwarded to him by the editors of the *Corriere della Sera*, the newspaper in which Leo's popular column, "Prevention Is the Best Medicine," appeared. Breaking with his usual habit, Leo, in one of his recent pieces, had not entertained his readers with a description of specific pathologies, nor had he provided a trite catalogue of recommendations for their health. For once, impelled by one of his idealistic impulses, he had taken sides and denounced the Catholic curia's "insidious boycott" of certain scientific institutions that had been engaged for many years in research into fundamental genetic questions. Leo had written (let's be specific: with the cautiousness imposed by his social position and the mildness of his character) that "the Pope should perhaps show himself more indulgent toward fervent researchers who are working for the benefit, certainly not the detriment, of humanity."

The last phrase—the one calling on the Pope directly—had caused a reader to fly off the handle, and, driven by contempt, send Leo a letter (neglecting to inform him that he had sent an identical one to the editor of the *Corriere*), in which, in a few very concise lines, he had spewed out all the bile in his body.

Below I cite the conclusion of the letter:

> How can Professor Pontecorvo dare to discourse on the conduct of His Holiness? Does Professor Pontecorvo know what Holy Institution he has dared to give his valuable advice to? And you, Dear Editor, how can you permit this self-described professor, this hypocritical scientist, this unbeliever in a white lab coat, to address His Holiness in this way, and in public? Perhaps Professor Pontecorvo would do well to think of the failures of his own religion, and the crimes committed by his co-religionists in the Holy Land, rather than occupy himself with Things that have nothing to do with him.

At the bottom, in place of the signature, was written: "Hostile greetings from a former reader."

"And how should I have addressed him?" Leo kept asking Rachel. "Can you explain it to me?" He couldn't let it go. And again: "Does it seem to you, dearest, that I addressed him in some way? If you think so, please tell me. Maybe this guy interpreted the expression 'insidious boycott' as a lack of respect toward the Pope. But you are the witness that it's not true. You know how much respect I have . . . And then all that extravagant use of capital letters. Doesn't it seem disturbing?"

Rachel was astonished by Leo's reaction to that letter. It was as if it had awakened the agitated obsessiveness that no one, outside the few people who knew him intimately, would ever have attributed to him. Leo had spent the entire afternoon pacing around the big glass table in the middle of the living room, in one hand the letter from the angry correspondent, in the other a clipping from the newspaper of the offending column. Every so often he stopped to reread a passage from one or the other. Then he started pacing again. And there was no way to calm him. Or to make him stand still. There was no way to bring the matter back to its modest proportions.

"Come on. Don't exaggerate. He's just a nutcase. He has the tone of a nutcase. The style of a nutcase. Why give him such importance? Why make such a big deal of it?"

"It's the excess of hatred, sweetheart. It's the resentment. It's the tone of contempt. The intimidation. It's as if this guy had a private argument with me. Such hatred boils over from this piece of paper! As if he wanted me dead. I don't understand these things."

"You don't understand them because they're incomprehensible. You don't understand them because you're a good son. You don't understand them because you don't know how far an anti-Semite can go in his hatred of you. You don't understand them because you would never do what that man has done."

"Which is?"

"Which is read an article and get angry to the point of grabbing paper and pen and writing this obscene letter."

At this point Leo seemed to calm down. But a second later, there it was, a veil of quivering panic spreading across his face.

"You know what I'm afraid of?"

"What?"

"How will the paper take it?"

"How should it take it?"

"Well, thanks to me it's lost a reader. Plus, a Papist reader."

"They must be in despair!"

"Don't joke. Please. Not now!"

"Come on, professor, be rational! Do you have any idea how many readers a newspaper like the *Corriere* has? And do you have any idea how many letters from these nuts it must get every day? They must have wastebaskets full of this garbage!"

"What if they take away my column?"

"For an idiotic thing like that?"

"Yes, for an idiotic thing like that."

"I didn't think your column was so important to you. You're always complaining about it. You always say you have nothing to write, that it distracts you from your work. It wouldn't be a tragedy. After all you're hardly a journalist . . . "

"Yes, but in fact I think it's important for my career. I consider it a kind of insurance for the life of my unit."

Rachel knew that his career and his department had nothing to do with it. That the column fed his vanity. But it didn't seem to her very nice to point out her husband's bad faith or his narcissism. And then she was really alarmed by the panic that had invaded him in the face of such a harmless misadventure. Was Leo's equilibrium so precarious?

Rachel had watched the passing of that small crisis. Yet her amazement at seeing her husband in trouble was equal only to her surprise in discovering that all it took to cheer him up was the weekly phone call from the regular editor, who asked, with the deference due a prestigious contributor, if the new piece was ready or if he was still writing. A second after he hung up the phone, Rachel saw him transfigured: there again was *her* Leo, at the peak of his emotional power. In shape, ready to start again. To Rachel that peak seemed even higher.

But what was happening to him now (the investigations and

all the rest) seemed a hundred times more serious. This Rachel knew. Nonetheless her husband's reactions astonished her.

As was to be expected, this time the paper couldn't put it off. After the first searches carried out in the hospital and the clinic, Leo had received a phone call from the editor, who very politely explained that it was perhaps necessary to "suspend the column for a while, not stop it." Rachel was there, facing her husband, as he was punished, like a student after a prank. She looked at him. He kept repeating, "I understand"; "It's clear"; "No problem"; "Of course, of course, it's the procedure"; "Yes, yes, don't worry"; "Thank you, I, too, am sure that everything will be in order"; "Of course, I'll happily come and see you." Even after hanging up the phone he had maintained his aplomb, as if it were not his wife beside him but still that editor who had aroused such submissiveness. Or even an audience eager to test his endurance. If Rachel hadn't known him so well she might have thought that her husband was perfectly serene. Sure of himself.

Too bad that she knew him. And so she knew that that very reasonable behavior was simply the other face of anguish. The paradox was right there. If in the case of a trifle like the offensive letter from an anonymous reader, Leo had found the strength to express his anguish, now, in the presence of a true threat, the courage to express himself failed. Poor dear, he must be so terrified he couldn't even vent. He was traumatized. This time the watchwords were hide, underestimate, look away, don't meet the eyes of the monster.

There was another small incident that Rachel would have interpreted in the same way, if only Leo had dared to tell her.

It had happened at the university, ten days before he received the phone call from the newspaper editor firing him. During one of the last classes of the second semester. Late May.

Leo liked teaching. He was good at it and did it with great care and a sense of detachment. He was endowed with natural eloquence, and was eager to communicate to the students the sacred fire that inspired him and at the same time demonstrate the self-sacrifice that had led him to the professorship. He had a sensual voice, which with the microphone sounded like a radio broadcast. And certainly he wasn't so ingenuous as to underestimate the weight of his own attractiveness. What do you think? He saw the girls in the first row, widening their eyes and resting their chins on the backs of their hands with an ecstatic gesture. He felt their gaze on him, intuited their comments, interpreted the flirtatious little laughs that, each time, blessed his entrance into the classroom. There was something theatrically sexual in those sessions, whose sacredness was sanctioned by the fact that for years now they had always been held in the same place, the same two days of the week, at the same time: Tuesday and Wednesday at six in room P10, on the ground floor of the Faculty of Medicine.

Anything could be said of Leo Pontecorvo except that he was a demagogue. He had a way with students, but stayed within the so-called academic formalities. He deplored the promiscuity between teachers and students so disastrously encouraged by the revolution of '68. But, similarly, he found any magisterial excess anachronistic. If he had to question a girl student he called her "Miss." With the boys, instead, he used the ironically paternalistic expression "dear boy."

As far as the students' behavior during class, he was inflexible. For decades (even in the rebellious seventies) he had devoted the first class to dictating the list of things that were not tolerated. They were not allowed to arrive late. Not allowed to leave early. Not allowed to chew gum. Not allowed to have a snack. Not allowed to interrupt the lecture with questions and comments. Not allowed to address the professor with colloquial locutions like "Hi." Not allowed to ask questions about the exams outside office hours. And so on . . . In exchange he undertook to be punctual, rigorous, sparkling.

There was nothing boring in Professor Pontecorvo's classes. Over the years he had learned the art of paring down technicalities and of stimulating the students' attention with cute anecdotes about hypochondriac mothers or tender stories about a sick child who, with tenacity and a fighting spirit, had given everyone a run for their money, starting with the doctor in charge.

That afternoon, in class, Professor Pontecorvo had been skillful enough to hide his distress. As he was driving to the university, in fact, the secretary of the clinic had reached him on the car phone with a rather unpleasant communication: a few minutes earlier the financial police had barged into the office with a warrant. Leo had answered her almost rudely, "Not now, Daniela! I'm on the way to class."

"But, Professor . . . "

"I told you I'm on the way to class. We'll talk afterward."

Imagine his apprehension as he crossed the threshold of the classroom. Imagine how he must have felt while he took from his soft leather briefcase the pad with his notes. And—to put off for an instant the moment when he would have to begin the class—he poured some water in the glass and began to sip it nervously. To his great surprise, when he began to speak his voice did not betray either impatience or uncertainty. Smooth as silk. No one could have guessed his nervous condition. Or imagine that only a quarter of an hour earlier that fascinating teacher had been informed that the tax officials were about to give him the third degree.

A weekend at the beach with Rachel and the boys (the first of the season) had given the professor's face an outdoor color. Which, besides, seemed to go splendidly with the tan cotton suit, the blue button-down shirt, the regimental tie, and the rich leather Alden moccasins acquired in the tiny shop on Madison Avenue.

In other words, Professor Pontecorvo was at the height of

efficiency and charm. He had even given some signs of exuberance in explaining how an excessive and sudden rise in the levels of alkaline phosphatase in the blood test of a child of eight or nine can already signal a diagnosis of rickets or some other bone deficiency.

Until he saw a student, a kid with an Afro and garish, to say the least, glasses, annoying a girl. The two were laughing in the third row. For a second the idea crossed his mind that they were laughing at him. For a second he was tempted by the idea of not intervening.

Nothing to be done: he lost patience.

"Would you like to share with us your private joke or would you prefer to take it outside?"

"I'm sorry . . . professor . . . it's my fault. I asked her a question."

"It was of vital importance?"

"Well, I asked if she had a pencil and paper."

"Ah, so you are telling us that you came to class without a pencil and without paper."

"It's that . . . "

"What is this for you, an outing in the country? Do you take this class for an amusement park? To me it seems a university classroom. And, as you do not seem to have realized, a class is in session."

Leo could have stopped there. He could have considered himself satisfied. But something drove him to keep going. To play the role, so unsuited to him, of the petulant professor.

"Don't you think that a university classroom is a place where paper and pencil should be at home? Or perhaps I am mistaken. Perhaps you have a completely different perception of this place. Maybe you're right? What do you others say? Maybe your colleague is right? Maybe this is a campground where we pitch our tents and tell jokes?"

It was the first time the students had seen Professor Pontecorvo indulge in that type of bitter, pedantic remark. Yes, they all knew that he insisted on certain things. But his reproaches always possessed the gift of lightness. Like the time he had reprimanded a girl who was chewing on something in front of him: "Are you full now? Are you refreshed? May I offer you something else? Coffee? A *digestif*? A cigar? A nap?" And they had all laughed (including the professor). Because Professor Pontecorvo's scoldings never crossed the line into humiliation and insult.

This time, however, he seemed eager to make trouble for that kid. His words were sharp and his voice was dripping with hostility. As if that terrible hair and the ridiculous glasses had aggravated his already strained susceptibility.

"So, will you answer me? How can you come to class without paper and pencil? What sort of behavior is that?"

And then Leo had said it. He couldn't contain himself. He had let slip the type of comment you should never let slip. Because it can always be turned against you. He waited a few seconds and then in a peremptory tone had said to the boy, "Aren't you ashamed of yourself?"

"And you, professor, aren't you ashamed of the billions of lire in taxpayer money you've stolen?"

This was the phrase the incessant memory of which had kept Leo awake for three straight nights. This was the epilogue of the incident that Leo had not had the courage to tell Rachel. No, he had said nothing to her, but he hadn't stopped thinking about it for a second. That little hippie bastard had put it out on the carpet in front of everyone. He had done in the classroom (or rather in the enchanted kingdom where for twenty years Leo had exercised his temporal power with great irony) what everyone would soon do in public: he had judged him summarily and, just as summarily, condemned him. That was why in the following days Leo could not help reviewing all the answers he could have given that provocateur, and hadn't.

Contrary to what usually happens when we think back over a missed chance to reply adequately to a provocation, to come up with a remark equal to the outrage that has been inflicted on us, in the end Leo was convinced that the behavior he had demonstrated under the circumstances was the best possible. He had been silent. He had pretended not to hear and not to be pained. He had pretended that his academic authority had not been forever crushed. He had taken up the thread of the subject where he had left off. Blood tests and all the rest . . .

What else could he have done?

But let's get back to Rachel and fear.

Rachel looked at her husband and spontaneously compared him to her father: Cesare Spizzichino would never have behaved like that. My father would have grabbed the bull by the horns. He would have been furious, my father. He would have made the lawyer's office quake with his yelling. My father would have stopped thinking about anything else and come up with a strategy to get himself out of the vortex.

But Leo in no way resembled the now deceased Cesare Spizzichino. And the irony is that Rachel had married him precisely because of that glaring dissimilarity. Although she loved her father very much, she was certain that there was only one thing more difficult than being Cesare Spizzichino, and that was to be related to him. An experience that meant you lived in a constant state of anxiety that an accident was about to happen. In fact that was how her father lived: waiting for (or invoking?) the blow that would crush him. There was nothing outside that he did not read as a promise of misfortune. The entire universe was scattered with evil portents. His stinginess, for example, derived from the fact that he was waiting for the Great Crisis (as he called it) that would change the face of the known world. In the same spirit in which certain messianic ecologists await the apocalypse that will annihilate the planet.

Was it possible that Rachel realized only now—observing the meekness with which Leo confronted the first true adversities of his existence of milk and honey—that all the fear her father had endured during the dangerous course of his life, and which he had chosen to confront boldly, was precisely what had allowed him to face with fury and strength the great sorrows that existence had exposed him to?

When Stella, his firstborn, Rachel's older sister, died in a grotesque accident (a bed, a blanket, and a murderous cigarette), Cesare Spizzichino had proved what sort of man he was. Before the burned body of his daughter he had cried like a slaughtered pig. He no longer slept. He never recovered emotionally. But, apart from those completely understandable reactions, as soon as the period of mourning ended he seized the reins of his life again, to watch over his surviving daughter with all his power. Yes, he had done it, even though Stella's death had provided him with the retrospectively incontrovertible proof that his fear was fully founded. And yet, just because he had spent his whole life studying the best way to absorb it, he had been able to react with courage and determination.

Fear produces contradictory behaviors: it can lead to an excessive reaction but also to an inadequate reaction. Rachel was discovering a very different way of being frightened. Her father used fear to protest; her husband, evidently, let it overpower him.

If only Leo hadn't hidden from himself that he was afraid . . . well, certainly now he would be reacting more forcefully and with a greater sense of responsibility. And instead there he was, busy denying to others and himself that he was terrified, and at the same time at the mercy of that terror. It was terror that drove him to surround himself with people he didn't need. He didn't want to be alone, like children who beg their mother to stay next to them at night while they sleep. Or like terminally ill people who somehow find the strength to get up and meet friends in a restaurant, convinced that there, in that convivial setting, death will not have the impudence to show up.

And Rachel, who saw all this, wished only to defend Leo both from the irresponsibility to which optimism had led him and from the grip of the fear that was paralyzing him.

And that's why the idea of that evening with the Albertazzis made her shudder and infuriated her. That's why Rachel was so worried. For weeks she had wanted to be alone with Leo, when he came home from the hospital or the university: to talk to him frankly, far from the indiscreet and judgmental gaze of any friend.

With the Albertazzis around Rachel knew that it would be up to her, not Leo, to parry the thrusts of Rita, that woman whose only interest in life had always been to demonstrate to herself and the world how pure she was and how everyone else was not.

"What do you bet that tonight that hyena Rita will not miss an opportunity to . . . " Rachel had shouted sarcastically after realizing that the dinner with Flavio and Rita was inevitable, and giving in yet again to her husband's wishes.

"I'll bet what you like."

On that bet the first round had ended. The second began the moment Flavio and Rita had left, after the usual canasta game of women-against-men, in which the men got the worst of it and they all (with the exception of Rachel the abstemious) tucked into the whiskey a little too much. And now the match between Leo and Rachel was set to establish which of them had won the bet.

Appearances solemnly pointed to Leo: he was the winner. No explicit allusion to his legal difficulties had been made either by Flavio or by the much more fearsome Rita. The impression was that the placid and affectionate Flavio had, for once at least, instilled in his wife a precautionary lesson, enjoining her to abstain from comments of any type. He must have told her to put aside ideas, indignation, and intolerance, not to mention her incorrigible passion for gossip, and appear understanding toward two dear friends who were going through a difficult period.

And she had followed the instructions.

At first there had been some tension. Above all in the way that Flavio had tried to avoid the type of question with which the two old friends generally started off. This time he had been careful not to begin with the classic "And so, professor, what news of the enemy?" "Enemy" was a generic word that for Flavio indicated any type of duty: work, university colleagues, the administration of Santa Cristina, the progress in school of Filippo and Samuel . . . in other words, everyday life. Maybe he was afraid that such a question might be taken the wrong way by a friend in trouble. It was obvious that Leo had problems at work. Pretending to ignore them was no less awkward than to take them for granted. So that Flavio for once was confined to answering the questions about his work that came from Leo. But he had done it with greater verbosity than usual.

Thank heaven at that moment, delivered direct from the kitchen, a silver tray full of hot tomato-and-mozzarella crostini, sprinkled with pepper and basil, had materialized in the living room, and Rita had fallen on it. Rita was one of those big eaters who never get fat and who, when you ask them how such a miracle is possible, give you an oracular answer like "It has to do with metabolism." Someone more malicious might have hypothesized that her entire body was a lethal waste-disposal factory. All the fire she had in her body, all the resentment, all the anxiety . . . This was devouring her from the inside.

On the other hand Rita that evening seemed calmer than her husband, and in general more tranquil than usual. Rachel had been silent, no more or less than she usually was.

Only for a moment during the meal, in a silence marked by the clang of silverware on plates and roast beef chewed by teeth, had it seemed that the specter of what was happening to Leo was there, in the center of the table, marble and mocking. But by the time they got to dessert (the usual *torta caprese*), the atmosphere had relaxed slightly, and Leo and Rita (who never stopped pouring cream on her cake) had begun to discuss politics: the subject that at that moment seemed to them most neutral.

It was the summer of 1986. A year earlier the great battle over yet another referendum that unleashed the fratricidal struggle between the Communists of the opposition and the Socialists of the government had ended. The latter had emerged strengthened by the referendum's defeat. Although the subject in itself was not among the most exciting, Rita had demonstrated a peculiar stubbornness in declaring that, with the referendum voted down, the workers had suffered one of the most outrageous humiliations ever inflicted by a "historically fascist" country "like ours." Her fierce hyperboles started the contentiousness, and it reached a peak of intensity when the argument fatally brushed the figure of Bettino Craxi—at that time (fifteen years before he died in his Tunisian exile) the flourishing head of the Socialist government, with his arrogant South American charisma and Kuwaiti life style—who, with his capacity to attract so much love and so much hatred, so much veneration and so much contempt, had become, in the families of many of his fellow-citizens, a kind of watershed that could cause divisions between peaceful individuals who until that moment had respected one another, making them the bitterest enemies.

The homicidal hatred that Rita felt for Craxi was no less grotesquely frenzied than Leo's veneration.

"The fact that my father, that piece of shit, has him in his house every other day," Rita thundered at a certain point, "is indisputable proof of what sort of man he is. Fifty years ago my grandparents, with the same deference, welcomed Benito

Mussolini. What can I do if my family is the seismograph of this country? If everything that is arrogant, everything that is fascist, everything that is authoritarian sooner or later ends up at my family's dinner table?"

"Nonsense, Rita. The same thing. The same argument. How long have we known each other? Twenty years? Thirty? You know, ever since I've known you you've hated *everything* that's innovative, you've fought against *everything* that tries to be healthily open-minded."

"It doesn't seem to me that you've ever found open-mindedness to be a healthy idea. Or maybe you've changed your mind recently?"

There's the comment, placed in a rhetorical interrogative form, and for that reason heavily tinged with sarcasm, whose interpretation Leo and Rachel, after their friends had left, began to fight about.

Rachel was enraged, convinced not only that her husband was responsible for Rita's nasty comment but that in a certain sense he deserved it.

"How could you even think of starting in on that subject?" she asked him.

"Why shouldn't I? Because it allowed that woman to say some stupid things?"

"Well, you should have been more cautious. You should have gone slowly. The way you defend Craxi, who has never done a thing for you . . . "

His love of Craxi. It was another of those disinterested emotions that Rachel couldn't bear in her husband. Plenty of people in their circle had taken advantage professionally, in the way of patronage, of certain political loyalties. Not Leo. For him the name Bettino Craxi was pure, melodious music. A poetry of intelligence and freedom. Which led him to expose himself publicly, especially on social occasions, by always taking his side. With a passion that, in an environment full of extremely refined Communists from good families, must have been incomprehensible to the point of being mis-understood.

How could Leo not see that among his friends there was not one capable of believing that an intelligent man could love with such disinterested enthusiasm a political personage whom they considered a pig, a criminal, a pervert? If Rachel (the lit-tle Jesuit, worshipper of discretion and hypocrisy) had always detested the way in which her husband laid himself bare before all those hostile people, of whom Rita represented a sort of epitome, it was much more difficult to tolerate now that—with the charge hanging over him of having received an aca-demic benefit from a friendship with Craxi (a friendship that in reality he couldn't boast of)—Leo presented Rita with such a dialectic advantage. Why not be silent at least this once? Why always stick your neck out to your opponent's guillotine?

"And meanwhile you got yourself called a fascist."

"You always see more in words than they say."

"Did you see how she looked at you?"

"In order not to admit that you lost the bet you come out with simple impressions. You were so anxious that it would happen that you saw it happen. But I assure you that Rita behaved in her usual fashion."

"And that same old story with Mitterrand?"

"What?"

"Was it really necessary? Couldn't you do without it?"

"I didn't start it. It was Rita who dragged in Mitterrand and all that squalid gossip . . . I hate gossip!"

"And you immediately took the bait."

"She seemed more eager than usual to deplore the dishon-esty and depravity of the Socialists in power."

"Yes. And who knows why!"

"Why? Do you want to know why? I'll tell you why. Because 'deplore' is her favorite verb. The one that's the most moving for her. Because Rita's life would be much more gray and colorless if she didn't have someone or something to deplore . . . "

"And you're a hundred percent sure that this time the objects of her deploring were only the Socialists in power? That her principal polemical objects were Craxi and Mitterrand?"

"And who if not?"

"Well, for example the most disinterested defender of their cause."

François Mitterrand. Another of Leo's passions. Another Socialist who had broken the bank. And, if possible, in a more grandiose manner than Craxi. In the French way: Napoleon, de Gaulle, in short, that sort of thing, you know the French . . . Besides, Mitterrand's extremely efficient grandeur was one of Leo's favorite subjects, especially recently. Ever since, just a few months earlier, he had taken part in a conference organized by the Insitut Gustave Roussy—one of the most avant-garde cancer centers in the world, where, among other things, Leo had at one time studied. A convention of luminaries hosted by the Cité des Sciences, or, rather, one of the great works inaugurated by Mitterrand during his term. At the gala dinner Leo had been introduced to Monsieur le Président, and had been able to show off, for a good two minutes, his very fluent French. From that moment his love for Mitterrand had taken the unvarying form of idolatry.

The trouble is that Signora Pontecorvo disapproved of her husband's love of all things foreign, no less than she disapproved of his idolatry. She found both too ingenuous for a man of his caliber and, at the same time, annoyingly partisan. Sometimes it seemed to Rachel that Leo went around the world with the sole purpose of noting, upon his return, how poorly his own country functioned. Rome, to hear Leo, was the worst place on the planet. He never came back from one of his trips without making a list of all the things in England or Germany that worked better. He uttered statements like "Landing at Fiumicino, after a week abroad, is always a trauma." An attitude that Rachel, in whose breast beat a soberly chauvinist heart, couldn't bear. Besides, in such circumstances, there was no subject of Leo's that did not sound tendentiously dishonest to his wife's ears. An ingenuous tendentiousness, true, but for that very reason more pathetic.

Like the time, oh yes, on that wretched trip to New York, when he had succeeded in dragging her along (usually she resisted his invitations, if only so she could then complain about never going anywhere). Rachel had been horrified one morning when, right after breakfast, Leo, as they left the lobby of the Sheraton and stood on Seventh Avenue, in the middle of summer, at rush hour, in a staggering din, had whispered, "I adore this fragrance!" There. That time, faced with such gall, she couldn't contain herself.

"What fragrance? What fragrance are you raving about? It stinks—can't you tell? A terrible stink. There's no place in the world that stinks like this."

"No, it's the fragrance of Manhattan. You just don't have the poetry to understand it."

"I may not be poetic, but this is the odor of garbage. And in Rome we have plenty of garbage. What is it that isn't right about our garbage?"

That was how Rachel had expressed herself that day in New York. Intolerant of the fact that her husband was so poetic in evaluating the stink of New York. And so prosaic about the Roman version.

Rachel, furthermore, had a problem with Paris. She felt for Leo's Parisian period that sort of tender and yet burning retrospective jealousy that wives who feel inadequate harbor for the life led by their husbands before marriage. From the way Leo talked about his time at the Roussy she could deduce that he had had a wonderful time. Not that he had ever told her in detail what he'd been up to during his Paris year. There wasn't that sort of intimacy between them. But Rachel felt that behind his reticence lodged a lot of indecent memories, for which her husband felt nostalgia.

And she wasn't wrong.

It's that in Paris, in 1963—the year when Leo had lived (God, if that is the appropriate word!) there—everybody was fucking. And Leo had been unable to resist all that promiscuity. Besides, apart from sex, he hadn't economized in any way. Which shouldn't be surprising. At least if you give due weight to the fact that little Leo had spent the first years of his life in Switzerland, toddling in short pants through the meadows of the Alpine village where his parents had sensibly gone into hiding in 1941. And that once he returned home his life in the postwar years had been more prosperous and comfortable than that allotted by fate to the majority of his fellow-citizens. And might have been even more comfortable if it hadn't been for the unbearable attitude of his parents.

They wouldn't leave him alone. They gave him no respite. They never let up. They were always on him. Did they perhaps mean to offer him, in an invasive form, all the protection that the Jewish parents of their generation—at least in Europe— had not been able to guarantee to their indiscriminately massacred offspring? Is that it? A kind of symbolic compensation? Or is it simply the overprotective syndrome of the parents of an only son?

Bah! In any case it explains the hypochondria of the father, the renowned, taciturn pediatrician who was constantly examining him, listening to his heart and lungs, administering pointless treatments (once he had practically sent him to his creator with a boiling chamomile enema). Similarly, it explains the suffocating attentions of his mother. But, above all, it explains why Leo escapes at the first possible opportunity. And, having earned his degree in Medicine and just enrolled in the specialty of Pediatrics, he accepts without hesitation a proposal from his mentor, Professor Meyer, to go to Paris to gain experience at the Institut Gustave Roussy. And why once in Paris he doesn't miss a thing.

He is assigned to a team studying, in the laboratory and in the field, neuroblastoma, the very particular type of cancer that afflicts only children, on which Leo did his brilliant thesis ("worthy of publication," of course).

In those days Paris deserved overtime! It could be said that Leo didn't sleep for all of 1963. As if a savage enthusiasm had allowed him to pare his sleeping hours down to the indispensable. All the novelties that surrounded him required dedication, because at that time Paris, in spite of its run-down appearance, in spite of the fact that everything was crumbling, insisted on declaring itself brand-new. In the morning you glanced at the papers and saw a continuous self-celebration: there was the new cinema and the new novel and the new morality and the new politics . . . Not too mention cool, alcoholic jazz, like the Martinis with ice that Leo gulped down in dark cellars on the Left Bank that smelled of cork, mold, and toilets.

It should be specified that, unlike the *vie de bohème* led by most of the young who gathered in Paris in that decade, Leo's was, to say the least, gilded. Thanks to Dr. Pontecorvo senior, in fact, the wallet of our young scion away from home was always equal to the situation. No poverty, therefore. No asceticism. No painful search for truth in misery. If anything a lot of amusement, and not at all cheap.

Which had not kept him from having his moments of poetry. At times—especially on Saturdays, when he could afford to prolong his carousing until dawn—on the way home (if the fifteen-square-meter studio in the Rue Jussieu could be called that), Leo, a touch high, had the impression that Paris was speaking to him. After an explosive night at the Caveau de la Huchette, the froglike cheeks of Dizzy Gillespie remained in his mind's eye, swelling improbably, allowing that great man of bop to blow into his trumpet like an angel on Judgment Day. He had just seen him perform, and was incredulous. But do you realize, my boy? The great Dizzy playing for you and a few others of the chosen? And then the smell of Paris at dawn—the butter of brioches just out of the oven and the sweetish damp of the river—encouraged epiphanic thoughts.

And, as for smells, there was one that Leo had not so easily freed himself from and which he was careful not to speak about to his wife. The one that, when he woke, he sought in the burning hollow between the neck and cheek of Gisèle Bessolet, the nineteen-year-old concubine who had begun to sleep at his house, on the wave of inertia that always seemed to be pushing her in the wrong direction. That is, if "sleep" is the right word.

There's no denying, that girl in bed really had nerve! At least that was the judgment expressed by a basically inexperienced fellow like Leo.

It should be emphasized, at this point, that the sensation of having finally understood, at the age of twenty-five, the meaning of the word "freedom" (the word that his parents played around with, overcome by emotion, when they celebrated the fact that, some years earlier, the Allied troops had screwed the Germans but which they tended to forget whenever the autonomous space to leave to their son was being considered), as I was saying, that whole crackling sensation of having discovered freedom just in time would not have had the aspect of rebirth if the cunt hadn't been involved.

If in a technical sense, in fact, it can't be declared that Leo lost his virginity in Paris, certainly it can be stated in an emotional sense. Let's say that the oppressive family he came from and the puritanical Rome of the fifties had joined forces to clip the wings of his promising masculinity.

Gisèle had helped to resolve the problem. And she was only the last in the list of his saviors. After Leo had been in Paris for a while he stopped being amazed at the fact that none of the girls he picked up in a bar, a park, at the home of a colleague, in the hospital—practically anywhere—refused at the end of the evening to follow him to his alcove. The first palpitations of a subversive sexuality? The first signs of the great depravity that would infect youths in the years to come? The female orgasm that finally returns, after who knows how many centuries of mortification, to the center of the world stage? Call it what you like. Our Leo called it life. Life as it should be. Life that lives forever.

During the day the work in the hospital, in the labyrinth of corridors where you lived in a constant neon half-light: difficult, dirty, killing, foul-smelling work but in a certain sense also exciting. In the evening music and pussy. Do you know of anything better?

The months in Paris, Gisèle, sex, jazz, research, experiments, the oncology department so ahead of its time . . . That had been his hour of air. Which, like all hours of air, turned out to be surprisingly brief and mockingly insufficient.

When Leo's father died, his mother had a pretext for recalling him home. And after the shiva, the week of mourning when the relatives of the dead man had to remain shut up in the house, Leo had not had the courage to leave again. He hadn't had the courage to abandon his mother. He had felt on his shoulders the responsibility of his father's pediatric office. No, he hadn't given up oncology, but he had to say farewell to Gisèle, to the city where he had been free, to the hospital environment where what he wanted to do in life was done in the best possible way.

Then, thank heaven, Rachel arrived. Small, voluptuous, and of a modest background (she had something of Gisèle!). And in time his work, too, had taken an interesting turn. Together with his mentor, Professor Meyer, and a handful of other intrepid colleagues, Leo had helped lay the groundwork for what would one day be the Italian Pediatric Hematology Oncology Association, and the first protocols in treating leukemia had been worked out . . . Then, with extraordinary precocity, had come the professorship, the hospital job, and the offer from the Anima Mundi clinic to house within its luxurious walls the pediatric office that Leo had inherited from his father. And meanwhile Rachel discovered that she was pregnant.

But just when everything seemed settled, the Parisian siren had sounded again: this time under the seductive appearance of a job offer that it was almost impossible to refuse. Not only did they want him again at Roussy, the hospital, in the suburb of Villejuif, where Leo had worked hard and passionately, but they were willing to offer him an appointment with responsibilities and a lot of money. He was the man they were looking for. The first choice.

Unfortunately this time not only the old Signora Pontecorvo objected but also the young Signora Pontecorvo. Daughter-in-law and mother-in-law, allies for once, did all they could to hinder him. Rachel didn't feel she could leave her widower father. She knew that, after losing his wife and a daughter, he considered the marriage of his second-born a kind of betrayal. All he needed was for her to go to Paris. Leo's mother, too, couldn't bear for her son to go back to live, probably forever, in France. The torrential force of these concerted protests had done the rest: driving Leo, with death in his heart, to give up that advantageous opportunity. Which had represented for him, and not only on the professional level, something more than a simple regret or a missed opportunity.

The recent Paris conference, the chat with Mitterrand, the visit to his colleagues at the Roussy, the nostalgic tartare devoured at the brasserie in the Rue Jussieu ("The same as it was then!")—everything had offered Leo the pretext for a thrilling nostalgia. For days he had done nothing but talk about it. Provoking in his wife a resurgence of the old jealousy of a girl of the people who sees her Prince Charming fleeing to places that are closed off to her.

But for once, hearing her husband gushing at the table, in front of the treacherous Albertazzis, about the Cité des Sciences, the steak tartare, and the other Parisian nonsense, and with all that apologetic enthusiasm in defense of Craxi, Mitterrand, the Socialists in power, Rachel had forgotten her jealousy. Concentrated as she was on her own rage and her own incredulity. Why did her husband again miss an opportunity to be quiet? Why did he open himself to slander? Why didn't he protect himself? Why couldn't he behave with some reserve? Why didn't he change the subject? Why did he offer so many details about those splendid days in Paris? In the marvelous Paris of Mitterrand? Why did he get so worked up about Mitterrand? Why did he defend him from Rita's specious attacks? Why at the moment when he ought to shut up, hide, retrench, was he instead blathering, demonstrating, exaggerating? What blasted suicidal program was this?

It's true, technically the bet had been won by Leo: neither Flavio nor Rita had in any way alluded to his legal troubles. But how could her husband not realize that, in reality, they had talked of nothing else for the whole dinner? How was it possible that he didn't understand that, in defending Craxi and Mitterrand with such passion, he had done nothing but accuse himself?

That was why Rachel was so furious now. Why she was pressing him so angrily:

"Did you really have to get so worked up?"

"I have no wish to hide. I've done nothing that I need to hide for. Let Rita think what she wants, but I'm not going to start being circumspect just because people like her believe certain things about me . . . "

"What I would have expected, at least tonight, was a little discretion."

"Discretion. That's your favorite word. The one you've devoted your life to. You and your working-class mentality. Don't be noticed. Hide like a sewer rat. Don't attract attention. Don't ever say what you think, people might hit you. For me it's different."

"No, it's not that! It's that . . . "

"Then what is it? Can you tell me how I should behave?"

Contrition. Prudence. Loyalty. That was the answer. That was what Rachel would have liked to reply to her husband. What she had been taught by that expert in adversity Cesare Spizzichino. But the only thing Rachel managed to say was:

"And shame? You don't feel any shame?"

"For what, God damn it? Tell me for what!"

For all this! For all that's happening to us! Rachel would have liked to say but yet again was unable to say anything.

"I don't know about you, but I have nothing to be ashamed of," Leo had retorted, full of rage. And for the first and last time in his life, he nearly hit her with all the strength he had in his body.

But now that the nation had been informed that a child had been molested, and, in addition, a child sentimentally connected (what an inadequate expression to describe the bond between two kids!) to your son . . . Well, now, yes, my old friend, you have something enormous to be ashamed of. Something so big that no one in this kitchen can breathe. Now that someone has found the strength to turn off the TV and the fire under the blackened coffeepot, and everything is sunk in an unpleasant silence, now ask yourself if the usual technique of acting offended by them, like a boy, can work. And you

answer no, this time it won't work. It's gone much too far for
a thing like that to work. That's a good system for times of
peace but not for the war that awaits you. This time not one of
the people you love most has sweet-smelling olive branches in
store for you. This time your old, well-tested sulk will be completely ineffective. This time, assuming you don't want to
spend the rest of your days in solitude, surrounded by a thick
hostility, it will be up to you to apologize, it will be up to you
to start off on the rough road of détente. It will be up to you
to win them back.

Those ridiculous letters, those meaningless letters, those
letters that the little psychopath blackmailed you with and is
now using in this indecent way. Why didn't you talk to Rachel
before? Why didn't you talk to the boys in time, when you
could have? Why this time, too, were you immobilized, waiting for everything to some crashing down? I know, now you'd
like to tell them that everything happened the way things happen in most people's lives: through a concatenation of ambiguous and uncontrollable events. And life is playing an ugly trick
on you. That you risk being destroyed by what seemed to you,
incapable as you were of assessing the consequences, the
behavior of a strange child. And that if there is anyone who
was lured, lusted after, deceived in this nasty business . . . well,
that person has your name and your appearance, which, since
the Paris days, you've always been too proud of, and which
now, in the light of everything that's happening, seem to you
repulsive. And yet you also know that the reason you didn't
tell them before is the conviction that they wouldn't have
believed you.

But if you were afraid they wouldn't believe you then, how
can you think that they'll believe you now? Now that the bub-
ble has burst. Now that it's completely obvious that you're trying to defend yourself by inventing alternative truths. How can
you ask Rachel, Filippo, and Samuel, at this point, not to be

satisfied with lazy appearances but to choose to believe your so improbable truths, if you didn't trust their capacity to understand when things were much less compromised? And if you can't hope to be believed by the only three people who would have an interest in believing you, how can you hope that the rest of the world will listen to you and trust you? How can you ask indulgence from the indifferent, the hostile, all those who stood outside there like hawks, waiting for that great man Professor Pontecorvo to make a false move?

Here it is, the false move. There's nothing left for them to do but tear you to pieces, get their revenge for all the success you've had, all the happiness you've won for yourself.

You feel the shudder of fear now? Do you finally understand that you need to fear for your safety? Do you feel the whole world preparing to do you in? It's a thought so enormous (the entire world, I mean) that you feel your equilibrium failing.

Outside are a lot of people who hate. The curious fact is that to hate you they don't have to know if you're innocent or guilty. They hate you and that's it.

They'll use this story to satisfy their Pantagruelesque resentment and to indulge their indignation. To gossip incredibly. This is what comes easiest to people who hate. Destroy you with the small arms of gossip. Make you pass for a pathetic pervert. For a parasite who too long pretended to be beneficial but has finally been unmasked. Then they'll move to the heavy artillery. They'll use that girl. That precocious little whore. They'll use her to strike at you. They won't show her publicly. They'll do it in a way so that she acts in absentia. They'll hide her, using her only to destroy you. She'll be guaranteed the maximum invisibility and privacy, while you will be marked by the greatest exposure possible. That's how they'll destroy everything you've constructed. They'll say you're a thief. Dishonest. Dissolute. And they'll do it to cleanse their own conscience, which is just as dirty as yours. This is the favorite sport of people who hate. Using the scalp of a powerful man who has been disgraced to cleanse the conscience of everyone else.

And what objections can you raise? None. How can you defend yourself from what seems incontrovertible? From letters written to a minor, from money lent, money stolen, and all the rest? The imbalance between you and the girl. That says it all. It's the most lethal weapon they have at their disposal. Your social power compared with the fragility of a twelve-year-old. That her power lies in her greater weakness? Yes, that's how things work outside these comfortable walls, stocked with carpets and bourgeois decorum, which you naïvely believed would protect you until the grave.

But the grave is getting closer. It presses you from so close that you already have the stink of a corpse.

A list of excuses sordidly similar to the ones any serial rapist might put forward. Is this the ace up your sleeve? You're afraid it is. Your explanations—so true and irrefutable for you—are precisely those which others are not willing to listen to. Everything that people wish to hear can be unearthed in the recesses of the painful, depraved correspondence of which you were one of the two incautious authors.

And that exchange of letters tells a story completely different from the one you would like to tell, and from the one you are sure you lived. The only *true* story—that is, the one everyone will believe—speaks of the moral corruption of a twelve-year-old girl by a fifty-year-old man at the peak of success (and already charged with a series of intolerable crimes). A twelve-year-old girl who has barely begun to menstruate. And who, among other things, was your son's girlfriend. Something that really turns the stomach.

And maybe the moment has arrived to realize that there is nothing to do, that anything will be useless. That you have your back to the wall. Trapped as you would never have imagined you could be. More and more certain that to proclaim your innocence, to explain to your family that it was *she*—she, Camilla—and not you, who started, carried on, and above all persevered obstinately, almost to the point of torture, will be in vain. That by now nothing will save you from the sentence that, in the inexperienced and innocent little minds of your sons and in the much more sensible one of your wife, has certainly already been imposed and carried out. The only thing that remains to you is this desire to weep. A childish, uncontrollable desire to start whining, to flood the organism with tears and never stop. But this at least you can spare them.

So it was that all Leo Pontecorvo could do—instead of asking his wife and sons to consider what was happening in its complexity, instead of reassuring them with generic formulas like calm down, everything will work out, mistakes are made just to be put right, instead of displaying the Olympian serenity that at least two of them until a few moments before had considered his outstanding quality, instead of barricading himself behind his proverbial optimism—all he could do was get up, open the kitchen door leading to the narrow stairs to the cellar, hesitate a moment, like a suicide before throwing himself into the void, and run down, into the part of the house appointed for his relaxation, to hide, to hole up, away from the people who at that moment he feared most in the world. More than the judges, the newspapers, public opinion, the father and mother of Camilla, more than all those who couldn't wait to flay him. He fled like a thief caught red-handed.

And although he persisted in repeating to himself that that flight was useful in sparing Rachel and the boys the obscene spectacle of his nervous collapse, the truth is that, at the most crucial moment of his life, he had chosen the behavior that most suited him, that most resembled him: cowardice. To flee

meant to remain utterly faithful to the child whom Leo—in spite of his respectable age, his gratifying professional and academic triumphs, the money earned, the style of life guaranteed to himself and his loved ones—in half a century of life had never, for an instant, ceased to be.

Here he is, Leo Pontecorvo, still the spoiled child of his mamma.

PART II

Seven months before fleeing (literally) from the kitchen, from his family, and from his responsibilities, Leo had fled, in a much more innocuously figurative way, from the urban routine, taking the family, as he did every year, to Anzère, a picturesque village in the shelter of the Swiss Alps.

That was where, for almost two weeks every year at Christmas, the Pontecorvos relocated. They rented an isolated chalet looking north, like all things beautiful and frozen, and forgot that in the world there existed alternatives to that exuberance of white and silence and sweetness.

Although Leo was relatively young, he had already been for some years what is called an eminent physician. And so his figure had begun to emit the aura of ashen authority radiated by tall, hunched lecturers who, before they speak, fumble in their inside jacket pocket in search of lost eyeglasses.

Thanks to the small photograph accompanying the health column in the *Corriere* and some occasional television appearances, he had discovered the pleasure of being recognized in a restaurant or on a train: he didn't dislike being a star to beautiful middle-aged hypochondriacs with rigid hairdos and affected smiles. And yet that celebrity hadn't given him a swelled head. Rather, if anything, one could say that Leo's charisma was made more compelling by the habit (or, if you prefer, the quirk) of not being conceited. Yes, Professor Pontecorvo was one of those luminaries who have worked out a very sophisticated method of being conceited by not being conceited.

A diversified career (in which oncology was the planet around which sparkling satellites orbited) had made him a more than well-off man. He often liked to boast to younger colleagues, with a mixture of cynicism and affectation, that his university salary (he had had the professorship for quite a while by now) served him at most as pocket money.

And perhaps he could have spared himself certain remarks in a world where only those over eighty were forgiven their wealth, or, rather, those with the good taste to be unable to enjoy all those good things anymore.

Anyway, in spite of that prosperity, in spite of such inappropriate remarks, and thanks to Rachel (a girl with her feet on the ground), the Pontecorvos did not like to show off their wealth. Except for Samuel, who precociously manifested a rapt passion for all that was, or at least seemed, expensive, the others had not been excessively infected by the hedonistic religion followed in those years by many families in their circle.

Just to be clear, they would never have gone on vacation to "the right places for the right people" (as a television ad very much in vogue then on the newborn commercial television had it), where Samuel would have happily joined his schoolmates. No Cortina, no St. Moritz or places like that. Certain ostentations were not admitted into the court of the Pontecorvo parents. Someone might object that to go every year to a pleasant and unknown village like Anzère could be considered an intensified form of snobbishness. But that had no importance for the Pontecorvos, who considered themselves at once above and below certain things. What counted was the fact that over the years they had established some sacred habits that made the stay in Anzère inadvertently easy.

Rachel began her day in the snow early. Sipping "in blessed peace" an entire pot of coffee (she brought it from Italy, like an immigrant) as every so often she glanced at the valley, which had the shape of an amphitheater whose sides were sharp peaks, uniformly snow-covered and at that hour, when the weather was clear, lacquered with pink and pearl-gray. Even the boys liked to get up early but for reasons different from their mother's: they wanted to get to the trails (who knows why!) before anyone else. They seemed to feel an exclusive satisfaction in observing that their father's sedan (it, too, had been loaded onto the train) dominated, in solitary splendor, the icy parking lot below the lifts. Besides, it was only the first contest won in a morning consecrated to competition.

Leo wasn't mad about skiing and in fact, with the cold, and the weariness that had accumulated during the year, would have taken his time in the morning. But he didn't want to disappoint Filippo and Samuel. It was as if for his sons there were nothing more sensational than to play a sport with him. You should have seen how those boys strutted when Leo, at the start of every summer, granted them the season's first, and last, three minutes of "passes and shots at the goal." There, in the yard at home, until his smoke-encrusted lungs and the piercing protests of his spleen enjoined him to throw in the towel, Leo watched his boys showing off for him with the fervor of a halfback on the junior team ready to hurl himself at every ball to impress the varsity coach. There they were, his boys: hyperactive, enthusiastic, full of energy and health, looking at him with such disappointment when he quit!

On the ski trails the atmosphere was the same. Ardor, adrenaline, competitive spirit. Filippo mocked his brother's fear of jumps. Semi, on the other hand, couldn't bear that Filippo, although he had been skiing for much longer, wasn't careful to keep his skis joined. And meanwhile, in the midst of these disputes, the father struggled on. The trouble was that, while Filippo and Samuel were at the age when one doesn't know the meaning of the word "fatigue," to the extent that they could ski for nine hours straight, for Leo the best part was the silence as he rode up in the lift. He let his head sink back, took off his gloves, poked his poles at the snowdrifts encountered along the way. He lighted a cigar. He inhaled, exhaled intensely the aphrodisiac cocktail of thick smoke and thin air. He felt the muscles of his legs go numb from a sudden blast of cold, and, when the ascent got steeper, returned to himself and was nearly in danger of falling.

Keeping up with the competitive impulses of his sons became more complicated every year. Until a few years ago he had been the one to instruct, wait, goad, but for a while now the roles had been reversed. In the meantime, it seemed, his style had become obsolete. And Filippo and Samuel kept pointing it out to him with impatient reproaches: "Come on, Papa . . . "; "Let's go, we'll never get there like that!"

Luckily his authority was still intact enough to allow him to impose a pit stop, at lunchtime, in the lodge, a cabin of dark wood shingles clinging nimbly to the icy slope, a dozen meters from the chairlift for one of the more accessible trails. Inside, it was more spacious than it appeared from the outside, and was welcoming even at the peak time of Christmas weekend, when it was crowded with skiers who, in their boots and silver uniforms, looked like participants in a conference of robots, astronauts, or medieval knights in armor. Thus, while the boys had a coke and a sandwich, he allowed himself a bacon-and-mushroom omelette, with roast potatoes and a couple of glasses. All accompanied by the usual comment: "Remember, not a word to the old lady,", alluding to the meal just eaten, which wasn't properly kosher.

The waltz of alcohol in his veins allowed him to enjoy the last postprandial descent. In the afternoon he didn't ski. The boys didn't even make an attempt to ask him.

Then for the professor the day in the mountains took a definitely more congenial turn. At home a long sit on the throne awaited him, followed by a scalding shower that lasted at least ten minutes, using up the hot water. ("Consuming the glacier,"

Rachel mocked him, always amazed by her husband's excessive use of the planet's natural resources.)

"Why don't we have a nice cup of coffee?" It was the standard phrase with which Leo addressed Rachel as soon as he came out of the bath, perfumed with cologne and talcum powder and with a cigar in his mouth. Both Leo and Rachel knew that what was wrong with that question was the use of the first person plural. That ecumenical grammatical choice was hypocritical and fraudulent: the coffee, which only he needed, would be made by her. The climb of the contemporary woman in pursuit of parity was in an intermediate phase. For now the wife continued to make the coffee, but at least she was asked politely, and, above all, in conditions that let a little uneasiness seep into the husband. At this rate the wives of Filippo and Semi—if those two confirmed bachelors should get married—would compel their docile spouses to make the coffee, and more than likely they wouldn't bat an eye.

After the coffee and a nap on the couch in front of the fire, Leo went to the village with Rachel. While she did some shopping, he, with a cosmopolitan attitude that the fluency of his English did not, unfortunately, match, bought the British and American papers. And sitting, freezing, on a bench he read them with enormous effort, dreaming of a dictionary.

As they headed home, the mountains on the horizon vanished behind a curtain of shadows, and the village lighted up. The windows of the shops on the main street began to sparkle. The precious goods, delicately arranged among red ribbons, wooden boxes, gilded balls, pinecones, branches of fir, asked nothing better than to be taken out for some air, be adopted, and, if possible, visit other countries. And luckily for them the right sucker was in town.

"Don't tell me that's the latest Nikon . . . " "Not bad, that pashmina! The salmon-colored one, a really fine cashmere";

"And those Blues Brothers Persols? Am I wrong or has Semi been driving us crazy about needing new sunglasses?"

Who, in those times, didn't dream of brand-new sunglasses? Who didn't dream of giving gifts? Now that the world was more or less peaceful, now that it offered so many opportunities, giving gifts was the best way of showing the people you loved that the worst was over and how important they were to you. A gift-giving euphoria that Leo was defenseless against. What could he do if those windows decorated for the holiday made him wish to remind his wife how indispensable to him she was, his children how satisfied he was with them, and himself how much he loved himself?

So began the usual pantomime. His insistence, her refusal. His certainties, her uncertainties. A pantomime whose result was taken for granted: in the end he would get his hands on the salmon-colored pashmina and the Nikon. And that was right. He needed nothing else. There was nothing else that interested him more at that juncture than to photograph with his new Nikon his wife wearing the equally new salmon-colored pashmina. He knew that to fulfill that dream he would have to confront—and rout—the trite objections of the beneficiary of such generosity. Which in fact were swift in arriving: "Leo, don't you think it's a little too expensive? And a bit gaudy? You're really sure it's my style?"

Coming out of the shop carrying the packages, he was all triumph while she hunched her shoulders and lowered her eyes, as if she feared that the God of Israel might track her down even there—in that frozen corner of paradise—determined to punish her for her vanity and her idolatry.

Returning to the chalet, while the boys had showers and Rachel took out the food she had just bought and put it on the plates (cooking was not her strong point), Leo finished reading the newspapers by the fire, transfigured by the milky fog of his cigar. Or he showed the boys, in their bathrobes, the latest purchases. Or he fiddled with the new Nikon while Samuel, thanks to his twenty-ten vision, read him the instructions. All this as he waited, still triumphant, to sit down at the table. Fresh bread, cheese, red wine, and a dessert that oozed Austro-Hungarian nostalgia. And finally beddy-bye.

Yes: all this, every year, for years, stupendously immutable.

Was it possible that everything had begun there? In such a pure and innocuous context? That the great misunderstanding that, seven months later, he would not find the moral force to explain to his family had begun to deposit its sediment right *there*?

For several minutes now Leo had been torturing himself with a lot of questions. Ever since, with enormous effort, he had managed to drag himself to the bathroom in the cellar. Now he is standing. In front of the mirror. He pees in the sink the way adolescents and drunks do. In his mouth the taste of a rotten cherry.

The idea of being able to give adequate answers to the useless interrogation he is inflicting on himself is no more reasonable than the hope of lifting his head to ask the mirror what has become of him in the meantime. Probably his face would reveal the killing effort he has lavished on trying to go to sleep. Two nights and two days. Or if you prefer forty-eight hours. That's what it took to break the siege of insomnia.

Which means that, after that utterly unrestorative sleep, the exile in the study-cellar is about to complete two and a half days. The two and a half longest, most stationary, most sleepless days of his life. The most interesting and the most banal. The most meaningful and the most useless. The most incontrovertible and the most mysterious . . . in other words, the "most," in every sense.

Leo, in any case, is still lucid enough to understand that his insomnia was not solely the result of the anguish for all that had happened and for all that was about to happen. There had also been an inconvenient technicality: in moments of crisis, it was impossible for him to relax in a place where Rachel was not within reach. To place his fingers on his wife's hip, slide down to her thigh, to play with those soft and familiar surfaces was the only tranquilizer that Leo had abused in all those years of marriage. But it seems that Rachel (not to mention her hip and her thighs) was unavailable this time.

For a few minutes after his flight from the kitchen, Leo had expected her. Embarrassed, terrified, incapable of believing that he could meet her eyes, but he had expected her. She is about to come down. We'll quarrel. We'll shout. We'll lash out at each other. Maybe we'll hit each other. But at the end she'll offer me a chance to explain. And things will settle down . . . Of this Leo became increasingly less certain as the hours passed. With the thickening of the shadows around him and the anguish within.

Then he had had a dizzy spell. He had felt his limbs stiffen. Was that tiredness? He remembered the discussion he had had with his wife, in the presence of a brawny furniture seller, at the time of the renovation of the cellar: Rachel who wants to buy a horrid little sofabed, Leo who has vowed eternal love to a useless, extremely expensive blood-red leather Chesterfield.

"You've furnished the upstairs like a space ship. Let me at least exercise down here the practical spirit that you despise so much." Lucky he had given in that time! Otherwise, now he wouldn't have had that makeshift bed at his disposal.

So, having transformed the couch into a bed, Leo lay down on it, certain he would collapse. But something had gone wrong. And the Calvary had begun: the search for impossible sleep.

All because he had made the mistake of turning off the light. In the darkness the space dilated in a frightening way: now the room was immense, like the cave of Polyphemus. His mother always told him—when he was a sleepless child—that damn story of Ulysses and Polyphemus. It seemed that she did it on purpose. (Leo had never been able to understand if that woman had loved him too much or too little.) But why just at that moment should he remember Polyphemus and his cave, when he hadn't thought of him for a thousand years? A cave the size of a giant, whose exit was barred by an equally giant mass. Children of the world, do you know of anything more terrifying?

In short, a second after turning off the light Leo had felt the pillow swelling under his head in a dismaying fashion. He had understood how it must feel to be a mere little fish in the immensity of the ocean. But just when, in order not to get lost in such an empty vastness, Leo, by a skillful manipulation of his fingers, had managed to reduce the size of the pillow, making it appropriate to the surrounding space—just then his breath was obstructed, as if the giant cave were rapidly growing smaller. A few seconds more and it would crush him.

So, increasingly short of oxygen, he got up, turned on the light, and started walking again. That was the secret: walk, get tired, like a child. And like a child keep the light on. Then throw yourself down on the bed again, waiting for the right moment.

Not to think. Not to think about himself. To forget for a few sumptuous moments who he was. Forget the story of which he was the incredulous protagonist. At times, in those two days of Calvary, the magic worked. Leo had been able to forget everything: why he was there, what had happened, what was at risk; and then Rachel, the boys, the TV news, colleagues, patients, the university, that damn girl, that damn girl, that damn girl . . . As if his organism refused to be constantly vigilant. As if his brain and body had called on the standard ration of oblivion and unconsciousness that allows us not to go mad.

But God only knows that Leo paid dearly for those instants of repose! The recurrences were frightening. Usually it was a

concrete detail, placed on the horizon of his abstract mental landscape, that started up the torture machine again: who knows, Filippo's French fries, Samuel's labored breath, Rachel's muteness . . . Then, like the man who has been diagnosed with a fatal disease and, waking from a tranquil sleep, suddenly remembers the death sentence hanging over his head, Leo felt a wave of panic rushing over him all at once. An anomalous wave that didn't come from far away but from within. The nightmare was concentrated in a few square centimeters of his chest. His legs shook, his ears buzzed, his blood burned. Leo would have hit his head against the wall to empty it out again. But now it was impossible. You can't go back. Now Leo Pontecorvo is no longer a human being. Now Leo Pontecorvo is all his embarrassment. All his shame. All his terror.

So he began to blather, or maybe to pray: "They're going to tear me to pieces . . . They're going to tear me to pieces . . . They're going to tear me to pieces . . . " Those words, a hundred times less powerful than their meaning, turned out to be a paradoxically effective exorcism.

Then, after two days of fighting, when he was sure that he would never make it—would never sleep again because insomnia was his punishment, his death sentence—Leo fell asleep.

Now he's been awake for several minutes. Dawn is making him wait.

He must have dreamed a river of tears. In the dream he was weeping continuously. So, as soon as he woke up, he touched his hands to his cheeks, observing that they were perfectly dry. Immediately afterward, his left hand hurried to seek a bit of warmth between his knees. While the other, following a course to the north, reached his skull, or rather the curly surface on which Leo's fingers had paused, in a pensive manner, for two nights and two days.

Now that same hand was fumbling with a skinny little dick, at an all-time low, aiming at the drain of the sink.

And so it happens, as his bladder empties, that (in one of those flashes which are so abundant in films and so rare in life), Anzère returns to Leo's mind. The light and snow of Anzère. Maybe because his brain, during those days of desperate interrogation, had always been more attracted by the opposites: the great and the small. Peace and terror. Sleep and wakefulness . . . And what could be a greater contrast, compared to the dense shadows in which he had wakened, than the brilliance of the days in the mountains? Was it possible that all that joyous shared light was implicated in this obscurity and this silence? Yes, in short, was it possible that to explain why he now finds himself here—in exile, terrified, peeing in the sink and determined never to look at himself in the mirror again—he has to interrogate something so lacking in pathos, so calm and relaxing, so starry and ineffable as the *last* vacation with his family in the Swiss snow?

To be more precise, the series of equivocal events that would conclude in the mountains had been set up, so to speak, by a state of tension. Nothing special. A small marital quarrel that had warmed their souls two weeks before leaving for Anzère.

Everything had begun with a seed planted by Samuel with his mother: that spoiled child wanted to take Camilla to Switzerland. Rachel had said she wouldn't even discuss it.

"Why not?"

What did he mean, "why not"? Did it have to be explained? Because he and Camilla were too young to go on vacation together. Because such a cohabitation would make Filippo and Papa uncomfortable, and this she could not allow. Rachel was surprised that Camilla's parents had agreed. And that they would lightheartedly deprive themselves of their daughter at Christmas.

"Her father said she could."

"And I say no! We're not going to discuss it."

"Then I'll ask Papa."

He had asked him. To Leo the matter didn't appear so unseemly: he didn't mind at all if Samuel brought someone. And for the same reason that, on certain Saturdays in June, he loved it when his sons' friends invaded his house and stayed for dinner. To have a "full house": this was one of Leo's favorite expressions. Above all if that fullness had to do with his children's friends. Not that he was present. He was careful not to go beyond two or three ritual phrases. But at the same time, in his heart, the idea that a dwelling so pointlessly vast was available for the entertainment of so many boys flooded him with an unspeakably sentimental warmth. And then there was the energy that Leo felt pouring out. The energy of adolescents. Something so radiant, fleeting, and smelly that even his youngest students had already lost it. And at the same time something so inescapable that it radiated even through the corridors of his hospital unit, full of small sick patients.

In short, the presence of Camilla in the mountains had the merit of proclaiming energy and fullness. And, further, Leo thought that if Camilla came his sons' attention would be focused on her. Maybe they would leave him alone. Maybe with Camilla around they wouldn't insist that he ski.

Leo had given his assent. Although aware that this would produce a breach in his married life.

The quarrels. Their exhausting and bellicose quarrels. The frequent clashes between Leo and Rachel, of which I've already given a taste, seemed to reproduce on a tiny scale and in a parodistic form the argument that, just in those years, was escalating within the tiny but valiant Roman Jewish community between two alternative conceptions of its own identity.

Beginning with the first fight, the oldest, which had set them against each other at the dawn of their married life, starting the day Rachel had found out she was pregnant: what name to give the child in her womb and, after him, the little brother or sister they would one day present him with. Leo thought the Biblical names that Jews, everywhere in the world, gave their children were pompous. He was for something normal, anti-septic, something like Fabrizio, Enrico, Lorenzo. Safe, sober, unencumbered. Something that would not immediately iden-tify them (after all, for that there was already their surname). Something that would one day make them bold citizens of the twenty-first century. Rachel, on the other hand, as you would expect, wanted her sons to bear one of those pretentious Jewish names: David, Daniel, Saul . . . In certain spheres that woman lost all sense of humor. The solution to the problem, as you will have already deduced, was solomonic: to the firstborn a Greek name had been given, to the second a Biblical one. And so not even this had resolved the internal dispute. A kind of creeping dissent that always placed Leo and Rachel on opposite sides of the fence.

The enormous publicity that the Jews got following the shocking news of the deportations and extermination had gone to the head of the Jewish case in point known as "the Roman Jew," throwing him into despair and making him cocky at the same time. The Roman Jew had discovered the existence, in distant lands, of Jews much more Jewish than him: strict and picturesque, tragic and brilliant, those Ashkenazi—with their brittle, magical, esoteric existence, always on the edge of dis-aster—appeared a thousand times more suited to (immeasur-ably more than the Roman Jew ever had) the task of being sac-rificial victims and peaceful heroes of the revenge visited on the Jews by History.

That awakening to their own inferiority had provoked in the more religious families a spirit of rivalry that translated into the adoption of customs and prohibitions that had disap-peared from the indigenous tradition centuries ago. All those alimentary shackles, all those turned-out lights on the evening of Shabat, all that fasting and prayer on the day of Yom Kippur, all those jackets torn in mourning were a postmodern quotation (literary and cinematographic) of a tribal Judaism that had little to do with the type that had been cultivated by the Roman Jews since the now distant time when the Emperor Titus had deported them to Rome. Forcing them to undergo in the following two millennia petty harassments in the heart of Christianity.

The fact is that the phenomenon of the radicalization of Roman Judaism had produced, by contrast, in the community's more secular and enlightened souls an impulse of mockery and impatience: a sarcastic spirit that Leo embodied perfectly, no less perfectly than Rachel played the role of the reborn Roman Jew.

This is the battlefield of the Pontecorvo spouses. She never stops finding new ways to make the life of the family less comfortable by unearthing traditions that basically have no more to do with her than the white tunic and sandals worn by Roman matrons in the time of Augustus. While he counts up all the secular Jews in the world who have been successful in cinema, literature, medicine, physics, and so on, forgetting that there is not even the hint of a Roman Jew in the group, and at the same time overestimating his own professional merits to the point of feeling himself part of the Jewish International of success.

And yet, although in essence the squabbles of Leo and Rachel always seemed to concern that alternative way of living Judaism, in reality this merely dissimulated the true reasons for their mutual aggressiveness: that is, the fact that they belonged to two different and in some measure antithetical social classes. In other words, the religious argument was the tin lid that tried to keep the caldron of class conflict from boiling over. About their relationship, in essence, there was not much else to know. The difference in social class, usually, explained much more than all the rest. It explained, for example, why Rachel's father had poisoned the life of his twenty-four-year-old daughter with endless prohibitions so that she, a step from a degree in Medicine, would stop going out, once and for all, with that fop of a professor.

Precisely the Leo Pontecorvo who, at the time still an unpaid assistant professor, had won her by initiating her into the other half of the universe, consisting of comforts and daily pleasures that that girl, who had lived under the strict rules imposed by her father and had been made romantic by a lot of Hollywood comedies, never imagined could be within reach. Their belonging to different worlds also explained why on the other side of the barricade the hostility was no less fierce: to the point where Leo's mother, using as a pretext the recent death of the husband of a dear friend of hers, showed up in mourning at the celebration in the temple of the much opposed marriage of her son to "the daughter of a tire salesman from the Ghetto."

Rachel owed the epithet to the profession of her father—a typical representative of the category of "street Jews" so despised by the well-off Jews—who had begun his economic ascent in the years right after the war, when, with an equally entrepreneurial brother, he had acquired the equipment for repairing trailer-truck tires.

Just at that time, the time of mass motorization, Cesare Spizzichino had rented a piece of land on Via Tiburtina, not far from the Pirelli factory, and there he had set up his little business, which had become the most prosperous in the whole region. The fact is that the fatter the wallet of Signor Spizzichino grew and the more prosperity flooded him, the greater was the desire to somehow free himself from his humble origins. This had led him to entrust to his two daughters the task, so dear to all the parvenus in the world, of gaining some social respectability through education and culture.

Stella and Rachel Spizzichino were the first two university graduates in the family: in medicine the living one, in pharmacology the dead one. A record that filled the massive body of Signor Spizzichino with such pride that tears came to his eyes.

A completely different history from that of the Pontecorvos, on whom the practice of the medical profession for at least four generations, together with assimilation, had bestowed a temperate affability that someone might have called condescension, if not negligence.

That these two worlds, different almost to the point of contradiction—now that they had been stuck together by a marriage that tenaciously endured, thanks to a strong emotion—seized on every irrational pretext to fight isn't so difficult to explain or to understand. Whatever certain enlightened souls may think, there is nothing more indigestible than diversity, and nothing more comforting than to fight what one can't understand. Loving each other and not understanding each other was the fate and the secret of Leo and Rachel, and of many other happy, stubbornly indissoluble couples of their generation.

In the autumn preceding the Christmas vacation in Switzerland the conjugal serenity of Leo and Rachel Pontecorvo was jeopardized by what later passed into history as the "crisis of Sigonella."

The night between the tenth and eleventh of October the carabinieri, employed by the Italian government headed by Bettino Craxi, had challenged the arrest of a handful of Palestinian terrorists by the U.S. Delta Force—directed from thousands of kilometers away by the no less resolute and bellicose Ronald Reagan. The theater of this psychodrama was the small landing strip of the military airport of Sigonella. On that tongue of asphalt, cooled by the fragrant night wind, Italian and American troops had come within a hairsbreadth of firing at each other. And certainly for a very juicy prize. The disputed terrorists were responsible for the kidnapping of the cruise ship *Achille Lauro*, whose conclusion had been the killing of the American Jewish paraplegic Leon Klinghoffer.

The interest, both practical and symbolic, of the Americans in capturing the murderers of their fellow-citizen was obvious. Equally obvious was the interest of the Italians in having their so-called territorial rights respected. In the end the Italian soldiers, without recourse to weapons but protected by nationalist pride and international law, had got the best of their opponents, like David over Goliath. Which had literally outraged Rachel, just as it had flooded Leo's blood vessels with patriotic pride.

And while the friction between Italian and American diplomats had been violent, never, not even in its most dramatic moments, had it reached the polemical force that at the same time, and as a result of the same dispute, disrupted the living room of the Pontecorvo house. It was as if the Sigonella case had sucked up into itself the already existing reasons for discord between spouses who were constantly quarreling. Beginning with the human and political judgment of Bettino Craxi, and ending with much more cogent arguments on Judaism and anti-Semitism, there was nothing on which Leo and Rachel could find agreement.

To Rachel it seemed emblematic (the closing of the circle) that that politician so adored by Leo should be stained with a crime that she considered among the most infamous—anti-Semitism. On the other hand for a man like Leo Pontecorvo, who since he came of age had carried in his wallet the membership card of the Socialist Party, and who, although he had never been active in it, followed its activities with the emotional partisanship of a soccer fan, to see Bettino Craxi express himself, on the runway at Sigonella, at the height of virile energy, well, it had been a joy.

A Socialist in power, a Socialist whose Socialist arguments prevail, a modern Socialist who wants to modernize the left, a Socialist who hates the Communists, by whom he is hated, a Socialist whom everyone respects and fears and, by virtue of that respect and that fear, has shoulders broad enough to bear any partisan gossip . . . and now, finally, a Socialist who holds back those arrogant Americans, who doesn't allow himself to be stepped on by that cowboy, that two-bit vaudeville actor Ronald Reagan. It was enough to give you an orgasm.

As you see, Leo's love for Craxi trumped his love of all things foreign, reawakening in him chauvinistic sentiments. Leo's indulgence of Bettino Craxi, which sometimes touched on complacency, found a sugary correspondence in Rachel's sentimentality toward the Jews. Which explains why the altercation over the Sigonella case had reached such a level of exasperation.

The place where that clash occurred was the one preferred by both. Leo, after his shower, was shaving his cheeks (he always did it at night) in front of the mirror, which was clouded by steam. While Rachel, in her small adjacent boudoir, was choosing (with her usual impatience) the clothes to wear the next day. Only at the end of the dialogue that I am about to transcribe did the two face each other, now in the bedroom: he with his neck mutilated, she in her nightgown, with the clothes angrily balled up in one hand:

"What does anti-Semitism have to do with it? You people think the world is divided into Jews and anti-Semites."

"Why do you talk as if it had nothing to do with you? As if you weren't in that world? You think that if instead of a Jewish paraplegic it had been a beautiful Catholic girl, what do I know . . . from Catania, your hero, your leader, would have shown the same indulgence toward those killers?"

"What indulgence? What the fuck indulgence are you talking about? I haven't seen any indulgence. If anything I've seen great severity. From a head of government tired of wiping the Americans' boots."

"Those same Americans who kept the Nazis from finishing that little job they began? It's those Americans you're talking about? What do you know about it? What do all of you know—you were in the mountains playing bridge among the cows."

"Do I have to be ashamed of my parents' far-sightedness, if they left at the right moment? Do you want to blame me for that as well?"

"I'm only saying that we're talking about the same Americans who liberated us. Who saved us!" (Here for the first time Rachel's voice trembled.)

"And for how long should we go on paying the bill? The *Achille Lauro* is Italian territory. Just like the airport where those shits wanted to make yet another surprise attack. Why shouldn't I be happy that this time they found a responsible head of state in their way? One with balls. One who doesn't get intimidated. One who knows how to stand up to fascists."

"And who might those fascists be? The Americans are fascists? Well, my dear, I think your ideas are a bit confused. Sometimes you talk like Rita and Flavio. The real fascists here are the pirates who seize a ship full of nice people and who—note—among all those present shoot a Jew in the head. The only thing I know is that your Messiah has managed things so that the guy who killed the *nth* innocent Jew gets off scot free."

"No one went free. No one. Now those shits are in our hands!"

"And Abu Abbas?"

"What about Abu Abbas?"

"Didn't they let him escape? You know where Abu Abbas is now?"

"I don't know. But I'm sure you're about to tell me."

"Eating lamb in cinnamon sauce and drinking mint tea to our health! That's where he is! He's out having fun with his

Bedouin friends, blessing the merciful anti-Semitic Italian people! And the instigators of this most recent massacre of the Jews are sitting at his table."

"Let me remind you that there wasn't a massacre. There was only one victim . . . "

"Do you hear yourself? You're talking like them! A single Jew isn't enough for you? To outrage you they have to be murdered by the truckload?"

"That's not what I'm saying. I'm only pointing out that whenever certain subjects come up you get carried away, you exaggerate. And otherwise you never do. Usually exaggeration is *my* prerogative. But when it comes to the Jews and Israel you surge past me. Like that time you wanted me to drop everything—hospital and patients—and go get the boys at school, because you were afraid that the demonstration against the occupation of Lebanon might, who knows how, involve them."

"I had every right to be worried. A classmate of Filippo's had called us murderers."

"Nonsense."

"Does the death of that child seem nonsense?"

"What child?"

"Stefano Tachè. Those pigs . . . If I just think that that day I was supposed to go to temple with Semi . . . " Here Rachel's voice wavered a second time. But rage won out again over emotion:

"Doesn't the idea of that pig now back in his own house, welcomed like a patriot because he cleansed the world of another Jew, make your blood boil? And that Klinghoffer's relatives, instead, have to swallow the usual bitter pill? A poor wretch, whose only crimes were to be a Jew and to be innocent. Is that why you rejoice? Because your fine Socialist government handles things in such a way that the murderers of Jews go unpunished? Is that what, in your view, we needed? Another anti-Semitic government?"

And at these words Rachel couldn't hold out: she had begun to sob. And only then did Leo, who couldn't bear Rachel's tears any more than he could bear the fact that he had been the one to cause them, end the quarrel by embracing her: "Come on, sweetheart, everything will be all right . . . "

Scarcely two months had passed since Leo and Rachel had been at each other's throat about the Sigonella case and here they were, on the eve of the Christmas holiday, clashing again on the appropriateness of taking Samuel's pubescent girlfriend with them. With less bitterness, perhaps, but for reasons that would have a much more devastating effect on their life than the death of poor Leon Klinghoffer. The tone was, as usual, sarcastic and melodramatic. The place this time was inside a Jaguar, barreling along at a hundred and thirty kilometers an hour on the Nuova Cassia:

"I refuse to take my twelve-year-old son's girlfriend on vacation."

"Don't be ridiculous. What can they do? They know there will be this she-wolf foaming at the mouth who is watching out for the virginity of her wolf cub! You won't believe it, sweetheart, but permissiveness offers some unimaginable strategic advantages. Defuses at its origin any transgressive desire. In other words permissiveness is a really good thing."

"It's not a matter of being permissive or not. This is all wrong and ridiculous. The wrong message given to Samuel."

"Oof, you're so obsessed with these messages you're giving."

"You remember how you and I had to win the right to go on a trip together?"

"So you want to take it out on Samuel?"

"I don't want to take it out on him. On the contrary. I want him to understand the value of certain conquests."

"Conquests? You want to make him some kind of Christopher Columbus?"

"Why can't a person ever speak seriously to you? I repeat, we had to sweat for it."

"Well, only because your father wouldn't give in! If it was up to him, you would have ended up like the pharaoh's horse: buried at his side . . . I saved your life! It wasn't my fault if Meyer didn't feel like teaching and sent me. And yes: at twenty-eight I was already teaching, and came to school in a sports car, like Dustin Hoffman. And you were the virginal student whom the depraved professor sunk his claws into. Lord, if you made me sweat, my love! Your pleasure, I mean, your love . . . "

"You are so vulgar!"

"You realize that our first non-secret trip was our honeymoon?"

"Exactly. It was so wonderful, so liberating . . . "

"You're right, maybe Samuel and Camilla should get married . . . "

"Please, stop it. You know how exasperating it is when you don't take what I say seriously. As I see it: the things you win on the battlefield are much more exciting."

"I know how you see it. In grand stereotypes. If you want we can lock Semi in the storeroom for a year. When he comes out he'll be full of life . . . "

"Stop it!"

"All right, I'm sorry. But it's hard for me to speak seriously about things I don't consider serious."

"Because, in your childish enthusiasm, you haven't thought about the practical questions."

"And what might they be?"

"The chalet isn't big enough. There's only one bathroom. Camilla is a girl, at a difficult age: she needs her privacy. It will be just as embarrassing for us to share the bathroom with her as it will be for her to share it with us. And then where does she sleep?"

"Well, it means Filippo and Samuel will sacrifice by sleeping on the couch in the living room and leaving Camilla their room."

"But really! Aside from all your apparent indulgence, even you must feel it won't work?"

Of course he felt it. And theoretically he would even have been inclined to say she was right. Nonetheless he didn't give in, for the usual reasons that husbands and wives don't give in: stubbornness, pride, desire to get the best of the adversary. And in the end he had won. His motion had, so to speak, passed. The careless deconstructive dialectic had routed the worn maternal anxieties and puritanical diktats of Rachel.

And how could he know, poor man, that by winning that little conjugal skirmish he had laid the foundations, like a short-sighted general, for losing the most important battle of his life?

And all because Camilla had chosen a bizarre and compromising way of thanking him. For his support, I mean.

Why should we be surprised? That girl was really an eccentric. The only thing Camilla shared with her contemporaries was age. Compared with the female friends of his sons whom Leo ran into every so often, and compared with the girls in his unit, Camilla stood out like one of those odd-shaped tomatoes thrown into a heap of shiny, plastic-looking, but also unfortunately tasteless ones, thanks to some industrial adulteration. Camilla was the type of girl for whom the antithetical assessments "She's older than her age" and "She's younger than her age" are both valid. Compared to her the others resembled each other in a depressing way, all with carefully brushed blond hair that made them grotesquely similar to the flawless girls whom Leo had found in his class in the early fifties and for whom he felt no nostalgia.

Was the world going backward instead of progressing? Was

it the excess of sex in the past twenty years that had produced this type of renaissance in the magic world of adolescence? The sensation Leo had had one afternoon, coming home earlier than usual to make an appearance at Samuel's birthday party, was so malicious and anachronistic: balloons, paper cups and plastic forks, big bottles of Fanta and Coca-Cola, and all those teen-agers intimidated by any suggestion of promiscuity, with the girls on one side of the living room and the boys on the other, as in synagogue. But, holy Jesus, what had happened to the sexual revolution? And alcohol? And marijuana? Of course, Leo hadn't expected an orgy, or anything like that. Nor had he hoped for it, at least not in his house. And yet not such a pervasive sense of vagueness and irresolution.

Most intolerable was the enclave of blondes with pink hairbands, tight jeans trimmed with paisley, and large shapeless sweaters, as if pilfered from a potbellied father. They seemed more like Teddy bears than like girls. Yes, nothing but dressed-up Teddy bears. So that in his own mind he had nicknamed them Teddy-bear girls.

A type widespread not only in his social class but more or less everywhere: you just had to make a little trip to the center of Rome on Saturday afternoon to run into slightly more vulgar clones of that type of girl. The world was becoming uniform. Aesthetically, anyway, class differences were disappearing, and fashions, although respectful of a pyramidal trend, were discovering the advantage of ecumenicalism.

Let's say that a perceptive shopkeeper, having acquired a stock of white or pink sweatshirts with large writing on the front, had managed to convince the most up-to-date girls of the most fashionable neighborhood that those pieces of fabric were really cool, well, you could be certain that in a few months that sweatshirt would have invaded the streets of Rome like a lethal epidemic, in a week spreading through the whole country and infecting millions of girls. So: the Teddy-bear girls who were overflowing Leo's living room and yard that afternoon could be considered, in view of their social origin, true unifiers of public taste.

Furthermore, these were well-brought-up and respectful girls, whose only fault (that is, if it could be considered one) was that they were rebelling against twenty years of rebellion, taking refuge in a conformism that, unlike that of their progenitors, had at least the good faith to appear as such. It's strange how so often the most conformist periods are also the least hypocritical.

And yet it pleased Leo (and in a certain sense Rachel, too) that the first girl their Semi brought home was not a Teddy-bear girl. The mind of the Pontecorvo spouses was philistine enough to believe that originality was in itself something good and instructive.

If there was an art at which that girl excelled it was an extraordinary capacity to disappear. To not be noticed. There was nothing in her person that did not seem to indicate a frantic quest for anonymity: the color of her clothes (sober and modest), which alternated between gray and dove-gray. Her elastic, supple body, like licorice: a thinness so excruciating that it made you think of certain diaphanous poetesses of the early part of the century but also of malnourished Pakistani girls. Her soft luxuriant hair, so red that the little Maoist was forced to restrain it in a peasant-style bun. The color of her skin—milk in dust—that seemed at the same time anonymous and restful. Not to mention an obtuse, obstinate silence, behind which she withdrew like a turtle in its shell.

And maybe this was why Leo and Rachel had scarcely noticed her when, a couple of months before the birthday, Semi had brought her home for the first time. When, during the dinner, just the four of them, that Samuel had compelled them to have, they, in order not to irritate the sensitivities of the two polite little sweethearts, had repressed impulses of tenderness and hilarity, delaying until they were in bed, finally alone. They had barely taken off the dressy clothes that Semi, for some reason, had demanded of all those present at that surreal dinner. And there they were, snuggled in the linen sheets, unable to stop laughing and gossiping:

"Did you see how our dear little boy could hardly breathe? Did you hear how his voice shook? And when he poured her water? And how he placed the napkin on her lap . . . "

"Did you buy that white jacket? He looked like the dwarf attendant on that TV show the boys torture me with . . . I hate that ugly dwarf! Him and his faggot boss."

"I can't believe that our Semi . . . "

"Our Semi what? That's what we male Pontecorvos are like. Precocious, decisive, enterprising, dressed in white and straight for the prize . . . but also extremely well behaved."

"I nearly grabbed that excited little face and covered it with kisses . . . "

You see? Not a word about the girl. Why concede any attention to a creature so colorless, when you can gush about your marvelous boy? Dressed like a South American playboy. His wavy blond schoolboy hair. His nose, whose slightly hooked profile betrays his ethnic origin and tempers his beauty, making it amusing, congenial, and in a certain sense romantic.

He was splendid. And Leo and Rachel felt so pleased as they remarked on it. It was so natural to comment on Samuel's behavior and neglect Camilla's. The garrulity that possessed Semi as he enumerated Camilla's various qualities was a thousand times more interesting than the sober and modest behavior with which the girl, her gaze full of incredulity, repulsed all those compliments.

That was why that night in bed, smelling the acidic fragrance of the sheets, which, when it began to get hot, Leo insisted be changed every day, they found themselves commenting on

Semi's embarrassment. The nobility of soul that that embarrassment symbolized. And they hadn't seen (how could they?) that right there was a girl destined to annihilate everything (linen sheets included).

The first time Leo really noticed Camilla was when he saw her struggling with her parents. He had met them on that occasion, Samuel's birthday, when they came to get her.

At their arrival, Leo still had the camera around his neck. Rachel had insisted, for once, that her husband make available to the family his dilettantish (and very expensive) passion for photography. And she had forced him into the humiliating role of official photographer for that tedious garden party crowded with Teddy-bear girls. Rachel had an outstanding account not only with the mountain of photos taken by her husband in the course of twenty years but also with all the photos that, in that same twenty years, he had refused to take. She couldn't bear the fact that Leo had filled their house with black-and-white landscapes, skyscrapers at sunset, insignificant details: crushed cigarette packs, chipped coffee cups, sandals abandoned on the beach. In other words: still-lifes. Rather, lifeless. That was the right word. Her husband photographed only dead things. And, even worse, he lavished all the care in the world on doing it. But ask him to take a "normal" photograph, who knows, the boys learning to ride a bicycle, his wife in evening dress or posing in front of the Eiffel Tower, the Louvre, or wherever the hell he wanted? Certainly not, not a chance. When you asked him, the artist felt outraged.

"What's the point," she asked him, exasperated, when, getting back the pictures from a trip, she was faced with that whole repertoire of whimsical images, "of taking pictures that look like postcards? What sort of souvenir is it if there aren't any people?" A comment that roused in the artist yet another gesture of impatience. As if to say: how vulgar!

But that afternoon Rachel had been clear: "I don't want pictures of rolled-up paper napkins. No floral details. I don't want an entire retrospective devoted to the roof tiles. I want pictures of my sons and the friends of my sons. Understood?" Understood. And the recalcitrant Leo could do nothing but keep scrupulously to the petty directives of the one who had commissioned him, spending the afternoon taking pictures of his sons and the friends of his sons, with special attention to the birthday boy and his little girlfriend.

At least until Leo, seeing that eccentric pair of adults come through the gate and make their way into the garden with a questioning and self-conscious air, had thought with satisfaction: finally, an interesting subject! So much so as to order them: "Stop right there!," with the authority of the painter who at last, after hours of searching, has glimpsed in the model's face the right expression. And those two strangers, astonished, had responded to the order with military promptness. Allowing Leo to shoot photo after photo with the enthusiasm of a professional photojournalist. It should be said that those two, framed by the perfect rectangle of the lens, made quite an impression.

They were an extremely vigorous young couple. You could be certain that he was the king of jogging and that she ate vegetables and patriotic salads of strawberries, white melon, and kiwi. The knowing wink addressed by the lady to the photographer revealed that good manners were perhaps not her strong point, but certainly when it came to aerobics she was second to no one.

Both were enveloped in honey-colored fur-lined suède sheepskins: an uncalled-for garment considering the mildness of the spring climate. Leo's eyes lingered more than necessary on the man's hair. It came down to his shoulders: a thing that, after the age of six, should not be allowed to any man (the color of that hair, by the way, explained Camilla's). Equally disconcerting was the contrast between the complexions of these two forty-year-olds, with a sparkling orange patina left by tanning cream, and the moonlike coloring of their pale daughter.

The chromatic difference must have been one of the many by-products of the overall difference that Camilla presented to the individuals who had given her life, and in whom she was unable to recognize herself. She was ashamed of them, just as they were completely unequipped to understand her oddness. Which explained why that evening she was in such a hurry to slip away and they were so eager to linger. To her there was no pleasure in showing her beloved Pontecorvos how inane and ridiculous her parents were, while they wished to understand what the Pontecorvos had that was so special as to lead their only daughter to spend most of her time with them.

In the light of her parents and her reaction to them it was easier for Leo to understand why Camilla, though just as pretty as her contemporaries, was animated by the desire to vanish and hide. If the genie of the lamp had granted her a single desire, she would probably have said simply, "Make me disappear from here." And the genie, "Where if not here, dear little girl?" "I told you, anywhere but here." This was what her beautiful eyes expressed, along with her body, which seemed to want to dissolve into a vertical line.

To understand this you had only to see the impatience with which, at that moment, she tried to intervene between the kind Pontecorvos and her parents. As if she wished to cover up, with her magic cloak of invisibility, even the individuals who were closest to her in the world but of whom she was most ashamed. It was clear that if it had been up to her she would have set fire to it all. To her father, to her mother, and to anything that had to do with them: including the out-of-season fleeces, the imperfect diction, the enormous over-accessorized Range Rover waiting outside the gate of the Pontecorvo house. Not to mention her father's manners, which displayed all the ceremoniousness of the boor who wants to impress the renowned professor.

They lost it too soon, Leo caught himself thinking, with the smugness of one who does not share an analogous fate. It's something that can happen. Yes, they've lost everything that Rachel and I have managed, at least for the moment, to hold onto: the affection, the respect of our children. It's something you see even in the hospital. There are fathers and mothers who still have full control of the situation, while others are totally at the mercy of these little monsters. Sometimes I have the impression that I'm still a hero to my sons. This man and woman have suffered a different fate. There's nothing that the daughter, at least to judge from the way she looks at them, would not reproach them for.

Ah yes, this ridiculous guy, with his sailor's tan, his Viking hair, and his Eskimo outfit, hasn't been his daughter's hero for at least five years. And to judge from the sweetness with which he puts the jacket over her shoulders so that she won't feel cold, his daughter's contempt must be the great suffering of his life. Made worse by the fact that it's a suffering he doesn't think he deserves and whose causes and extent he is incapable of perceiving. And shit, probably he has done everything for Camilla, a hundred times more than his parents in his time did for him, and what is the gratitude he gets from her? A look of tremulous embarrassment. And yet this embarrassment is precisely what Camilla is so precociously forming her personality on. But I swear, if one day my sons should look at me like that . . . yes, I swear . . .

So Leo reasoned, with sympathetic pity, after lowering the camera, after politely introducing himself to those two ill-at-ease people, after calling Rachel and asking her, in turn, to call Camilla, and after noticing the expression painted in Camilla's eyes on seeing her parents in conversation with him. Yes, so Leo reasoned, observing with pleasure that, if Camilla was so apprehensive and doing all she could so that he and Rachel wouldn't realize what common clay her parents were made of, that meant that she considered the Pontecorvos people of a certain rank. While Leo reflected on these things, glancing with one pitying eye at Camilla's father and with the other, much more proudly, at himself, Camilla gave evidence for the first time of her oddness, by addressing her father and mother in French. There would have been no harm if, for example, that had been some private game that they habitually played (like characters in a Russian novel). Or if, following another hypothesis, the French nationality of one of her parents had inclined her to that bilingualism which transforms some families into an irritating Tower of Babel. But suppose that neither her mother nor, much less, her father, was French, that neither could utter a single word of French, except perhaps *merci* and the very popular at the time, not to say annoying, "*Oui, je suis Catherine Deneuve.*"

The reason Camilla spoke that language so confidently and with a beautiful accent was that, since the start of her school-days, she had attended the French school at the Villa Borghese named for Chateaubriand. You shouldn't be surprised that they had sent her to that school: since it was a very fashionable institution, for those poor devils loaded with money but disastrously ignorant the idea that their daughter should go to the Chateaubriand, speak French almost like the French, and spend time with the children of ambassadors and similar things was moving to the point of tears. So that when she was six they asked her to speak to them in French just for the pleasure of hearing her speak French.

For some years after that, they had had, in the small villa in the Argentario where they spent a good part of the summer— a villa acquired by Camilla's father thanks to his colorful leather-goods shops in the center of Rome—a so-called au-pair. A Sabine, a Monique, a Charlotte, whose only job was to practice French with the girl. The trouble is that, increasingly over the years, the girl in question, taking advantage of that ephemeral presence, had excluded her parents from her life through a language that to their ears sounded like an enigmatic music. To the point where once, at the beach, when Camilla and her au pair Monique wouldn't stop chattering to each other, her father, at the height of irritation, had yelled "Shit, that's enough!"

From then on Camilla had got in the habit of speaking French to her father whenever she felt the need, and he, who wouldn't have hit her for anything in the world, of taking it meekly.

Evidently that moment with the Pontecorvos was a propitious one. The context was among the less appropriate, but (and this was the most disturbing fact) the sentences were, after all, apt for the circumstance, like: "*Oui, Papa, la fête a été magnifique!*," "*On y va, Maman? Je suis fatiguée.*"

Leo, who knew nothing about that whole business of the French, wondered what in the world had got into her. Why was she talking to her parents in French? To get out of that impasse in a situational way? To draw attention to herself and annihilate forever the objects of her shame? Or, more simply, was it a way of embarrassing her parents so much that they would leave and take her with them as quickly as possible, putting an end to the nightmare? Leo didn't know, but if the last was the explanation and if such were its purposes, then Camilla's strategy had worked perfectly. Since her parents, with the swiftness of Cinderella when she abandons the prince, had said goodbye and hurried off, while that small eccentric continued to speak to them in a delightful ancien-régime French. The moment was so unpleasant that Leo couldn't even find the courage to ask Semi what the hell had got into his girlfriend. And yet Samuel's indifference to that bizarre scene might lead you to think that to him it was nothing special.

Since then, Leo hadn't thought of Camilla and her eccentricity. At least, not until he was informed by Rachel that their second-born had set as a condition on his presence in Switzerland Camilla's inclusion in the party. So Leo had begun to suspect that that girl, besides being a little strange, was also a precocious manipulator. But he had thought it with good-humored amusement. If there was something he was proud of it was his own tolerance.

Samuel, that sweetheart of a kid, that exemplary twelve-year-old, dictates conditions? Confronts his parents with an either-or? With blackmail that he has neither the authority nor the balls to carry out? Unbelievable! Delightful nonsense!

What could Leo do if he found all this partly laughable and partly touching? If he couldn't share all the worries that seemed to torture Rachel? If Rachel's attitude seemed to him an upsurge of maternal jealousy?

About the fact that it had been Camilla who inspired Samuel with the idea of taking her to Switzerland there was no doubt. Samuel certainly was not so enterprising as to come up with such a thought. But while for Rachel that influence represented a subject for anxious reflection, for Leo it was something amusing and adorable. To see Samuel at the mercy of that strange girl was a sight . . . In light of her behavior with her parents, it made sense that Camilla wanted to avoid immersion in the usual Christmas vacation: the company of relatives she hated, completely taken up with unwrapping monstrously expensive gifts and stuffing themselves with food. Yes, the idea of being able to avoid this nightmare was really too alluring for her. And that the Pontecorvos, apart from certain freedoms that Leo took (some presents for the boys in order not to make them feel too alone in this boundless world of impenitent Catholics), did not, for obvious reasons, celebrate Christmas, was for her marvelous. She couldn't let this opportunity get away. And so she had conceived her "operation Anzère."

Bringing it to a successful conclusion.

In Switzerland, in the odd company that created a situation so unprecedented yet basically congenial to her nature, Camilla had felt the need to thank the person who had helped her make a dream come true.

That thank-you had taken the form of a little letter.

The first of those letters, thinks our prisoner, now that—having washed his face, taking care not to meet the eyes of his greenish double in the mirror—he has started pacing the room again, dreaming of a cup of coffee the way the man lost in the desert dreams of the refreshing jet of a fountain.

Certainly, even before the letter made its appearance, Leo had been able to observe how right his wife had been about everything. Camilla's presence had inevitably spoiled the tried-and-true Helvetic mechanism. Filippo had protested about having to sleep on the sofa bed with his brother. And Samuel, although he was unable to protest in turn (being responsible for the inconvenience), had since they arrived suffered from insomnia, out of a sense of guilt at having caused distress to his brother, who needed more space to perform the rite (beating his head on the pillow in time to music) by which, ever since he was in swaddling clothes, he had invoked sleep.

Then, there was the fact that Camilla not only didn't ski but had no intention of learning. Which meant that Rachel had to be with her all morning. Not to mention the more dangerous issue, that Camilla suffered from asthma (the information had been provided to the Pontecorvos after they had already given their controversial assent to Camilla's coming). The parents had appealed to them. Which drove Rachel to take special care in the cleaning in the morning. To keep always within sight and reach the little inhaler containing adrenalin, and, in the case of a more violent attack than usual, the syringes and the vial of hydrocortisone. Not counting that at the last minute Telma, the maid, had defaulted and hadn't come to Switzerland with her employers, as she usually did. And so Rachel found herself compelled to take responsibility for the domestic duties that the tiny Filipina's sweet presence usually relieved her of.

Leo for his part had had to sacrifice the most pleasurable, solitary part of the day in the mountains. From the start, he no longer found his seat on the throne and his endless shower thrilling. How could he enjoy himself knowing that, beyond the door—in the warm, damp living room, where the fire, with some difficulty, crackled amid sighs and sobs—there was that girl? Who he felt was waiting for him. If the idea of appearing in front of her in his bathrobe wasn't so terrible (Leo came from the type of open family where no state of undress is met with censure), entertaining her was tremendously difficult. Finding something reasonable to say to her. And in any case that possible conversation would ruin the rest of the program (walk with Rachel, newspapers, buying the *petits cadeaux* et cetera).

From the first day Rachel wanted to give Leo a taste of his afternoons for the next two weeks.

The second her husband returned from the ski slopes, in fact, Rachel went out, not before reminding him to watch Camilla's asthma. And Leo knew his wife well enough to know that the message directed at him as she left the house, slamming the door, went more or less like this: "See, you wanted to bring her with us? Now you deal with her."

How could he blame her? It must not be easy to always be right and never be listened to.

So, apparently, it was his job to take charge of his son's girlfriend every afternoon. Of that freckled nuisance called Camilla. A real problem. A problem from every point of view, which Leo hadn't taken account of.

Although he had two sons more or less the same age as

Camilla, although his unit was swarming with kids, although he was used to being around the twenty-year-olds who packed his classroom at the university, Leo wasn't sure how to deal with a teenager.

Basically all his ties with the world of childhood and adolescence were governed, so to speak, by a comfortable social order, in which he occupied a set role. The secret lay in the solidity of his position, which was as immutable as that of all the other parties.

Although his relationship with his sons was not marked by the taciturn formality adopted toward him by his father (the seraphic Professor Pontecorvo senior), nonetheless even a relationship that intimate had all the requirements necessary to be described as "old-school." When Fili and Semi were very small, Leo loved to play the part of the father who doesn't want to have the children around. So Rachel had affectionately nicknamed him Herod: a nickname and a reputation that Our Man didn't dislike, in fact he liked to confirm it with remarks such as "With the type of work I do, for me vacation means not having screaming kids underfoot."

And as for his little patients . . . well, with them Leo could bring out the typical paternalism of the caring doctor, just as for his students he preserved an ironic professorial conventionality.

But what self could he invent to entertain that crazily silent, mysteriously complicated girl? Leo was timid the way certain tall, handsome, absent-minded men are. And confronted by a twelve-year-old with whom he was called on to make light, casual conversation, he was in danger of playing the part of a timid adolescent, and transforming that nuisance of a girl into an experienced and condescending woman. Already he had been entangled in awkward monologues. Yes, the most annoying thing was that what awaited him in the living room, saturated with warm humors—a room that had given him so many solitary pleasures in preceding years—was an unpleasant experience of regressing to adolescence.

The confusion of roles. That was the biggest trap.

For the first two days he had managed by giving her a sort of third degree about Samuel, asking her what type of boy he was, how he behaved with others. Then he had tried to generalize that boring subject by finding out what kids their age did and what their future plans were (really, quite a question to address to a twelve-year-old!).

Camilla's near-silence led to further embarrassment. And then there were her big eyes, with their amber glints, that, although bewildered, were so fearlessly aimed at her adult interlocutor. Something that disturbed Leo in a way he could not explain.

By the third day it was clear that they had run out of subjects. He had shot all his arrows. As for Camilla, Leo began to doubt that she had any arrows to shoot. And that was why, that day, he managed to prolong his stay in the bathroom, hoping that the abundant afternoon snowfall would inspire an early return by his sons. But, for the third time in a row, she had managed to annoy him even before he set foot in the living room. With that damn Christmas song. Since they arrived she had not stopped listening to it. She had brought the forty-five with her and had taken possession of the record player that the landlord put at their disposal. And for three days she did nothing but play that song, and only that song. At very short intervals. Constantly. Stubbornly. Leo was an expert in that type of childish compulsion: Filippo, if he fell in love with a song, listened to it ad nauseam. And yet Camilla's obsession was unrivaled. It was that goddam song (now gone down in history) in which a beardless George Michael—who in those days favored a hair style worthy of a Rodeo Drive coiffeur—never stops lamenting some past Christmas or other.

That was the soundtrack that accompanied what used to be Leo's lovely moments in the bathroom. A tune for faggots! If there was something that Leo was intransigent about it was bad musical taste. All to say that she was doing her best to make him angry and herself a nuisance.

In that state of mind Leo, the third day, appeared in the living room already dressed and with his hair wet. And seeing that girl with her nineteenth-century Irish look near the record player and in front of the fire, and not knowing what to say, he had made a remark that sounded so ridiculously literary and antiquated that, after uttering it, he could have killed himself:

"The Goncourt brothers haven't been discouraged by the blizzard?"

Now, to call a "blizzard" that placid snowfall was an even more pathetic exaggeration than to call his sons the "Goncourt brothers." And yet for the first time Camilla smiled at him. Almost happily.

"Why the Goncourt brothers?" she asked. A question. Finally a question. Too bad Leo had no idea how to respond.

Leo had nicknamed his sons the Goncourt brothers some time ago. When he had confessed to Rachel the irritation that he sometimes felt at the bond between Filippo and Samuel, so close that it bordered on symbiosis.

"You don't worry that Samuel can't get to sleep without his brother? Maybe it wasn't a good idea for them to sleep in the same room together all these years, in that bunk bed."

"No, Semi is just a little afraid of the dark and the silence. Even though he denies it."

"Maybe, but Filippo told me that every night Semi asks him not to fall asleep first, otherwise he can't get to sleep. On the other hand, Filippo has to shake his head like an autistic child, or like a Hasid at the Wailing Wall . . . Some pair! Don't you think? Maybe they were born to live separated."

"I told you. Children—and Semi is still a child—hate darkness and silence."

"All right, but mightn't it be time to split them up a little? Separate schools, separate vacations . . . "

"Why are you so eager to do something so cruel? Something that will happen soon enough naturally?"

This bitter statement of Rachel's—reinforced by the chilling thought of the sister she had lost so many years earlier?—led Leo to extricate himself with a pedantic remark.

"Because I don't want to be the father of the Goncourt brothers."

Of course, it wasn't that Leo knew so much about the Goncourt brothers. He was the virtuous product of those classical studies which even in his day were invariably referred to in the past tense and thanks to which you had unfailingly, and of necessity, become aware of the existence of the Goncourt brothers. And which, without insisting on the actual reading of any of their books, required you to know that they were nineteenth-century writers, kept a kind of four-handed diary, and fucked the same girl.

But evidently that allusion to two French writers (although unknown to her) had made such an impression on Camilla that she couldn't stop smiling with happiness, like one who, after a long search, has found her soul mate. A joy so solid that it gave her the courage to formulate her first question:

"Why the Goncourt brothers?"

"You don't know who the Goncourt brothers are?"

"No, but from the name I'd say they're French."

"To be precise, they *were* French."

Seeing the girl's questioning gaze, Leo felt he had to explain: "They've been dead for some time."

But when the Goncourts died did not seem to interest Camilla any more than it interested her to know what the hell they had done to live. It was something else that had caught her attention, as was clear from her next question (she was making progress):

"Semi told me that you lived in Paris for years."

Leo was pleased that Camilla had used the formal "you." Every so often on the ward he dealt with children, for the most part from modest backgrounds, who used the informal *tu*. This not only irritated him but, worse, put him in a difficult position and saddened him. But here was a well-brought-up child. Her parents, however crude, had taught her that with an old man like him you use the formal pronoun. And, on the other hand, at her elegant French school Camilla must have acquired the transalpine taste for formalities. You're in trouble if you don't call the professors Monsieur and Madame. Trouble if you don't address them with a stilted *vous*.

"*For years?* That's what Samuel told you? That I lived for years in Paris? That megalomaniac boy! A year only. I lived in Paris for a year."

"A long time ago?"

"More or less a million years ago. You remember the Punic Wars? You remember Hannibal? Well, more or less then."

At that remark she had again laughed, and this time, it seemed to Leo, like someone who is about to let go. And he nearly caught himself thinking: how lovely to make a woman laugh! And how lovely to see a woman let go! But just as he was about to say it, an imaginary hand grabbed him by the scruff of the neck and a no less imaginary voice shouted at him: do you see women in this living room? No? So what woman are you raving about?

But then why, if Camilla was only a child, was he so eagerly acting the man of the world?

What had he said? "You remember the Punic Wars? You remember Hannibal?" and she had laughed. She had laughed because the Punic Wars, unlike the Goncourts, were familiar to her, probably she had just studied them. Evidently her happiness depended on having got the allusion and understood the joke of such a sophisticated man, one who had lived in Paris for a whole year in the time of Hannibal.

"What's it like to live in Paris?"

"Have you ever been there?"

"Never. Though maybe next year my school is organizing . . . And then maybe . . . And Papa has promised me that . . . "

"I envy you. It's wonderful not to know Paris yet."

There we are again. He had fallen for it again. He had again begun to play a part. For a second, listening to himself speak, he felt like the protagonist of one of those forties comedies that Rachel and Samuel liked so much, where a slender Fred Astaire or a sullen Humphrey Bogart, usually a millionaire in crisis, charms—thanks to his mature fascination, veined with skepticism—a sweet young girl with a funny smile and a raw beauty, who, although she's just come from an orphanage, has aristocratic manners and refined speech. But neither Fred nor Humphrey, thought Professor Pontecorvo, regaining possession of his faculties, could have been forgiven for a pompous remark like "It's wonderful not to know Paris yet."

"Do you go there often?"

"Every so often I have to. For my work it's indispensable. But if I can I avoid it."

"Why do you avoid it?"

Yes, why? Leo realized that now he was speaking the truth. It was true, he never went back to Paris willingly. Who knows why. Still that story? Still regrets? Come on! All things considered, the balance, on the scale of his fifty years of life, was more than a surplus. Everything in him indicated happiness and prosperity. There was not a comma of his life that he would change.

And so why the covert sadness? What does sadness have to do with it? What does it mean? I wouldn't want it to be of no value: the self-indulgent melancholy that pushes us all to cultivate mawkish, inapt regrets. The road not taken and all that romantic nonsense.

In any case, and in any way he wished to put it, one thing remained true: Leo did not go to Paris willingly. To Milan, yes, to London, too, not to mention New York and Vancouver. To Paris no.

"Is it because of a girl?"

That was the voice of Camilla. It was the voice of Camilla calling him back to reality and tearing him away from his interior wanderings. The strange fact is that she did it with a question that had nothing to do with reality. With a totally inappropriate question.

"What girl? What girl are you talking about?"

Leo immediately regretted the irritated tone of his voice. He hoped she hadn't noticed his sudden apprehension.

"Semi told me. He says you had a girl in Paris."

"Ah! So says Semi. And what else does he say?"

"That if you had chosen that girl he wouldn't be born now, so he's happy that you didn't choose her. And so it makes me happy, too."

Gisèle? Is she talking about Gisèle? Did Semi talk to his girlfriend about Gisèle? Leo felt confused. How was it possible that a twelve-year-old child was talking to him about Gisèle? Leo looked around. There was nothing that at that moment did not speak in the tender and familiar language of the usual. He was in the same chalet that he and Rachel had rented for more than ten years. Ever since Filippo had had his first skiing lesson, and had learned to climb up the school slope and come down in a snowplow. The air was full of smoke because the fire was sputtering. Outside the window the snow was still falling, with the insidious grace of a symphony. Where had Gisèle come from? Because, as far as he knew, no one had any idea about Gisèle, he had never even talked about her to Rachel.

Or maybe he had? Maybe he had talked about her soon
after they met, who knows? It was possible. Telling her about
Paris he had let slip the name of Gisèle and she had done the
rest: guessing what Gisèle meant to him, or, rather, had meant.
The road not taken and all that romantic nonsense. Yes, but
what did Gisèle *really* mean to him? Absolutely nothing. A
good lay. A good lay but too brief. When his body held up.
When his dick held up. That's what Gisèle was for him. And
so why thinking back did he feel that sense of childish bewilderment? Was a slightly less surging virility enough to make a
man of middle age disastrously sentimental?

Then Leo wondered if the story of Gisèle might be one of
those which Rachel often told the boys. The stories that sent
Filippo into raptures. Like the time at the hotel in Monte Carlo
when he had eaten and she hadn't. Suddenly Leo felt angry at
Rachel. Her lack of tact. Her capacity to take apart anything.
Her talent for recycling and manipulating pieces of Leo's life
to entertain the children. And to think it was she who always
accused him of indecency! Sometimes Rachel talked to her
children about their father as if he weren't there. Sometimes it
seemed to him that Rachel was increasingly similar to that
mother-in-law she had so fervently hated.

Or maybe Gisèle had nothing to do with it. Maybe Camilla,
that strange girl, was inventing. Improvising. That's all. From
the little that Leo knew her, it was a more than legitimate
hypothesis. Camilla hadn't said a name. She had talked about
a "girl." She had not said "Gisèle." That there was a girl, that
at that time there had been one, was so normal and likely that
for a mind drawn to certain Parisian romanticisms it must not
have been so difficult to imagine it. She had imagined it, that's
all. No panic.

"What do you say, shall we have some tea?" Leo then asked,
to get out of the little emotional impasse in which he had gone
hunting.

"What a good idea . . . tea . . . yes, I'd like some tea," she had said enthusiastically.

This time, too, Camilla's reaction was surprising. Why did Leo have the impression that whatever he said was interpreted by that girl the wrong way? Why such enthusiasm for a cup of tea? It was afternoon. It was snowing. It was as cold as the gallows. Tea was very appropriate. And so why all this enthusiasm?

In the kitchen Leo managed to calm down. He put the water on to boil. He got two teabags from the package of Twinings Earl Grey. He cut the lemon slices and poured some milk in a little pitcher. His only fear was that Camilla would appear. Who knows, to give him a hand. Thank heaven she didn't. She confined herself to turning on the stereo and starting "Last Christmas" again.

Returning to the living room Leo found her standing near the fire, now nearly out. She was trying to rekindle it in the frantic way typical of someone who has never dealt with a fireplace.

"Leave it, leave it . . . " he said. And, after putting the tray down on the low table covered with Filippo's comic books, he went over. Gently but with extreme propriety he took the wrought-iron implement from her. It seemed to him that Camilla, before letting go, resisted a few seconds too long.

And why did she stick to his side? Why didn't she go sit on the sofa? Now really she was up close to him, leaning over the fire with a piece of paper in her hand.

"No, no—no paper! It burns instantly and it's useless." Leo felt one of her little hands graze his side, as if she had been tempted to lean on him as she got up. While this laborious operation was completed Leo felt threatened by the sharp, bitter odor of a sulking girl: the diluted, feminine version of the stink emitted by the rooms of adolescent boys. And yet again he felt in the air the extremely unpleasant impression of lust.

An impression. Which, now that the fire had flared up again and Leo had sat down, didn't disappear. The question was: who was lusting for whom? Not him. But on the other hand there was nothing in that girl that expressed either an explicit or even implicit wish to provoke him. But if she wasn't provoking him, then why had he started to think of what until that moment had never entered the anteroom of his brain?

It was as if Leo had suddenly realized not only that before him was a girl but that she was his Samuel's girl. And that if she was there now, in the living room where for years the Pontecorvos had perpetuated their blameless family idylls, she owed it to him. Precisely, to Leo. It was he, the irresponsible father, who had allowed his barely adolescent son to take his girlfriend on vacation with him. As if he were an adult. Only now did Leo understand what Rachel had tried in vain to explain to him weeks earlier: the presence of Camilla was not appropriate. And that if it happened it would be unpleasant. And that it wasn't a question of morality, of puritanism, of prudery, and all those fancy words with which Leo had demolished his wife's objections. It was simply a question of good sense.

That was Samuel's girlfriend. His Samuel, the happier and less complicated of his sons, the child for whom everything came with extreme ease. For that very reason it wasn't so odd that already, at twelve, Semi had a girlfriend. Precocity had always been one of the two characteristics (the other was eclecticism) that made his parents so proud of him. The only surprising thing is that the gifted little man had such an irresponsible father.

Yes, this was Samuel's girlfriend. Which means that, although in an embryonic form, the two must have had some physical contact. This banal observation made an impression on our professor. And, all right, he was a doctor, and a children's doctor. Certain things he was aware of and he knew. He remembered the time when a nurse had burst into his small office at the Santa Cristina clinic and breathlessly told him she had just caught two kids in the bathroom, in a position that was to say the least intimate . . . But why use euphemisms? They were fucking. Those two little leukemia patients were fucking. "Like adults," the nurse explained, and he had wondered if there were others.

Leo recalled that he had stubbornly defended—first to the nurse, and then to Loredana, his psychologist friend—the right of those two poor kids to enjoy themselves a little, given the terrible reception that life had reserved for them. He recalled with how much insistence, and with what eloquence, he had defended the rights of nature.

Too bad that now it was not a matter of any two kids. Too bad that now, if he thought of his Semi with Camilla, something seemed wrong to our luminary.

Suddenly he felt so uneasy. His own thoughts embarrassed him. He had to turn away from her, afraid that his eyes were focused on details of that small body, sprinkled with freckles, that had welcomed the caresses of Samuel and who knows what other.

There is no lust without intimidation. This is a hard natural law. If lust is explicitly aggressive, invading, brutal, then it's not lust. And perhaps this explains why Leo felt so confused. On the edge of something he didn't know or refused to recognize.

Was it that sense of shared intimacy, triggered by an allusion to two French writers (Camilla's France, or, rather, freedom, the imagined world against the experienced, the fantastic universe into which she withdrew in order to escape from the vulgar world of her parents), that impelled Camilla, on the fourth day, to write to him? Or was it the mounting sensation of promiscuity and violation that evidently Leo was not the only one, in that room, to perceive?

It's what Leo is now asking himself and can't answer.

Not bad for only the third day in the mountains, he thinks, with the crumb of irony that remains to him. But was it really like that? Or is this a classic retrospective distortion? What do they call it? Hindsight? Maybe Leo simply needs to remember the third day like that. He needs to dramatize it. To give it depth through pathos. Just because if he didn't remember it like that all this would not make sense. Only by overinterpreting can Leo convince himself that things could not have gone otherwise. That he would not have been able to modify them in any way. That this is his story, period. And set his mind at rest.

Probably if things had gone differently that third day it would not have persisted so obstinately in memory. Nor would it have become such an obsessive object of study. And perhaps he now would not remember it with the sacredness that is conceded to milestones. Or really he would not remember it at all. In other words, if that first letter had never arrived, if Camilla, impelled by who knows what, had not written to him, Leo would not now, seven months later, be here analyzing the third day in such minute detail.

Besides, other things had happened on that unforgettable third day which could have led her to the insane gesture full of inappropriate initiative. The letter, I mean.

In the end Fili and Samuel, because the snow began falling more thickly, had in fact returned earlier than usual, to be precise five minutes after Rachel, who had likewise returned early. Seeing the Pontecorvo brothers enter, transformed by the circumstances into a pair of walking snowmen, Leo had felt a sudden relief.

The five minutes spent alone with his wife and that girl hadn't been a big deal.

Rachel was put out by the fact that Camilla, seeing her come in loaded down with packages, hadn't gone to meet her, but sat there with her nose in a book. Leo knew how annoyed Rachel was also by the fact that, since they'd been there,

Camilla had never once offered to help, not even to set the table. If she had offered, she would certainly have been refused. But that Camilla had not even once made the gesture Rachel found intolerable.

It was one of the small rules of behavior that Rachel had learned in her modest family and from which she never deviated. In the place where she came from, work was the only, the unique, value. It was what gave dignity to people's lives. Thus, whenever a carpenter, for example, showed up in the early afternoon at the Pontecorvo house to put up a bookshelf and brought with him a son or an adolescent apprentice, Rachel would rush breathlessly into the boys' room, where, after lunch, they were camping out on the bed reading comics or watching TV, and order them, "Come on, get up, the carpenter and his helper are here."

As if they, too, were supposed to help. It would be terrible if the carpenter or, especially, his helper were to see her sons lolling in dissolute idleness. How shameful! It was better if they appeared pointlessly active rather than busily playing. They should be on their feet, at least. If for no other reason than respect for that boy, their contemporary, who was working. It was for analogous reasons that when, just to give another example, the upholsterer came to take away two heavy divans to reupholster, Rachel, during the journey from the living room to the van parked in the driveway, made her muscles available to help (in reality hindering) the potbellied brute the upholsterer had brought with him to help out.

For Rachel Pontecorvo it was better to present an unrealistic idea of yourself as a worker or a pain in the neck than to give the impression of the idle chatelaine who watches others work. This was the work ethic inculcated in her by that Stakhanovite father from whom she had in no way succeeded in freeing herself. Inevitable, then, that Camilla's insolent immobility seriously annoyed her. But what could she do?

(All right, come on, Rachel, tell us what you don't like about this Camilla. What it is that oppresses you. Vent all your discontent. Don't go on hiding. Don't be a hypocrite. Don't go on elaborating practical reasons, or reasons of principle. Explain what is intolerable to you. Explain once and for all that if at first it was sweet, touching, even moving to see your little Samuel cooing like a dove in love, as time passed the thing began to worry you. And now, in spite of the pair's tender age, the whole business is assuming dangerous and unacceptable proportions. Explain to everyone why your inner sirens have been blaring madly for weeks. Admit, if you have the courage, what is wrong with that girl. And what will always be wrong. Confess that, in spite of the irresponsible tolerance of your husband, the fact that Camilla isn't Jewish is a problem. An insurmountable obstacle. For God's sake, spit it out, tell it all: you didn't bring two fine Jewish boys into the world to feed them to the first shiksa who comes along!)

Filippo and Semi's early return from the slopes helped to relieve the tension Leo felt, crushed between the two women (one a woman in miniature but it comes to the same thing), both in full temperamental turmoil.

By the mere act of re-entry, Filippo and Semi gave their mother the opportunity to do her female five minutes of venting. All the orders she hadn't dared address to Camilla she was now taking out on Filippo and Samuel. It was all do this and do that. And, in response, nothing but leave-us-alone and let-it-go, Mamma.

A few hours later, at the dinner table, the boys took care to finish exasperating their mother and again offered their father the chance to distinguish himself heroically in the eyes of Camilla.

Filippo and Semi were in the state of excitement that often

drove them to a form of demented, exclusive camaraderie, inducing in others the suspicion that they weren't intelligent enough (or not stupid enough?), or in any case not competent enough, to participate in an esoteric conversation between initiates. It was a complicity that in a moment could become, for that very reason, irritating and unpleasant.

The truth is that their coded language was the most visible and least attractive aspect of the symbiosis between Filippo and Semi. It made use of an infinite series of materials, whose bibliography, if someone had really been interested in compiling it, would have been pointlessly tortuous: movies above all, but also phrases of Leo's or Rachel's transfigured by time and by the thousand occasions and most disparate contexts in which Filippo and Semi had repeated them; expressions typical of superheroes from cartoons or animated cartoons on TV; some grammatical howler produced by the uneducated assistant in the after-school program; an especially clever vulgarity formulated by a schoolmate or the judo teacher.

That was their papier-mâché world. A parallel universe consisting of an irrepressible and utterly private chatter, in which it was as easy for them to indulge as it was difficult, once inside, to abandon it. A game whose preferred victim was Rachel. Who, struggling to comprehend, asked her husband, "Do you know what they're saying? I can't understand them!"

"Forget it, they're just two idiots talking nonsense!"

Their mother's lack of comprehension only increased the boys' hilarity. Then Filippo would ask her, "How could a stupid woman like you have given birth to two rad guys like us?" And Semi appeared both proud of and amused by his brother's audacity.

Well, that evening Filippo and Semi were in top form, and especially obnoxious, and there was nothing the others could say that did not inspire them to some new, incomprehensible joke. In particular the doomed targets were Rachel and Camilla (with their father they didn't dare).

Leo had already observed how Semi's behavior toward his girlfriend changed in relation to his brother. In Filippo's absence, Semi behaved toward Camilla in the clumsy, cloying manner that he had demonstrated the night when, the preceding spring, he had introduced her to his parents, during that absurd dinner when Leo and Rachel had had to endure candlelight and so many other sickening things . . . But here, in Filippo's presence, Semi's behavior toward Camilla underwent a radical transformation. He became insolent. Sometimes, with real rudeness, he didn't answer the questions she asked him. Or he withdrew when she approached him. It was as if Semi wanted to prove to Filippo that, in spite of that girl's arrival in his life, nothing between them had changed. He was still on his older brother's side. And their fraternal bond would certainly not be called into question by despicably giving in to a love affair.

Another of the techniques used by Samuel to demonstrate to his brother the degree of his loyalty to the cause was to gang up on Camilla with him. Like that evening, when, after refusing to sit next to her at the table, he started looking at her derisively, which seemed to provoke in the girl, who was usually so enigmatic and indifferent, bursts of dejection. It was as if her childish eyes wouldn't stop asking, What did I do to you? Why are you treating me like this? Why are you a different person when your brother is around? What is it that I don't understand?

The sense of exclusion was transformed into a fairly pathetic attempt, not at all natural to her, to join the conversation. Leo had noticed how every so often Camilla tried to get Samuel's attention by inserting some completely banal comment. It was a suicidal strategy, to judge from Semi's behavior, as he became increasingly contemptuous. Suddenly, perhaps in a desperate attempt to be noticed, or maybe trying deliberately to make fun of him, she had said to Samuel, "You're all red, you got too much sun today!" Leo naturally thought back to the embarrassing tan of Camilla's parents. And he deduced that the remark hid a not too veiled reproach.

Semi gave no weight to that reproach, which provided him, instead, with the opportunity to make fun of her in a way that would certainly amuse his brother.

"Too much sun, too little sun. Too much water, too little water . . . " Semi shouted triumphantly.

And Leo recognized a line from *Bianca*, a film of Nanni Moretti, which his sons had liked enormously and which had increased their vast repertory by a dozen more quotations.

Camilla was frozen by yet another joke at her expense, while Filippo laughed hysterically. Camilla's sad expression and the boys' boorish, inappropriate insistence on firing off their incomprehensible nonsense caused Rachel to ask her husband, with a light pressure on his hand, to intervene actively. Rachel knew how much the boys respected their father, just as she knew the physical charisma (bordering on fear) that Leo's slender figure exercised over Filippo and (especially) Samuel. Leo, no less irritated than Rachel, scarcely needed to be asked:

"Cut it out, God damn it!"

Then he waited for his sons to be quiet to lend greater strength to his scolding:

"Do you think it's polite to behave like this? Don't you hear how unfunny it is? Don't you find it pathetic that you are the only ones laughing at your jokes and allusions? Haven't you had enough of all this self-reference? I can assure you—and I would ask you to trust me—that you are not witty, you are not polite, you are simply irritating, to anyone looking at you and anyone listening. You're acting like idiots. Not to mention that you're repetitious and boring. Even Mel Brooks, Woody Allen, Nanni Moretti jokes—all of which, for the record, I taught you to appreciate—repeated three hundred times become tiresome. Now stop it. Understand?"

And then, but in a tone that had moved on from intolerant to become definitely Biblical:

"But above all I forbid you to make fun of your mother, who refuses to understand you, because she is too intelligent and too sensible. And I order you not to exclude our guest from the conversation."

The great savior. The hero of women! So he must have appeared to Camilla. He who arrived at the right moment to restore order and chivalry. His words had an extraordinary effect. Filippo and Semi giggled nervously. His lecture had silenced and mortified them. A sudden change that Camilla could observe more clearly right after dinner, when Filippo went out with his mother to the village to get a strudel and ice cream and Samuel returned to treating her with the usual sappy attention.

And now Leo recalls the sense of peace he felt that evening, after dinner, when he said good night to Samuel and Camilla, sprawled on the floor in front of the fire. He recalls his own voice saying, "Don't lie so close to the fire!" Just as he recalls Samuel's cries: "Papa, come, please come, Camilla's not breathing! Please, Papa, come here . . . " That is the cry for help that Leo heard a few moments after going to his room and lying down on the bed to read. He recalls his sprint to the living room. And he found Samuel, terrified, bending over Camilla, her body contorted by retching and by her gasping attempts to cough, in search of the drop of air that her body needed more every second. Her bluish face, her hands, literally livid, at her throat.

And suddenly all the timidity that Leo had until then felt toward that girl, who inexplicably embarrassed him, disappeared. In the moments following the violent asthma attack (caused perhaps by the smoke from the fire or perhaps by nervousness), Leo Pontecorvo, the great pediatric oncologist, used to managing much more complex emergencies, displayed an exemplary calm and sang-froid.

He opened the door of the closet where Rachel had placed the first-aid bag. He took the inhaler, the syringes, and the vials. He approached Camilla. He pushed Samuel aside with a gesture of his arm, and performed all the necessary actions. First he made her lean against the wall, then, almost violently, he stuck the inhaler in her mouth, flooding her with adrenalin, and finally, since that first intervention seemed to have resolved the problem only partially, he took the vial and the syringe and—with what manly efficacy!—injected into the girl's veins that diaphanous liquid.

Two minutes later it's all over. Camilla lies on her back on the sofa, breathing heavily. Samuel, next to her, can't stop whimpering, and Leo, Olympian, in the decisive and assertive tone that in the past minutes has transformed him, says, "I'm going to make you both some chamomile tea. I'm afraid you need it."

Was it the calm and tranquility with which he had faced the emergency that so struck Camilla? Was it the affectation of manliness? Had she confused the intervention of a consummate professional with a truly heroic gesture? Was that the mistake that inspired such audacity in the little psychopath?

It might be. Who knows how many times she had seen her parents, the friends of her parents, the teachers at school undone by the violent manifestation of those attacks which, although they had always afflicted her, continued to terrify her.

At those moments the extreme tension clarified into a broad, definitive lucidity, which allowed her to see her Semi's father in all his cool and poetic efficiency. He had treated her as she wished to be treated. He had taken care of her as she wished to be taken care of. He had touched her as she ought to be touched. With resolute, precise gestures, stripped of any

violence, cleansed of any excitement. Was this what Camilla had let herself be so influenced by? Not taking into account the fact that he was on his home ground. That he was swimming in his own sea. That this was his job, a kind of routine. But how could she know that?

Or maybe she did know it?

In the altered state in which Leo is living (he has curled up again on the bed and now has both hands on his neck), as he recalls all the events of the recent past, he is struck by the suspicion that she faked it. That she used her superb acting and manipulative abilities, not to mention her experience, to simulate an attack. Knowing that that was the only way she could flush him out. Is that what had happened? Had she set him up from the start? Leo doesn't know. He can't say. He is so alone, so confused, so delicately balanced over the abyss.

In short, on the fourth day at Anzère the first letter arrived.

The first strange clue: the place where it was delivered. Leo—in bathrobe, towel over his shoulder, and bare feet—had gone into his room and closed the door. He had taken off the bathrobe, thrown it on the bed, shivering, and mechanically opened the drawer of the dresser where, the day they arrived, Rachel put his underpants, socks, and undershirts. Just then, reaching in for his boxers, he had felt against his fingertips a papery roughness. Probably an envelope. He had grabbed it, sure it was a mistake or a joke of Rachel's. But on the back the words "For Professor Pontecorvo," in a handwriting of looping and graceful precision, had appeared to him another unequivocal clue (or at least it seems to him now, as he thinks back to it).

It wouldn't have disturbed him so much if, just an hour earlier, going into the bathroom for his regular shower, he hadn't found a still more unpleasant surprise. Lying on the shelf under the window was a panty liner, evidently just discarded, faintly stained. A sense of irritation took possession of Leo. He had thought it was Rachel's forgetfulness. Except then he considered the fact that in many years of marriage a thing like that had never happened, and he understood that the bloodstained panty liner belonged to Camilla. And he dismissed it as the typical lack of awareness of a thoughtless adolescent.

But now? Well now, in the light of that envelope containing a letter whose contents were definitely inappropriate, that used panty liner took on a completely different relevance. Had it been left there deliberately? But why? To prepare for the arrival of the letter? A kind of treasure hunt with scattered clues? And, in that case, what was the final prize? Was it perhaps a perverted message of love, or a threat? But really what could one expect from someone who was always silent and then found fluency in another language? All this was definitely annoying. Rather, more: indecent and unacceptable.

What should he do? Go out there, give her back the letter without even opening it, reproach her harshly, tell her she must never again leave such souvenirs in the bathroom or stick her hands in the dresser where an adult keeps his piles of fucking underwear . . . Speak to her with the same severity he would have used with one of his sons, and explain to her that a girl of twelve does not write letters to fifty-year-old men.

That's what he should have done.

Let's say he had, what would have happened? Certainly she would have burst into tears. Camilla's anxiousness. The bizarre disproportion of her reactions. That was something it was right to be afraid of. The risk was that Rachel and the boys would find her like that, humiliated, in tears. At which he would have had to explain to his family several unpleasant things: starting with what Camilla had done. The vacation would be irremediably spoiled. Then he would have had to face the bitterness of his younger son and Rachel's irritation. And it wouldn't end there. He would have had to speak to Camilla's parents, those two uncouth types (the Viking and his concubine) and explain to them the unpleasantness of the matter. Because of the way they looked at their daughter, the way they excused her, and gave into her on everything, because of the extraordinary number of times they had telephoned her since she had been there, and the fact that they had agreed to let her go to the mountains although it had obviously upset them, it wouldn't have been difficult for Camilla to convince them that he had been the one to lead her into such inappropriate behavior. He tried to remember if the preceding afternoon, when they talked about Paris, he had said something unseemly.

All these hypotheses—as he stood there, naked, dripping, cold, with the envelope, now also saturated, in his hand—tormented him.

Maybe it would be better to wait for Rachel. Maybe better to put the whole business in the hands of the most practical woman in the galaxy. Yes, of course, it should be Rachel who spoke to Camilla. It should be Rachel who spoke to her parents. He didn't want to get involved in this business. And suddenly the idea that his Rachel would, as usual, take care of everything calmed him.

It should be explained that if in his profession Leo Pontecorvo did not lack the audacity and initiative of people who have been successful, in the face of certain practical difficulties he displayed all his tremendous inadequacy.

Since childhood he had been accustomed to delegate every managerial complication to his mother. And to concentrate first on his studies and then, right afterward, on his career. "Race horses don't organize the races, race horses race." This was the catch phrase of his extremely obliging mother!

The result of such self-denial in his studies and such ineptitude in practical matters was paradoxical: even today, at almost fifty, the great teacher, the fearless luminary, the fascinating lecturer, adored father and faithful husband would not have known where to get in line at the post office to send a certified letter and would have had great difficulties in paying a bill. Suffice it to say that he became agitated whenever he had to sign a check. Luckily when his mother died and he was overwhelmed by the weight of all those tasks and responsibilities, Rachel had been at his side.

In other words, this utter lack of pragmatism combined with success in his profession made him a man with a dual personality: extremely efficient in things that interested him, childishly inept in the management of all other business, toward which, in time, he had begun to feel a kind of superstitious uneasiness that in the face of the most aggressive and inquisitorial bureaucracy—or rather ordinary justice—became true anguish. It was enough for a traffic patrol to stop him for a check to make him go nuts. There he is, fumbling in the glove compartment of the car in search of documents with the ardor of an inexperienced drug dealer who, stopped at airport customs, pretends not to know how to open the two suitcases whose false bottoms are stuffed with cocaine.

All to explain why, a moment after connecting the letter to the pad, and both objects to Camilla, Leo began to tremble. And why his overexcited brain was crowded with the apocalyptic hypotheses that infect the life of paranoiacs. Making him feel suddenly trapped. And leading him to blow up the whole business to the point of seeing himself already in the dock. That also explains why he had only to think of Rachel to calm down and dismiss his torments as the ridiculous product of neurosis. But above all that explains why suddenly, after vacillating for some time, he had opened the letter, forgetting that the preliminary condition for him to remain totally clean was that the letter be delivered to Rachel sealed and untouched.

The fact is that, once he had calmed down, he was overcome by curiosity to see what was written in it.

Perhaps there was no malice. But then why put it there?

Why not deliver it by hand? Maybe it had seemed to her a safe place, where he would find it without anyone else seeing it. But wasn't that just what people call "malice"? Creating an exclusive complicity with a person you should treat with formality. And in any case what sense would it make to answer her in turn with a note? However polite and cold his response might be, it would still be a compromising document. It would be the note that a father of a family sent to a girl of twelve. The proof that he had responded (and hence given importance) to the provocation of a girl. It would take nothing to convince them that he was the corruptor.

(You see? Every time Leo Pontecorvo found himself at such an impasse he began to think of the world in the third person plural. The entire world became a generic "they" eager to harm him, get him in trouble, trap him.)

These new distressing thoughts kept him, if nothing else, from tearing the letter out of an envelope that by now had been opened.

The inconsistent part of the matter is that anxiety, which should have induced him to care and caution, directed him rather toward error, carelessness, contradiction. This usually was the road at the end of which he met paralysis. This was the vicious circle: great fear produced carelessness, carelessness took shape in an irresponsible gesture. And it all resulted in paralysis.

Leo had presented the same terrible evidence of himself some time earlier, with Walter, one of his assistants. Then, too, he had made a big mess of things. But yes, Walter, the young fellow who always showed up late at the university and always with the dark-circled eyes and drawn face of one who has stayed up till the small hours. A really gifted kid, one of those whom Leo liked immensely and Rachel was allergic to. ("Why do you bring him home so often? Why does he always come here to eat at night? Doesn't the obsequious way he treats us bother you? Those compliments, that flattery? He's such a sweet-talker." "Yes, we laugh at it. But come on, he's a good boy. He wouldn't hurt a fly. He amuses me. He knows a lot of things. He's so enthusiastic. Among all the students I've had he's certainly the most promising. He's got some trouble at home. I like helping him.")

Well, this very fellow, about whose supposed agreeableness or disagreeableness Leo and Rachel argued quite frequently, one day, right after class, had lingered with Leo in his office longer than necessary. Until at a certain point he had asked for a loan.

"How much do you need?"

"A fair amount, Leo."

"Yes, but how much?"

"Around ten million lire. But look, if you can't . . . "

"Calm down, I didn't say I can't . . . but you also understand that it's a large sum . . . and also that I'll have to talk to Rachel about it. You know, she's the one who keeps the accounts . . . you know me, I'm hopeless in such things."

"Then no, thank you. Better not. I don't think I'm so popular at your house . . . "

"Don't talk nonsense. Rachel adores you."

"No, Leo. Better not. I'd rather anything than cause problems for you with Rachel."

"Calm down. After all, it's my money. I sweat for it daily. All I said is that I'll have to speak to Rachel about it because she's the one who keeps the accounts . . . Can I ask you what it's for, at least?"

"Well, it's something painful. Mortifying . . . "

"If you don't want to or can't tell me it's not important . . . it's just that . . . "

"No, no, I'd like to tell you. Rather, it seems right to tell you, I don't need to hide anything from you . . . It's my mother."

"Your mother?"

"Yes, my mother. Since Papa's been gone, since he died, well, anyway . . . she hasn't been the same. You know, my mother is the type of woman who relies completely on a man, one of those women who live in symbiosis with their husband. Who without their husband don't exist. And my mother without my father doesn't exist. And I don't know how to tell you how hard it is to witness this painful spectacle. And how terrible for me to know I can't intervene. Especially since I also have a lot of problems to resolve."

"I can imagine."

"I think I'm at fault. For not having been close enough to her in these last two years. For not having seen what was happening. Or anyway for becoming aware of it too late . . . "

"Yes, but of what?"

"Leo, my mother has become an alcoholic. I still have trouble believing it. And I can't believe her problem has any other name than that: alcoholism. It's really just like they say. It starts slowly, and you fall into it gradually, until suddenly there you are, hooked. And then it's too late . . . Poor Mamma, everything began with those damn aperitifs. You know, I can't even stand to hear the word 'aperitif'? The word turns my stomach. When she says, 'Shall we have an aperitif?' I have to stop myself from smacking her. She has a totally degenerate way of pronouncing the word 'aperitif' that irritates me!"

"And how are things going now?"

"You should see her, Leo, she's like a ghost. It took a while for me to understand what was happening to her. One day she tells me that a quick drink before dinner is good for her, picks her up. Because evening is the most difficult time. And she needs to get through it somehow. Relax. And so then the glass of wine, the Aperol, the Martini before dinner . . . Then, you know how it is, one glass leads to the next . . . By now her life is one long, exhausting aperitif that begins when she opens her eyes in the morning and ends when she goes to sleep, completely drunk. Every morning I find her in a different place in the house: on the toilet, the couch, a stool in the kitchen. She prefers anywhere to her bed. There's not a moment of the day when she doesn't stink of alcohol. She's never sober. She raves. She laughs. She cries. She's paranoid. She lies, Leo, she never stops lying. It's been six months since I've been fighting this thing, and I'm beginning to think it will end badly. That the situation won't stop getting worse. And I can't take it anymore, Leo. I can't take it."

"Who have you talked to about it? Before today, I mean."

"I talked to Loredana. I asked her for advice, a professional opinion: basically addiction is a psychological problem. She gave me a couple of addresses of colleagues of hers who run clinics, who work with addictions. You know, Alcoholics Anonymous and all that other nonsense. I've been there. I've seen how and where they work. I've seen the people who go there. It's terrible, Leo. Like zombies. I can't see my mother among all those people. She's delicate, a person not used to suffering, she has a bad relationship with suffering. I can't put her there, it would destroy her. One of the many reasons she hasn't been able to recover after my father's death is that, without his income, she's had to reduce her life style drastically. I think she drinks not to see all the squalor she's besieged by. That's why I can't put her in one of those places, with those people. She wouldn't come out alive. Or she'd come out thirstier than before."

"And so what have you decided?"

"I was almost desperate. Until a little while ago, a friend I confided in gave me a brochure for a kind of clinic. A fabulous place, Leo. On the coast, near Amalfi. A pink villa on the sea. A garden looking onto a marvelous cove. I read this booklet at least ten times and I realized that it makes no mention of alcoholism or drug addiction. I ask my friend what the place is, and he tells me it's a private clinic where important people go to dry out. Celebrities can count on the maximum of efficiency and professionalism together with the maximum of discretion. Last weekend I also did some investigation. I talked to the director. And I understood immediately that it's the right place. That maybe there my mother could go back to being my mother. I don't know if you understand. The trouble is that the treatment costs an arm and a leg. We can't afford it, at least at the moment. I'm trying to sell a small property that my father left me. I'm sure that to get a good price I just have to wait for the right moment.

"So, now you know my sad story. If you can advance me the money for the first three months, I'll undertake to pay you back a little each month. At least until I can sell the house and pay off the debt all at once. And then with me your loan is safe: no one better than you knows how little I earn now and how much I could increase my income in the next years. Look, Leo, I've given you the reasons and I've given you the guarantees. It's all straightforward, isn't it?"

Very straightforward for Leo, but definitely not for Rachel, who, once informed of the situation by her husband, without hesitating to hide her sarcasm, had said:

"And naturally you gave it to him, without batting an eye?"

"What should I have done?"

"For example, not given it to him."

"Calm down. I took my precautions. It's a sure thing. Walter is about to sell some property. He'll give it all back sooner than you think."

"Have you seen this property?"

"I'm hardly a real-estate agent."

"Did he show you some document?"

"I'm hardly a bank director."

"Where is this property, Leo?"

"I don't have the slightest idea. Does its location seem important to you?"

"It seems important to me to know if it exists. It seems important to know if it really belongs to him. If it's not already mortgaged. It seems important to establish whether he really used the money you gave him to take care of that sob story he sold you. Or if it was just the right amount to settle an account with some bookie or loan shark. Knowing him . . . "

"I don't see why an assistant of mine, a good kid, besides, whose career is in my hands, should extort money from me by deceit."

"A good kid? A megalomaniac, if anything. A bullshitter. A liar. Let's say even that the story he told you is true, couldn't he send his mother to a center? He had to send her to a five-star hotel? And at our expense?"

"I'm astounded, Rachel. Astounded by your insensitivity. Astounded by your sarcasm . . . And let me say, sweetheart, that sometimes your distrust dismays me. Why you obsess about the details without taking into account the scenario."

"And, my dear Mr. Scenario, in what way did you give him this money?"

"Not certainly in cash. I wrote him a check. Something official, in other words. You wouldn't want me to be taken for a loan shark?"

"And when is he supposed to make the first payment?"

"In one month, exactly. To demonstrate his good faith he told me that the first month he'll pay back a sum amounting to more or less one and a half installments. Calm down, love, I have everything under control. I told you, it's a straightforward deal."

A straightforward deal indeed. Too bad Leo couldn't know that some time later Walter would publicly charge him with usury. And would reveal to the judge that he had been first blackmailed and then fired by that wretched loan shark. And that to confirm his charge he would hand over to the investigators a receipt signed by Leo certifying that that bastard of a usurer had been repaid a figure fifty per cent larger with respect to the agreed-on installment, taking further advantage of his momentary state of need. A truly unsustainable rate of interest.

One of the most significant and paradigmatic examples of Leo's gullibility. But also one of the most spectacular.

Leo's problem—in his work as well, both in the hospital and at the university—was that confronted with formalities of a bureaucratic nature he became so dazed that in the end, simply in order to get rid of them, he delegated. Every time someone showed him a document he signed it rapidly, whispering, "You take care of it." As if speed in removing practical things from before his eyes diminished his responsibility. Like those bulimics who are always on a diet, who eat quickly, under the illusion that that way the organism can't absorb all the food they're gorging on, Leo devoted as little time as possible to the paperwork demanded by his profession.

The worst bureaucratic abominations could happen under his jurisdiction without him even noticing. His attitude in the hospital was similar to that of certain landowners of earlier times: in order not to be troubled and not to concern themselves with things they considered beneath them, they delegated everything to shrewd, crooked agents, only to find themselves later, after generations of dissipation and theft, swindled, with their patrimony almost completely mortgaged. Rachel trembled for her husband's haplessness, the negligence that was the opposite of what had been instilled in her by a very prudent parent. But the therapeutic brilliance, the successes Leo piled up, the river of money with which he flooded her would not allow her to reproach him as she would have liked to and should have. Although every so often she couldn't restrain herself and asked him some embarrassing questions about the management of the accounts.

"Why hasn't the clinic sent the November bills yet?"

"How should I know? If only one could work in peace, without all this nonsense!"

"Will you tell me that you might have lost those bills?" To which he, to cut it short, with the typical arrogance of the moron and out of a desire not to open the Pandora's box on which he sat his precious behind all day, answered, "Do you think that with all the number of colleagues around to take care of my affairs I should be the one to worry about these things? The bills will go out."

I think this picture gives an account of the mental state of anguished questioning that torments Leo, who is still standing there with that envelope in his hand (by now open), in the completely irrational—for now, at least—terror that in a few seconds sinister-looking Swiss policemen will come to arrest him, accusing him treacherously of corruption of minors and who knows what other infamies.

And yet . . .

And yet, amid the inner chaos that feeling of excited curiosity advances. Of course, the excitement is linked to the desire that our worst nightmare may end up coming true. But beside this type of insane excitement is another, much more ordinary, that has to do with vanity. Yes, just that. Basically, beyond the artificial barriers erected by the occasion, this whole business can be reduced to a letter that a woman, although very young, has written to a man, although getting on. If we leave aside the age of this woman and this man, forget their place in the world, and disregard the closest family ties, the essence of this reduction is a male and a female. One confronting the other. In that relationship of permanent seduction through which nature perpetuates itself.

Now, there is no male who doesn't derive at least a little flattery from rousing the interest of a woman, even if she seems for various reasons most inappropriate. And it must be said that Leo (although he would never admit it) is susceptible to the pleasures of erotic vanity. Rather, I would say that vanity is alive in him with such dominance as to have prevented him, by antiphrasis, from betraying Rachel even once since they were married.

And I assure you that that sort of faithfulness, in the world Leo lives in and the environment he comes from, is an eccentric rarity. There is no old family friend, not even a colleague at the university or the hospital, who hasn't embarked on at least a small relationship, or who hasn't yielded to the call of a little adventure at a conference or a flirtation on the unit. Not Leo Pontecorvo.

God knows he could have!

But Leo had always preferred to shake off with style the incomparable erotic advantages that a prominent position in two emblematically promiscuous places like the University and the Hospital brings with it. And yet to be concentrated on his affairs and royally uninterested in all the rest certainly did not prevent him from noticing the sexual interest he was the object of on the part of the brighter students, the more capable nurses, the more enterprising colleagues. And even the mothers of his patients, sometimes, above all when their children were out of danger. And yet to rebuff those advances had never been too difficult.

He found it gratifying enough to feel how, for many women, his position in society, joined to a robust, youthful body with a few tufts of blue-gray hair on the chest, represented an irresistible carnal provocation. People underestimate the erotic euphoria derived from not giving in to the offers that turn up at random intervals.

The milieu in which he had grown up (the Jewish fifties, filled with the desire to live) had been too libertine not to have caused in him, by contrast, a profound nausea for flirtations, for dalliances. He detested his colleagues who used their petty power for erotic blackmail. No less than those who wrecked their families to chase some little piece of ass from the suburbs. Just as he deplored those who addressed unpleasant remarks to students or nurses, playing fluently on the ambiguities. Nothing gave him greater pleasure than to distinguish himself from that type of male. That was why ignoring any sexual provocation entered into his idea of masculinity. An aesthetic question even before a moral prohibition. But for goodness' sake! He had only to imagine himself next to a young woman to be attacked by a sense of the ridiculous and to see his fifty-year-old body instantly shrivel.

Nonetheless, on those occasions when he had received a more or less explicit erotic offer, he never failed, a moment before rejecting it and a second afterward, to experience a subtle pleasure: the joy of feeling that he was still a man so desirable mixed with the pride of remaining faithful to his wife and his principles without too much effort.

(Even today the human material that inspired his masturbatory activity, moderate but punctual, as in all middle-aged men, was presented to him by the perfumed army of women to whom he had said no.)

This was the tenor of his feelings, while Leo couldn't stop turning over and over in his hands the damp, open envelope. He felt excited. Not by the fact that a twelve-year-old had written him a letter (there was nothing desirable in her or any other twelve-year-old). But perhaps by the fact that the twelve years of that girl broadened the range of his virtual hunt. Titillating the idea of omnipotence that devastates the character of many men kissed by success. It was as if Leo were saying: not only nurses, not only residents or students. At this moment of your life you can have them all . . .

That may be why, having worked up his courage and taken

the letter out of the envelope, and having carefully unfolded it, he found himself so disappointed by such a note:

> *Monsieur Pontecorvo,*
> *Je tiens à vous remercier de m'avoir invitée chez vous avec mon Samuel.*
> *L'amabilité de votre famille rend très agréable notre séjour.*
> *Cordialement à vous,*
>
> *Camilla*[2]

You didn't have to speak perfect French to know that the language used by Camilla in her little note would have been more suited to a business communication than to a private message. A bureaucratic French, and so doubly inadequate. Such that the whole thing appeared a pointless, pleonastic formality. Not that Leo had expected a real confession. But at least a thank-you for the way he had taken care of those two rude sons of his. Not to mention the energy and style with which he had saved her life.

But then why put a letter like that, with no content, no revelation, in with his underwear and socks? Why announce it with a blood-stained panty liner? What the hell did all this mean?

Finally the idea crossed Leo's mind that it simply meant nothing. The girl was just a little odd and very mixed up. He was the idiot, to have been swamped by all these useless reflections. What could you expect from someone who spoke to her parents in French but that she would write pointless letters in French? Evidently for her it was a pattern. She took refuge in French whenever she was embarrassed. She had done it that day with her parents, she did it now with him. After he had seen her in such a bad way, so fragile, spluttering . . .

---

[2] I wish to thank you for inviting me to your house with my Samuel. The kindness of your family has made our stay very pleasant. Cordially yours, Camilla

It was that mixture of disappointment, worry, and frankly a certain relief that led him into the living room, after he got dressed. There was nothing in Camilla's behavior signaling that something had changed. She was there, as usual dressed in pale clothes, lying on the sofa in front of the fire. The heels of her bare feet dangling off the sofa were slightly flushed by exposure to a fire that had stopped crackling. She raised her head from her book and rested her large eyes on him for a few instants, but immediately immersed them again in her reading. She had brought with her the whole garish company of Little Princes, young Buddhas, Jonathan Seagulls who poison the literary taste of thousands of adolescent readers. That literary trash occupied a royal place on the table next to the sofa.

She didn't seem disturbed to find him there. Much less showed signs of a general conversation. Which meant that she didn't expect a response? Or that it was enough for her to have brought twenty minutes of confusion into the life of an adult? What was it, a joke? Did she want to test him, make fun of him? Everything was possible. And maybe none of what was about to happen would have happened if he had not decided in turn to play.

When Leo wonders why he did it, why he chose to get on that merry-go-round, he can't find an adequate answer: only a contradictory catalogue of nebulous retrospective explanations. He acted out of boredom. Or maybe out of disappointment that in Camilla's first letter there was no sign of what for a few seconds he had been certain of finding there. As a challenge. A challenge fed by the fact that she hadn't pressed the accelerator as she should have.

Was it that tiny disappointment that reawakened the libertine instinct kept at bay for decades with hordes of young women at his feet? The fact is that that girl, who wasn't all there, had somehow succeeded in getting what no one before her had ever got.

But Leo knows very well that wondering how she succeeded is no less idle than wondering why people get cancer. In nature everything obeys the perverse logic of madness. It's not only the cells of your prostate or your colon that suddenly go mad, without warning. You, too, go mad.

And yet before diving into the fire, the cautious Leo had again put fate to the test. On the morning of the fifth day, he had put a letter of response, no less brief and no less pointless than the one written by Camilla, into the same drawer of the same dresser, full of underwear and socks, before going to the ski slopes with the boys.

A game. Nothing but a game. A small prank in response to a prank: let's see if she's so clever and enterprising she can sneak into my room a second time, and so smart she can guess where I hid the letter. Leo had enjoyed thinking about this. Except that all morning he was in a state of anxiety that Rachel might intercept that letter. And then, yes, he would certainly be in trouble! How would he justify it? How to explain to his wife that he had hidden among the underwear a letter addressed to his son's girlfriend? Well, some things are simply unjustifiable.

All right, there is nothing in that letter. But the sole fact of writing it, the sole fact of having conceived of writing it, and then having hidden it . . . well, that already makes you a sick and irrational man.

That's how Leo was transforming the fifth day's skiing into a nightmare. A real pity, given all that splendid fresh, swishing snow under his skis, the magnificent sun, the sky enameled with a fierce cobalt. It wasn't like him not to enjoy the omelette and the roast potatoes. His only racking desire was to go home and see what had happened to that letter. To check if it was still there. I swear that if I find it there, that disgusting letter, I'll burn it, along with this whole ridiculous business I've let myself be dragged into.

He nearly broke a leg going down the valley in a crouch, imitating the boys, forgetting that a man of his build can reach really dangerous speeds. And all because he was bursting to find out as soon as possible if someone, whether Rachel or Camilla, had found the letter, or if it was still there.

Not to mention speeding in the car over the icy asphalt, on his feet only his wet socks, since, in the urgency of the moment, he hadn't even put on his soft after-ski shoes.

Then, having parked in front of the chalet, he affected composure. He took his sneakers out of the trunk, put them on, and with his heart in his throat went into the house.

Finding it silent and in disarray had really given him a shock. Where had the two of them gone? It was the first time they hadn't been there. Where had they run off to? And why was the house still a mess? Leo hurried to his room. He opened the drawer. The envelope wasn't there. Someone had taken it.

The door that opened and the demeanor of the two women (a woman and a girl who, to judge from their slender build and the look of friendly complicity that animated them, might be taken for mother and daughter, or anyway aunt and niece) put an end to the two most frightening hours of his life. He had only to look at them—bright, tired, happy—to understand that, whichever of the two had found the letter, he had nothing to worry about. And yet he had been in such a state of anxious prostration that he couldn't help attacking them heatedly:

"Where the fuck have you been?"

"Are you crazy? What kind of talk is that? Forgive him, Camilla, my husband never expresses himself like that unless he's really angry. We just have to find out why he's so angry."

"I'm not angry. I was just worried. I come home, I don't find you. Everything is a mess. After what happened to Camilla last night. I was thinking the worst."

"You're right, sweetheart. It's that Camilla suddenly wanted to go out this morning. She seemed so happy. She asked if I'd go for a walk. And you know she never asks for anything. So we took the bus to Crans and did a little shopping, like two real ladies. That's all. By the way, do you like these?" And she took out of a bag two wool turtlenecks, one blue, the other rust-colored: "This is for Fili and this for Semi."

It was as if in half a day of shopping all the distrust that Rachel felt for Camilla had dissipated. Now look at them, they seem like the best friends in the world. That complicity lasted for the whole afternoon. This time, Camilla helped Rachel make dinner. And Leo, as he piled logs on the hearth to light the fire, heard them laughing like two schoolgirls. But what had happened to the letter? For a second he wondered if by chance Rachel, knowing him so well, had contributed to a scene that at that moment seemed to Leo more a joke. But no. Rachel didn't make jokes like that. On the other hand Leo regretted that Camilla had seen him so beside himself. That a man of his age and position had let himself go like that: that was really undignified. He felt ridiculous. This was something that had been happening more and more often lately. And he didn't like it.

All right, it's time to put an end to this sordid business. That little sociopath sent me a ridiculous letter, I thanked her, adhering to her code (ridiculous) of behavior. Enough now. The matter ends here. My friend, you've simply found a way of torturing yourself a little with your paranoias. This, too, is classic. Now let's retake possession of our life. At this point she certainly won't respond.

Dear Leo,
You don't know how angry it makes me to see you so sad with your wife. I thought my father was the saddest man in the world. But knowing you I've seen that there's something worse. So I want to save you. Save you from the revolting

mess you live in. It's hard to tell you what I feel. But it's the most special feeling I've ever felt since the beginning of my life. I love you. And now I love you more because I know you love me. I've known it for a long time. That day in the mountains I couldn't believe that you answered me. But when I saw your letter I said to myself, "He loves you." And then I understood that I had to help you at all costs. Now, at the age of twelve (almost thirteen), I understand what I have to do in my life. I have to help you get out of that marriage.

*   With all my heart,*

Camilla

"I have to help you get out of that marriage"?

And God only knows how she would manage it! Yes, Camilla would succeed in the greatest, most useful, and destructive of undertakings: removing Leo Pontecorvo from the marriage he had always wanted to be in; and she would succeed in the ridiculous and paradoxical form that seemed to her most congenial. With those mawkishly and threateningly ungrammatical letters. By which Leo's life was invaded in the weeks following their return from the mountains, as if by an avalanche. Those increasingly long letters, increasingly passionate and increasingly resentful that awaited him every day in the dressing room, in the underwear drawer (the young lady was not then so original as she thought was), and that unfailingly shook him with nausea. Like the example I gave a few lines above: the fifteenth letter in all and the eighth after the return from Anzère.

Months of words, months of emphatic phrases, months of limping syntax and shallow vocabulary, in which Camilla gave wonderful proof of how her brain had cut off every relation with the universe. Of how the dear old concept called "actual facts" in her hands was inverted to the point of losing all meaning.

It was then, in close contact with that verbose epistolary

176 · ALESSANDRO PIPERNO

garbage, that Leo became conscious of the intolerable isolation in which he was floundering, in which we all flounder. It was then that he discovered that his absolute solitude was dictated by the impossibility of revealing to anyone the grotesque comedy of which he was the reluctant not to mention clandestine co-protagonist. He was already in a situation in which he was unable to tell anyone that he had lost control, that something unbelievable was happening to him and he could do nothing about it. There existed no confidant, no psychotherapist, no rabbi to whom he could explain such a story.

The most loved and protective person in his life—that is, Rachel, the woman who had perfectly replaced his mother— was also the last being in the world he could tell. If he had, he would have had to explain too many inexplicable things. Above all, why he hadn't told her everything when that first letter arrived? And then what had induced him to answer it and to continue to do so the next times, when the whole business was taking an increasingly monstrous turn? He would have had to explain to her how a child had managed to checkmate a man like him. And how a man like him had let himself be conned by a child. How he could have let himself be intimidated and terrorized in that way. He would have had to explain why under close analysis the denials that he continued to present to Camilla would appear on the page so affected and irresolute. He would have had to say to his wife that the reason he had not taken that grotesque little redhead aside and said to her, "Listen, honey, you've been a pain in the ass. Don't you dare put your crazy letters in with my underwear ever again, and now get out of my house forever, out of my life and my family's life" was his lack of courage, of far-sightedness, of virility, of moral strength, of initiative, of trust in his neighbor, and on and on. And that it was precisely the lack of these qualities, qualities that a man of his age and his background should have possessed, which had led him to respond, point by point, to

Camilla's letters with messages in which he very gently ordered her (rather, entreated her) to stop.

And at that point he would have had to explain to Rachel that it was precisely that meek and conciliating attitude which had provided Camilla with the evidence demonstrating the existence between them of something that in reality had never existed. Expressions like: "It has to stop here"; "What's been has been"; "We have to return to our lives" sounded like an implicit admission that there had been something between them.

Well, Leo would have had to explain to Rachel that he had used that tone and had had recourse to such expressions just to satisfy her. Because he was afraid of her. Because he had seen how furious Camilla got whenever he denied that there had been something between them. Maybe—he had thought irresponsibly—if I indulge her a little, if I explain that I'm sorry, it will be easier to get her to stop bothering me. But, naturally, allowing her to extort the concession that there had been a kind of semi-relationship between them had simply confirmed to future readers of those letters that he had had a passionate love affair with a twelve-year-old, who was, besides, the girlfriend (in the way you become attached at that age) of his younger son.

The trouble is that when he realized what was happening it was already too late. That is to say that the "too late" had arrived very quickly. That girl already had the dozen letters that could trap him. Letters in which he asked her to cut off a relationship. But in which he did not dare to remind the recipient that that "relationship" had existed only in her psychopathic little head. There, and, now, on the page as well.

As in those fatal diseases that go into remission, simulating improvement, just before killing you, Leo had occasion to nourish an unreasonable hope, which deluded him that the situation was resolving itself.

It came out of terrible months. For the first time, on the professional front as well things were not functioning as they should. The tax authorities, through avenging angels dressed in gray, were doing an audit on the Anima Mundi, the private clinic where Leo had his pediatric office. And this had filled him with an anxiety that by now, knowing him, you will be able to imagine.

On the other side, the family idyll in which he had always found relief from his professional troubles seemed a distant memory. There was almost no evening when his torturer wasn't at dinner. That little whore had insinuated herself into their family so deviously. She was always following Rachel. It seemed that, having overcome Rachel's distrust, she had really managed to win her over. Leo knew how much Rachel had wanted a girl. There, now she had her girl.

Every night Leo hoped that there would not be a letter waiting for him. Every night he was disappointed. Now he didn't even read them. He opened them, was gripped by the nausea that madness and lying bring, skimmed a few lines, and then hid them in the drawer in his study. He locked them there and good night.

He had stopped answering her: his last, desperate move to free himself from that situation. Maybe, no longer finding replies, Camilla would get tired. Considering the number of letters he received in the days following his resolution not to reply, one might say that the only result of that punitive measure had been to infuriate her. The frequency of the letters was in itself a threat: for some time Leo had been reading only the first three lines before hiding them in the drawer in his study. Three lines were now sufficient for him to understand the general tone. And that unreasonable number of letters appeared definitely threatening.

Until the last letter arrived. So it proclaimed on the envelope: *Last Letter*. Only for that reason had Leo read it to the end. At first he had looked at it with real fear. What did it mean that it was the last letter? Had she got the message: there was nothing more to do? The madness had to stop here? Or otherwise, after that letter, she would carry out an extreme act intended to destroy the lives of them all? Leo had fiddled with envelope for several hours. Finally, at three in the morning, in the bathroom, trembling and bathed in sweat, he had opened it.

And here was yet another delirious, senseless, grotesquely romantic letter, in which Camilla, after expressing a tortured farewell, made a last request, which at first appeared to him reasonable.

The girl wished to have her letters back. Then she would disappear, along with her grief. She would leave Samuel and would vanish from their lives. She would relieve that family, which had given her so much, from the weight of her presence. The only condition she imposed was that: to have back the concrete symbol of her love and suffering. Those letters.

The thing appeared extraordinarily reasonable to him. On the fifth consecutive rereading of Camilla's last letter (last! Get it? Thank heaven), he felt he was, after so long, a free man. Free to reappropriate his life and make of it what he wanted without having to take account of that little madwoman. He read the last four words (written in French, naturally)—*Adieu, mon ange adoré*—and he couldn't help laughing. The indulgence of the triumphant.

Thus—impelled by the usual insane ingenuousness, by irreproachable candor—Leo gave back to his tormentor the only evidence of his condition as a victim of blackmail and persecution. And he had given it back without thinking that a responsible man, before restoring those letters, would at least have had the wit to photocopy them. Without thinking (in spite of the fact that the elements of the thought were all within reach, like one of those elementary puzzles for children), I was saying, without thinking that his correspondence with Camilla could one day reappear in his life, with a power of plausibility in inverse proportion to the real unfolding of the facts. Without thinking of the possibility that she (or her easily manipulated father) would deliver it to the authorities and the newspapers, in a speciously mutilated version: from that substantial file they would be able to leave out ("to protect the identity and the feelings of a criminally corrupted minor," the noted journalist of the noted weekly who was covering the noted "Pontecorvo affair" would certainly write) all Camilla's letters, and all those in which Leo sought to free himself from the grip of that obsession.

At that point, after such purposeful mutilation, there would survive of the original correspondence only the disgusting pet phrases "my little one," and "dear girl," with which poor Professor Pontecorvo had tried to flatter his persecutor.

Phrases that, removed from the original context, made a really nasty impression.

But these are only hypotheses made (if retroactively) by the narrator of this story. Leo doesn't know anything.

Hidden in his bunker for almost three days now, like a Mafioso, locked up in the secrets of his own castle like a deposed monarch, he doesn't know, nor can he know, what is happening outside or what is about to happen (of course, he doesn't even know what's happening on the floor above). He doesn't know because no one comes to call him, or to get him. He has only the vague information given by the TV news. He has only that gratuitous and generic bomb. He can't know anything else. He doesn't want to know anything else.

He imagines that outside the walls of his catacomb is the inferno. That for him, now, the world is a hostile place. He imagines that the man accused of tax fraud, private interest in official acts, embezzlement, loan sharking will, in the light of what is announced as a new, horrible accusation, appear even more obscene.

What remains to him—while his eyes are wounded by the bloody light of sunset, and the specter of another sleepless night materializes—is the ninety square meters of the cellar. In the end, carelessness, fear, neurosis, irresponsibility have been punished. Leo should be angry. Shout his innocence to the universe.

But he's paralyzed. He wasn't brought up to resentment. He's not equipped for that type of aggressiveness, he's unfit for war. He's like those center forwards who score goals by the handful in easy games but, catapulted into difficult matches, into more violent battles, disappear into the cocoon of their own timidity. He is the classic type who succumbs.

This drives him on to lofty thoughts. He seems to understand what he always said he couldn't understand: the submissive attitude of so many of his co-religionists who, several decades ago, let themselves be loaded onto freight cars without blinking. Let themselves be carried to distant, frozen lands, to be murdered like mice. Yes, there isn't much left for him now except to be murdered. Without forgetting, however, that the three people who were closest to him, by whom he always felt protected, and whom he, in his way, loved more than anything, overwhelming them with kindness and offering them the comfort of a life of opportunity, are now his worst enemies.

PART III

B ut, darling, I thought Rabbi Perugia taught you that a twelve-year-old cunt isn't kosher."

An inappropriate remark addressed to a man devastated by anxiety and insomnia, his blood vessels saturated with drugs he has self-prescribed, and Leo has to repress a gesture of contempt, not to mention a desire to turn on his heels and leave. He doesn't do it because he can't do it: he's the one who asked for this appointment. He's the one who needs it.

And he doesn't run because (although he won't admit it immediately) that phrase carries a whiff of old times, and, after an instant's restraint, he can only give in to its bracing effect. He feels a burning heat rise up inside to free his guts, which for days have been clamped in a steel vise. A beginning of gastric release that fills him with an unhoped-for peace, and is followed by an immediate awareness: it's been days since he has put anything in his mouth, since he closed his eyes, since his body has been ill. And in that same instant Leo realizes how important and wonderful it is for a man to be able to eat, sleep, defecate with ease.

A twelve-year-old cunt isn't kosher?

Just the sort of creative cynicism (and in essence tender and tough) into whose secrets Herrera Del Monte initiated him, when they were the worst-matched pair of friends in the little gang enrolled in Rabbi Perugia's bar-mitzvah preparation course, in the early fifties.

Not coincidentally is it Herrera Del Monte who comes out

with such a vulgarity. Leo went to see him in his office. Importantly spread out over two adjacent apartments on the top floor of a pink stuccoed building, on the most glorious stretch of Via Veneto—the Fellinian strip of sidewalk that divides the Café de Paris from Harry's Bar.

Finally, after a short wait, Leo was led into the dark cave where Herrera, his childhood friend, spends most of his days, from eight in the morning till ten at night, with the sole purpose of getting men whose power is equal only to the degree of their corruption and despicableness out of trouble.

And there he was, behind the enormous glass desk, neurotically neat and sparkling, after thirty-five years exactly like the stocky kid whose almost dwarf-like stature had been the distinguishing mark of the perfect martyr to the proverbial meanness of twelve-year-olds: the mirror image of the successful boy, at that time cheerfully embodied by the radiant and long-limbed Leo.

The long-ago years of early adolescence, when physical appearance is all. When the world, in its beginnings, still seems divided between gods and pariahs. When social hierarchies are decided by the sweetness of a pair of eyes and the gracefulness of high cheekbones rather than by any moral credential or intellectual merit. The age when appearance says of you everything that others want to know. And of course the relationship between him and Herrera was based on that treacherous aesthetic opposition: the attractiveness of the one who asks nothing better than to be reflected in the ugliness of the other.

Girls found his ugliness revolting, because it was accompanied by the mad hygienic neglect that (who knows why) many boys not favored by nature indulge in (as if to give artistic perfection to their own repulsiveness). But, in spite of everything, Herrera had Leo. Herrera, like those who are poor in spirit but fervently religious, rejoiced in Leo, obtaining in exchange from his idolized friend the kindly, disdainful benevolence that is granted to followers. This at least was how it looked from the outside. From the inside things worked differently. Leo admired the dwarf's ability to be sarcastic about anything. To illuminate the dark side of existence. From the height of his physical attractiveness, Leo was able to intuit that the iconoclastic spirit he so admired in his friend was the effect of a life spent continually parrying the blows that his physical repugnance provoked.

Blows that fell on a being who was extremely gifted intellectually, with a sensibility, so to speak, sharpened by a mother as fierce and intelligent as her son.

If from a mother you seek protection and hypocrisy, then beware of one like Maria Del Monte. She hid nothing from her son. Rather, she never stopped reminding him that everything would be more difficult for him than for anyone else. So she had risked destroying Herrera's life. By hiding nothing from him. Developing in him the tragic sense of his own inadequacy. Cultivating in her only son, whom she pretended not to be proud of at all, the preventive disappointment that in fact Herrera set up as a bulwark in confronting any adversity. Here's how, by means of a Spartan upbringing, Signora Del Monte had made a real hardass of her son.

Leo loved to hear his friend talk about his mother. Because he managed to do it in the irreverent and at the same time sorrowful way in which Leo would have liked to speak of his.

"Mine is the only case of Oedipus unrequited," Herrera said. "I love that woman to die for, and she, well, forget it . . . "

"In what sense?" Leo asked.

"You know why she called me Herrera?"

"Why?"

"Not certainly because she loves soccer or Balzac. That is, my mother doesn't give a fuck about soccer or Balzac. She did it in honor of my speech defect, my bloody French 'r's. She gave me the first name that popped into her head with at least three 'r's in it. The bitch obviously wanted her son to find even the pronunciation of his own name to be an embarrassing experience."

"Come on! How could she know that you'd have the French 'r'?"

"Statistical calculation. Genetic probability. Darwin and all that other nonsense. My father has it, my grandfather had it. In other words, it was likely that I would, too . . . And then, do you believe it? My little witch has divining skills," Herrera added, with unusual tenderness. "And now here it is, Herrera Del Monte, a name worthy of an enemy of Zorro!"

And he'd conclude with a sentence like "If that woman loved me a quarter as much as I love her . . . well, it would be enough for me!"

Leo knew that Signora Del Monte didn't hate her son at all. The punishments and nastiness that objectively she inflicted on him derived from a perverse (and very Jewish) conception of pedagogy that could be summed up in a simple phrase: "Stay calm, my boy, there is no injustice that the world will one day inflict on you that your mammina hasn't already."

You, too, can see how the comment on the presumed passion of Leo for the twelve-year-old cunt is perfectly in line with the spirit of the long-ago days when Herrera taught him that if there's one thing that doesn't deserve to be respected, well, it's your personal tragedy. And yet the same comment is completely indifferent to the professional delicacy that an important lawyer should use toward those who show up in his office as future clients.

And Leo wonders if that irreverence, which has opened an unexpected crack in his already fissured spirit, is part of a shrewd strategy, the product of careful reflection. Perhaps Herrera, with keen intuition, has understood that his old friend, at least in this area, doesn't need a professional consultation, or even some phrase suitable for the occasion, much less the self-serving sympathy that some might have shown him at every turn in recent weeks. And he has probably also cornered the market in reproaches and insults.

And maybe, considering the inferno that the life of his one-time hero must have lately become, Herrera wanted to submerge him in the moral atmosphere of the past. Drag him far away, to a world where to be Leo Pontecorvo was a good thing. To a time when Leo was decidedly at his ease in the role of himself. When Leo was a happy kid, hugely entertained by the nihilistic remarks of his unhappy friend. Evidently Herrera hasn't lost the gift. Which consists in pleasing Leo by means that are not at all pleasant. In fact, he has really refined that talent, making it a vital tool of his profession. The art of reading inside you. Of understanding what you need even before you understand it. And serving it to you with coarse arrogance.

Suddenly Leo is glad he came to see Herrera. After so many wrong things, here's one right. He hesitated far too long before turning to his old friend. He had been thinking about it for weeks. Even before he was hit by cyclone Camilla. Becoming more and more convinced of what Rachel had explained from the start: being a client of the same law firm that represented the hospital was suicidal. And now, although the girl's defamatory slander has not yet produced any reaction, Leo is sure that something is about to happen. Soon the prosecutor's office will be in touch. The thing is too gross for something not to happen. And this time he has to be prepared. He needs a specialist in dirt: someone tough, fierce, implacable. And it so happens that Herrera Del Monte is one of the most established and controversial criminal lawyers in the city. A real courtroom shark, whom Leo's more enlightened friends, the snooty type, despise apocalyptically. As if he were a kind of sewer capable of receiving, disinfecting, recycling, and putting back in circulation all the feces in the country.

Several times in the thirty-five years that have now passed since his bar mitzvah, Leo has chanced to run into his friend's public exploits. Once, in the dentist's waiting room, he was distractedly leafing through one of those glossy women's magazines when suddenly he found himself facing, in the center-fold, a very grainy photograph that showed his friend at the beach.

Herrera looked furious. A hairy whitish gnome with an adorable potbelly. His hair was the same: uncombed and almost too black (like the artificial hair of a toupee). The photographer had caught him spreading lotion on a television star-let who at the moment was the desired prey of the paparazzi, and who that summer was consorting with, according to the caption, the "famous Roman criminal lawyer." Yes, Herrera seemed really furious. One hand was busy spreading the lotion and the other inveighing against those goddam busybodies. And Leo couldn't help laughing. God only knew how well he was acquainted with the fury of that silly dwarf. His bursts of anger. It seemed to him that he could hear Herrera's voice at the moment of the click: harsh, croaking, trembling with anger. Maybe—Leo had thought with the good will of another era—the anger had to do with the squalor in which he felt impli-cated. The dwarf and the chorus girl. Beauty and the Beast. Herrera had too much good taste and self-awareness not to know that that scene on the beach was repulsive. The fact is that, although Herrera had pursued, as a sort of intellectual vocation and a protest against the Heavenly Father, all that seemed to him eccentric and original, evidently he couldn't resist the banality of lusting after those big blond ibexes. Six-foot-tall giraffes who should have compensated for his short-ness, but instead only emphasized it grotesquely.

In the dentist's waiting room Leo had thought back to how his friendship with Herrera Del Monte had been destroyed by one of those Valkyries. The reason that the memory of their break was still so vivid in Leo, after many years, was a result of the mortifying astonishment with which he had seen a decades-long alliance crumble because of a little business that hardly deserved mention, but instead . . .

No, Leo hadn't forgotten that September Sunday. How could he forget? It must have been in the mid-fifties. They had just enrolled in the university. As on all Sundays when Lazio was playing at home, Leo had showed up at the Del Montes' elegant apartment, at 15 Piazza Barberini, on the seat of his metallic-gray Vespa, and waited for his friend to come down. Leo's outfit was the usual: the same good-luck jeans and the same good-luck blue sweater that he had been wearing since the day when, years before, his friend Herrera had initiated him, in his own particular fashion, into the absurd torments of the soccer fan.

Herrera had come out of the entrance without his usual quickness and bounce. It was the first Sunday of the championship. Mid-September. The two friends had been anticipating it since the start of summer, and Leo would have expected greater enthusiasm. Instead Herrera seemed upset. Leo also noticed that his own tan made Herrera look, if possible, even more like a fairy-tale character than usual. His dumpling-shaped red nose gave him a striking resemblance to Grumpy, one of the seven dwarves. A Grumpy who, at least on that day, seemed to have no wish to grumble. On the trip to the stadium, he had kept to himself. He had let himself be driven without opening his mouth.

Herrera's behavior once they reached their usual place in the stands was no less indecipherable. He was silent. He was gloomy. And the match on the program that day—Lazio-Naples—should have kindled his competitive ardor. Herrera hated the Neapolitans. To tell the truth he also hated the Florentines. Not to mention the Milanese and the Juventists. If you thought about it, Herrera hated them all. And he had taught his friend to do likewise, explaining to him that sports fandom is, above all, a matter of hatreds. That's why Leo would have expected the usual behavior: a range of gratuitous insults addressed to the opposing players but also to those on his own team, the usual stream of floridly scurrilous remarks, veins swollen and arms waving. Instead nothing. He had sat through that sad match without opening his mouth. Only on the way home on the Vespa had he let out:

"I think I'm in love."

Herrera Del Monte in love? But come on, does that make any sense? Leo had never known him to gush over anyone. For a long time Leo had doubted that his friend was even interested. He changed his mind when Herrera gave him some photographs of bare-breasted women:

"I'm entrusting them to you, my friend: it's the best that life has given me."

Herrera the wanker. Herrera the self-ironic masturbator. This made sense. Herrera the misogynist. This was in the order of things. Not Herrera in love. Not Herrera tight-lipped and sappy, saying things like "I think I'm in love."

So that Leo couldn't find the right thing to say, as if the other had just confessed he had a fatal illness.

"My mother has naturally blessed her."

"What?"

"When she's in a bad mood she calls her the shiksa. If she's in a good mood she calls her the *haver*. In her moments of happiness she's 'your German.' She says she goes out with me because of our money. And many other unpleasant things which I prefer not to mention . . . "

"Where did you meet her?"

"In the mountains. She works in a shop, you know those local emporiums that sell everything. Newspapers, cigarettes, toys, brooms . . . Next week she's coming here by train. My mother said I must not bring her home. That I must not name

her. I could care less about naming her in front of her! Just
think, she asked my father to cut off my money until she leaves
and I come to my senses. If it were up to her I'd be masturbating until I retire. If it were up to her."

That's the Herrera of yesteryear. He had just announced
that there was a woman in his life, and he continued to rant
about his mother and his jerking off.

"And your father?"

"My father, poor man, what can he do? He's at the mercy.
An order from the matriarch is never under any circumstances
discussed . . . Well, in short, the point is . . . I wanted to ask
you for a small loan. I'll pay it back as soon as possible and I
promise that in exchange one of the nights she's here I'll introduce you."

There. It wasn't comments that Herrera needed. He
wanted a small loan.

"Will you at least tell me what her name is?"

"Valeria. Her name is Valeria."

The break between the two friends occurred exactly two
weeks later.

And it all happened rapidly. They were on the Vespa,
returning from the usual game. Not even the defeat of Lazio
that had just taken place before their eyes could explain
Herrera's dark mood. In other words, what was going on?
Where was his Herrera? What had they done with him? There
was not a trace of energy in him, as if they had dried him up.
What was the matter? The fight between his mother and
Valeria? This was really intolerable. The most stoic creature
Leo had ever met was finally revealing his breaking point? The
only thing a man like that couldn't bear was the atavistic clash
between the rights of his mother and those of Eros? And why
was Herrera so unfriendly toward him? Why, sitting there on
the Vespa, didn't he say anything? Why didn't he show off with
one of those pyrotechnic invectives against defeated Lazio or

his meddling mother? Why didn't he indulge in one of those orations that would one day surely make him a better lawyer than his father?

But just as Leo was thinking these things about his friend, the other had stung him with the most absurd statement. Herrera had got off the Vespa, in front of the entrance to his building, and, just like that, in passing, as he repaid the loan, had whispered, "I don't want to see you anymore," in the same tone in which he might have said "See you tomorrow" or "Call you later."

Leo had barely managed to ask, "Why?"

"Because I've decided."

"Sorry, but what have I done to you?"

"You haven't done anything. Not deliberately. But you've done a lot of things maybe without realizing it. Maybe by accident. Because you couldn't do otherwise. And that is the most serious thing. And that's why I don't want to see you anymore."

Leo was incredulous. He couldn't say a word. He was offended. And if he hadn't been so disconcerted he would have been angry. And Herrera no less: all red, flushed, as if he were about to explode. As if that painful conversation were wearing him out. He was ending things there. Period. He had nothing to explain. He wanted only to go.

"Come on, don't be an imbecile. I understand that something happened. But why should I have to pay for your bad mood? I think I deserve a decent explanation. At least tell me what happened!"

Leo was truly stunned. And he was also upset. Never in his life had anyone dropped him like that. He didn't know what it meant to be dropped. That was why he was upset. And then he was irritated by the words he was uttering, too similar to those of a man who asks a woman who has just dumped him for the reasons. If he thought about it his state of mind was not so different from that of a husband abandoned without warning and without explanation.

And Herrera had only exacerbated that feeling of painful dismay with another of those generic and oracular utterances: "You know, that was really terrible the other night." And he had said it with such wretched misery.

The other night? What had happened the other night? Then a vague memory emerged, something uncertain and wavering like a drunk man walking. And in fact the evening when Herrera introduced Valeria to him, Leo had consumed more alcohol than usual and more than was necessary. Maybe in that alcoholic altered state he had done something inappropriate? But now, no matter how hard he tried to remember, he was almost positive that he had maintained a standard of behavior well above the threshold of decorum.

Of course, he had been astonished by that large garish girl. With her martial tone of voice and her Trentino accent. He had had to control himself in order not to laugh at the sight of the dwarf next to that Viking. A circus scene. But he was certain, good Lord, that he hadn't laughed. That he hadn't let out any potentially outrageous thought. He had behaved very well. He had drunk only a little. And he had also talked a lot. Yes, this, too, he remembered. Just as he remembered Valeria's eyes. Valeria's eyes that were drinking in his words, and Herrera sitting silent in a corner.

The sense of inadequacy. The sensation of being unable to compete with a friend so handsome, so loquacious, so capable of being in the world. Was that the point? Was that the reason Herrera was cutting him off, like a maid caught in the act of stealing? Certainly that was it. Leo suddenly remembered the vague sense of guilt that had come over him, at the end of the evening, a moment before they parted, when, transformed by the alcohol and his loose tongue, he had told Valeria a stupid little story that he should have kept to himself. About the time he had bought cigarettes for Herrera and the cashier had said, "Aren't you ashamed to be buying cigarettes for your son?" Lord, how Valeria had laughed. Frighteningly. Lord, how Herrera hadn't laughed. No less frighteningly. Why had he told such a stupid story? It's true, it was amusing when the two of them recalled it. But to tell it to Herrera's girlfriend, Herrera's first girlfriend, that was intolerable. Herrera's face at that moment! It expressed such humiliation. Such complete shame and disbelief.

Leo was now thinking back to that face, after Herrera had said, "You know, that was really terrible the other night . . . "

And at that instant Leo understood why when Herrera was with him he was always so amusing, so full of interest, and why, instead, in the presence of others (especially of the female sex) he withdrew into a shell of hostile awkwardness. It was a matter of shame. He was ashamed of being what he was. Shame followed him everywhere. He *was* that shame. Was it possible that Leo understood it only now? They had known each other for so long. Their parents had been friends forever. And he understood him only now. And so why was he astonished that his friend cast him off without explanations? There was nothing surprising about it. And above all there was nothing to explain. It had all been there, for years, within reach. He had only to pay attention. His own fascinating presence made the shame of being Herrera Del Monte all the more bitter.

How could he not have thought of it before? How difficult, how terrible to live that shame. You could never relax. There was not a single being on the planet who would not look at you with disbelief and scorn.

From then on, starting that Sunday, outside of public or social occasions, they hadn't met. So that day at the dentist, seeing the picture of Herrera in the women's magazine, seeing his friend, older but still full of rage, Leo had smiled tenderly. It's still him, he had thought first: a mixture of shame and revenge. Assessing the anger with which Herrera was chasing off the photographers, Leo had thought, You haven't changed a bit, my friend. You got everything you wanted. You're rich as Croesus. You're the most talented and controversial lawyer in Italy. You can fuck all the Valkyries you want. But that shame—the shame of being Herrera Del Monte—well, that certainly has not passed.

It was natural, then, that Leo, at the greatest impasse of his existence, should think of Herrera. Herrera was what he needed. Not only someone who could help him out of his troubles but the only one who could understand Leo's state. A true master of shame. A world-class expert.

Everyone had abandoned him. But Herrera would support him. Because he knew what it means not to be able to look up out of fear of seeing depicted in the eyes of a stranger all the disgust that the sight of you provokes in others.

In short, for days Leo had been pondering the idea of going to see him. Asking him for help. If he hadn't done it from the start it was because of his usual sloth, embittered by the wretchedness in which he was living. Now that his wife had stopped helping him, now that Rachel had abandoned him, now that she behaved as if he didn't exist, now that he was living in that sort of bunker lined with records, books, and memories, Professor Pontecorvo was adrift.

If a serious and deplorable event hadn't taken place, Leo wouldn't have called the Del Monte office, or made an appointment with Herrera, or found the strength to get in his car to visit him in his bunker on a hazy, hot Via Veneto.

Just that morning Camilla's father had appeared at the gate of the Pontecorvo house. Along with his wife and the beloved .9-caliber Beretta he had bought for the protection of his shops. The idea was to empty the entire cartridge into that dickhead. And do it openly. In the early light of dawn, to imprint his revenge with Homeric vigor. Premeditated murder? Jail? Life in prison? Kill an unarmed man? Kill him driven by vague, generic accusations, still to be verified? And then deliver himself to the police? Or, in the manner of certain serial killers, take his own life right after shouting "You'll never get me!"? Why not? There are worse things in life. Like leaving that pig unpunished. They still haven't arrested him. What a shitty country! Some pointed out that Leo no longer left his house. Big deal, they can all stay shut up in that palace!

For days Camilla's father had been going around in a rage, saying that pig would have to pay. As if the pretentious and somewhat exhibitionistic indignation typical of certain uneducated and excessively virile men had lodged in him. This pushed him to take refuge in a sampling of rash and melodramatic statements, like "I want to see him dead!"; "Hanging from a hook at the butcher's like a side of beef"; "For certain crimes we need the electric chair"; "The thing you can't forgive is the betrayal of trust"; "It's a disease"; "If I just think of my child . . . " and so on. The truth is that Camilla's father couldn't wait to show off in front of his adored daughter, who for too long now had despised and rejected him.

So there he was, engaged in his sordid show. First he had tried the intercom, and then he had begun to shout: "Come on out, dickhead. Out! Try to get out . . . I'm waiting for you and I'll show you . . . "

And Leo, no less inclined to melodramatic gestures in those days, didn't make him wait. He asked nothing better than to do something reckless after yet another sleepless night. So he appeared in T-shirt and boxers before that man who was preparing to be his murderer.

This was the unseemly picture that was served for breakfast to the extremely seemly neighbor: an exceptionally tanned man with long red hair holding a gun, and an unrecognizable Professor Pontecorvo in a state of undress.

The obvious loss of weight and an unkempt beard made him appear even lankier, and even more like a penitent character from an El Greco painting. Written on his face is: "Shoot. Please. Shoot, what are you waiting for? It's what everyone wants. And what we want." And, to be even clearer, Leo goes down on his knees. In front of his executioner he kneels. And not with the gesture of one who asks for mercy but with the self-possessed, compliant, and impatient motion of the man condemned to death who asks only to get it over with as soon as possible. The polite and implacable gesture of one who is ready for martyrdom.

The ironic part is that Leo chose to kneel down on the same narrow strip of earth where, not so many months earlier, at the end of Samuel's birthday party, he had welcomed Camilla's parents: when he had ordered them to stand still so that he could photograph them. Just like that, Leo kneels in the same place where, in his time, he was able to display the benevolent sense of superiority induced by the sight of those two embarrassed boors. Now the situation is definitely reversed, and all to his disadvantage. Now it's he who has to be ashamed. Now it's he who's at their mercy. Now he's the helpless one. With the same politeness with which they made themselves available to his camera, he makes himself available to their gun. But it's one thing to photograph someone, it's another to shoot him. This banal observation explains why that lout can't do it. Why he can't do what he came here to do. Why he can't shoot.

Demoralized by that painful docility, astonished by that Japanese-style courage, or suddenly aware of the consequences of such an act performed in front of such a numerous audience, he lowers the weapon; his cheeks are streaked with tears, and he begins to whimper like a child. Mumbling his words. And after him his wife, too, begins to sob: "Please, dear, let's go, leave him alone . . . please, sweetheart, it's no use . . . don't you see what sort of worm . . . don't you see, love . . . "

And then Leo weeps, too. No longer on his knees but on all fours. He weeps. And he doesn't even know why. Until that moment he had managed not to (except in sleep), not in front of his family or in the prostrate solitude in which he spends his days. But now yes, now that they're all watching, he manages to cry. As when he was a child and before starting to cry he would wait till his mother was there, so she could comfort him.

The contagious collective weeping spares only Filippo and Samuel, who are watching the scene from behind the French window that opens onto the garden. Seeing them so catatonic, close together, almost embracing, as if to give themselves courage, one would say that they are ready to witness the execution of their father.

"Do you know your father is a pig? Do you know it or not? If you don't know it I'm telling you! You, Samuel, you know your father is a pig? You know what he did to me? What he did to us?" Thus the father of Camilla to the Pontecorvo boys.

Until, collapsing with weariness, he gets in the car, escorted by his wife, who is sobbing even harder, and disappears into the rosy air of morning.

So it was after this trauma that Leo had found the courage to pick up the receiver, dial the number of his old friend's office, and ask for an appointment. To hear him say:

"About time! I thought you'd never call," in the familiar and slightly resentful tone of a friend you usually see frequently but whom you've somewhat neglected lately. In reality, apart from the wedding of a cousin of Herrera's, three years earlier, it was a very long time since they'd been friendly. The only thing Leo managed to say was "It's that . . . " But Herrera immediately interrupted him: "Come on, I'm here, I'm waiting for you. Come right over and explain."

How would Leo explain what was happening to his life now? How to explain the state of terror in which he had been living for days? The claustrophobia that alternated with agoraphobia, according to whether the cellar was perceived by his senses as a narrow cave dug into the earth or an immense empty square. And then that terrible sensation, which had suddenly possessed him, of no longer being part of the human assembly? Of being an undesirable?

Only a few days earlier, after some time had passed, had he found the courage to go out, to abandon his household bunker and drive around. And he had immediately realized that he hadn't gone out by himself in years. He didn't know where to go. Obviously not to the restaurants where he used to go with Rachel and other couples. Certainly not to the movies, which would intensify the sense of claustrophobia that tormented him. The world, now that there was no place to return to and be welcomed, seemed an infinite wasteland full of things that were indistinguishable from one another.

So he had found himself having a drink in a place packed with kids in the neighborhood of Corso Francia. He didn't even know how he had happened on a place like that. He remembered only that he had got in the car making sure that no one in his family saw him. And that he had traveled kilometers and kilometers as if in a trance.

And had found himself there. A cheap vodka in his hand. A meaningless din. Surrounded by kids with tanned legs all dressed the same way: shorts, Lacoste shirts with the collar raised, boat shoes. The paranoid sensation that they were all pretending not to look at him. From the waitress to the other customers. Had they recognized him? Was it possible? And why not? As far as he knew, it wouldn't be strange if, since the day the nightmare began, his photograph had appeared obsessively in the papers and on the news shows.

Suddenly he noticed that he was dripping with sweat and that he had a troublesome, banging headache. He was agitated by an unprecedented cardiac arrhythmia. He would have liked to ask for help but he was afraid someone would say, "Drop

202 · ALESSANDRO PIPERNO

dead, you fucking pervert." So he left, and headed toward the car. Behind him he heard someone calling: "Sir, sir! Hey, sir, I'm talking to you!" There, that's it, he thought, now they're going to lynch me. He turned. It was the waitress, out of breath and definitely irritated.

"Sir?"

"Yes?"

"You didn't pay for your drink. I've been following you . . . "

"Oh Lord, I'm sorry . . . Here, keep the change, I'm sorry . . . "

No, the world was no longer for him. There was nothing around him that did not arouse fear. Terror vanquished any nostalgia.

And Leo was right to be afraid and stay alert. Because, even if he had chosen not to know it, all this happened in the very days when the national press had declared its prurient love for this ugly story, examining it in its embarrassing details, attributing to it pretentious allegorical significance: if only the Famous Writer and the Renowned Journalist had resisted the temptation to offer a penetrating account of the Fall of the One Above Suspicion or the Unmasking of the Imposter. Of course not. That August the beaches along the Italian coast were transformed into a piazza, where herds of mad philosophers wished to have their say about greed, betrayal, lechery, illegality.

And to do it they took as an example the story of the doctor who treats children stricken with cancer and finds nothing better than to make money off their misfortune and, in his spare time, seduces twelve-year-olds (Did he fuck her? wonders the envious pervert devouring the morning paper).

Evidently the combination of illness, violated childhood, political collusion, academic iniquity had given the common people the illusion of being substantially more honest and deserving than all the Leo Pontecorvos in the country—those with power, those with money, those with women, those who'd had everything in life and therefore believed they could profit from it, and who now deserved to die in ignominy.

On one thing they all agreed: a man like that could not remain free. A man like that should be arrested.

That was what was happening. That was what Leo could have asked Herrera's opinion about if only he hadn't cut off all contact with the external world, if only he hadn't chosen prudently not to watch TV, not to buy newspapers, not to answer his phone, which rang continuously.

The truth is that at this point Herrera knows the story much better than Leo. That's why he welcomed his friend to his office with a remark of such vulgar insinuation. The crowning touch was to call him "darling." The phrase with which, many years ago, in their world (that of the solid Jewish bourgeoisie that had emerged unharmed from persecution, of the rowing clubs and the long summer card games in the shady pinewoods of Castiglione della Pescaia), men used to address one another ironically. The odd affectionateness with which Leo's father could have consulted Herrera's father and vice versa.

That that phrase had been carefully pondered is demonstrated by the fact that never again—in the course of the conversation that followed and those of the succeeding weeks, when every morning Leo would appear exactly at nine at the office of his childhood friend—did Herrera allow himself a similar intimacy.

Now that he has given that suffocating man some air, now that he has put Leo back at ease (the vigorous co-religionist who in life, all in all, at least up to that point, had been as fortunate as he, but on whom fate some time ago began to turn its back . . .), now it's time to treat him as a client, and try to get him out of trouble. Not before having clarified certain preliminary conditions:

"The advance is seventy million lire. In cash, tax-free. My

secretary will wait for you in the lobby of the Hotel Cicerone the day after tomorrow at five. If you agree to be defended by me, you have to agree also to the idea that I will be your rabbi, your confessor, your psychologist, and above all your general. You'll have to answer to me for everything. And you'll have to do what I say. First, you have to fix your residence at my office. It means that all the documents relative to the investigations will come here. Second, I forbid you to watch TV and read the papers. I forbid you to poison your life with all that shit. Third, I forbid you to talk about the case with anybody (and you have no idea how many shitty anybodies there are around) without first talking to me about it. Fourth . . . "

So far it's all easy. I've been ignoring the papers and television for weeks, and then who would I talk to, if no one speaks a word to me? Leo catches himself thinking, again pierced by anguish. But right afterward he feels a voluptuous pleasure: someone is treating him like a child. Isn't this what he most needs? Someone who will treat him like a child. Someone who will present him with a strict set of rules.

"Listen, could you explain one thing?"

"Shoot. But don't get used to it. Usually before opening my mouth I want to see the money. My eloquence is more expensive than a Porsche."

"So many things I don't understand. The news of those letters. Coming out like that. On TV. Implying who knows what. . . Well, in other words, I would have expected to get a legal communication from the court, a notification, a summons. Why doesn't anything happen? Sometimes I want so much for something to happen. This nothing happening is killing me."

"I don't know what to tell you. I'd have to know the details, the charges . . . But I can make some hypotheses. Apart from any dark moralistic considerations there aren't sufficient grounds for prosecution. Of course, it's not a very seemly thing to write and receive letters from a young girl. It's the sort of thing that brings discredit to a man with a fine collection of existing charges like yours. And yet it's not a crime. Not at all. Molestation. Violence. Those are crimes, and you can rest assured that if there was evidence that you'd committed them they would have come to get you already! With all the unpleasantness in the air. But evidently they have nothing in hand. As for the other crimes . . . well, it's plain that if they were afraid that you could tamper with the evidence or slip out of the country they would have arrested you. But they're not worried about this. It's not like Leo Pontecorvo to flee. Not the Leo Pontecorvo I knew. A Leo Pontecorvo full of good citizenship and a sense of responsibility. An example of bourgeois respectability. Not a common fugitive."

These last comments seemed to Leo full of sarcasm. He heard in Herrera's voice a not very veiled reproach. Was Herrera taking his revenge?

Leo chooses not to notice. He has other things to think about. All in all he's pleased. He feels protected, in good hands. Isn't this the important thing? Herrera's innate nihilism, which now seems so brutal, if properly directed can prove very useful to his case.

Suddenly Leo feels a profound affection for his friend.

"You know, you look splendid!" he says, lying and telling the truth at the same time.

"Seriously? Well, after all my life hasn't been the failure decreed by my mother."

"I know, I read the papers."

"God, my mother . . . it's a year since she left me."

Leo knows. He used to read the obituaries in the newspaper. But, since at the time he chose not even to send a telegram of condolence, he pretends to be surprised and dismayed.

"What do you want?" Herrera continues, as if talking to himself. "My girl was old. A lot of ailments. And recently a serious senile dementia to drag around. I must have found a hundred caretakers for her, each one better than the next. She drove them all away. She didn't understand anything anymore, her brain was mush, the only thing she knew is that she didn't want to die with those girls, she wanted to die with me, her only son. And in the end I convinced myself that maybe it was the best thing. So during the day I worked and at night I stayed with her. You're a doctor. You know how devastating it can be. You want to know what she said to me the night before she died, when I was putting her to bed?"

"What?"

"'Darling, I love you very much.' There, the only affectionate thing my mother said to me in her whole life. And, the dirty whore, she whispered it to me when her brain had already gone haywire!"

Yet again Leo feels a sense of closeness, of solidarity. A friend. My friend. Here he is. He's come back.

If Leo spent the first part of his life under the guardianship of his mother, and the second under the attentive and loving gaze of his wife, now it's time for the legacy of the two women in his life, each having failed for a different reason, to be collected by Herrera. It's up to this fearless lawyer, this spiteful and determined dwarf, to accompany him on his perilous new path. And there is something enticing in this. Something poetic, which should not escape a man made sentimental by misfortune: at Herrera's side his life as an adult Jew began, and with Herrera it will have a new beginning or a tragic conclusion.

He has merely to set foot outside the office of his new lawyer, his new mentor, still under the bracing effect that the encounter—the stream of memories and the sudden flash of some glimmer of hope—left him with, and find himself on the street in that equatorial climate, overwhelmed by hot gusts of August humidity, to feel again all the weight of what is happening to him.

He runs awkwardly to his car, parked in one of the side streets that flow into Via Veneto. Calm down, my boy, it's nothing. Nothing happened. In fact, it all went better than you imagined. So pick yourself up, relax, and think of the next moves.

He has decided to follow the orders that Herrera imposed. He has the childish and military illusion that if he sticks to the instructions things will slowly return to order. It's then that another thought, no less pernicious than all the others, slips in and almost makes him faint.

The money. Where to get all that money? A substantial sum: well within his means, certainly, but tremendously difficult for a super-incompetent of his type to obtain. Leo doesn't know how much money he has. He's not the one who thinks about those things. It's Rachel who takes care of the bookkeeping and the bank accounts. He knows he has a good income and he has nearly unlimited trust in Rachel's administrative capacities. He has always been grateful to her for not keeping him informed about the family accounts. For never having put a telephone or electric bill in front of him. For not keeping him up to date about her financial maneuvers.

That's how he has always wanted to live: like one of those monarchs with unlimited credit, kissed by the privilege of not having to think about what for the common people is the dominant thought (yes, much more than love). He knows that over the years she has invested in real estate. But it's all he knows. Like a spoiled child, he has been provided with credit cards and checkbook. Through those two sublime instruments he can count on all the money a man of his background and life style needs. And it has never occurred to him to be excessive in his purchases. He is immune to certain compulsions.

Now he realizes that he doesn't even know if the apartments that Rachel bought are in his name. He remembers going several times in recent years to Emilio, a notary, also a childhood friend. And signing some papers while Emilio, as if he were in synagogue, recited some very boring litanies, written in an impossible style. He remembers typewritten sheets of ruled paper and he remembers above all the feeling of sleepiness that assailed him.

Evidently his terror of bureaucratic things manifests itself in a strange form of sloth and torpor, whose result is that now he doesn't know what he has signed. The transfer of all that he has to his wife and children (which until a few weeks ago would have been fine)? Or the acquisition of some new possession? Who knows? And who could he ask? Maybe he could call that ridiculous religionist Emilio and get an accounting of what he owns? What impression would that make? It's out of the question. He needs anything but Emilio's unctuous voice. But then how the hell can he get, without going to Rachel, seventy million in cash? There's no way. Who could he ask, on the other hand, except her?

He has a burst of anger. After all it's his money. He broke his back, he studied and worked tirelessly for all those years. The money belongs to him. And what's the use of making so much money if you can't count on it for serious matters of health or some legal mess?

The problem is that Leo hasn't spoken to Rachel since the hot July night when he fled from his family, abandoning them to their questions. She has done everything to avoid him, and he's not at all sorry about it. At least until he has found himself having to face practical questions. Those which up to now he happily delegated to her. And he has had to confront all his own incalculable ineptitude. Luckily he had the idea of going to Herrera. But without money Herrera doesn't exist. The way to grasp the new opportunity called Herrera is a big pile of cash. Without that, bye-bye opportunity called Herrera. Having to ask for it from the person who, of all of them, Leo imagines is the most enraged at him, would be like professing a genuine friendship with Camilla's father. Without that money the sole possibility he has of starting life again shatters.

Since this business began he hasn't gotten mad. But now it's as if all the violence accumulated toward the unprecedented series of charges that have reduced him to a pariah of society had decided to explode. He hates Rachel with his whole self. Her damned intransigence. The way she doesn't listen to you. That conviction, which seems to come from God, that she can distinguish what is right from what is wrong. Her moral sense is so fierce it makes her unjust. What use is her religion if not to inspire pity and understanding? How can she not feel pity for him? How can she not see what they are doing to him? Every day, her husband is mashed to a pulp, they've taken everything from him, even a reason to live, they've made him a clown. And all this though he has done nothing. Nothing.

Even she, his Rachel, believed Camilla's accusations. That damned little whore got him. That fucking psychopath who speaks to her parents in French, who writes raving-mad letters, who enjoys subjugating and torturing adults.

And that's why a bulldog like Herrera Del Monte is indispensable to him. Because only he, with his tenacity, his ability to debate, his shrewdness, will have the strength to destroy that absurd, tentacular edifice of lies. That's why he dreams that Herrera will seize the head of Camilla, that of her Viking father, that of the profiteering assistant and all the others, all those who are angry with him, and put them through a shredder. That's the cry of revenge of this poor count of Monte Cristo. That's Leo Pontecorvo's Biblical dream of revenge. Which will never come true if he can't get his hands on that money first.

Now here he is in the car, at two in the afternoon, the air conditioning on, the windows up, an atrocious heat outside, and he can't move: the mere idea of putting in gear his beautiful French-blue Jaguar and, after looking into the rearview mirror to make sure that no one is coming up behind him, leaving is more than he has the strength for. He's paralyzed. He's hot and cold. He's afraid. He's furious. He wants the money that belongs to him but he doesn't know where it is or how to get his hands on it.

And in a burst of extemporaneous sentimentality he says to himself that after all the money isn't for him. No, not for him but, rather, for something superior to him. That's what he'll say to Rachel the Intransigent, if only he can find the courage to ask her. "This money is not for me but for a higher mission. Justice. Truth. Things that you, my darling, should love as I do . . . " These abstractions, conjoined with an affectionate appeal to his wife, make him cry.

And so a man of forty-eight, protected from the world like a fish in an aquarium, in a nice comfortable dignified vehicle—inside of which the air-conditioning blows like a polar wind—finds for the second time during this long day the courage and the cowardice to cry. Sobbing like a lunatic, he suddenly realizes that a child outside the window is enjoying the scene. So he tries to compose himself and, still overcome by sobs, waves and smiles tenderly at him. But a second later he regrets it. He remembers that he is not in a condition to be tender with anyone, especially an innocent.

Mechanically, and not without paranoia, he turns around to see if by some chance anyone saw him smile at a child. The jackals are everywhere. In ambush. At least he has learned that lesson. There is nothing you can do now, even in exemplary good faith, that someone, at some point, could not use speciously to destroy you, to confront you with a responsibility you don't have. That's what Leo Pontecorvo has learned from human sociability. Others exist to destroy you. We are born to be destroyed.

The more he thinks about the money he needs, the more tormented and enraged he becomes. No problem, I'll go home and tell her without hesitation: "I have to pay the lawyer. I need my money." At that point she can't continue to ignore me. She'll have to give me an answer. If she says yes, well, good. If she refuses, I'll let her see what I'm capable of. Again this violently aggressive thought soothes him.

Turning onto the Cassia, two-thirds of the way home, Leo realizes in anguish what will happen if she really won't give it to him.

On the other hand she could well refuse him. Rachel isn't the same. Rachel stopped being Rachel no less than the world has stopped being the world. Or at least it seems that way to him. Rachel is now a ghost in his life. Or maybe he is a ghost in Rachel's life. It's the same thing. Well, not to give him that money, to refuse to help him, would be a perfect way for her to get revenge, but also to underline his irrelevance in her new life.

And if she said simply, "I'm not giving you anything. I forbid you to touch our money." Or, still worse, if she continued her silence? What would he do then? Nothing. If he had any strength for reacting he would have deployed it a while ago. Exasperation has a paradoxically calming effect on him. He will withdraw into the cellar, where he has been sleeping for several weeks already. He will throw himself on the pullout bed. He will try to sleep and won't succeed. Oppressed by that apocalyptic heat. He won't show up at the Cicerone with the money. And so he will lose his last chance to get out of this mess.

Is this how Rachel will get her revenge? Is this the way? By not letting him get the best defense he can? She's like that. He knows her well. Her devotion can be absolute, but, once you disappoint her, she'll punish you forever. You can't win back her trust. Leo knows her intransigence. He admires it. He loves it, that intransigence. Maybe partly because, at least till now, he has never been the victim of it.

He recalls the completely crazy way in which, when Filippo was three and was having a tantrum because he wanted another

212 · ALESSANDRO PIPERNO

cookie, of a kind he was very fond of, she had said to him, "All right, Fili, now I'll give you your cookie, but you have to promise Mamma that you won't ask for another one." Filippo had given a little nod of assent. Sealing a pact that to the child in the circumstances evidently seemed reasonable. Yes, if she gave him another cookie he promised that he would stop whining. Except that Filippo, once he had eaten his cookie, started whining for another one.

Leo had been astonished by his wife's reaction, as she continued to say, "I don't like this, you promised! You promised you wouldn't make any more fuss. We made a deal and now you're going back on it. I'll give you another cookie, in fact, wait, I'll give you all of them, you can eat them all, eat them till you feel sick, but know that you are not a trustworthy person."

You are not a trustworthy person? To a child of three who wants another cookie? The thing seemed so grotesque to Leo that he thought it right to intervene. "Sweetheart, aren't you overdoing it?"

"Now, Leo, don't get involved. We made a pact and he's breaking it."

"Yes, I know, but calm down. He's your son, he's three years old, he doesn't even know what a pact is. At his age the word 'trust' has no meaning. He reacts instinctively. He doesn't even understand that he promised something. And even if he understood he doesn't consider his promise so prohibitive. Don't give him the cookie if you think it will spoil his appetite but, please, don't give him your Biblical curses."

This is the person he has to get money from? This is the person he has to be forgiven by? A woman who was incapable of understanding a three-year-old who didn't keep his word? Well, he's screwed. Rachel is sweet, she is the most willing and helpful person in the world, she is an extraordinarily altruistic woman. But if you slip up you're finished. If you put yourself outside her idea of morality (which has nothing to do with the vulgar puritanism of many other women of her milieu but is invested in the highest sphere of human virtues: loyalty, sacredness of one's word, and so on . . .), well, if you go outside her idea of morality there's no escape. You can't expect any mercy.

After he's driven through the gate and parked the car in the driveway of his villa, Leo stays there for a bit, enjoying the air-conditioning and tormenting himself with the thought of what awaits him. Then he goes into the house. Hearing the sound of dishes coming from the kitchen he goes in and sees her there. Helping Telma do something. Telma sees him and starts, then whispers, "Hello, professor." But not her. She doesn't turn, or even start. And so Leo, trying to give his voice a little authority and a crumb of authoritative detachment, says, "I need seventy million in cash for tomorrow. It's for the lawyer." Still nothing. "Did you hear what I said?" Of course she heard. And just because she heard she didn't answer.

So, after a terrible night spent lying in front of the basement door that opens onto the stairway at the end of which is his marital bedroom, right next to the one where the boys sleep; after a night when he has conceived thoughts of suicide, homicide, flight, and who knows what else; after a night in which he has done nothing but think of the best way to try to reoccupy the domestic spaces that after all belong to him, unable, in reality, even to turn the knob to open the door that divides him from the upper part of his dwelling—after a night like that, he woke at midday on the pullout bed still dressed. Next to him he found a briefcase full of bills. He counts them as well as he can, noting that the figure corresponds more or less to what he needs.

He can still save himself.

Slowly, the Pontecorvo family's well managed little nest egg started to vanish under the enormous weight of the legal expenses and the lack of income. At intervals of seven days, Leo would leave a note on the kitchen table with the figure he needed written on it, and the next day punctually the same briefcase with the money was there waiting for him on the same table.

If Leo paid scrupulous attention to the punctual payment of the honorarium and the other orders imposed by his lawyer-mentor-parent, the same cannot be said for the prohibition on reading the papers. This was indeed strange. Because until that moment Leo had not read them, avoiding them had come naturally. He had guessed that to be uninformed was the only way open to him of preserving his sanity. But as soon as that natural self-protective impulse had been regulated and institutionalized by Herrera's authoritative and explicit prohibition, Leo, like a new Adam, couldn't keep himself away from the noxious seduction of the poisoned apple of the national press.

Every morning, after the usual sleepless night, at the first light of dawn he slunk out of his lair, by way of the garage, so as not to occupy the kingdom where his family lived and which was now forbidden to him; he went to a newsstand (one a little farther away from the one he had always gone to, a few kilometers to the east, just outside the neighborhood) and bought every sort of newspaper. Then he came home, and, with a mixture of pleasure and pain, paged through those sewers of newsprint. Although the press had less and less interest in him, although his *affaire* had slipped discreetly to the back pages of the dailies—from the national news to the local—nonetheless he never failed to find some little article.

Leo had got into the habit of reading everything carefully, not missing even a line. With the meticulous rigor with which he had once examined the test results and clinical files of his patients or with which he prepared the notes for his learned articles, he now underlined all the small journalistic inaccuracies. He was called "the forty-five-year-old Roman oncologist." "The well-known cardiologist." "The fearless Milanese oncologist." Also Camilla's age fluctuated, according to the article.

Between one newspaper and the next, that little bitch went from nine to fourteen in a flash.

Hunting down these imprecisions, which at first had exasperated him because of their injustice, their indecency, with practice had become a puzzle-like entertainment. Similarly underlining them, clipping them, putting the clippings in a box and then showing them to Herrera with satisfaction: as if the obsessive monitoring of the uninformed and malevolent press that would not let go of him could in some way be helpful to the work that his lawyer, in another office, was doing in a certainly more constructive way.

There was no occasion when Herrera didn't reproach him. Why did he waste so much time on that lunatic nonsense? Why didn't he stick to his orders? This was the road to the madhouse, not the way to win the trial that they would soon have to face together.

"Rest, read, exercise, think about other things . . . Your wife doesn't want to see you? Find yourself a twenty-year-old to fuck. If you want I'll get one for you. But distract yourself, for God's sake. I want you fresh, tough, and ready, when the time comes to fight. I want you to be in shape. At the height of your psychic and physical powers. You understand what I'm telling you?"

"Of course I understand. But do you realize that this shit says I favored one milk company over another for reasons of friendship, for reasons of patronage? And this one calls me a degenerate? A child molester?"

"Leo, no serious person charges you with anything at all. Only that shit of a journalist. And thank heaven journalists aren't the ones who run trials."

"But do you know how many people must have read that article? Do you know how many people who know me and who don't know me believe I'm the monster who did all these things?"

"It seems to me that you're somewhat idealizing the average

newspaper reader. The majority have trouble reading the head-lines, and the minority who embark on the undertaking of starting an article are already limping at the fourth line. The scant few heroes who get to the end, well, they forget the entire contents in the act of moving on to the next article. And that's what you should do. Forget. Forget the whole business. You don't realize it because it has to do with your life, because the thing burns you, which is natural, and also because you can't have my objectivity, but your affair is going out of fashion. *You* are going out of fashion. And this, I assure you, can only play into our hands. I shouldn't tell you this, but I nourish many hopes. The more I examine, the deeper I get into this business, the better I understand the impressive series of mistakes, con-jectures, strained interpretations. In the end we'll make it. I promise you. All you should be thinking about is what will become of you when this business is over. You should be think-ing of yourself, your health, your family, how to get back on track. You don't give a shit about fucking a twenty-year-old? At least find some way of talking to Rachel and the boys. Remake your relationship with them. Regain their trust. If you want I'll help you. I'll talk to Rachel. I'll put before her all the incontrovertible proof of your good faith and your foolishness. I'll show her in detail how the story of the girl has no criminal implication, I'll show her how that girl literally subjugated you, blackmailed you, leading you to the brink of despair . . . "

"No, please, I beg you, Herrera, I'll do what you want. But don't say anything to Rachel, leave the boys alone."

"But why? You don't think they'd like to know that their father and husband isn't the monster that some would have us believe?"

"No, no, please. No. Promise you won't do it."

"All right, all right, I promise, but don't get excited. I won't say anything. But you can't go on avoiding them. Being ashamed in front of them. Leo, you don't have anything to be ashamed of. Absolutely. The person telling you this makes his living by defending habitually devious sharks who should have a million things to be ashamed of but, God knows why, don't even know what it means to blush."

Herrera was preaching, as they say, in the wilderness. The problem was that Leo was that wilderness. The funny thing was that what had, in part, impelled Leo to go to Herrera was the conviction that he, better than any other, would be able to understand the shame that Leo couldn't in any way purify himself of. Evidently Leo had calculated badly. Not only for him had things changed over time. They had for Herrera, too. He was no longer the despised dwarf he had been. Now he was a successful man. Through his virile charisma, through his satanic cleverness and his acrobatic eloquence he had made the world forget his height and his appearance. And, despite all his empathic capacities, how could that renowned lawyer imagine the life Leo had been leading? The abyss he had fallen into? The most recent period of his human experience (the only granted to him) was rigorously devoted to shame.

Did Herrera know anything about what it means to be aware that your sons are looking at you unperturbed while you're on your knees in front of a man who is about to shoot you? What it means to imagine what your children are suffering because of you? But, so it is, Leo would never have been able to explain to a rational man that, when you are so involved with shame, the only thing you wish for is more of it. To bury yourself under it, like a man who has just been shot and every so often presses on the wound to feel where the pain is. That was why all that documentation was useful, all those scrupulously filed newspaper clippings: it kept him attached as tightly as possible to his shame, so that he wouldn't forget it or underestimate it for a single instant.

Or maybe yes, Herrera was right. Maybe he was going mad? But was there anyone, at least in their world, who under those circumstances had more right to go mad?

The picture that I ruthlessly reproduce on the facing page managed to put Leo's nervous system to a hard test.

It appeared suddenly in a couple of newspapers, accompanying articles discussing his *affaire*. Finally they have what they wanted, Leo thought, overexcited. They have their ace in the hole. Other evidence that had developed, other abominations were of no use. That photograph said all there was to say. That photograph could have served as a publicity poster for the campaign to raise public awareness whose final, by now obvious, objective was the elimination from the social organism of the bacterium Leo Pontecorvo.

Leo didn't even know how they had dug up that photograph. He already heard it, the voice of the classic, very sensible simple soul (the world is full of them), who would reassure him by saying that it was no big deal. It didn't show him naked, or dressed as a woman, or in dubious poses, or with a gun in his hand, not to mention drunk. It hadn't caught him in a compromising position with Camilla, or engaged in any of the infinite number of corrupt acts that were attributed to him. Nothing like that. Why are you getting so excited? the very sensible soul would have asked, basically all this photo shows is a man mounted on a horse like a thousand other men who practice the anachronistic art of equestrianism. But it's exactly that! Leo replied inwardly and at the height of agitation to the hypothetical sensible soul. That is the point. That is the secret. That is the low blow. It's an insinuating, specious photograph, full of double meanings and false bottoms.

He, who now knew the system from the inside (that majestic and insidious incinerator), could conceive the iconographic power of a photograph like that. A power such that this time not even Herrera could minimize it. With his subtle intuition he would certainly understand.

"We're back on this stuff? But didn't you promise me that . . . ?"

"Yes, I know, and I swear I've kept it . . . rather, I've tried to. But it's not so easy and maybe not even so intelligent to ignore this stuff. I have the right to check, to monitor. You can't keep an eye on everything, and your colleagues can't, either. I know, I know, all day they're working for me. But these things they can't understand. You'll agree with me that it takes our intelligence, our upbringing, our maturity to understand certain things . . . "

"Calm down, Leo, calm down, nothing is happening. Now I'll give it a glance, as you say, just calm down a moment . . . "

"Why are you telling me to calm down? I don't want to calm down. I can't calm down. How can I calm down when they continue to publish this kind of slander?"

"But what slander?"

So Leo put it down in front of him again. And Herrera, without losing control, resumed:

"Look, I've seen it. It's a photograph, that's all. Maybe it doesn't show you at the height of your attractiveness. Maybe you're not the most photogenic man in the world. But, good God, it's a photograph. The photograph of a man on horseback dressed like a shit. I've seen a million. All you have to do is buy the magazine *The Horse* not to mention *Show Jumping* or *Dressage*, and you'll find another thousand."

This time that cynicism didn't amuse him, that brisk irony didn't make him feel at home or intimate. It made him indignant. And made his heart sink. Leo had no desire to joke; he wanted to be taken seriously. He expected a serious response. He was spending his last cent, reducing his family to poverty, to get serious answers. So he ought to give him a serious answer.

"O.K., sorry, no joking. I swear to you, my friend, that I can't understand what you're saying. I can't understand why this picture should be more dangerous or more defamatory than all the ones that have been published so far."

Was it possible that he didn't understand? A man of his

subtlety, his cleverness, his sensitivity didn't understand. Probably to understand certain things you have to be in the middle, you have to be involved. Everything in life has a meaning. This entire tragedy has a meaning. Is it possible that you, Herrera, you, don't understand it?

Leo really needed to believe in it. In the meaning of what was happening. But he didn't know how to convince his lawyer that that photograph was connected to that notorious meaning. So he tried to calm down. Or, rather, to play the part of the man who is calming down.

"You're sure there's no way to make them withdraw this photograph? To get it pulped? I don't know, charge them all with defamation?"

"You see? I don't understand what you're raving about. What's happening to you? You're losing control. I repeat: it's a photograph. All you have to do is not look at it. Don't buy the newspapers and don't turn on the TV. That is the only prescription against paranoia."

"So now you're calling me paranoid? What does paranoia have to do with it? I'm paranoid just because I realize, because I register meticulously what's happening? Everything that's happened to me seems to you like paranoia? You know what I'm going through? Do you have any idea how alone I feel? Overnight I became a worm. A reject. No one is willing to grant me anything. You remember the conference at Basle, the one they invited me to? Well, yesterday evening a girl, a shit with a very polite voice, left a message on my answering machine. You know what she said?"

"How should I know? That they changed the time of the coffee break?"

"That at the last minute they had had to cancel the conference. That they were dismayed, they didn't know how it could have happened, but that because of a regrettable series of circumstances . . . and all that other Swiss rubbish . . . "

"Well?"

"Well what?"

"What's the moral?"

"The moral, Herrera, is that they're killing me. The moral is that for a while everyone has been killing me. Including the Swiss. But you know why they decided right now to finish me off?"

"Why?"

"But it's so clear, holy Christ! Because they saw the photograph. Think about it, Herrera. I've thought about it, since last night I've been thinking about it, and it hangs together perfectly. This fucking newspaper is available in Basle, right? Of course it is, I found out. Evidently it ended up in the hands of some idiot bureaucrat. That bureaucrat showed it to the committee. And only then the committee decided. This photograph convinced them. I see them all in a little knot looking at it, commenting on it, judging it . . . I see it all."

"And you don't think they barred you because of everything that's happened to you in recent months? When you told me about it you said you were surprised that they hadn't revoked the invitation, with some excuse. And now, look: they've done it."

"Yes, but why just now?"

"Because they've come back from vacation. Because the conference is approaching. Or because they only now remembered you. How should I know? And above all, who gives a shit? Do you really think that one of the organizers, after coming across this photograph by chance, had a revelation? And only then withdrew the invitation? This is what you're telling me? This is your brilliant deduction?"

"Exactly."

"Well, my friend, as you see, the stopper is out of the bottle . . . I told you not to read that shit. It's that shit that is turning your brain to mush. You're not the first I've seen reduced to this state. You've stopped thinking straight. I repeat: you're not the first I've seen reduced like this. And I knew it might happen. Well, let someone help you who still has his feet planted on the ground: unbelievable as it may seem to you, this photograph says nothing more about you than any other I've ever seen. Yes, it's true, it shows you in a sporting activity. Maybe the sport you're engaged in isn't among the most common, in fact, let's admit, it's a bit snobbish. Maybe this will make some people angry. Some working-class guy, some populist. Maybe the concierge will say to the butcher's boy, 'Just look at this shit of a pedophile, this thief, this loan shark, this shitty Jew with all his billions. I would've bet he'd go horseback riding dressed like someone going foxhunting.' Yes, I don't deny that that could happen. But between that and saying that this photograph is the product of a great plot intent on destroying you, well, there's a big difference."

Seriously, Herrera, the extremely intelligent Herrera, didn't understand? And yet to him it seemed so obvious. Or maybe he absolutely understood. Maybe he understood and wanted to make him appear crazy. But of course: he's not my friend, he's not my ally. He was the one who broke off with me at the time. He was the one who at a certain point in our life decided he didn't welcome my presence. It was my height, my look, my attractiveness, my self-assurance that irritated him. Made things difficult for him. Humiliated him. This guy has hated me since we were kids. How could I rely on him? How could I put my life, or what remains of it, in his hands, if what at the time for me was friendship was merely hostility for him? What for me was affection was for him envy. He's drawn me into his trap by deceit. He's bleeding me dry. And now he has awarded himself a front-row seat so he can enjoy the spectacle of my destruction. He was just waiting to see me reduced to this to enjoy his revenge completely.

And why? Because of an unfortunate remark that I let slip out when I was half drunk in front of that Valeria, or whatever her name was. If only he had explained what he felt. If only he had told me what he had inside. But not him. He was proud. He didn't ever want to expose himself. Only at the end, when the situation had become untenable, then he kicked me out of his life. Like that, without warning, with a ferocity and a premeditation that left me breathless. Has he been lying in wait for me since then? Never underestimate the blasted rancorousness of a dwarf! Why should I be surprised? He has always been like that: eloquent and ambiguous. And now the moment has arrived to make me pay the bill. This nasty flea-bitten lawyer, whose stomach hair is longer than he is, pretends to help me, to be with me, while he is ditching me.

Until suddenly Leo had an illumination.

"You remember the question you asked Rabbi Perugia about Jewish iconoclasm? And you remember his answer?"

This sentence came out of his mouth before he even knew why.

"Now, what does Jewish iconoclasm have to do with it?"

"Come on, don't look at me like that, don't treat me like a madman, I'm perfectly lucid. You remember or not? Of course you remember, but you don't want to give me the satisfaction. And to think that every time you argued with the rabbi I looked at you with such admiration. Maybe it didn't show, but I was ecstatic. Your argumentativeness, your love for anything that wasn't obvious, your ability to challenge those anachronistic superstitions . . . "

"All right, all right. Thank you. I agree, it was amusing to make fun of that ninny, and attack his granite convictions, but I can't understand what it has to do with that photograph and everything else that's happening . . . And I don't remember anything I asked the rabbi or any of his answers."

But by that point Leo had lost the desire to explain to his friend. Or to remind Herrera what the callow Herrera had said to Rabbi Perugia so many years earlier, and above all what Rabbi Perugia had answered. That exchange between a stammering young rabbi and a thirteen-year-old gnome suddenly appeared to Leo so profound—such a definitive prophecy!—that to tell it would seem like a pointless violation.

Leo was in a trance now, placidly saturated with that memory: the long, boring lessons given by Rabbi Perugia to the meager group of preadolescents on Sunday mornings in the basement of the Tempio Maggiore. He remembered everything. The soccer games that preceded those exhausting immersions in religion, and in which Herrera gave evidence of all his bitter combativeness. The dusty neorealist air you breathed during those games—those battles!—in which the local, working-class Jews used their only encounters with Jews from middle-class families to thrash them. But also the dancing parties that followed the lesson and that usually took place at the Pontecorvo house. Gay little parties that Herrera stayed away from, out of timidity or pride or in order not to spoil them by his presence.

How was it possible that Herrera didn't remember the morning, thirty-five years earlier, when, a few weeks before their bar mitzvah, he, Herrera, had asked Rabbi Perugia why God had refused to allow Jews the comfort of images? Why had that capricious bearded entity, with whom Herrera seemed to have a score to settle, forbidden his people to make a portrait of him? The Catholics are always painting their beautiful Jesus, glowing and trim, and we are not even granted a little holy picture. Why? Why?

A question typical of the boy Herrera. His typical idle curiosity of those years. The quibbling, the intellectual exhibitionism that were to make up for the physical disagreeableness. And at the same time a challenge with which he wanted to destroy everything around him. Which provoked in the other kids (especially the girls) distrust and incomprehension. And which went so well with the distrust that his body aroused in everyone.

Why was that horrible dwarf so interested in these things? How could it be important to know why God did not want to have his portrait done, if in a few hours everyone would be in the living room of the Pontecorvo apartment dancing to records that had just arrived from America? How could a boy of thirteen prefer those pompous questions to Glenn Miller, Cole Porter, Bing Crosby? Why, if none of them—dragged out of bed on Sunday morning for what they considered a supplemental ration of school, reserved for Jewish boys—gave a damn what the rabbi was saying about God and his whims, was Herrera so interested? Why did that ugly, timid child show such pugnacious energy only in soccer games and when he was argumentatively challenging Rabbi Perugia?

The curious thing is that, if Herrera's verbose insistence was incomprehensible to his companions, it pleased the rabbi, who, in fact, said to him, "With that head you should be a rabbi!" To be answered by that extremely precocious thirteen-year-old: "But, I'm afraid that you, Rebbe, have too much faith in the Law of Moses to be a lawyer."

Have too much faith? Come on, that's not the way thirteen-year-olds talk. And yet that's how Herrera talked. Like a novel.

Well, that time the captious eloquence that Herrera in the years to come would put in the service of his clients and make fruitful for his bank account, and now uninterested in persuading rabbis of the eternal Father's inconsistencies, was fixed on the question of images. Why didn't God want a portrait of himself? Herrera didn't understand it. And who knows why Leo—although at the time he belonged to the category of sleepy slackers who, during the lessons, did nothing but stare at the clock, in the hope that the torture would end as soon as possible—realized that he remembered both the rabbi's first answer, definitely ironic, "Well, maybe the Poor Old Man isn't as vain as they say he is," and the second, extremely serious: "Or maybe the Lord wants to teach us that the truth is everything that images don't express."

In recalling this second answer, Leo felt another shiver. A sense of elation. As if those words would explain how things stood. The reason for everything. He was happy that the rabbi had checkmated his best student, and that now that same student, who had become a famous lawyer, could be checkmated again, by the same phrase. Yes, dear old rabbi, tell this conceited man how it works. Tell him the only reasonable thing about my present situation: *the truth is everything that images don't say.*

And so, thirty-five years later, Leo decided to repeat that sentence to the person who had triggered it: "Do you remember, Herrera? The truth is everything that images don't say? Do you remember, Herrera? Please, tell me you remember."

"Leo, calm down, I don't know what you're talking about. I'm afraid you're raving mad."

"But really, come on, what an extraordinary answer! I understand it only now! Now that I'm confronted by that photograph, I understand it. I understand how photographs lie. It's photographs that are the problem, you see? Those bastards use the photographs to destroy your life. Like that night when they broke the story on the TV news. Behind the anchorman there was a photograph of me. When I heard him talking about me, I looked up at the TV, incredulous. And I saw myself there, next to that guy. It was me but it wasn't me. That photograph showed me but said nothing about me. Photographs are the problem. They're what ruin everything. It's because of certain photographs that later your wife won't ever speak to you again, that your sons don't want to ever see you again, that you hide in the cellar like a madman, like a thief. And it's because of photographs like that that I'm ashamed. Tell me you understand. Tell me you see what they've done to me. What they're doing to me."

"Yes, I see, Leo. I see it very well. Now calm down. Sit here and calm down. You'll see, we'll make them pay. They'll take it all back."

"No! You see you don't understand. I just want you to say that this photograph produces the same feeling of terror in you, too, that it produces in me. Mystification, distortion, deception. Those are their weapons."

And although Leo had the tone of a fanatic, although part of his perception of reality was by now almost completely compromised, you couldn't deny that that photograph was at least so stupidly grandiose as to border on a lie. What was more fallacious than the photograph that Rachel kept, ironically, in a frame set on a small table near the entrance (who had taken it from its spot and given it to those hyenas?), far from indiscreet eyes, and put there to remind him of what he would never again do? The photograph captured him in an impeccable riding outfit, mounted, reins firmly in hand, on a bay with a light-brown coat and black mane, shins, and tail.

There did not exist a photograph, among the thousands taken of him in half a century of life, that more poorly represented a man who had chosen good taste and self-irony as codes of survival. But who would explain to the distracted consumers of newspapers and television news that the horseman in that picture, if not exactly innocent, was guilty in a much more debatable way than that picture seemed to suggest?

Rachel had taken it the previous spring at the riding school in Olgiata, when, after years of inactivity, he had decided, on the advice of a nutritionist colleague, to take riding lessons and, yielding to the vanity of the beginner who believes he can hide his ignorance behind correctness of equipment, had acquired form-fitting cream-colored pants, shiny brown leather boots, and a ridiculous checked jacket. Anyone who knew how to ride would have seen in Leo's posture the signs of inexperience: heels up, back bent, cautious rigidity. But how many equestrian champions are there around? A handful of snobs and riders who probably don't read the newspapers and don't watch TV because the fresh air is better.

That photograph was destined to produce the completely opposite feeling: something that led people to be suspicious of such unexpected self-confidence, a suspicion that easily degenerated into anger and aggression. A person who today agrees to be photographed decked out like Beau Brummell, a person who has lost the sense of the ridiculous to the extent that he'll pose for the lens like an equestrian statue—from such a person you would expect certain nasty pathological crimes. Only a big shit in jodhpurs can, unlike many contemporaries of his background, face the crisis of middle age not by buying a custom car and fucking his wife's aerobics instructor but by embarking on the road of no return that leads to corruption, loan-sharking, pedophilia . . .

And no one gives a damn that the photograph doesn't represent you. Indeed, that that photo is the spectacular denial of everything you've tried like mad to be. Because that photograph is stronger than your life. It's truer than you. More definitive than any sentence, more persuasive than any witness for the prosecution, more circumstantial than any expert evidence or testimony. That photograph is you as others believe they know you. That's why it's so vibrant. So potent. So cruel. Why it says to the world what the world wants to hear: that nothing goes better with depravity than vanity.

Four men in uniform violated the peace of his basement office early on a late-September morning. And they did so with seemliness and discretion. Knocking and waiting, before entering, for a sign of life. Although Leo, whose sleep by now was extraordinarily light, heard the cars parking in front of the house, the voices of the policemen as they approached, the front gate buzzer, and then the front doorbell and the indiscreet shuffling above his head, he started when someone knocked at the door.

Who could it be? Who would dare knock at the wicked hermit's door? Rachel? One of the boys? Telma? Maybe the plumber? Maybe his toilet wasn't the only one where the water pressure had decreased? Maybe it had happened in the whole house. And maybe the diligent Rachel, who, in a certain restricted form, was still taking care of him, was sending the plumber to fix the problem down there, too . . .

Whoever it was, Leo preferred not to answer. He pretended it was nothing. Unable to restrain the emotional upset that the idea of an intrusion caused, of whatever nature it was. For a moment he even entertained the impulse to hide behind the flowered sofa that for some time now had functioned as a bed. In essence it could be anyone. Nothing would have surprised him. Not even a gang of boys with sticks arriving to beat him. Or Camilla's father, who had finally come to a decision . . . But it wasn't fear for his own safety that kept him from answering; if anything it was a sudden modesty. Embarrassment at hearing the sound of his own voice. It's true: when he went to Herrera's office he talked, he talked excessively. But when he went home, to his bunker, the mere idea of uttering a word seemed to him sacrilege.

After another volley of increasingly harsh blows the four policemen, having grown impatient, entered.

The sight reassured Leo. And yet he remained silent, melodramatically offering them his wrists so that they could handcuff him. But one of the four, a kid (he couldn't have been more than a few years older than Filippo), said, "Professor, there's no need."

Leo's surprise at seeing those kids in uniform had been no less intense than that of the police officers at finding themselves in the presence of a man completely different from what they had seen in the newspapers and on television.

The ruinous fall into the abyss of such an improbable destiny had taken the form of a somatic revolution: an involuntary loss of weight and the whitening of his stylishly cut hair had distorted his aspect. Then something must have happened to his coloring: the florid copper color of his complexion was blemished by gray-blue highlights, and the skin, especially on his hands, was marked by coffee-colored stains, of a type usually manifested at a more advanced age.

Which merely emphasized an even more revolutionary metamorphosis, that of character: presenting, during this morning blitz by officers with an arrest warrant, yet another public performance in which Leo gave proof of a striking timidity, as if he wished to demonstrate to those four incredulous cops and to himself that a few months had been enough to eliminate from his nature any trace of arrogance or pride.

More than two months had passed since he had last slept with Rachel and since he had seen the boys, except every so often by chance through the high, narrow windows of the cellar. Two months since he had left in the morning to go to Santa Cristina. Since he had received any phone calls except from Herrera, from some latecomer busybody, and an obscure, methodical, yet raving bearer of threats. He had relieved his family from the weight of an unwelcome presence, like the wary and diffident Gregor Samsa . . . Not surprising, therefore, that he was inclined to welcome any living being who knocked at his door, but at the same time also frightened.

Maybe because of the long isolation, the surprise, the headache, and the ferocious weariness that afflicted him, or maybe because meanwhile, after a month and a half, he was losing faith in Herrera's thaumaturgical powers, but there was Leo, exhibiting an incongruous hospitality toward the men who had come to arrest him, the men who stood there, with the handcuffs attached to their belts, ready to take him who knows where. This is my new family, Leo thinks, with emotion. And that's why he is so polite. Maybe he would have shown the same gratitude to anyone who came to free him from that domestic nightmare. In essence one confinement is the same as another!

Even to that guy who called up and threatened to kill him and then piss on his corpse he was in some way grateful. Yes, he was grateful even to that psychopath, who said things like "You enjoy yourself with little girls, right? You go out with them? But God sees these things and I see them, too. I see them, too. Professor, may you hope only that God finds you before I do . . . " Anything, even the words of that maniac, was better than the silence by which he felt besieged, that absence of tender human contact (God, Rachel's smooth hip! Did it still exist somewhere?); anything was better than those crushing thoughts, as heavy as reinforced concrete, and those sudden revelations of consciousness, in which he took note of the inexorableness of what was happening.

The fact is that any of his acquaintances who had seen him in that situation, up against the boys in uniform, would have been goggle-eyed at that compliance, which was on the point of dissolving into emotion.

In other words, where had the well-concealed pride of Leo Pontecorvo gone? With which he had always kept his neighbor at bay, ever since the days when he was the top student in Professor Meyer's postgraduate course? And what was the source of the obsequiousness with which he prostrated himself before his jailers? Was two months of isolation and social unfitness enough to transform a great man into a timid, whimpering creature?

Believe me: much less would be enough!

The police, besides, showed themselves perhaps too accommodating. After sparing him the humiliation of the handcuffs, the boy, the most obviously inexperienced, defying protocol and the anger of his superior, had whispered, "Professor, you certainly won't remember, but you treated my brother's daughter," in a tone indicating that the daughter of the young policeman's brother was in excellent health. She was on the list of former patients who had made it, some of whom came to see him every year, to demonstrate that if they were still there they owed it to him.

A very untimely confidence, the young policeman's, which led the higher-ranking one to intervene: "Excuse me, Professor, I don't want to make you hurry, but it might be best if you take some personal things. It's possible that tonight, anyway . . . yes, well, *you understand* . . . "

What is there to understand, in the end?

The wall that separates your beautiful marital bedroom from the cell where at any moment they might throw you is much thinner than your presumption of social inviolability led you to believe. Is this what you're supposed to understand? Well, it doesn't take a genius.

Leo let them escort him out as if he didn't know the house where he had lived for so many years and which had cost him a lot of money. He was relieved to observe that on the journey from the cellar to the front door there was no one. Probably Rachel had arranged it in a way that no living soul would be present at his arrest. Sparing him a mortification or sparing herself and the boys. And things went smoothly. Coming out into the open air, Leo was greeted by a sparkling sunny late-September day. The apricot-colored light of the morning was like dawn in Jerusalem. On the horizon a solitary, polished front of white clouds had assumed the form of a shark with its mouth half closed, alert, ready to hurl itself on its prey.

Those September days. He had always loved them. When everything in the house started up again. He, worn out by

August at the beach, returned to work. Rachel returned to being the unopposed mistress of the house. Filippo and Semi returned to school. There was something touching and reassuring in that inexorable *return*. In the morning, before he got in his car and rushed to the hospital, Leo took a short walk to the café just outside the northern entrance of the compound, which the boys called "the ditch." He got coffee and newspapers for himself. And hot croissants for Rachel and Telma.

Those September days. It used to be the time of year when Rachel devoted at least one afternoon to getting the boys all their school supplies. She went to stationery stores and the big department stores to get binders, notebooks, pen and pencil sets, backpacks. It was a habit that Rachel particularly cherished, and which had also infected the boys. Semi, for the whole five years of elementary school (or, as he said at the time, "nementary"), before his consumer desires shifted to clothes, couldn't help asking his mother every year, "Will you buy me the set with the compass and magnifying glass?"

And she: "We'll see."

And he: "We'll see means no."

"We'll see means we'll see."

Rachel had to restrain herself in order not to get the boys everything they wanted. Still vivid in her was the frustration at not having the same supplies as her schoolmates. For Rachel school was important. Unlike her husband, she had always loved it. She had been an exemplary student. For her school had been a gym, an alternative to the dreariness at home. Not for Leo. For Leo school had been above all an obstacle. Getting up at dawn was painful. He belonged to the fraternity of night owls who wake up at midday. If there was one thing he thanked heaven for it was that at a certain point school was over and no one could force him to get up at that insane hour. That sweet and caressing air must be the same as those mornings when his mother crept into his room, opened the blinds, placed the milky coffee on the night table, gently pulled his soft, sleep-warm feet out from under the covers, and put on his socks. An incomparably tender gesture which nevertheless was the prelude to a reluctant awakening.

As the agents escorted him out of the gate and opened the car door for him, Leo wondered if that year Rachel had found the strength to take the boys to buy new school supplies. Probably not. They were too old for such pastimes. And then how could what had happened not have had an impact on the family's daily behavior? Leo no longer knew what to hope. He didn't know if he preferred that the events had left a mark or that nothing had left a mark. His mark on his sons. This was truly a terrible subject. On which he was afraid to question himself. His sons were an atrocious mystery. They had always been. And certainly they would never stop being one.

Although he lived one floor away from them, Leo knew nothing about his family. He was wary of asking Herrera or anyone else, just as he was wary of even a minimal attempt to make peace with his wife. That time—the time for making peace—was over. She had always been the one to make the first move.

Getting into one of the two police cars, which smelled of apples and onion, Leo had felt his nerves release, as if they were taking him away from a nightmare.

The twenty square meters of damp, stale twilight where they threw him is definitely overcrowded. And not exactly with gentlemen of his type. The air reeks of urine, sweat, dripping pipes, rust, wet dog, and many other equally fragrant things.

Everything here says that it's an intermediate stop on the sinister journey to the unknown that he has been compelled to undertake. All this filth and all this excitement, all this take this one out and stick this other in, makes Leo think of the waiting area of an emergency room. Yes, evidently this is the place where the new arrivals are sent before . . . before what?

There must be a mistake. Leo remembers that Herrera told him that in prison they usually don't like to mix up people of different backgrounds. Or maybe not? Maybe he didn't say that at all. Maybe Leo dreamed it. He had placed one of his last hopes in class prejudice. What did you think, my boy? That they would put you in with some kleptomaniac member of the Lincean academy?[3] With a depraved baroness? With Dr. Mengele or Silvio Pellico? What did you expect? That for big-shot professors of your lineage, for a man endowed with your good manners, there was a special area outfitted like the V.I.P. lounge of an airport? What do you say to a good cigar and an aged cognac?

Instead they had no compunctions. Why should they? Justice is blind (as is injustice). They put you in here: a small space crowded with shady-looking brutes, who, thank heaven, are minding their own business. With the single glance he felt able to cast around, he observed a great extravagance of T-shirts. The rest is what you might expect: several-day-old beards, tattoos, curly hair, some pierced earlobes from which the earrings had been confiscated. The aesthetics of crime. The banality of crime. When Leo entered he was greeted with a welcome from a dozen brown distracted eyes. The behavior of these thugs—from what Leo could understand (for hours now his buttocks have been sinking into a worn mattress thrown into the room, which is already so full of twin mattresses that it's almost impossible to walk without stepping on them)—savors more of indolence than of intimidation.

Why is Leo here? They haven't explained it to him. Nor has he had the courage to ask. Not even the young cop, the nicer one. Who, alas, disappeared before his colleagues. When the police officers handed him over to a prison guard, Leo was

---

[3] An Italian science academy founded in 1603 by Federico Cesi.

tempted to ask the latter why he was there. But looking at him he resisted. A flabby little man with the knot of his regulation tie loose and his beret cynically askew. His massive arms burned by the sun, but only up to where the short-sleeved shirt began, which allowed one to glimpse, from the biceps up, a disturbing whiteness. No, he wasn't the person to ask what was happening.

And so whom to ask? Leo's mind was about to explode with questions. And it's terrible to have so many questions, all those people around, and no one to ask.

Why did they come to get him today and not that day in July when everything started? What happened in the meantime? And why at dawn on Friday? Before the weekend. Entering the vast prison courtyard, bounded by massive walls, like ramparts, Leo shuddered, a small attack of claustrophobia. Not to mention that the atmosphere is more relaxed than someone like him might have imagined. Something discarded, forgotten, as if time there languished in an eternal swampy August. If you thought about it, it wasn't very different from the air one breathes on September Fridays in the hospital and the university. The days are still long and beautiful. Why not take advantage? People still want to go to the beach. Yes, the last seaside weekends. There's no harm in that. But then why drag him here on this particular day? Why not pick him up on Monday? Leo is dying to ask someone this question. Certainly his new fellow-tenants are much more knowledgeable than he is about such things. But he doesn't dare to interrogate them. Naturally—he doesn't even dare to look at them. The only thing he remembered to do is ask that sort of menacing guard (an instant before he threw him in there) to call his lawyer. At least this time he adhered to Herrera's directives.

"If they come to get you," Herrera had urged him many times, "try to call me as soon as possible. Even at four in the morning if necessary. Since you know I can't sleep more than three or four hours a night. Of course, it's just a scruple. It seems to me highly unlikely that they'll arrest you now. As I was saying, if they wanted to do it they would have done it already. You're not a common criminal. You have a clean record. You're not going to repeat the crimes and there's no advantage for you in absconding . . . so . . . "

So, Herrera's irreproachable logic has been routed by the indecency of the facts. In truth Herrera also told him that "preventive detention" (as he had called it) would have been justified only if they had acquired new, even more crushing evidence or if there had been a new crime, probably more serious than the earlier ones.

Is that it? Is a new crowd of accusations hanging over his head? Why not? With all the people who have recently felt compelled to accuse him of something, it's plausible that a new detractor has come forward.

The truth is that the answers Leo seeks are in the right-hand pocket of his pants. That's where he put the copy of the arrest warrant that was given to him the morning they came to get him. Everything's written there. The explanation of why they brought him to this place.

But something is keeping him from putting his hand in his pocket and glancing at those few pages. Her prefers not to know. He feels that his nerves are so delicately balanced that a comma in the wrong place would make him collapse. So no paper and blessed ignorance.

One thing is certain: Leo has been here for hours and of Herrera not a sign. Maybe they didn't let him know. Or maybe yes, they told him but he, for some reason or other, is taking his time. Maybe they notified him, he came, but they won't let Leo see him. Or maybe they notified him, he came, and now he's working to get him out. Probably that old Levantine is bargaining with the judge.

Yes, the judge. Who knows who the judge is? Since it all

began Leo has always had trouble imagining the human beings who were doing this to him. He has always found it incredible that whoever was doing such harm was a person like other people: wife, children, dog, insurance, and everything else.

One of the kids from the police, alluding to the judge, referred to him with the honorific "doctor," referring to his law degree. With respect or sarcasm? Who knows!

"Has the doctor arrived?" he asked as he handed over to his fellow-jailer the package called "Leo Pontecorvo." Just then Leo had read his own name written in block letters on the file that the two cops were exchanging. That was what he had become: a file. There was nothing that described his current condition better than those creased, dirty pages. Not bad for a man who for his whole life had avoided every bureaucratic trifle. In short, when one of the two men had asked the other if the "doctor" had arrived, the answer had been among the more evasive: "I don't know if he's coming today."

He doesn't know if he's coming today? How can he say that he doesn't know if he's coming today? There's a chance that he won't come till Monday? Or even that he won't come until he finally considers it proper to show up? Which means that Leo will have to stay sitting on this mattress for who knows how long (he is terribly thirsty). He'll have to stay here staring at the filthy floor of the cell in which they temporarily park detainees waiting until the formalities of admitting them to prison are completed.

(Yes, "temporarily," the most far-seeing of adverbs.)

What time is it? Leo doesn't know. At the entrance, along with a handful of other personal items, they confiscated his watch. To judge from the heat that has loosened its tentacles and from the late-afternoon light that filters through the high, sealed windows, eight hours must have passed. Leo has been shut up there for hours with a bunch of other people. And he still hasn't spoken a word to anyone. A real record. Leo is the

type who when he is facing a long trip on a train or in an airplane in the end feels the need to bother his neighbor with some stock phrase: "There's a bit of turbulence" or "Do you know what time we're supposed to get to Milan?" But what are the conventional questions to ask a cellmate? "How many have you murdered?" "How many old ladies did you rob last weekend?" That sort of thing? . . . Better to be silent. Go on minding your own business. Wait. Something will happen, something has to happen.

Afterward, Leo was put in isolation, as per the "doctor's" orders. And now here he is talking to his father and mother. And he has been for some time. They've come to see him here: in his "single room," flooded with milky moonlight. They must have flown here from the cemetery, which isn't far away. It's where, in a small, decaying neoclassical chapel in the old Jewish cemetery, Leo buried them, a decade apart. It's where, in a tomb on whose front is written "Pontecorvo-Limentani," to signify that it is full of putrefied Pontecorvos and Limentanis, his parents, until a few hours ago, were resting in blessed peace. Maybe, seeing their son in trouble, they decided to wake up. (Leo imagines it was his mother who took the initiative and tugged her husband by the sleeve—or what remains of it.) And after a brief parley they flew to him.

They don't seem to want to give him advice the way they used to. Nor do they want to reproach him. Rather, they do what, in life, they were never able to do: they listen to him. They sit there seraphic and smiling and listen to him. For hours. That is to say that in the cell he doesn't breathe the dark atmosphere of chaos that accompanies the dead king in the presence of the young Hamlet, nor does Leo feel terrified, like Don Giovanni before the ghost of the Commendatore. Not at all. As I was saying, the atmosphere is relaxed. So much so that Leo not only isn't afraid but he has never been so talkative. He hasn't felt such a strong desire to smoke a good cigar in a long time. He doesn't have one, but it's as if he did.

Although it's not cold, Leo is shivering. Pleasant shivers. It's the third night he's been there. Alone. And those shivers, before his parents arrived, are the most poignant thing that has happened to him since he was put in isolation. He has even managed to sleep for a few hours. Maybe because in the mean-time he has learned the art of not thinking precisely about any-thing. The art of detachment. Of no hope. Precious skills, capable of putting in perspective, if not actually canceling, the weight of time. Whenever they bring him food or ask if he wants to go out for a walk, Leo starts. The door of the cell emits a sinister sound that makes him start.

But beyond these moments of panic the stay in the cell is unexpectedly innocuous. It's the first time since it all began that he has stopped thinking about what's happening to him. He doesn't give a damn what Herrera is doing. He doesn't even wonder anymore how it's possible that, four days after his arrest, he hasn't even showed up. He doesn't wonder anymore if Herrera has forgotten him or if someone (who knows why) is preventing him from seeing his client. Leo doesn't think about what people are saying about him. People don't exist. The world doesn't exist. A desolate empty land. That's what the universe has become. He doesn't think about the judge, the notorious "doctor": the man who is taking his time, and who Leo, in all conscience, doubts will once more show up for work. The signature for Leo's arrest. That was the last act of the "doctor" before he retired. Before exiting the stage. Leo doesn't even think about Rachel, or Filippo, or Samuel. He begins to wonder if they ever existed. If they do exist, how is it possible that they aren't with him? How is it possible that they could allow this to happen? What perverted intransigence, what altered sense of justice could have led them to show such a glacial indifference toward him?

Yes, there, finally, he feels protected. No one can hurt him. He has seen that his infinite mildness, his meek behavior, induces in the guards who bring him the meal tray a strange, precious compassion. No one has been so kind to him in a long time. In short, Leo is comfortable there. All he does is nap. He has so much sleep to catch up on. He begins to believe that prison is underestimated.

Until Mamma and Papa show up. It must be very late. The moon and the stars have taken care to illuminate the inside of the cell. From outside comes the magnificent perfume of the Roman night: damp of the river, freshness of eucalyptus. And Leo can't stop talking.

The food here is really terrible, he is saying now. And not only the food. Everything is disgusting. This smell is disgusting. To help you understand, Mamma, it's a much, much more disgusting smell than the one that came out of my suitcase when I got back from the Jewish youth camp. Remember, Mamma? When you became obsessed with the UGEI, the Union of Young Italian Jews? It was time for your son to socialize. Spend time with his people. He was such a pretty child, your son, so intellectually precocious, so athletically high-spirited, and yet held back by his condition as an only son. And by a solitary temperament. And maybe by all that Jewish overprotectiveness that he was the object of. Those years in Switzerland saved his life, of course, but they also slowed it down a little. Here's the kind of conversation that at a certain point you started having at the table. Papa and I were eating and you were talking. You never stopped talking. And it was incredible some of the things you said. You, the inspiration of my precocious misanthropy. You who alone were responsible for my compulsive lack of sociability. You who had done everything possible to shelter me from the inordinate number of traps that this planet conceals. But, lo and behold, with one of your unexpected strokes of genius, you decide the time has come for emancipation. And that that emancipation has to pass through the bonds of blood. And what is better for emancipating a spoiled child than to send him to a fine Jewish summer camp? You remember how desperate I was? How I clung to you? You remember how I cried? That I didn't want to get out of the car?

"Come, little bear, look what a nice view you get from here. Look at the sea, and all those kids. You'll have fun here. Tomorrow your friend Herrera arrives. And then Mamma and Papa are only an hour away by car."

And in fact the view was beautiful. The colors were so vivid. The yellow of the earth, the blue of the sea. And, yes, Herrera was about to arrive, even though nowadays you'd never suspect it. It gives me shivers to remember it, Mamma. But it was terribly hot. Not to mention the mosquitoes, the dirt, the slovenliness! Life in that camp was like life in a kibbutz. And maybe that was the basic idea: a bit of real socialism translated into a little colony of Jewish kids camping in a pinewood in the Maremma. The bigger ones take care of the little ones. The little ones respect the big ones. Sooner or later everyone has a turn in the kitchen. Or in the latrines. Sooner or later everyone has to take a turn as night watchman. Night watchman? Exactly. Flashlights, sticks, whispers . . . As if the Jews didn't feel safe even in Tuscany. Something truly ridiculous but so exciting.

Yes, Mamma, I was starting to have fun. As usual, you were right. After the first bewilderment, after winning the battle against my rich kid's squeamishness, I started to feel better. After crying for several hours because I had been abandoned by you, I almost forgot you and began to enjoy myself. And I did enjoy myself. All those boys, Mamma. And all those girls, Papa. And Herrera, so comically squat . . . A magnificent vacation. And now, remember the shock you had when you came to get me? That wasn't your son. That couldn't be your son. Your son wasn't so thin, so dirty, and so scruffy. Your son wasn't a street urchin. What had happened to him? Had those austere *gnevrim*[4] not given him enough to eat? Made him work too hard? Neglected his cleanliness? Wretched UGEI!

"I never smelled a stench like that."

It was you, Mamma, who said that, when you opened my suitcase. After two weeks at the camp. As if that suitcase contained all the sweat and all the grime of a lifetime. You remember that stench, Mamma?

Well, it's not even comparable to the stench in here. I know you don't like it when I talk about these things. And in such an explicit way. But if I don't talk to you, then whom do I talk to? That's in essence why you came to see me, isn't it? That's why you ventured all the way here. That's why you're reincarnated. So that finally I can let everything out. So that I can tell you, rather, inform you, of what is happening to your son. You know, they nearly brutalized me. It was terrible. A horrendous fellow, Papa, with an accent and monstrous breath tried to brutalize me. He and his thugs tried to inflict on me a torture that I can't tell you about. And they got close. And I thought that was the worst thing. When the guards saved me, when they pulled me out of that nightmare, I said to myself: that was the worst of it. From now on things can only improve. Now I will have the consolation of mercy that is owed to those who have suffered so much. And so unjustly. That's what I thought the moment after I was saved from that nightmare. What innocence. What naïveté. The nightmare had just started. Now it was the guards' turn to have their fun.

Understand, they did neither more nor less than what the prison rules provide for. Mostly paperwork: the ID photos, the fingerprints. Then they made me strip completely. They confiscated the gold chain you gave me for my bar mitzvah, my wedding ring, and even your watch, Papa. Then, completely naked, with just a cloth around me, I was taken to a boiling-

---

[4] "Jews" in Roman dialect.

hot room. They left me there for a long time. They took their time. After a while they came back. They weren't alone. There was a doctor with them. A doctor, white jacket and rubber gloves. He put his hands everywhere. Yes, even up my ass. He put two fingers up my ass, Papa, as if he were checking my prostate. And they all stood there looking at me. The doctor and the two guards. They gave me such looks. As if my naked-ness weren't enough for them. As if they wanted to strip me even further. If it had been up to them, if their wishes had been granted, they would have skinned me alive. No, no, the doctor was not at all rude. The doctor was kind. A bald, skinny type, younger than me. For someone whose job is to stick his hands up the ass of prisoners he was really friendly, and yet there was something repugnant in all that friendliness. You can't receive a human being in a hot room like that, you can't make him wait for all that time, and then come in and as if it were nothing stick your hand up his ass, and do it with such cheerful friend-liness, besides. That affability has something demonic about it. Affability is the worst thing. The true mortal sin.

Then luckily they put me here. And left me in peace for a while. You don't know what a surprise it is for me to see you. You know? I miss you insanely. I've never missed you so much. Maybe because there's nothing you wouldn't have forgiven. To be a son is the most beautiful thing in the universe: because there's nothing a son can't be forgiven for. You, Mamma, you were always saying as a joke, when I got up to one of my tricks, "Your children will avenge me." You couldn't know how right you were. Maybe you would never have been able to conceive the intransigence of your grandsons (about your daughter-in-law you had some suspicions. This I must acknowledge). Their lack of compassion. The problem of becoming a father and husband is that you aren't forgiven for anything. Right, Papa? You no longer enjoy full immunity. They're all there, ready to tear you to pieces. All there with their fingers pointing. They can't wait for you to slip up. Yes, they seem to expect no less. They just hope that the dad and husband does something really stupid. Something he will pay dearly for. With an incurable resentment.

Now Leo is talking to his father and mother about a documentary he saw a few months ago with his sons. One of the last programs he watched with Fili and Semi. When for them it was a privilege to watch television with their father.

The show is called "Quark." You wouldn't know it. The host is a man named Piero Angela. An elegant, skillful, ironic man. The type whom you, Papa, would like. With whom you'd enjoy talking about politics and society. Not to mention you, Mamma. You'd go mad for a man like Piero Angela. He would captivate you with his British charm.

Anyway, I was watching with your grandchildren a documentary produced by the BBC and impeccably introduced by Mr. Angela. I have to say that the title of the documentary immediately struck me. A truly literary title.

"Nature: Stories of Parents and Children."

It was all in the title. An exhaustive title. A magnificent title. Don't you also think all nature is contained in that? In that infinite relationship. Which repeats. Which goes on repeating itself. You should have seen the images. The lioness with the lion cubs. The gazelle with the pups. Even repulsive animals like the boa and the frog prove to be loving with their children . . . Everything expressed a single feeling. A fierce, desperate desire to protect and be protected. You understand, my dear ones, a desire to protect and to be protected. And this is the most important thing. The thing I miss most . . . Yes, I know you understand me . . . See? You haven't abandoned me. You are here. You have joined me. It couldn't be otherwise. Really, it couldn't be otherwise . . . But don't stay there, come closer. Yes, just like then. Just like when I was scared and sneaked into your room. I knew you would protest. I loved those protests.

But I also knew that in the end you would give in. I was electrified by the absolute power that I had over you and you over me . . . I was euphoric in a bed that seemed so big to me. Your mattress of wool. Here, now, come. Settle yourselves here. Since you weigh nothing. You're very light.

Thus Leo fell asleep held like an infant, or like the filling in a sandwich, in the arms of his mother and father. Who went on caressing him. Soothing him. Who continued to whisper: don't worry, everything's all right, you're not alone, don't be afraid. Mamma and Papa are here. And Leo slept very well. Deeply. His father's aftershave, the camphor-like odor of his mother. He slept sweetly. As he had not for many months.

During those months, Leo, in a completely arbitrary fashion, had attributed to the investigating judge (or group of judges), who was doing all this to him at least a hundred different faces and bodies.

His imagination had worked hard! It had done overtime, scaled mountains. Sometimes portraying the "doctor" as the small unhappy fat man who can't wait to crush the balls of a good-looking guy like Leo. Then as a lean, lanky, peevish character. Then it had been the turn of the ignorant, vigorous cop, quickly replaced by the quick-tempered sharp dresser, by the inexperienced new graduate, fanatical about the Law. And a throng of other more or less unlikely human types who from time to time had a turn.

But he hadn't been able to imagine anything resembling the man he found himself facing when, finally, on the morning of the fifth day of detention, two guards came to get him and led him, through endless corridors, to a stuffy, disorderly room where the gray, the beige, and the yellow lived unhealthily together.

Opposite the door of the public prosecutor's office Leo found Herrera waiting for him. A disheveled Herrera. An irritated Herrera. And more, much more: an enraged Herrera!

Leo, at first, seeing the wild eyes of his lawyer, observing the state of muttering agitation he was in, thought that he was the object of that fury. Why not? He was inured to people who got angry at him for no reason. Here's another one, he had thought, but without getting too upset, with the stoicism that prison in just a few days had taught him.

But as he approached he understood that Herrera's stammering invective—"It's intolerable, unheard-of. It makes no sense. It makes no sense at all!"—was not addressed to his client. But rather to the sheets of paper that Herrera was holding. And that Leo immediately recognized. It was a copy of the arrest warrant. A clone of the one that Leo still had in his pocket and had been careful not to look at. In there was everything that Leo had tried not to know during his detention. That is, why they had arrested him. On what charge. Why they had put him in isolation. Why they had kept him for five days from seeing his lawyer or any other human being . . .

The astonishing thing was that Herrera, far from being interested in the condition of his client, was so obsessed by those pieces of paper. As if they were a certification of his impotence, a personal affront. That Leo had had his first, traumatizing ration of prison seemed to interest Herrera completely incidentally: Leo's imprisonment was only a collateral effect (one of many) of the aberration represented by the papers that Herrera was savagely clutching.

Might there be a risk that as soon as the door opened Herrera would attack the judge with the recklessness he seemed in the grip of at that moment? That he would be unable to restrain his dwarf's resentment?

Leo naturally hoped not. That was all he needed! In essence, Herrera had kept urging on him coolness and composure . . . and now he was the one losing control?

Leo suddenly felt like the boy who is brought by an angry parent into the presence of a feared principal. A father who wants to express all his indignation at the treatment of his son by the mathematics teacher. A parent so wrapped up in his own fury that he doesn't realize his son will pay for that attitude later, with interest.

Leo wasn't pleased. He didn't like the fact that Herrera was in that state: I wouldn't say *about* to explode but more than anything *already* exploded.

It was more or less then that Leo Pontecorvo remembered that he was Leo Pontecorvo. And boldly reappropriated his identity and his place in the world. It was then that Leo began to tremble. And felt his colon contracting in sudden and insidious spasms. Increasingly conscious that beyond that threshold was the most important thing in the world. That in a few seconds the mother scene of his whole life would be consummated. For which was required an exceptional performance, and so a general condition different from the one he was floundering in.

All this while his lawyer couldn't stop blathering: "This piece of shit tricked me. But don't worry. Now we'll make him explain what sort of comedy this is, now they're going to tell us why they kept you from seeing your lawyer, as if you were a Mafioso. Stay calm, Leo. Leave it to me. Look at me. Take your time before you answer. In fact, answer as little as possible. If you have any doubt that the question might be a trap that means it doesn't merit an answer. You understand?"

And this was the great lawyer? The infallible lawyer? The shark of the law courts? This agitated little gnome who couldn't do anything better than poison him with his tension? Shouldn't he be reassuring him? Wasn't that one of the reasons he got so much money—for his capacity not to lose control at moments like this?

Maybe Herrera's problem was Leo. Why not? He always had been. Whatever they say, people never change. If an individual provokes ambiguous feelings in you in adolescence it's likely that he'll continue to provoke them even in full maturity. An exemplary career and widespread approval aren't enough, women aren't enough, money isn't enough to free you from the frightened and bitter child who languishes inside you. Leo could have written a treatise on the subject.

Certainly when Leo regained possession of his faculties it wasn't the best of moments. Right at that instant the detachment, the indolence, the stoic acceptance of his destiny, which had protected him until a moment before, went to the dogs. Which didn't help. He wasn't content with a return to being Leo. Leo confronting his drama. Leo facing the most perilous test.

The most perilous test. Exactly. The most difficult and torturous examination. There was no doubt about that.

You could hardly consider Leo a creature of exams. He never had been. Everything he had obtained, starting at a certain point of his life, he had had to win by hard work. He had had to keep in check an overflowing emotionality and struggle against an innate apathy. He had had to reconcile an inclination to creative contemplation with a tough competitive spirit. And, on the subject of competition, the family he came from, as far as scholastic results were concerned, would not have tolerated any faltering in its only offspring.

It's true, certain things came naturally to him. Translations from Greek, for example. Those he could do. During high school he had only to come face to face with an ancient-Greek text to see the right words emerge from a deep and unknown place in his consciousness with unusual spontaneity. The rest was simple. Seize those words, fill them with meaning, copy them neatly onto the page and wait for the enthusiastic approval of a teacher-admirer. Leo had a real talent for Greek. A skill as fantastic as it was impractical. What was the use of knowing how to translate texts, written in a long-gone language, that celebrated the deeds of men who had been dead for millennia? None.

Mathematics. That was useful, yes. Or at least everyone thought it was: a pity that Leo had no talent for it. It was the black beast that pursued him along a decent but far from exemplary school career.

It's that when he was confronted by all those numbers and all those symbols he was overcome by a bovine, almost invincible somnolence. Pursued by anguish. What was the sense of working so hard in an exercise of such inhuman abstraction? All he did was wonder about it. A first response to this philosophical question arrived in tenth grade from the mathematics teacher, who made him retake his final exam in September. See how this lazy fifteen-year-old was given the opportunity to meditate all summer on the indispensability of that soporific subject. And also to reflect on how dishonorable it was for a Pontecorvo to repeat an exam. All that summer term, in fact, until the stain was washed away, his vacation at the beach was punctuated by looks of disapproval and the factoring of polynomials. Three laborious and humiliating months. Three months of graph-paper notebooks. No going out, no going to the beach, not even the evening walk for ice cream with his friends, because he had to settle fully his debt to society. But above all three months in which he had learned that, although in other things his parents were basically indulgent, in that area they would not accept a misstep. School no. That's no joke. You have to repeat the mathematics exam? It means that you haven't sacrificed enough. That you haven't tested yourself fully. That you've given up too soon.

That was the most important lesson Leo learned that summer. Apart from equations, which instantly disappeared from his mind. What he learned was that everything he had (and he had much) he had to deserve. And that that implicit blackmail was the basis of the education they were giving him. Bourgeois education. Old school. More draconian than a biblical precept. Whose unique commandment solemnly decreed: "You have to be better than your father and you will bring into the world individuals who will do everything possible to be better than you."

He was a thoroughbred, and had to behave like one.

A lesson he remembered in his first year of university, when he had had to confront a new insurmountable obstacle: the chemistry exam. Again that somnolence. Again that sensation of vacuousness. Again a confusion of mixed-up formulas in his mind, impossible to memorize. What torture! But by that point the horse had been trained. By that point Leo knew how to behave. And he did his best to pass the most difficult exam of the first year of Medicine with the biggest bastard of a professor. That old madman who insisted that you learn the textbook by heart. Who did all he could to make you nervous. Not to mention that he was a close friend of Leo's father. But the same bourgeois morality that compelled a privileged student like Leo to repay his parents with an impeccable university record kept his father from saying a word about his son to an old friend.

Leo remembered the day he went to take the exam. The fierce humidity of July. The bastard who, for some reason, wasn't sweating. He remembered when that man had asked, in an incredibly patronizing tone, if by any chance he was the son of his dear friend Gianni Pontecorvo. Leo remembered how he had followed his father's instructions and said no, he wasn't the son of that Pontecorvo. He was the son of another Pontecorvo. The son of some ordinary man, who, in order to pass that difficult exam, had to start where everyone else started.

Lord, the pitiful state he was in as he lied about his identity to that notorious bastard. His mind was empty. Or, rather, so packed with formulas and bad omens as to be unusable. He came from four months of depraved study. He was nauseous. He hadn't slept for the past two nights and had even taken some pills to keep himself going. He felt close to fainting. He

254 · ALESSANDRO PIPERNO

wished he had a passage of Thucydides in front of him to translate. Or a fragment of Sappho to interpret, and to give meaning to. Then indeed he would have prevailed, could have shown what he was made of. Leo was one of those athletes who get excited when they play at home and are disproportionately depressed in an away game. And there was nothing that resembled a hostile away game more than that humid classroom, in the shape of an amphitheater, where the bastard and his assistant bastards evaluated the students with the systematic indifference of a firing squad retaliating for some wrong.

And Leo had made it. The triumph of self-denial. He had come out alive and triumphant from an unequal contest. That time he had made it. And from then on he had passed every exam he faced, always relying on force of will and betting on the efficacy of sacrifice.

But what would have happened if he hadn't passed the chemistry exam? What would have happened if, by some chance, betrayed by emotion or ineptitude, he had said something foolish? What would have happened if the bastard had suddenly, with a characteristic gesture, thrown the book in his face, saying, "We'll see you in six months"?

Nothing would have happened. Nothing more serious that what had happened a few years earlier when he had to retake the mathematics exam. He would have had an extra ration of study. He would have had to put off getting his degree by a few months, and hence his emancipation from the family. He would have had to face his parents' anxiety. Their disappointment. Their anger. That's it? That's it.

And now, on the other hand? Now what would happen if, during the interrogation he was about to undergo, he didn't give the right answers?

Well, Leo was about to find out.

So this was the enemy. This his face, this his body. Or rather what Leo had tried to imagine for all those months and, to judge from the individual standing on the other side of the desk, had in no way succeeded in portraying with any verisimilitude.

So this was the persecutor. The Grand Inquisitor. The Torquemada on duty.

By a series of coincidences (not random at all?), the man who opened the door and invited them to come in, the polite but not in the least formal man who told them to sit on the other side of the desk, had been assigned the majority of the numerous investigations involving Leo. It meant that, for almost six months now, a great part of his working life had been devoted to gathering evidence capable of proving that Leo Pontecorvo was a thief, a malefactor, a pervert. It also meant that it was he who had signed the piece of paper that was responsible for the five most ludicrous (certainly not the most horrific) days of Leo's existence: the piece of paper that Leo still had in his pocket and whose contents he insisted on ignoring.

Herrera had presented a petition to ask for a formal preliminary hearing after his first meeting with Leo. The prosecutor had rejected the petition, but before Herrera was able to present his appeal, the public prosecutor had arrested Leo.

"That shit got in there before me!" were the words that Herrera kept muttering, growling.

Why such passion? Why get angry at him like that? Why should he be obsessed with a human adventure that was basically not so different from that of other fathers of families, other eminent doctors, other professors? Leo had wondered innumerable times.

But now that he was in front of him, now that he could have had an answer, he didn't wonder anything of the sort. Now it seemed to him that everything was perfectly linear and logical.

That was the job of the investigator. Which he carried out with no less commitment and no less dedication than Leo, in his time, had put into his.

Leo thought again of all the speculating he had done with Herrera, who, like many lawyers of his generation, was convinced that everything came from a political prejudice.

"That man hates you," Herrera repeated.

"Why do you say that?"

"You can tell from the way he writes the orders that he hates you. He hates what you are. He hates what you do. He hates your damn column in the *Corriere*. He hates your Jaguar. He hates the doll's house that you shut yourself up in. He hates Craxi and your pathetic Craxian idealism."

"But why? Can you tell me why?"

"Because he does!"

The investigator's wholesome appearance spoke of his perfect good faith. He acted like that because he couldn't act otherwise. If a judge learns of some crimes it is his duty to be concerned with them and to pursue whoever committed them. The penal code says so but also common sense. And, even if you knew, as Leo knew, that a considerable number of the charges lodged against him were unfounded, you couldn't help appreciating the diligence with which this man performed the tasks that society had entrusted to him.

Leo remembered the time when he had asked Herrera if he had ever had anything to do with that man.

"Of course. Besides, I had to meet with him several times for your case. But I already knew him by reputation, everyone knows him. He was just transferred, or had himself transferred, I don't know."

"From where?"

"Calabria. Aspromonte, to be more precise. He was in the trenches. They don't joke around there. And it seems that our friend stood out there, too, for a certain stubbornness, let's say.

And there, too, he pissed off quite a few people. That's why they gave him a team of bodyguards. Threats, intimidations, letters with unexploded shells. In short, the usual grotesque means by which mobsters let you know you're a pain in the ass. Maybe that's why they transferred him. Or he had himself transferred. You remember those Piedmontese idealists, rock-solid, whose dream, from the time of university, consists of going to the South to restore, at last, the rule of law? That's it, something like that. Good books. Loves music. In short, the classic type to watch out for."

"But aside from that, what type is he? As a judge, I mean."

"What type is he? A type like Adolf Hitler: harsh but fair."

Thus, with one of his cynical and hyperbolic digs, Herrera had let his client understand that it was a taboo subject. This was a matter that Leo should absolutely not get mixed up in. Stuff for lawyers and not for clients. Even though that sarcastic remark had had the effect of further transforming in Leo's eyes the essence of the man who was now facing him. The name of Hitler had vanished. The pair of adjectives endured: harsh but fair.

If he really was like that—harsh but fair—well, Leo had nothing to fear.

Except for some muttered greetings, the investigator had still not addressed a word to Leo or to Herrera. For now he was involved in giving instructions, in a low voice, to those who must be his colleagues, assistants, or underlings. One, little more than a boy, sitting in front of a typewriter, would probably be responsible for the report. The other, getting on in years, would be making sure that the tape recorder, with its large reels, which was placed on a small table beside the desk, functioned properly. They must be from the investigative police. Two assistants. He sensed in them a great but at the same time affectionate respect for the investigator. Leo got the idea that, being in a government office, one breathed an air of cooperation and understanding. As if it were a fine family held together by a father who was *harsh but fair*.

Finally there was a woman. Also rather young. Whose lack of attractiveness and irritating thinness were remarkably summarized by her hair, pulled back in a stiff dark-brown bun. Maybe the magistrate's assistant. Now the two were talking. Probably she would take part in the interrogation.

In that atmosphere heavy with concentration and expectations Leo recognized the same emotion that preceded a surgery. Although he wasn't a surgeon, he liked to be present at the operations that, all too often, his small patients had to undergo. If only to be sure that those butchers didn't get out of hand. So that's how a child must feel a moment before the anesthesia, amid all those adults who were talking to each other, organizing, giving one another orders. Those adults got up like astronauts, who would soon be laying their hands on him.

Even the light, so bright and artificial, evoked an operating room.

Leo, noticing the way the young woman looked at the public prosecutor, was sure that she must be in love with him. Of course, madly in love! More in love than that and you'd die. Yet how could it be otherwise? Who wouldn't be in love with a man like that? Finally Leo allowed himself to look at the man attentively. To grasp the elements of such an unmistakable fascination. He was still turned toward the woman.

There are men whose pants, because of their meager backsides, hang with an impeccable and therefore unsustainable precision. Those men who have no ass are for the most part lacking in compassion and insufficiently provided with emotional resources, and above all they are cold, precise, and without mystery, like solved puzzles. That's what the flat ferocious ass of the investigator said: it said everything about the severity of this young man, but very little about his temperament.

When at last the man turned toward him, Leo was struck by his radiant virility. No more than five feet seven, lean if not exactly athletic, the investigator wore a sky-blue shirt open discreetly at the collar, the sleeves clumsily rolled up to the elbows. His summer pants of custard-colored cotton were part of a suit whose jacket drooped over a chair. His perfectly spherical head, which was perfectly shaved and shining, reminded Leo of that actor Rachel liked so much, what was his name? Ah yes, Yul Brynner. Then, there were the eyes, whose blue displayed a Flemish clarity.

A terribly painful nostalgia for life. For his life. Leo felt overwhelmed by this. Seeing a man so at his ease in his own pants, with no belt. Seeing a man who was allowed to do his own job freely. Seeing a man at the height of his energy, at the peak of efficiency and power, Leo felt such envy. For a second he found himself longing for—yearning, with ardor—the purloined goods: all that they had stolen from under his nose. He thought, at random, of his wardrobe, his students, emergencies at the hospital; he thought of successes and failures, of conferences and the coffee breaks between one session and the next; he thought of Rachel, of Filippo, of Samuel, and even of Flavio and Rita; he thought of the fragrance of Telma's *torta caprese* just coming out of the oven; he thought of vacations, of the lagoon, of the snow, of Saturdays, of Sundays but also of Tuesdays; he thought of the great Ray Charles, the voice of the great Ray Charles, he thought above all of that . . . In an instant everything returned. Everything he had lost. Along with fear. Fear of the sinister ritual that was about to be performed, in which he had been assigned the difficult role of lead actor. Goodbye stoicism. Goodbye fatalism. This was life. In its densest and most unequivocal form. Here fatalism had no usefulness, philosophy was a pointless waste of time.

What had happened to Herrera?

Having vented all his anger outside the door, once he was inside he seemed to calm down. Which Leo didn't mind. What distressed him was that, compared to the judge, his lawyer seemed an impotent, derelict creature, without authority.

"Signor Del Monte," the judge said, in a voice that was disappointing, not the equal of his appearance: not equally firm, not so warm, not at all that of a great man. With too any irritating high notes. And languid in a way that was unmistakably Turinese.

"Signor Del Monte, if you have no objection I will begin."

"All right, but first I would like . . . " Herrera replied with a calm and a severity that Leo both liked and disliked at the same time.

The judge immediately interrupted, as if he hadn't heard him: "If you have no objections, we can take as read the indictment and the state's evidence. I imagine that both you and Professor Pontecorvo have had time to . . . And as for time we have already wasted enough."

We can take as read the indictment and the state's evidence? What a bizarre expression. Leo guessed that probably they would skip the preliminaries and the courtesies, that they would get straight to the point. To the interrogation. Without passing through the reading of the indictment. Which would only delay further the moment when he would learn the nature of the crime that they were accusing him of and for which they had thrown him in jail. Leo went back to tenderly patting the pants pocket where he kept the pieces of paper.

"No, no objection, Dottore."

"Professor, as your lawyer must surely have told you, some days ago I myself went to your house for another search . . . "

"On that subject . . . " Herrera interrupted again, "you must understand that Professor Pontecorvo and I have not had time to talk about anything . . . In short, I would expect . . . "

Again Herrera's tone alarmed Leo. It seemed resentful, like that of someone who is about to explode but can't afford to.

The exact opposite of what it should be, not to mention the exact opposite of the judge's, which displayed a seraphic calm.

Leo was content, nevertheless, that they both referred to him as "professor." It seemed to him that it was a thing among gentlemen. Among people who belonged to the same rank. The Judge, the Lawyer, and the Professor. A fine trio. The longer he was there, the more Leo felt he ought to trust that man. And answer to the point. Because he was a trustworthy type. Remember? Harsh but fair. The kind of person Leo wanted to deal with. Not an enemy but an antagonist. Not the wrinkled mathematics teacher who, in her time, had made him repeat the exam. Not the bastard who taught chemistry at the university. Not Camilla, and not even the wretched father of that wretched girl. Not the anonymous, obsessive dispenser of telephone threats. Not all the hack journalists who stubbornly insulted his integrity. In short, not all the people who wished him harm and who suddenly seemed to be crowding this vast world. A harsh but fair man. In search of the truth.

And so Leo would have liked to tug on his lawyer's sleeve and say to him: come on, that's enough now, stop it, don't go on quibbling, let the judge speak. Let's clear up this situation and go home.

"Dottore, you must realize that since the professor and I haven't been able to talk to or see each other in the past few days . . . " Herrera began, as if alluding to an ordinary impediment and not to the court injunction that had forbidden him to have contact with his client for five days and five nights.

"And so what shall we do, professor? Would you like to avail yourself of the opportunity not to answer? Admit to the allegation? Or do you want to clear yourself?" the judge asked. And Leo couldn't tell if his tone was sarcastic or meant just what it said. Or if it concealed some threat. The only thing he knew was that he didn't like it and that again it had been triggered by Herrera's quibbling.

Why was he dragging it on like that? Leo wondered. Why irritate the judge, who seemed so serene? Basically Leo had a tremendous desire to answer. Leo had never had such a desire to answer as at that moment. Now that he finally had before him a man with the right questions, to which the right answers could be given.

"So shall we begin, sir, or not?"

And Leo saw out of the corner of his eye that Herrera was assenting, still with that very guarded manner.

Meanwhile the judge had turned to the young woman, who without hesitation handed him a substantial file. Doubtless some of the documentation that had been gathered over all those months.

"So, professor, yesterday afternoon a search was made in your house. Over which I presided. It lasted some hours, and was conducted in the presence of your wife."

He said these things in an extremely impersonal way, as if he were reading a report. Even if it was obvious that he was reading nothing.

Rachel? The judge and Rachel had met? They had been in the same rooms for some time? They had spoken to each other? While he was rotting in isolation? It was something that he really couldn't imagine. For the first time since he had sat down across from that man, Leo felt an impulse of hostility toward him.

What was it? Jealousy? Or shame? Or both?

Certainly Leo had some trouble picturing Rachel and the investigator going through the house, laying hands on his things. He wondered how Rachel had faced that further humiliation. After two months of having had no relationship with his wife, Leo could say with certainty that he no longer had the slightest idea of who that woman was. That's how things go. It had taken twenty years to get to know her and he had forgotten her in a few months. Was that why he encountered so many difficulties in imagining how she had reacted to the violation of domestic intimacy by a group of thugs directed by the judge? A mad thought led him to consider that she, in her ridiculous zeal, had helped them, thanks to the same scruples that led her to help carpenters and upholsterers. Another, no less irrational thought suggested that she had protested. Had flown into a rage. Shouting that they could not take such liberties, it wasn't possible, this was not something she could tolerate. Another still (perhaps the most likely) was that she had docilely submitted to the will of those people. Her husband was a frightening criminal, her husband had put *them* in that position, demonstrating a lack of responsibility equal only to his perversion: it was right that she should allow those people to do something so serious and humiliating. Because only a thing so serious and humiliating could throw a little light on that endless terrible history.

A search. Is there anything more contemptible in the world? Leo thought of the January day some years earlier when, coming home from Anzère, he, Rachel, Telma, and the boys had found the house turned upside down. During their absence thieves had gone in and cleaned it out. Leo remembered Telma's shrill whining as she kept saying, "Signora . . . signora . . . " But he also remembered the sense of rage and humiliation that had assailed him. The sense of rage and humiliation that had assailed them all. A disbelief charged with of bitterness. How could someone dare lay hands on their things? Money, pictures, silver, Rachel's jewelry, the boys' television, his watches, even some of his records, and many other things. But the stuff was the least of it, it could be replaced. And if it couldn't, you could live happily without it. The problem was the violation. The outrageous violation. Those hands everywhere. Hands in the most tender place of all. In the place built with tenderness to welcome and protect the Pontecorvos. That was the frightening thing.

A spasm of anguish made Leo's stomach contract and filled his mouth with saliva as he imagined the judge and his henchmen who, before Rachel's sorrowfully compliant gaze, stuck their hands everywhere.

At that point the magistrate, who up until then had behaved impeccably, said something that to Leo seemed definitely out of place.

"I must say, professor, that you have a remarkable record collection."

How could he take such a liberty? Was he trying to be funny? Or was he speaking seriously? In either case it was a shamefully inappropriate comment. What? You throw me in jail, after tearing me to pieces, and now you start talking about records? My records? My wife and my records? As if to emphasize that while I was rotting in here you were enjoying yourself in my house, with my family, with my kinds of comfort? For a moment the surreal thought surfaced that soon—with him out of the game—this man would take his place in his life, would install himself, like the most arrogant of the Suitors, in his home, listening to his precious imported records. But he immediately chased that absurdity from his brain.

Yet Leo still hoped that he hadn't heard right. That he had made a mistake. He was ready to be asked "Where were you that afternoon at that time?" He was ready to be asked "Do you have someone who can testify that you were there that day?" He was ready to have addressed to him all the questions he had found in the paperback mystery books he had been so fond of as a boy. But he wasn't ready to talk about records. And he was also very surprised that Herrera, till then so quick to interrupt out of turn, had not taken to task this son of a bitch. Who, in fact, continued his meditations unperturbed.

"Your Ray Charles collection: really priceless. You've got some amazing records."

No, the amazing thing was not that, over the years, Aunt

Adriana had sent him from the United States some "priceless" Ray Charles records. The amazing thing was that this man— the fierce prosecutor of Mafiosi and camorrists, the incorruptible judge—wouldn't stop talking about records. And that the only response of his lawyer (a shark of the law courts) was to remain stubbornly silent. And that the assistant, without turning a hair, continued to transcribe every word without looking at him in suspicion and astonishment. That was what was amazing. Certainly not the priceless records.

Was it a joke? Or a brand-new interrogation technique, just imported from the United States, to make both the guilty and the innocent *sing*? First you get them talking about their passions, then you catch them? Watch out, Leo. Watch out.

"Thank you, sir," Leo hissed, trying to impress on his voice all the sarcasm he was capable of. Hoping that this would irritate both the judge and Herrera. Or at least force them to come to their senses.

"And also books, I must say. Really not bad. You have taste, professor."

And Herrera still nothing.

"You know, I looked at those books," he added. "Rather, we all did," he corrected himself, taking in with a single glance all the people there, as if they were not in a cramped little room in a maximum-security prison but in a sophisticated book club.

"And we formed some very precise ideas about your tastes. And your likes. Truly refined, professor."

Leo no longer had the strength to thank him or to reply. Professor. Professor. What at first had seemed a sign of respect, a recognition of his social position, now began to be irritating.

"We noticed that you also have the habit of underlining in books. With a pencil, of course. A pen would be barbaric. With a pencil you can also erase."

"Meaning?" Leo said, encouraged. And immediately he felt

a tug from Herrera. As if he were being called to order. It's true, he thought, Herrera had said to him, "Never say yes or no. Don't comment. Speak as little as possible." He had repeated it ad nauseam. But this wasn't a normal circumstance: the investigator was talking about books. About books underlined in pencil. Was it possible that Herrera didn't have the authority to bring the interrogation back to something logical? Possible that Leo was the only one who felt how out of place everything that was happening was?

"So, professor. I marked some sentences you underlined, which seem to me very interesting. Which deserve comment, reflection. For example, listen here. A passage underlined by you in a very famous book. 'The norm of Roman law on the basis of which a girl could marry at twelve was adopted by the Church and is still in force, if tacitly, in some States of America. The age of fifteen is legal everywhere. There is nothing wrong, both hemispheres declare, if a forty-year-old brute, blessed by the local priest and full of alcohol, tears off his underwear, dripping with sweat, and thrusts up to the hilt in his young bride. In temperate and stimulating climates . . . girls mature near the end of their twelfth year.' Interesting. Professor, don't you find it interesting?"

"To tell you the truth, I don't understand why you're reading me these things. I don't know what you're talking about. I don't even know what book it is."

"You don't understand, eh? And then let me read another passage underlined by you. Same book, same author. 'Marriage and cohabitation before puberty are not at all exceptional, even today, in certain regions of India. Among the Lepcha, eighty-year-olds copulate with girls of eight and no one cares. After all, Dante fell madly in love with Beatrice when she was nine . . . '"

The investigator wouldn't stop reading. And Leo began to understand what he should have understood some time ago. It wasn't so difficult. Those passages evidently underlined by him were, according to the investigator and his group, proof of his perversion. Was this what he had in hand? Was this one of the reasons they had arrested him? Because he had underlined certain passages in a book? If he had underlined passages that discussed the slaughter of the Armenians would they have indicted him for genocide? Was this what was happening?

"Dottore, I don't see," Herrera finally interrupted, "the relevance of all this to . . . "

"You don't see the relevance? And you don't, either, professor? Not even you see? Then here's another of your books. This one is also very famous. Listen. This has also been underlined: 'A forty-year-old dishonors a girl of twelve: might it have been the environment that incited him?'"

"I still don't understand," Herrera was saying. "What do you want to know from the professor?"

"It's obvious," said Leo, by now careless of all caution and increasingly angry. "Don't you see, Herrera? The honorable judge prosecutor is making insinuations. The honorable judge prosecutor is skillfully, or perhaps only clumsily, reconstructing the psychological profile of a pervert."

"Quiet," Herrera said to him. "Christ, be quiet."

"No, don't be quiet. Go on talking. Tell me. Is that what you think I'm doing? What we're doing? A psychological profile? Very interesting. Really very interesting. Well, apropos. Here are some other nice things we found in your study in the basement. They were hidden behind your precious records."

The investigator had the woman pass him another folder, from which he took some fairly well-creased pornographic magazines. Which Leo immediately recognized. He had bought them on a long, solitary lecture tour in the United States. Erotic and pornographic magazines. Having in common names that alluded to the young age of the models who were depicted in more or less explicit poses. *Just Eighteen*, *Barely Legal*, *Lolitas*, and so on.

For Leo it was a real shock to see those magazines, which for years had been lying behind his records. But not because they had any meaning, not because they proved who knows what. All of them in that room knew that they were perfectly legal magazines. Magazines for adults that any adult could buy. And that a responsible adult like him had taken care to keep out of sight of his underage sons, by hiding them.

The reason Leo was so stricken was that in his mind he pictured the scene of the discovery of that pornographic material, which had presumably happened in the presence of Rachel. Leo thought of Rachel's humiliation. Now, all wives worthy of the name know that their husbands every so often need that type of material. All wives with common sense know that conjugal sex is one thing and jerking off another. And that, despite the fact that jerking off is so depressing, it's a thousand times better than adultery, habitual or occasional. But the idea that Rachel had seen those magazines. The idea that they had been found in front of her. The idea that after the discovery she had been looked at with censure. The idea that she could imagine her husband in the bathroom masturbating over that stuff. Those girls. Well, that was an intolerable idea. Which humiliated him, annihilated him, and made him even angrier.

"And what are these things evidence of, sir? You want to ask me if a respected and respectable professor in his forties with a beautiful wife and two fine sons still masturbates? Well, yes, he still does. Where's the problem?"

"It doesn't seem to me that I said anything about problems. There is no problem. You are doing it all. You do and undo. I am confining myself to showing you some things that intimately concern you. Like this."

This time the investigator picked up an art catalogue and a photographic catalogue.

"What can you tell me about these articles? These, too, belong to you. They were in your bookshelf."

"What can I tell you about these? Let me see. This is a catalogue of a show that my wife and I saw in Switzerland some years ago. Of one of the most famous contemporary artists. Balthus. And these . . . let's see. These are postcards. They also come from some exhibition. These are photographs taken by a great writer. A writer wrongly considered a children's writer. In reality he was an outstanding artist, whose weakness was that he photographed pubescent girls. I treat them. He photographed them. His name was Lewis Carroll. My name is Leo Pontecorvo. This photograph, if I'm not mistaken, shows Alice Liddell playing the part of a beggar. As for this one who is pretending to play the violin I don't know what to tell you. But I find it very beautiful, very expressive. I find very evocative both the sepia color of the photograph and the melancholy expression of the girl. That's how I imagine *Alice in Wonderland*. Just like this. You know, I've always loved that book. I even made my children read it. But I believed everything, everything, except that one day I would find myself in Wonderland. Because that's what this place is called, right? Wonderland? You know it, sir, Wonderland? But of course you know it. You are a sophisticated man, honorable judge. You know very well that the photographs of Lewis Carroll have no significance. Likewise you know very well that a catalogue of Balthus means nothing. Balthus paints only naked girls? Carroll photographs them? Try to arrest them if you can. You try to enter Wonderland."

"Professor, you are not the one to decide whom I should or should not arrest. Besides, I have other things to show you."

"What is it this time? You want me to listen to a choir of angel voices? Or the latest record from the Mickey Mouse Club?"

Leo continued to be sarcastic, and Herrera didn't intervene. Herrera was in a daze, as if he found himself in a nightmare. Drowning in something over which he was unable to exercise any control.

"I don't think, professor, that you are in a situation to make jokes," the judge said, in a glacial tone.

After a further pause, he took some photographs out of another envelope, and laid them out on the table in front of Leo.

"You took these?"

Leo picked one up with an attitude that expressed even more disappointment and sarcasm. Then the others.

"Yes, I took them. And?"

They were pictures from Samuel's birthday . . . the year before. To be more precise, they were the pictures that Rachel had compelled him to take and which, if it had been up to him, he never would have taken. What is criminal about that? What is illegal about giving in to the wishes of a nagging wife? How many wives and husbands like that are there in the world? Leo, at first glance, didn't understand. He didn't understand what the judge was driving at. Those photos meant nothing. Except that his wife was obsessed with souvenirs. Rachel was that way: she wanted a photograph for every occasion that she in some way considered an event. Her horror at the inexorable passing of things, her petit-bourgeois idolatry impelled her to collect testimony for everything. Impelled her to accumulate useless mementos and never throw anything away. If one of her sons simply put on a jacket and tie for a party she would ask Leo to do a photographic feature on the embarrassed dandy. If the Pontecorvos got dressed up to go to the opera or the bar mitzvah of the son of a friend, Telma or some other unfortunate would be summoned to immortalize that stylish moment. Leo didn't even dare to think what that woman would do when one of her children got a diploma, graduated, married, or, who knows, became a government minister!

Until Leo, leafing through the small pile of photographs that the investigator had put in his hand, realized that the author of those snapshots had lingered in an at least suspicious way on the girlfriend of the birthday boy. Then he understood.

There was the point. There was the trap. The snare set for him. The final piece of evidence. Perhaps Leo should have explained to the investigator that it was the birthday boy who insisted that his father-photographer devote himself in particular to his girlfriend. What was indecent about that?

Nothing. Really nothing.

But the terrible fact of this whole business is that—although by now Leo had been sitting on the chair across from the investigator and next to the stupefied Herrera for several minutes—no specific charged had yet been made against him. Nor had he been questioned regarding his presumed crimes. Only insinuations. Only a crazy collection of evidence gathered by a herd of incompetent bureaucrats too hung up on psychology to be considered respectable people. In short, what were they accusing him of? Leo was certain that they must have more significant evidence. If they didn't, surely they wouldn't have dragged him here. No, they would never, ever allow themselves to destroy the life of a human being without having in hand something other than those meaningless and overinterpreted relics. Leo was sure there was something else. There couldn't not be something else. And so why this torture? Why this infinite prologue? Why not get immediately to the point? Why not let the shoe drop? Where was the ace up their sleeve? That was what Leo couldn't understand, that was what goaded his sarcasm and his indignation.

Basically, if you thought about it, the only question that up to now they had addressed to him—all right, no one had put it in explicit terms, but it was so—was somewhat sinister and metaphysical, and sounded something like this: why are you Leo Pontecorvo?

This is what the investigator would have liked Leo to explain. This is what the investigator had been asking him for quite a while, beating around the bush, cravenly. It was as if he were angry with him just because he was who he was. And certainly it was difficult to exonerate himself from a crime like that. The crime of being Leo Pontecorvo. The crime of having lived up to that point as Leo Pontecorvo and, if necessary, of preparing to die as Leo Pontecorvo. How does one exonerate oneself from a crime like that? The rest—all that stuff they kept putting in front of him—was pure pretext, an incidental digression, an idle waste of time.

For a moment Leo felt tired. For a moment he lacked the will to explain. For a moment it all seemed to him so empty, so formless, so distorted. He wondered if it was true that, in the eyes of the world, so much evidence of his perversion existed or if, much more simply, there was no individual whose personal story could not be so speciously manipulated.

"Professor," the investigator said suddenly, "do you know Donatella Giannini?"

Donatella Giannini. Of course he knew Donatella Giannini. That woman's name transported him for a moment into a tidy, aseptic, efficient place, totally different from the one where he was now. Donatella Giannini. She was one of the nurses at Santa Cristina. One of the best. One of the most industrious and cooperative, one of the most exacting, the most resourceful. A point of reference for the ward: adored by the patients, by the parents of the patients, by the doctors, by her nurse colleagues, and by her aides. By all, in short. A sweet and charismatic head nurse, who was dedicated to her work with passion and modesty.

"Do you know what Donatella Giannini told us?" the investigator asked, pulling out of yet another envelope yet another piece of paper.

"How could I know, sir?"

"She told us that, in your ward, you encouraged sexual promiscuity between sick children."

"But that's not true . . . it's not like that . . . Donatella couldn't have said anything of the kind . . . Unless she's referring to that business . . . something that happened some years ago . . . but I said so to speak . . . Two kids were found together by Donatella . . . she came to tell me . . . she was upset . . . and I said only that . . . but not in that sense . . . not the way you understand it . . . Donatella couldn't have told you . . . It's true, there was a disagreement, we argued about what happened. I said some things, but like this, so to speak . . . in an abstract way. A challenge."

At the word "challenge" Herrera interrupted, energetically: "That's enough now, Leo. Now be quiet . . . Your Honor, enough of this. My client avails himself of his right not to respond . . . enough of this. Really."

"No, it's not enough, Herrera. You don't understand. You don't understand what they're doing to me. You don't understand how terrible what they're doing to me is. It's all so absurd. You don't understand and you don't say a thing. I gave you a lot of money so that you would say something. I made you rich so that you would defend me. But you sit there in a stupor. You say nothing."

"Leo, I said that's enough."

"I'm telling you that you don't understand! No one can understand. If you're not in it up to your neck, if you're not drowning in it, you can't understand it. What these people are talking about amounts to ridiculous trifles. Underlined books, exhibition catalogues, records. And you pretend it's nothing. That woman looks at me as if I were Mengele. And that other one writes . . . and I . . . It's the absurdity that's the most terrible thing. It's the paltriness of the invention that is most odious."

"Please, come on, stop it . . . Your Honor, let's stop here."

"No, I'm not going to stop here!" Leo said, getting up.

"Professor, I must ask you to stay seated. And to lower the tone of your voice."

Leo heard someone behind him open the door and enter. A guard who had become alarmed?

"No, I'm not stopping," he repeated in a lower voice, sitting down again. "What's going on? All our strategies? All our conversations? And now you say nothing? You just sit there, completely silent? You always have advice for me. You always have something to reproach me for. You always know what to do. Except this time. This time you don't know . . . "

"Please, Leo . . . come on, really, let's end here."

"We're not ending a damn thing. Do you understand that we're not ending a damn thing? It's been months since I spoke. Months that I've been listening like a bad child being punished. Months that I've trusted everything that's said to me, that I've been pretending that everything that's happening to me makes sense. And that I, in some way, deserved it. For quite some time I've let myself be treated by you with sarcasm, I've let these people torture me. And I can't take it anymore. I can't bear it. My days are hellish. You don't know. You don't know what happens in here. You should carry out an investigation into what happens in here . . . But you, Herrera, whose side are you on? Will you tell us whose side you're on?"

"Leo, if you go on I'll be forced to abandon the brief . . . "

This time it was Herrera who rose, producing a much less threatening effect on the onlookers.

"Is that your only worry? Abandoning the brief? Not getting mixed up with me, with what's happening to me? You're afraid of being dragged into my hell? Well, you can set your mind at rest. It concerns only me . . . Do what you like. But at least I want to tell you what I think."

"Not now, not here, what do I have to say to you? Listen, Your Honor, it's better if . . . "

"I told you, Herrera. I tried to explain it to you. They trick you with the photos. They put some photos in front of you and think they've understood everything about you. They think they know everything about your personality. For them those photographs are the truth. If only one could live without leaving a trace! And if only all of you knew how irrelevant the traces I've left are. If only I could explain to you what it means to be checkmated by a twelve-year-old girl . . . "

"What do you mean, professor, by 'checkmated'?"

Speciousness, nothing but speciousness. Here we are again. It's crazy, the ambiguity of words. The destructive power of that ambiguity. The more you justify yourself, the deeper you sink. The more you explain, the murkier it becomes. You can never get out of this situation, maybe Herrera is right: the best thing is to be silent. But I can't be silent anymore. I never had such a desperate desire to express myself.

" 'To be checkmated,' Dottore, means 'to be checkmated.' I don't know how else to explain it to you. To feel threatened, blackmailed, at the mercy of something enormous, frightening, and uncontrollable . . . "

"Are you speaking of your drives, professor? Is that what you're talking about?"

"No, I'm not talking about my drives. I don't think I have uncontrollable drives. I don't think I've ever had them. No more than any human being endowed with objectivity and common sense. I'm speaking of the fierce, odious, foolish behavior of a little twelve-year-old whore, who, God knows why, decided to destroy my life. To annihilate everything I created, everything I love. Like that, in a deliberate, satanic way . . . "

Leo felt short of breath and he had a desire to weep. But he also felt that he had finally taken the right path. He was telling the truth. Isn't this what respectable people do? Tell the truth.

"And who might the 'little whore' be, professor? Who is it that you call a 'little whore'?"

"Leo, please, stop it! Leo, I beg you, don't answer . . . "

"You know very well, sir, who the little whore is. I can't even bring myself to name her. I will tell you more. I am terrified by the idea of naming her. Here I am, a large, tall man. I'm almost six feet tall and I can't utter the name of that little whore."

276 · ALESSANDRO PIPERNO

Leo, although his mouth was dry, his back soaked, and his heart racing, was still lucid enough to realize that every time he uttered the word "little whore" (and God knows in what a liberating tone he uttered it), the meager body of the investigator's young assistant trembled, as if it had been shaken by an electric shock. Leo felt the eyes of that girl—yes, girl, she couldn't have been much over thirty—fixed on him with indignation and disbelief. Because the word "whore" disturbed her? She was the assistant of a judge. She must have seen and heard much worse. Leo suspected she was one of those frustrated feminists so detested by Rachel. Those unhinged paranoiacs who interpret even the most conciliating male gesture as an intolerable aggression. One of those girls with no sense of humor who feel on their own bony shoulders the weight of all the centuries of abuses suffered by women.

What did that girl think of him? It wasn't so hard to understand: he was the atavistic enemy to be beaten. The ironic fact is that outside there were starting to be a lot of people who considered him the atavistic-enemy-to-be-beaten. Which was truly incredible, if you took account of the sort of life he had led, if you took account of his good nature, his very rare talent for *not* hating anyone. There, maybe that was the reason that so many people hated him. They hated him because he was incapable of hating and those who don't hate can't defend themselves. His insufficiency of hatred was unforgivable. Yes, maybe that explained a lot of things.

So Leo, seeing the assistant tremble at every "whore," wondered if maybe Camilla was destined to become a woman like that. And if all that she had done was the apprenticeship for becoming that type of woman. A woman who hates. It was the first time he had thought realistically about the motive that had impelled Camilla to do what she had done. In the past months he had been so preoccupied with defending himself from the attack launched against him by that psychopath of a girl that he had never wondered what was going through her head all that time. What had armed her. Love? Hatred? Meanness? Revenge?

The only thing certain now was that, at every "whore" uttered by Leo, the hatred of the investigator's assistant expanded. Every "whore" was a lash. This pleased him. As if he perceived the power that he finally had available. The power of leading her to exasperation. The power to disgust her and make her feel worse and worse. That advantage led Leo to insist on that epithet, to stick it in every two words, purposely:

"No, don't ask me to say it. I really can't utter the name of that little whore. I don't even remember it. I have in my mind only whore, whore, whore . . . "

All just to see that woman suffer, that grownup Camilla!

It was then that the judge decided to speak, solemnly this time, pronouncing his words carefully and ostentatiously waving another piece of paper. And he did it with the satisfaction with which a professor of mathematics writes on the blackboard the exact solution of a difficult equation:

"The girl of twelve whom you call by such an unforgivably vulgar word, professor, might she be the same one who accuses you of attempted rape?"

So that was the charge. So that was why they had arrested him. So these were the words written on the piece of paper that Leo had in his pocket and which for five days he had not had the strength to read. Camilla had accused him of having done yet another thing that he had never done and had never dreamed of doing. Camilla, like the diligent and conscientious girl she was, had completed her masterpiece.

PART IV

He sees it immediately, as he goes through the gate. It's on the inside of the wall surrounding the house (which has meanwhile been brightened by a mild, red autumn), still fresh, drawn during his absence, probably on a recent night, by some vandal. No one has had the decency to remove it: a graffito that reproduces in a childishly stylized way the figure of a man on a horse. A Marcus Aurelius drawn by an immature hand. Both the man and the animal have nooses around their necks.

Really? They want him dead? And not only him but also his imaginary mount? The horse in that wretched photo. Leo is tempted to point out to Herrera that he was right in the end. That photograph had its importance. But just as he is about to say it he realizes that it doesn't matter to him anymore. To persuade Herrera. To dissuade Herrera. To argue with Herrera. What's the point?

It wasn't easy for Herrera to get him out of jail. Not after the disastrous interrogation. Not after Leo's appalling outbursts. Not after they had to take him bodily back to his cell. Leo was confined there for twenty more days. So they told him: twenty days. Even though his own perception tells him that it could have been twenty minutes or twenty years. In any case, Herrera had managed it in the end. Finally he had done something right.

And, not content, Herrera came to get him. He gloriously, or vaingloriously (add a prefix and everything changes), appeared

282 · ALESSANDRO PIPERNO

across from the prison in his Mercedes 500 the color of a hearse. Everything has to be big. Size is Herrera's weakness. There he is, in the driver's seat, in the huge interior of that sort of steamship on wheels. One of those ostentatious square cars that get old immediately and after a few years become the property of sophisticated gypsies and mediocre crooks.

And now there they are, next to each other, staring at the wall in silence.

"I'll call someone right away to get rid of it."

"No, no, leave it. It doesn't matter."

Meekness is becoming a sort of vice for Leo, but it can't keep him from violently slamming the door of that monumental car when he gets out and heads, alone, toward the entrance to the basement.

The singular thing is that the drawing has quickly turned into the sweetest element that his house is able to offer him. As was to be expected, in fact, Leo has not found a brass band waiting for him. Imagine. With what's happened. Prison, the new vile charges that hang over his head. If Leo needs human warmth it's just as well that he is content with the graffito of a hanged man.

And that's what he has done. He has grown fond of it, like a child with a stuffed animal that's lost its fur. More and more frequently he gets up on a stool and from there, from his study-prison, through the high little window, stares at his new friend.

Days pass, weeks. Leo is still getting thin, he keeps getting thinner, he grows a solemn beard: white, thick, hieratic, suitable for Moses. That beard is his response. A vanity tending to mysticism is the antidote to the inexorable and the inextricable that are poisoning him. The look adapts itself to the new tenor of life, the tenor of life to the new conception of the world. Even his way of dressing, ever since Herrera got him out of jail, has become more austere. He wears a sweat suit, of the type he would never have worn in good times. To signal an indomitable and rigorous path toward redemption.

Winter is at the gates. An army of dark clouds, swollen, spectral, has reached the Pontecorvo house after a triumphal march from the Urals, along the expanses of northern Europe and through the Alps and the Apennines: and now it is stationed there, on the horizon, ready to do battle. It has brought with it the first cold and extreme dampness. The pergola of Virginia creeper that until a few weeks before displayed dazzling red and orange foliage is completely bare by now, reduced to a knotty tangle of stems, like a petrified forest.

Leo, frightened by the falling temperature, knows he can't count on compassion from Rachel. She is, as usual, stinting on heat (she will stint at least until the middle of December). Then, driven by the boys' protests, she will be generous. So more and more often Leo, especially early in the morning or late in the afternoon, starts shivering. Down there the dampness is threatening. When he gets too cold he puts on over the sweat suit an old ski jacket that he dug out of a store room where Rachel keeps the old and now unwearable clothes (liberating terms such as "throw away" or "give away" do not belong to the genetic vocabulary or the emotional dictionary of the lady). The jacket smells a little too much of moth balls, but Leo doesn't mind. In the storeroom he also found a comical gray wool cap. Like the ones that athletes wear jogging, or with which fishermen protect their ears when they go out before dawn. It seems made just for covering the white receding hairline. Sometimes at night he falls asleep with the cap on and wakes up with it still on in the morning. Which gives him a strange euphoria, like an old salt.

Herrera didn't have to make too great an effort to persuade his increasingly laconic client not to appear in court. (Meanwhile the trial has begun.) Better not to show up, Herrera explained. It's more prudent for an individual's actions

284 · ALESSANDRO PIPERNO

to be judged, rather than the flesh-and-blood individual . . . and blah . . . blah . . . blah. These old tunes no longer deceive Leo, the strategies are repugnant to him. Herrera has remained the windbag he always was, he had his chance to show what he was made of. He wasted it. Now he can say or do what he wants. He can explain or be silent. Leo isn't interested.

The only request he has made to his lawyer is to be informed in detail about every court session. Herrera calls every night and Leo has him recount everything: and meanwhile, with schoolboyish diligence, he takes notes. He always has with him a kind of note pad (another article provided by Rachel's storeroom-junk room), on which he very precisely records his lawyer's summaries. And while Herrera speaks, Leo imagines the courtroom where the trial is taking place, where these people argue about what he did and what he didn't do, about what he said and what he didn't say. Where is the trial taking place? In one of the many courtrooms at the Ministry of Justice. Leo pictures the horrid grandiose edifice, the useless swarming, the odor of cappuccino from the machines. A ferment worthy of an anthill. An immense anthill. Where everyone speaks loudly or in whispers. Never normally.

From the way Herrera describes it, the inside of the law courts is fake, like a set at Cinecittà. The paving is cobblestones, just like the ones that could be found on an ordinary Roman street in the sixteenth century. And the lamps are the ones typical of a Roman square. The square, exactly. The forum. The rhetoric of the forum. The place where the people gather. The place where the people debate. The place where, in the name of the people, judgments crucial to the life of the individual are made.

"All citizens have equal social dignity and are equal before the law, without distinction of gender, race, language, religion, political opinion, personal and social condition."

There you have Article 3 of our constitution. Splendid, inflexible, so well-intentioned. Leo imagines it reproduced in synthetic form in the gilded inscription on the woodwork that is placed between the empty seat of the contumacious defendant and the judges:

ALL ARE EQUAL BEFORE THE LAW.

Which in general is true, but also depressingly irrelevant. Who gives a damn about the law? The law might even have the best intentions in the world. What counts is what people think of people. What people make of people.

And, on the subject of people, to listen to Herrera, the Pontecorvo *affaire* is attracting less and less attention. But Leo isn't interested in this. He wants to know everything that is said. Herrera for the most part satisfies him, giving him exhaustive summaries.

And he, as he listens, no longer gets angry about the slanders that, in his absence, rain down on him. He has become astonishingly habituated to lies and, in a strange paradox, averse to the truth. Here's a thing that really enrages him: when Leo scents the odor of truth, he shudders. Just a little is sufficient, all Herrera has to do is tell him that he presented to the court the receipt for a plane ticket showing that the defendant could not have been where his cleverest little accuser claims he was on that day, owing to the simple fact that he was present at an oncology conference in Anversa . . . All Herrera has to do is tell him that, after displaying the receipt, he threatened to call as witnesses thirty individuals ready to declare that Professor Pontecorvo (as Herrera insists on referring to him) was there, at the conference, at an international meeting with prominent colleagues, drinking Scotch and smoking Cuban cigars provided by generous pharmaceutical companies. The intrusion into the courtroom of a definite, incontrovertible date in his equivocal and unstable past is enough to make Leo feel dizzy.

It's as if the truth brought back to him a self that he broke with a long time ago. So fuck the truth, let's concentrate on the lie.

Leo continues to eat at night. Some kind soul leaves the food ready in the oven, and he, like a thief in his own house, goes upstairs for provisions. The first time he found that single portion of food ready for him his appetite disappeared, put to flight by the emotion provoked by a gratuitous gesture of kindness that he doesn't think he deserves, and whose anonymous maker he will never know. But as the days pass that, too, becomes a habit, and the emotion vanishes. Every night, a little before midnight, he enters the kitchen, opens the oven door, takes what has been left for him, and goes back down into his cave.

Reluctantly eating that warm food Leo thinks of death, and makes an effort to do so by mixing the old materialism of a man of science with the comforting pantheism of certain men who, before they die, convert to some abstruse Oriental philosophy.

I will merely crumble, he says to himself. Yes, nothing will happen to me but this: crumbling. Which means I will not vanish, but in fact the cells that make up my body will go joyfully out into everything. Floating like pollen. What a marvel! And through a sort of instinct full of affection they'll stay around. I'm here, Rachel, my adored sweetheart, my love, I won't abandon you. The ashes I am about to be transformed into will watch over you, over our boys . . . The atoms of my body as it decomposes will always be here with you. They will accompany you. They will caress you.

Usually it's this macabre form of sentimentality that leads him to put down the fork and pick up the pen. And write. These days, he does nothing else. Especially at night, like the poets of yore. It's typical of individuals of his social class to write when things go badly. Never does a man at the peak of success start writing in order to exalt his satisfied life. Take a week at Bora Bora with deep-sea fishing! Write? Are you kidding—they only remember it when things take an ugly turn. Writing is a business for the unlucky. Writing is to put things in order. So that all this emptiness takes shape in a purpose. Now that his case has gone stale, and everyone is forgetting about him, he doesn't need a lawyer to rehabilitate him. He doesn't need a public rehabilitation. And since, given the behavior of his family, he can't even hope for a private rehabilitation, then it's worth trying to write.

After all, it might be the last chance he has to reestablish the truth.

But Leo is no longer interested in the truth.

And that's why, instead of sitting down at the desk and energetically dashing off a memoir full of hatred and anger, spelling out everything; instead of using the pen like a club, which he would have the right to do; instead of putting his rhetorical skill in the service of a battle against falsehood and in favor of decency; instead of writing how a herd of hospital bureaucrats got him involved in shady deals; instead of writing about how an assistant he had helped first swindled him by extorting money from him by deceit and then charged him with loan-sharking; instead of writing how a little flirt trapped him, and how the father of that flirt demonically manipulated the letters so as to make him appear a pervert in the eyes of the world; instead of writing how an entire media-justice system distorted his story to make it into a kind of emblem of the corruption of the whole country; instead of writing how his wife, whom he loved, respected, and never betrayed, to whom he gave all the well-being that a woman can expect from a husband, condemned him without appeal to a life as a reject; instead of writing how his sons have eliminated him from the face of the earth . . . Yes, in short, instead of writing what he should have had the right and the duty to write, Leo began to reflect on Leibniz.

Yes, our little moron began to philosophize, reheating old

notions he had learned during high school. Of all the things that his experience could have taught him, the only one that Leo feels he has learned is that men are monads "without doors or windows."

And . . . yes, maybe it's true, monads, as Leibniz says, have neither doors nor windows. But the cellar in which he has trapped himself, well . . . that at least has one door (even if it is increasingly impassable), and also a row of windows, although they are small, set high up, and through them one can enjoy a very partial view of the world outside.

Those two little windows, those two portholes, constitute the only bond with what, in spite of everything, Leo continues to love most: Rachel, Filippo, and his Semi. Too bad that the only thing the two peepholes allow him to see are the feet and legs of the beloved persons. The most glorious moments of his long, methodical days are those when he sees the legs of his sons and his wife walk on the driveway toward the car. It's seven in the morning. Leo, after a nearly sleepless night, sits at the window to watch those beloved legs and feet going along the driveway, swaying and dragging, in sun and rain. They climb into Rachel's S.U.V. And finally Leo sees the gray Land Cruiser maneuver on the porphyry paving in front of the garden and go through the gate. That is a moment of great euphoria for him. It has an emotional tone completely opposite to the one that assails him when the same Land Cruiser returns at the end of the day and the legs and feet of Filippo and Samuel, much more dynamic than in the morning, jump out of the car and run to the door. Or they stop a moment to kick a ball while Rachel warns good-humoredly, "It's time to do your homework. Wasn't tennis enough? Don't you ever have enough?" And they shout, "Five minutes."

All normal: no one worries about the prisoner who is down in the dungeon. As if he no longer existed. As if they had succeeded in annihilating him. For a while the boys had had some restraint. They didn't let themselves be seen, they played ball with great circumspection. As the days passed, they appeared increasingly less aware. Yes, it really seems they have forgotten where their father lives.

And those are the moments, in the evening, when his family comes home, that Leo feels he can't make it. He feels he is on the edge of something terrifying. If only he could pay attention to his body he would open that door, go up the stairs, return to live with them. But he is so upset that he fears they won't recognize him. Or, even worse: they won't see him. As if in the meantime he had become a specter.

Even Christmas passes. From the little window he sees the firs and magnolias of his neighbors decorated for the holiday, the lights that blink on and off and the driveways swept by the Pakistani gardener Mohammed, whom the whole neighborhood employs. He sees mothers getting furtively out of cars with bags full of presents. Leo can't believe that everything began exactly a year ago. The thought of the quantity of things that, since then, might have happened differently is too unbearable for him not to look again at the graffito of the hanged man and find a little comfort in it.

I mustn't forget you. You are my whole life, when I feel like this. When I think of the past I have only to look at you, and it all returns to normal. Everything is back in place.

New Year's arrives. And Leo, still with his face pressed against the glass, sees the midnight sky exploding with colored lights that intermittently illuminate the graffito of the hanged man: bathed in all that many-colored psychedelic light it comes to life, and at the end it almost seems that it has decided to tell him something. Loud explosions. The dogs whimper and bark desperately. And finally, after four-thirty in the morning, a long silence. It's 1987. Maybe things will adjust themselves. Maybe 1987 will be a whole other story. Maybe the problem was really 1986. Maybe Rachel has just been waiting for the year to end.

Certain things are important for her. Superstition. Kabbala. Such things are all to her. And maybe she's right. Maybe she was always right. In a few minutes I'm sure she'll come in with the boys. They're giving me a surprise. They'll come to say hello to me. And then we'll start fighting. All of us together, as we've always done.

Leo spends January first of 1987 waiting for someone to enter. But no one comes.

And the days continue to pass.

The only miracle presented by the new year is snow. Snow in Rome. Leo is looking outside, and there, suddenly, the landscape he knows best—the corner of the cosmos framed by the glass of one of the two little windows—is transformed. The slow, swaying waltz of an immaculate manna that has the power to slow down time and immobilize space. An image of agonizing eternity that is moving to our bearded poet-philosopher. The scene is so strange and unexpected that he doesn't even feel the usual need to attribute esoteric meanings to it. The world is only giving a demonstration of how white, beautiful, harmless it can be when it wants to. That's all. Nothing else to say, nothing else to explain.

For hours and hours, Leo's eyes are glued to the window, watching the implacable gentleness with which the snow manages to transform everything—path, garden, terra-cotta patio, porphyry driveway—into a gauzy white expanse. Smoothing wrinkles, softening roughness: that's the healthy effect of those thirty centimeters of snow. The only irregular elements in the increasingly soft and uniform whiteness are Rachel's dried-up flower beds, which the snow has transformed into white lunar craters.

The snow lasts a couple of days. Then it begins to melt. And what remains after it melts is a landscape of ugly brutality.

Like a flayed human body.

One night—it must have been three-thirty (an hour that Leo has always considered unpleasant)—the house's extremely loud alarm starts to intone a percussive, sharp, penetrating singsong. Leo gets up from the sofa bed with a start. That device is ringing for the first time since they installed it (the year before, when some villas in the neighborhood were robbed). Leo recalls the installer, a goggle-eyed kid who at the time explained to him how, although the device was reliable, it could possibly, at times, be set off for no reason. "What do you mean, no reason?" Leo had asked. To hear the reply: like that, no reason, set off by an imperceptible excess or activated by some natural calamity—rain, lightning, thunder, wind. Leo had been amused by the fact that the kid treated the device like a living organism, subject to sudden switches of mood.

But hearing the sharp wail now, in the night, he seems to understand what the kid meant. The sound is like the cry of a slaughtered pig, a lobster submerged in boiling water. A tortured whistle.

Whatever has happened, the alarm is sounding. If there are thieves in the house that gadget will cause them (or must already have caused them) to flee. If instead it's a false alarm, so much the better: Rachel, or one of the boys, will take care of turning it off. They were also present when the installer explained how it worked. On the other hand, until someone disengages it the alarm will continue to shriek; then it will go silent, only to start up again in a few minutes. And all this indefinitely.

At the first interruption Leo gives a sigh of relief. But when the alarm starts wailing again, he is frightened. What's happening? Where are Rachel, the boys, Telma? Maybe they don't know how to turn it off or maybe the device is broken? Or maybe . . . No, that he doesn't even want to think . . . Maybe they are hostages of some thug (and in Leo's mind the thug immediately acquires the features of one of the frightening guys in the first prison cell).

Leo had decided to get the burglar alarm at the time—defying Rachel's contrary opinion (she is hostile to technology and unwilling to accept the hypothesis that crime could threaten her family)—after reading in the paper about three sons of bitches who one night broke into a villa on the Cassia, not too far from one of the entrances to Olgiata. Leo also recalls the details of the robbery. The owner was bound and gagged, the valuables obtained by means of threats and beatings. And, to make the horror more unforgettable, right before the eyes of the gagged man, his wife and sixteen-year-old daughter were raped. And a steaming pile of shit left on his marriage bed.

Meanwhile the alarm continues to sound, and no one is turning it off. While the distressing contents of the article he read last year return to poison Leo's mind along with the face of that man in prison. What's happening? Did they get in? Are they threatening, beating? Maybe they are raping Rachel, or Telma, or one of the boys? And what should he do? Be bold, open the door, go upstairs, find out what the situation is, intervene? For a second a petty thought possesses him. A heroic gesture. Yes, maybe that would restore things. If he saved them he would win that sort of rehabilitation he stopped hoping for some time ago. It would be worth it even if he died in the attempt. Posthumous rehabilitation.

Until the alarm is silent again. That sudden pure silence is no less chilling than the noise. Leo puts his ear to the door. Nothing. No sound. No one seems to be aware of anything.

Maybe this time they've turned it off and gone back to bed. Here, this is the right moment. I could go up and take a look. If they catch me, I have a reason ready. Excuse me, Rachel, I'll say without any trembling in my voice, I was checking to see that everything is all right. I just wanted to be sure . . . Yes, those are the words ready for her if only he could rouse himself, open that door, go up the stairs, and take a few steps into the living room. Those are the words to speak if he should run in to Rachel, sleepy, in her nightgown.

Just as he is fantasizing about this clarifying nighttime encounter the alarm yet again sounds the trumpets. No, they haven't turned it off. Didn't they hear it? Maybe, even though they've heard it, they aren't able to deactivate it. And, yet again, a trite flurry of anguished thoughts. Interrupted by a new idea.

Or maybe they've left. Yes, that's the explanation. Who can say that they haven't gone away? In fact, in recent days the house has been more silent than usual. No floor waxer in the morning, no patter of feet. It's the first week of February. Not far from Valentine's Day. The time of year then Rachel takes the boys skiing. Maybe they're on a skiing vacation. There, yes, they've gone skiing. All explained.

But then who has left the food in the usual place? Maybe Rachel instructed someone to leave food for her husband. One of her little men. That's what she calls them: "little men." It's funny to see that small woman, whom everyone respects, giving orders to her "little men," gently but with authority, and the affection they feel for her is obvious. That's why it's been only cold food for the past few days. Yesterday evening some cheese. Today dried meat. That's what it must be . . .

A noise. He seems to hear a noise. A noise plunges him again into agony. What does he want, anyway? All you have to do is open the door, go up a few stairs. You've done it millions of times. Why can't you do it?

Although all night that wretched alarm continued to go on and off at regular intervals, although he was furious at himself and at the world, although he could not take his hand off the doorknob, Leo stayed there for all those hours, petrified, cheek and ear against the door, chewing the bitter pill of his own cowardice. Continually falling asleep and waking up.

Until some sounds from the garden waked him. In an

294 · ALESSANDRO PIPERNO

instant he remembers everything that happened. And he stands up. He feels a great pain in his side, after the night spent on the floor leaning against the door. He limps to the window and looks out, and the scene grips his stomach in a hot vise.

The legs and feet of the three people he loves most and who don't want to see him anymore are still there. They walk along the path, toward the Land Cruiser, as if nothing had happened. Leo sees Filippo's hand holding the squares of milk chocolate that Rachel has given him every morning since he was very small. Then he sees an edge of red down and the gray sneakers that belong to Semi running breathlessly to the car.

What happened the night before? Why, if they were there, did no one dare to turn off the burglar alarm? Why didn't anyone move? Why? Why? Leo would never know.

Another day—and outside the green shoots of Virginia creeper were a luxuriant promise of spring—Leo had been suddenly invaded by a hope. Vague, ridiculous, outside the time limit. But, whatever, a hope. He had stopped hoping long ago. Maybe because along the way he had learned to appreciate the formless, safe, slight comfort offered by despair. A despair that leads you to choices and actions that are rational and dignified.

For several weeks now, he had stopped listening to the detailed reports from the trial furnished by Herrera almost every evening. During them Leo was silent. Keeping up with all that stuff made him seasick. All those charges that were brought against him. Five charges. Really, too much. All that attention on him. All that enthusiasm for sticking their hands into the muck of his life, not so different, basically, from the muck of any other life. The whole business was revolting.

The verbose court sessions must be so brutal. With an insulting repetitiousness. With such bureaucratic mendacity. Why talk about it so much? Why still talk about it? Why drag it on so long? Did no one share his nausea with the whole situation? How could one live talking only about those things? How could one live attempting to establish the wrongs and rights of Leo Pontecorvo?

His life as it was recounted by those old fogeys in the courtroom had to be so dark. Just as the one recounted by Herrera had to seem so rhetorically virtuous. Was that all right with everyone? Well, for him it wasn't. He couldn't bear it anymore. He was exhausted.

But no, it's not that he was angry with the behavior of those men of the law. There was nothing outrageous in fulfilling as well as possible the duties imposed by one's profession. There was nothing bad about being so detached. In fact, if he thought of his previous existence, he saw clearly how he, too, had lived happily for many years beside so many terminally ill people and so many corpses. So many people who were suffering and so many others who wept for their suffering. For him, too, it had been an achievement to insure that living with pain and death did not influence the tone of his life. He wasn't sick, he wasn't about to die, he was only the caring doctor, who very often had to yield to the power of nature: the desire of nature to renew itself through destruction. It's a hard thing to accept. But in that type of job you have to learn to take it on before the age when you have little time left to live. You have to learn it in your youth. That is, right away. As soon as you enter the hospital. Cynicism? Call it what you like. Spirit of survival, common sense. So Leo had learned to call it.

After a while death had stopped interesting him. It had become a job. Like an executioner, an undertaker, a soldier, Leo had managed to separate those two parts of his life. The happiness from the horror. Like a psychopath. As the saying popular among garbagemen goes: "It's a dirty job but someone has to do it."

Leo remembered clearly a night when he had come home particularly upset by the death of a patient. It wasn't the first time he had seen a child die and witnessed the anguish of the parents. It was his job to fight with death for the children. Nor was it the first time it had happened under his medical juris-diction. He was a thirty-five-year-old oncologist. He had behind him plenty of chilling experiences. Not to mention that it wasn't a special child. Then why feel so badly for that partic-ular child? Leo didn't know. But it was a fact that that child had triggered something. It was a fact that for him that child hadn't been like all the others. And that that child had begun to be dif-ferent from all the others once he hadn't made it. Just as it was clear that if he, Professor Leo Pontecorvo, hadn't settled accounts with that child he would have been unable to take care of all those who followed after.

His name was Alessandro, and he was nine. He was a lively child, one of those who laugh at everything. One of those who teach you a lesson with that mixture of good humor and toughness. One of the bold ones, who like to talk to you about what is happening to them and what might happen to them with a lucidity that you wouldn't expect even from a brave adult. One who had a way with the nurses, a really bright nine-year-old.

He had a blood disease, but not among the most devastat-ing. And maybe one of the reasons that Leo became fond of him was precisely the possible remission of the illness. And he seemed to have been right: Alessandro got better. His illness was beating a retreat. Leo agreed to discharge the child from his ward with some satisfaction. Feeling like a God the Father.

But a few months later Alessandro's parents brought him to the emergency room. They had been at the seaside, on the beach, when blood began to gush from his nose and his par-ents couldn't stanch it. Then a sudden weakness. Delirium. A fever so high his brain is about to fry. Leo gets a phone call. He is also at the seaside for the weekend. He has to go to the hospital immediately. Alessandro's parents need him. Alessandro needs him.

Leo certainly didn't have to wait for the tests to know that it was serious. A recurrence. Extremely violent, pitiless, like all recurrences. And unexpected. This time the treatments had no effect. Things deteriorated quickly. Why? the young doctor asked himself. Simple, because things deteriorate. Because no case resembles another. Because no patient resembles the one in the next bed. Because each adventure is its own adventure. Because to seek comfort in statistics is a scientific perversion that a doctor endowed with common sense and experience should never give in to. A knowledgeable doctor should know his enemy. A knowledgeable doctor should know that his enemy is that capricious and unknowable thing called the human body. And he should know that nothing is more fragile than a fledgling human body. People say that the psyche is unknowable, is a mystery, but, if there is one thing that's unknowable and mysterious, it's the body.

And then, a few weeks later, after he had told the parents that their son was no more—those same parents to whom he had said, only a few months earlier, that Alessandro was out of danger, that he needed to be watched but was out of danger, that he would have a life different from that of other children, under the threat of the treacherous disease, but anyway he would have a life—Leo had taken off his white coat, returned to his car, driven to his house at the seaside, with its view over a beautiful lagoon, and there had found waiting for him a young wife who was nursing their newborn second child and scolding his rowdy older brother. A scene that celebrated the triumph of life.

A scene so sweet-smelling and so stinking. And he had felt guilty. He had felt dirty. For a second he had been tempted by the moralistic shortcut of not accepting the joy of his house, the joy of his life. But then he had understood that he was wrong: his work was his work, his life was his life. The two things often met. They lived together on a very fine thread, suspended a thousand meters above the ground, under which the abyss opened. But if one didn't want to go mad one had to keep them apart.

There, the same was true of the courtroom. It resembled his unit. The battle was inexorable. Strangers spoke with pompous gravity of things that wouldn't change the course of *their* life. And this time the only life in play was his: he was the terminally ill person in this circumstance. He the child whose life was in danger. Everything around him was scenery.

And now he understood those sick people who stop fighting, who seem to have found an inner peace. Who no longer have the strength to complain. Whose only impatience concerns the treatments whose object they are, and which have no use except to sharpen the agony and cruelly postpone the time of nothingness. What he was going through in court was nothing other than therapeutic persistence, there came a point when he was unable to bear it any longer and had pulled the plug.

That's why he stayed home, in his hole. Placidly resigned.

At least until that day.

That day when he was captured by a ridiculous hope, triggered, paradoxically, by yet another piece of bad news. A telephone call on his private number. Herrera. Camilla had asked the judge to be heard a second time, she had new revelations to make. It meant that they were ready for a final encounter: her parents or the psychiatrist would have her say painful and devastating things.

"Why are you talking about it?"

"I'm afraid they'll increase the charges. They might be fabricating more nonsense: I want you to be prepared. It might be something really terrible for you and your family. If that little lunatic should make revelations of a certain type, the spotlights of the press might go on again."

"What type of revelations are you talking about?"

"Something even more serious."

"What do you mean, more serious? What could be more serious than what they're accusing me of? What are they coming up with this time? An orgy? Cocaine? That she showed up with some luscious little friend from nursery school?"

"Leo, don't talk nonsense. Don't joke. And, for heaven's sake, not on the phone. I don't know what there is that's new. I know only what I told you. It's a rumor. But you have to prepare yourself. You have to remain cool."

Leo had listened calmly to this further madness. The sarcasm with which he had received the news testified to his calm. After Herrera's reproach he had made no other comments. Except when Herrera said that he would come and see him, that they would talk about it. Then Leo confined himself to whispering that he didn't want him around.

But now, right after he hung up, an old rage possessed him. The only thing he could still feel was a sense of frustrated contempt. What else did they want to do to him, the little whore and that lout her father? All this was not enough? When would their hunger for revenge be satisfied?

Revenge. Might it not be time for him to take revenge? Leo was seized by a passion for revenge against that girl. It was just the gratuitousness of the folly and cruelty that continued to enrage him, even on the emotional Aventine to which he had withdrawn.

It should be said that there was nothing positive about Leo's rage. It was all devoted to negativity. The days were over when he took pleasure in imagining the rise to public rehabilitation. It was a long time since he had fantasized about the scene in which he descends the marble steps of the Palace of Justice, in a rain of roses, applause, and tears. It was an infinity of time since he had imagined the faces of Rachel and the boys bursting with pride for the redemption that had taken place. Hope had become, so to speak, so rarefied as to disappear. At the end of the tunnel there was no virtuous happy ending waiting for him. At the end of the tunnel there was only another tunnel. At the end of which there was yet another. And so on.

But now, now that his rage was rekindled, now hope, too, was rekindled: it reappeared in his eyes in a less noble but more exciting form. He wanted to see that girl shown up as a liar, annihilated. He wanted to see Herrera make fodder of her publicly. Only a bloody scene like that might give him some joy. In other words, it was bitterness that had rekindled the fire of hope. And it was the desire for revenge that kept it burning.

And to think that the hours preceding Herrera's phone call had slipped by in grotesquely comforting reflections on the most hygienic way of clearing out of this world in a hurry, if possible on tiptoe. Not exactly a specific thought, rather a pastime with which he had been amusing himself for several weeks. For a need like his there was a word: suicide. But it seemed to him so emphatic. So literary . . . he preferred to think of an instantaneous break.

If only I were like Camilla's father, one of those fascists with a gun . . . if only I lived on the top floor of one of those nice big apartment buildings . . . if only that time I had listened to what Luigi, the anesthesiologist, said about a lethal combination of drugs . . . if only I had the courage to hang myself . . .

It isn't that Leo had had enough of life. He liked life. He absolutely liked it. He still had dreams sometimes in which he miraculously wore again the clothes of the man he had been before this obscene business defiled his existence. Well, the good god of dreams is a witness of how much Leo, in the role of his former self, had enjoyed himself. The pleasures, the many innocent underrated pleasures of the civilized individual, of the blameless ordinary man. There was not a single instant of his new life in which Leo had committed the sin of disowning them. There was not a single instant when he had not celebrated them with fervent nostalgia. The Friday evenings when Rachel picked him up at the hospital: he was too tired to drive, and so he left the car in the parking lot. He took off his tie and got in Rachel's car; as usual she showed up a few minutes late. They barely arrived in time. They entered the theater breathless, almost always last, stumbling over the knees of their neighbors to get to a seat.

After the movie they always went to eat at the same place: in the world there was only Berninetta. Leo ordered a mug of ice-cold beer, a vegetarian fritto misto, an extra-large pizza margherita, and that inimitable sour-cherry tart (the secret is in the short-crust dough, Leo explained to his wife every time). Then it was time for the cigar and coffee, in that order, for goodness' sake. On the way home in the car, Leo napped. That's what I mean by the pleasures of life. Napping in the car beside your Rachel after a perfect evening and a week of killing work.

No, Leo did not belittle the power of those delights. He wasn't angry with life in general, but with the particular turn that his had taken lately. The suicidal thoughts he toyed with were nothing but the fetid dross of mental tiredness. His brain was exhausted by the most idle of thoughts: all that might still be if things had happened differently. The specific weight of that useless thought was really too demanding for a single brain. Leo didn't want to die. Leo wanted to turn off his brain, at least for a little while. He wanted to nap in the car beside Rachel in the hope that the journey home would last an entire year at least. But since that was no longer possible, then there remained only option B. The plan in reserve. An option and a plan that, just because he knew death so well and in his life had seen hundreds of cadavers, made him shudder with terror.

He was at the mercy of that horror when the telephone

rang. And he had only to exchange a few remarks with Herrera to feel that horror diminishing. Replaced by a ferocious will to live: a vitality in the form of contempt for that crazy little bitch. And an ardent desire to kill her.

It then had occurred to him that perhaps, somewhere in the house, there might be a letter from Camilla, one of the most passionate and one of the most threatening. Leo hadn't read it all, to the end. But he was sure that right at the beginning that psychopath had written him that she felt the moment had come to give herself to the man she loved. That is, to him. Too bad that that letter had been written a couple of weeks after the presumed carnal violence they were accusing him of. (At least, so it seemed to him.) In short, that letter not only exculpated him from the most lurid accusation but at the same time revealed that girl's madness, her spiteful intentions . . . Hence it would make the entire structure of the accusation collapse. As if in a flash Leo remembered the evening when he had found that letter, in the usual place. He had started to read it. Maybe because of the irritation and the fear that the sexual offer roused in him he hadn't realized that Rachel was entering the room.

"What are you reading?" she asked.

"Nothing, a circular from the Santa Cristina administration . . ."

"They've started writing the circulars in a pen with fuchsia ink?"

"In fact it's just a draft that the director sent me to look at before he makes a clean copy and sends it out." He had closed the subject without losing his courage.

And without paying too much attention, and without even finishing it, he had hidden the letter somewhere. Yes, but where? He had been sitting on the bed. So maybe he had hidden it in the nearest place, the drawer of the night table, inside a big folder stuffed with other papers. Yes, it must be there.

And where if not. Crazy to remember it now. Might his fool-ishness, his messiness, have been advantageous for once? Yes, the letter must still be there. Undeniable proof of that girl's madness. The letter would demonstrate that if there was some-one who had been violated, brutalized, well, it was him.

He was so pleased with the opportunity that life had sud-denly presented to him, so anxious to recover that sinister evi-dence. So elated at the idea of revenge. But at the same time our poor cockroach was so frightened by the prospect of mak-ing a journey that would expose him to the risk of running into one of the three people in the world he least desired to encounter . . . For that reason he couldn't do anything but sit there, in a daze: his senses strained and his nerves an instant from breakdown. Over time his fear of finding himself face to face with Rachel, Filippo, and Samuel had become a supersti-tion. Leo knew that the only domestic space allowed him—according to an agreement tacitly reached with his immovable jailers—was the kitchen. He was allowed to enter only at night, within an extremely restricted time, somewhere between eleven-thirty and one. Which was more than sufficient, since the stairway that went up from his study-prison led directly to the kitchen, which at that hour would be empty, clean, and tidy.

For that reason he was now there, near the stairs, unde-cided what to do, afflicted by palpitations and the sort of nau-sea produced by excitement about a dangerous mission. He wanted to ascertain as soon as possible if that letter was still there. So much time had passed. So many things could have changed. No one could guarantee, for example, that his bed-room still existed as he remembered it. There was even the possibility that since then Rachel had cleared everything out. That she had decided to get rid of everything belonging to her husband. Yes, this could not be excluded on the face of it.

In the end Leo—like the night when the burglar alarm

began to screech—allowed prudence, allowed cowardice to have the upper hand: the disappointment he would feel if the letter wasn't there would have been much more intense than that aroused by the pain of not being able to get there. Yet again his cowardice seemed to be extraordinarily protective.

Or at least it had been until that Thursday. If things in the life of his family hadn't changed, then Thursday was the propitious day. In the afternoon Telma went out, Rachel took the boys to tennis lessons, and usually, then, she went to the hairdresser. Which meant at least three hours to carry out his mission.

So, at four-thirty on a late-spring afternoon Leo goes upstairs. He violates the boundary that months ago he ordered himself not to cross: the threshold that divides the kitchen from the rest of the house. Finding himself in the place that for so long constituted the ordinary background of his daily life does not rouse in him the overwhelming emotion he imagined. Rather, there is something irritatingly sad about such a display of unchangeability. And then he feels affronted by all that cleanliness. Don't these people know that they live above the lair of a cockroach? Don't these people know who the cockroach is? It's incredible how families immediately get used to their own hypocrisy. How little it takes *to become* that hypocrisy. Everything around him demonstrates that, after the July night when all hell broke loose, everything has gone back to moving on its proper path. Leo doesn't feel nervous. He is so disappointed that he's no longer afraid. If someone comes in? Come on in. I'm a grown man, I'll know how to face it.

Finally he's in his bedroom. He merely has to open the door to recognize the bluish half-light that Rachel wants that room to have. And this time the emotion is strong. There is something soft and relaxing in that space. Maybe the regal orange leather armchairs near the window, or maybe the two Art Deco lamps bought on the Rue de Seine, in Paris, on the way back from their honeymoon, or maybe the cotton bedspread with its candy-colored pattern, the strips of rosewood parquet . . . who knows what.. but it all lends the room a welcoming sweetness that Leo didn't remember. And it's as if just then he felt on his shoulders the accumulated weight of all the insomnia of that year of life-not-life. He would like to lift up the covers and slip inside. He would like to fall asleep in his bed and never wake up. He is so overcome by emotion that he has almost forgotten the reason he's there: the letter, the trial, Camilla, all that garbage . . .

To distract himself, and at the same time to revive the diminishing sense of exultant surprise, he goes into the walk-in closet. But this time the surprise is of an opposite nature. If earlier Leo was offended by everything in the house that hasn't changed, now the moment has come to be offended by all that has. The small room that functions as a closet, with two large mirrors that challenge each other from opposite walls, has been emptied of every trace of his earthly presence. What happened to his pinstriped suits, his tweeds, his shoes, scarves, jackets, hats, gloves? There is nothing anymore. This is the walk-in closet of a lady, a divorcée, a widow. Leo feels a ridiculous hatred for Rachel. For her common housemaid's diligence. For her damn moral fiber. For her obstinacy. For her mania about hygiene . . . Because it's hygiene that drove her to eliminate every trace of her husband from that closet. Where his clothes used to be, now—hanging on the brass rail that runs from one end of the room to the other—are only Rachel's jackets, coats, pants, skirts, which, seen in a row like that, look like a herd of well-dressed ladies lined up at the post office.

The sight of his many wives—which the game of mirrors comically replicates—makes him dizzy. So he sits down on a low chest of drawers. Next to so much disappointment he feels a strange, and decidedly inappropriate, happiness stirring.

Something that has to do above all with the senses. And meanwhile he breathes very cautiously. He absolutely doesn't want to get used to the odor he has rediscovered. The odor of his wife. The odor of a suddenly cut-off intimacy that, if you think about it, would soon have been entering its twentieth year. To keep it alive Leo holds his breath for a few seconds, and then sticks his nose in the sleeve of an old raincoat of Rachel's. He is desperate. And, just as when he was desperate as a boy, he feels an untimely desire to masturbate. How long since he's ejaculated? Too long. His sexuality, his masculine brutality have been trampled on by the many humiliations he's endured. The persistence of embarrassment has been his bromide.

And now he finds himself desiring Rachel in a new, unthinkable way, even more passionate than when, in the early days, she, like a good Jewish girl, wouldn't give in to him. No, Leo has never desired Rachel with such exhausting passion. Not even at the beginning of their relationship, when she refused him in the car and our young professor's pants swelled with contained vehemence. Not even then.

Leo feels that, just like a child, he would come in an instant. He has only to yield to the impulse, take it out, touch it a little. He is so excited and so desperate. His mind does nothing but select and isolate delicious moments in the long list of conjugal couplings. There is nothing more terrifying than nostalgia for conjugal sex. There is no perversion more lethal than to masturbate while thinking of your wife. Leo is thinking about this. And then of the first times with Rachel. The beauty of the first times. The barriers they had overcome in the course of years. When he deflowered her a few days before their marriage. The first time she took him in her mouth. The first time he convinced her to let him come in her face. The first time he licked her. The first time he took her from behind. Yes, all the first times condensed into a single image, a sole instant, trapped in the fibers of that useless raincoat. All that explosive material is there, in his mind, in his body. It took nothing to set it off. And to keep it alive very little is needed: he has only to press the sleeve of the raincoat against his nose with greater force and breathe in more violently.

But now another thought gets in the way. Something that resembles jealousy. How has Rachel been behaving in these months? Other men? A steady relationship? Everything that's happened to Leo in recent times proves that there is really nothing that can't happen. That the unthinkable is around the corner, waiting for you, with a smile.

The jealousy that starts to torment him is what makes him capitulate. In the end Leo can't resist: he pulls out his penis, which demonstrates an adolescent reactivity. And he starts masturbating, as every man knows how to do. As every man learns to do at thirteen and never forgets. Nothing odd about it. Men are made like that. You're always ready to jack off, at the most inconceivable moments and in the least appropriate places. Ever since the beginning, when your body discovers the glory of those stickily mysterious spasms and asks nothing more than to make them happen again and again and again . . . ever since it has been natural to take that solitary gymnastic syncopation for an exorcism. The last depraved resource of your nerves to keep from giving in.

It's the same for Jews who, when they leave a cemetery after the annual visit to their dead spouse, feel the obligation and the need to eat something. Life is reclaiming its rights. Life requires respect and dedication. But it's also the only way that's left to vent frustration and confront disaster. A bad grade at school? Your girl has cheated on you just because that guy had his butt in a Porsche Carrera? You're upset by the idea of a new Ice Age or the inexorable desertification of the planet? Have no fear, my boy. Run to the bathroom and masturbate. Jack off. Let go. Ardently, violently. It's the best way to get through it. A sacred gesture, blessing and cursing at the same time. A feral, ancestral instinct like that of the dog who pees on the roots of a tree. It so happens that this time Leo's tree is his former conjugal boudoir, orphaned by his dazzling collection of clothes and saturated with the tormenting odor of Penelope.

But, just as he's about to come, he's distracted by something, a noise behind him. Is someone observing him? He turns his head suddenly but sees no one. Another noise. Faint as fabric sliding on a floor. Panic. Has someone seen him. Has someone seen him jerking off on his wife's raincoat? Was it Telma? Or one of the boys? Was it Rachel herself? Was it a ghost? Was it no one? Embarrassment once again disengages his virility. Leo, after composing himself as well as he can, runs away to bury himself again.

I will never go out again. I swear. Yes, that was the last time.

Then summer erupted: a month early with respect to the calendar, as sometimes happens in Rome. The days of Leo Pontecorvo were attended by two contrasting feelings: a renewed and meditative fatalism and the sensation that someone was keeping on eye on him twenty-four hours out of twenty-four. A shadow. A sprite. Something supernatural. This impression had been with him ever since he had had to abandon his plan to masturbate on the raincoat of his wife. The excitement had disappeared, but not the presence that had made him flee.

He no longer had much desire to eat. For several days he hadn't even gone to the kitchen to get the food he needed. On the fifth day of not eating, he found the tray with the food outside his door. And from that day on that's how it was. He was glad the tray was there, and he wondered if the presence he felt around him had put it there or a family member who preferred to remain anonymous. They wanted him alive. Evidently that thing didn't want him to die, didn't want him to waste away. Evidently that thing needed Leo to endure, to live. But nevertheless every day he ate a little less. He was discovering the pleasure of not eating.

Then true summer arrived. And it was giving the best of itself in the perfumed warmth that arrived form the garden. The boys had just finished school, and one of Leo's greatest pleasures was to look out through the window to watch their legs playing ball in the garden. He recognized both Filippo's and Samuel's. It was so poignant to recognize them. To witness the miracle of obsessively repeated moves, which Leo never tired of. He felt a pang of grief when the game ended and the teams of four against four, which his sons and their friends formed every morning, broke up, to agree to meet there at the same time the next morning.

Samuel played defense. His vehemence as a defender, the passion with which he stuck to his opponent and kept on him were in contrast with his temperamental and capricious character. Although in life up to then he had been successful in everything he did, Samuel never gave the impression that he could become deeply involved in something. The price you pay if life functions too well for you. If it hadn't been for that nice gift that Leo and Camilla had given him the year before, his life would have grazed perfection. At least as far as his father knew.

He often wondered what was hidden in the little heads of his sons. What did they feel? What did they want? Who were they? The distance between people who love each other is a mystery no less profound than the oceanic abysses. What fine phrases did our prisoner conceive. Samuel, his Semi, so it seemed to Leo, was born under a good star. That's why it was amazing that he put so much grit into playing soccer: it wasn't what you'd expect from someone for whom things have always gone well. Filippo's style of play didn't in any way represent his life, really, either. Filippo was regal and charismatic when he played. But his life wasn't that way. In life he had always given a bad account of himself, from the start, I would say.

An incident during one of those games tested Leo's nerves yet again. Likewise his courage and his cowardice. There had been an incident. Filippo tackled by Semi. They never played on the same team. Semi couldn't bear Filippo's reprimands, any more than Filippo could bear his brother's lack of style and his excessive fervor. That's why there was a general opinion among that tribe of adolescent soccer players of Olgiata that the Pontecorvo brothers should always play against each other. And it was precisely Semi's impulsiveness, so irritating to Filippo, that provoked the disaster. Semi had slid into his brother's ankle. And, to judge from the way Filippo was now writhing and from his whimpering yelps, it seemed likely that he had broken it. The sharp wail that seems to mix crying with laughter, horror and disbelief, emitted by athletes, especially young ones, when they are faced with the outrageous impotence of a broken bone. Leo saw very clearly, from what for once turned out to be a privileged position, his son's foot dangling. Likewise he saw his other son, desperate, unable to stop calling, "Mamma, Mamma! Hurry up . . . hurry . . . "

Leo, no less desperate than his sons but if possible still more frustrated, found a way even at that moment to conceive a self-flagellating thought: observing that not even then did Samuel call him. Not even in an emergency. For a moment the mad idea that he was dead crossed his mind: maybe he was dead and he was the only one who didn't know it. Maybe death was just this. Persisting in believing you're alive while all those around you have accepted your nonexistence. Maybe the presence he felt around him was merely the trace left by his life that had now passed. Maybe he himself was nothing but a trace. The trace of a trace.

Of course not, he wasn't dead. They had simply forgotten him. For them, between him and that spider near the window that was doing gymnastics on its own spider web there was no difference. Yet again he was tempted by the idea of emerging.

Going to help his son who had broken his ankle. Comfort the other, reassure him that it wasn't his fault. That he shouldn't take it like that. That these are things that happen. And while he thought of what to say to Samuel to console him it occurred to him that, to tell the truth, Filippo was especially prone to certain accidents. He was a subscriber to catastrophe. He always had been. If that day the Omnipotent had decided to sacrifice the bone of a boy playing ball in the yard of his house, well, you could bet that that bone would belong to Filippo Pontecorvo.

A difficult relation with the universe. A divorce from the creation. This was Filippo's distinguishing feature. Was it his fear of the universe that had made him such a wary and silent being?

When he was four or five the only thing that he enjoyed, and from which he never wanted to be parted, was the giant books that Rachel gave him for his birthday: those pure, biblical anthologies from Disney with egotistical titles like *I, Donald Duck, I, Mickey Mouse, I, Scrooge McDuck*. Filippo consumed those big books the way a rabbi consumes the Torah. It seemed that all there was to know about life could be revealed by the adventures of Scrooge in the Klondike. By Donald's lovable blunders. Or by the bold arrogance of Mickey Mouse in solving puzzles.

At first it was Rachel who was responsible for the evening reading from the enormous volumes. One story a night. That was the agreement. And Filippo looked at the pictures and listened to his mother as if the spell were constantly renewed, as if it were always a surprise. After a while Rachel could recite those books from memory. And yet it was still not enough for her son. So that from time to time, during the day, Filippo picked them up, with immense difficulty (they were almost as big as him), and began to patiently leaf through them, as if he were inspecting every minute detail of every picture. As if he were concentrated on the drop of sweat on Donald or never had enough of the "sgrunt!" of Scrooge McDuck. Every so often he laughed, and sometimes his face was sad.

At one point, the year before Filippo went to elementary school, Leo tried to teach his son to read. He wanted him to have a totally autonomous relationship with his sacred books. He wanted his son to read by himself those comic books that he knew by heart. And it wasn't because he was tired of reading to him, or because he wanted to relieve Rachel of that tedious task. No, he wanted him to read so that he could discover the electrifying pleasure of autonomy.

Leo had been dismayed not only by his astonishing incapacity to learn but also by the opposition he put up to an activity so prosaic. As if writing and reading were for Fili a defeat. As if they would destroy the spell cast almost automatically by those drawings. Yes, after a while Leo had had to surrender to the fact that the only exercise in comprehension performed by his older son was to take in the drawings, feed on the images. Filippo was like a prehistoric man, unskilled in writing but with a well-developed sensitivity to shapes.

His problem with writing and with the alphabet—of which Filippo gave evidence the following year, in first grade, when a more sophisticated teacher recognized the unmistakable signs of dyslexia—was only the latest skirmish in that great war against the world that had been, until then, his very short life.

It was the conscientious teacher at the American school (it was customary for the Roman bourgeoisie at that time to send their children to some foreign institution) who called Rachel to tell her that Filippo had problems with the alphabet. She wondered, among other things, if it was prudent, given the circumstances, to send him to an institution where his mother tongue wasn't spoken. Miss Dawson belonged to that category of robust New England ladies who, though they have a strong

314 · ALESSANDRO PIPERNO

314 · ALESSANDRO PIPERNO

accent, speak a correct Italian, articulated with flawless syntax and provided with a rich lexicon.

"You know, it's already more difficult for him than for the others. At least eighty per cent of the children who attend this school are native speakers. It's normal that the remaining twenty per cent, to which Filippo belongs, should encounter some difficulties. But if you add to this handicap a problem with the alphabet, then . . . "

"What do you mean?"

"That for Filippo there is no difference between a 'p,' a 'b,' and a 'd.' And although I've tried to suggest it to him, there seems no way to make him understand. Anyway, it's not something that's so alarming in itself. It's a problem in which one can intervene. I know people of great talent and great success who have suffered from it . . . "

Rachel had taken no comfort from the generic reassurances of Miss Dawson. And even less from her husband, whose only comment, when she reported the teacher's words, had been: "Well, come to think of it, the 'p,' the 'b,' and the 'd' are rather similar. I always thought that Filippo wasn't the type to be splitting hairs."

That was how it worked between Leo and Rachel: when she was worried he played the role of the blowhard, and vice versa. Leo still knew today how that remark, at the time, was more useful to him than to his wife. But what was wrong with that child? Why was there always something? Why was what came naturally to others perplexing to him?

On the other hand Leo had guessed before Miss Dawson that something was wrong, although, incapable of facing up to problems squarely, he had prevented the suspicion from reaching the level of consciousness. Distinguishing "b" from "d." He had tried his best with a thousand examples to get his son to understand that they were two different things.

"The 'b' looks like a man with a big stomach," he had said.

"whereas the 'd' is a man with a large bottom." And to be even clearer, he had pointed out to the child his own stomach and bottom. Although Filippo had laughed at this joke of his (children find both anatomy and scatology very funny), nonetheless he couldn't learn to recognize the difference between the two consonants. Evidently it was something too big for him. An undertaking.

The teacher had said she didn't know what to do anymore. Also, that incapacity made Filippo extremely aggressive toward his schoolmates, who, by that point in the year, had already learned the alphabet. And at the same time it caused him deep shame.

"The other day he hit a classmate," Miss Dawson said to Rachel.

"Hit? What do you mean hit? Why?"

"I'm afraid the boy was making fun of him because of his trouble writing." When Rachel told Leo, he remembered that Tuesday when he was taking Filippo to school and had asked him:

"Do you like playing with Francesca?" Francesca was the speech therapist.

"Yes," Filippo had answered, "but I don't want to play with her in the morning anymore."

"Why?"

"Because then I'm late for school."

"Well, isn't that better? What do you care? You have an excuse. If only I'd had an excuse for coming an hour late at your age. If I had one now . . . "

"But if I arrive late they say I'm sick."

"Who says you're sick? Why do they say that? You're very healthy."

"They say I'm sick because I arrive late. And also because I play with Francesca."

Then Leo had thought that some shitty mothers must have

said to their shitty children that the reason Filippo Pontecorvo came late on Tuesday and Wednesday was that he was sick. That he had problems with learning the alphabet. And then Leo was furious. Goddam mothers. Goddam children. Goddam humanity. And goddam also my little Filippo.

Because Leo knew, he remembered: dyslexia was only the latest alarm that Filippo had sent out. The first had been speech.

Leo and Rachel had had to wait four years before Filippo gave them the satisfaction of uttering a sentence with a meaning. If pressed, he would respond with little grunts and monosyllables. Initially, they had attributed to timidity and shyness the fact that, compared with other children, he was slow to speak. Filippo had been an exceedingly placid infant, one of those who don't cry much and sleep a lot. Which had allowed his parents to believe that that persistent silence was a new sign of his capacity for self-sufficiency. Filippo was silent simply because he had nothing to say. This Leo and Rachel told themselves in the early days. Not to exaggerate the thing was the right attitude: of responsible parents, modern parents. Filippo was a bit slower than necessary in expressing himself in words. No harm. For what he needed gestures were enough, words would come. Filippo was like that. One who took his time.

But after they had been telling themselves this little story for a while, Rachel and Leo had stopped believing it. Filippo was almost three and God alone knows how much his parents yearned for him to utter, even just once, those two momentous words: "Mamma" and "Papa."

They were tired of being satisfied with the monosyllable "ta," which in Filippo's extraordinarily primitive language seemed to indicate all the adults who had some authority: parents, grandparents, babysitter.

For Filippo they were all "ta."

There was no way to make him say anything else. And they

kept trying: "Sweetheart, say at least ta-ta, yes, say it twice, double it, ta-ta. That's all, it's already a big step forward."

It was typical of Leo to give these articulate speeches to a child who didn't seem very inclined to conversation. That was also the way in which he followed the instructions imparted by Loredana, who, before giving him the phone number of a speech therapist, had said, "Talk a lot. Never get tired of talking to him. Hearing you speak is all Filippo needs. And you'll see that in the end he'll be unblocked."

And so here's the diligent father entertaining his son with long, useless disquisitions. At those junctures Filippo looked at him in bewilderment. And if Leo persisted, exasperated, "Ta-ta, ta-ta, it's not hard," then the angelic little face of his son became red. He would turn toward the wall in dismay and start rhythmically banging his head against it.

Filippo was ashamed.

He was perfectly aware of what was happening to him. Both of how he was different from other, talkative children and of the pain he caused his parents. And this made him ashamed. So when his father insisted too much on his talking, he would let out one of those terrifying, prehistoric deaf-mute cries. And beat his head against the wall.

Shame. That feeling demonstrated that his son was deeply sensitive. Life was too competitive for Filippo. Everything seemed to wound him.

And the rage that sometimes assailed him—the angry frustration he showed whenever he couldn't do things that others did naturally—was so in contrast with his angelic beauty. Who wasn't in love with his beauty? Fine blond hair, blue eyes, a rosy round face. He was the idol of supermarkets and restaurants. A pop star to the young women who stopped him everywhere he went, swooning over his beauty: "What a stupendous child," "What a little angel," "He's irresistible, I could eat him up with kisses."

Wherever they brought him, in his stroller, with that regal face and the elegant, modest clothes in which he was sent out by his young well-to-do parents, people stopped to look at him, and sometimes they complimented Leo and Rachel, who quivered with pride. But from him nothing. Filippo didn't react to all the love, all the admiration, all the tenderness he was capable of arousing. He didn't indulge in the vanity that usually affects beautiful children. He was indifferent, impenetrable, wrapped up in himself, always absorbed in a sort of intense and exclusive feeling. That lack of response had the effect of rousing a further impulse of affection in the adults who looked at him with such admiration. The boy didn't see their flattery. He also had an inner beauty. If life were only freedom and self-sufficiency, Leo thought sometimes, Filippo would have a radiant future. But unfortunately beyond freedom and self-sufficiency there existed something else: society claimed its rights, the world wished to be taken into consideration. No one, not even such a beautiful a child, can afford not to respond to the infinite solicitations of the universe. That's why he would have to speak, just as one day he would have to learn to write.

And yet that spectacle of freedom and self-sufficiency was so thrilling. Almost all children are whiny in the car. They have no patience. After a while they become impatient, fidgety, unbearable. They protest, they kick, they demand attention with savage cries. Filippo did not fall into the category of little annoyers. In the car he took on a serious and contemplative air, even melancholy, you might have said. He looked out the window, brooding like a poet. You called his name, he gazed at you for a second without changing expression, then returned to the window. An attitude that Leo and Rachel found both charming and praiseworthy.

Basically Filippo had always been an independent sort.

Leo recalled how, coming out of the bathroom in the morning, he would find that little imp, with his blond bangs ("like a member of the Hitler Youth," joked our proud father to his friends), crawling happily. At that time his favorite toy, which he refused to be separated from, was his father's underpants. He looked at them, he put them on his head, he cleaned the floors with them. He could play for hours with those underpants. There was no game that entertained him more than those underpants. Leo called to him. But Filippo gave the first signs of his timidity and his difficulty in communicating. The more you called him, the more absorbed he became in his private world, him and the underpants.

That was the way Leo was first confronted with his son's strangeness. Only then had he begun to pay morbid attention to other children the same age. And only then had he noticed how Filippo was simply different from everything that was normal. And this had filled his heart with shame. A shame that Leo was ashamed to feel. Which Rachel seemed to have countered not only with a fierce pride (all right: her son was odd, and so? what was so great about normality?) but also with a desire not to hide it, rather to display it.

Painfully Leo remembered the day Filippo turned four. Rachel, spurred by the speech therapist ("You have to surround him with an atmosphere of affectionate sociability"), had organized a party in the garden. Filippo had been born in May: in that season the garden offered a shining, lush spectacle of colors and scents, especially welcoming to children's parties. Leo had wanted to be present, driven in part by curiosity to see how Filippo managed with his contemporaries.

The truth is that Leo wasn't happy about that birthday. For him it represented the final confirmation of his son's oddness. Everyone had been constantly telling him that up to four it's normal not to speak. That up to four there's no need to worry about it. There, now Filippo was four and he still hadn't opened his mouth. All right, in the meantime he had learned to say "mamma" and "Papa." But Leo wasn't satisfied. And finally he felt he had the right to be worried. He had the right to shout his worry from the rooftops. Too bad that that opportunity, generously offered by fate, gave him no relief.

That wretched birthday party. What anxiety!

It was the first time that Leo had seen him in action. Ever since Filippo had started going to the nursery at the American school, Leo had always managed to invent an excuse to give Rachel, and himself, in order to miss the numerous recreational activities in which his son was involved. He hadn't been at the traditional afternoon Halloween party (many years before that holiday became popular in Italy), thus sparing himself the sight of a goggling zombie who sat in a corner eyeing sweets of every sort. Nor had he wanted to go to the school Christmas pageant, in which his son had played (to listen to Rachel, "with masterly skill") a motionless tulip, who, in spite of the script, when the scene changed to winter, had refused to wither along with the others, producing great mirth in the audience and in his mother yet another embarrassment veined with tenderness.

And Leo had not attended any of those children's parties precisely in order not to be exposed to what on that birthday he couldn't escape: that is, the spectacle of his son's horribly precocious maladjustment. His son who couldn't fit in even when the entire world was mobilized to honor him. His dissonance, his oddness.

It had been truly unpleasant to observe how Fili, even in the presence of so many companions, appeared detached, closed off in a permanent private game. Always clinging to those wretched comic books. Blasted Donald Duck, blasted Huey, Dewey, and Louie! What do they have that we don't? Why, my little one, are you always with them, why not come out here with us, who love you so much?

Suddenly the mothers of the other children, perceiving the unease aroused by the bizarre behavior of the birthday boy, had grabbed their children and led them over to Filippo.

"Come, won't you play with him?" one said. And Leo felt deeply pained. In that woman's voice was an insulting note of pity. After some insistence three children gathered around Filippo. The mothers returned to their chat. Leo observed how confidently the three talked, and how they tried in some way to involve Filippo. But he refused. He stayed on his own. Until one of the children impatiently addressed to the others a phrase that Leo would never forget: "Leave him alone, he doesn't understand anything. Filippo is stupid."

Little bastard! The cruelty of children. The frankness of children. It had been such a blow to Leo. To the heart of "affectionate social relations." No, there was nothing affectionate about social relations. Social relations are cruel. And he, Leo, knows it well.

When you have a very small child (particularly if this child is the first) you tend to magnify any problem he has, imagining that, just like the problems of adults, it's doomed not to be resolved . . . And you are scarcely aware that, while you're torturing yourself with the doubt that your son will ever speak—because if he hasn't learned to do it up to now he probably never will, because it's evidently something too complicated for him—suddenly, almost overnight, he begins to speak with utter naturalness. But then on the horizon a new problem appears, which to you, poor fearful father, doesn't seem any less insoluble than the previous one. So it was with Filippo.

In the end Rachel had been right: after a while Filippo began to speak. At first he struggled, distorting his words in a sweet, funny way. Saying "I don't lighe" instead of "I don't like." Getting confused about some verb persons: you might say to him, "Am I wrong or did my Filippo eat a little too much today?" and he, all polite and offended, would answer, "I'm wrong, I'm wrong!" Later his language became impressively correct.

But with the arrival of words, which were increasingly clear and precise, and before Filippo revealed his helplessness with the alphabet, another odd thing had manifested itself, which disturbed Leo and Rachel in a way that was different, perhaps, but no less pointed.

They noticed that, in order to fall asleep, Filippo had got in the habit of beating his head violently against the pillow. And he usually did it in time to music. This had started when Rachel bought a brightly colored child's portable record player, made just for 45s, which were all the rage in those years. And Leo had inaugurated the machine by inserting an old single by Ricky Nelson, one of those hard-to-find records that the same American aunt every so often sent Leo, her Italian nephew, when he was a boy.

The record was from 1957. At that time Ricky Nelson was a teen idol. And that single, titled "Be-Bop Baby" (what audacious alliteration!), had for several weeks been at the top of the charts in the United States. Which had inspired the diligent Aunt Adriana to get it and send it to her nephew. It was a catchy tune, typical of the time. Leo had always liked it. Maybe because it was connected to some memory stored in that romantic jewel box that was his youth. He certainly hadn't the slightest suspicion that he would come to find that song intolerable because of the hundreds of times his son forced him to listen to it. For Filippo it was the only song that existed. You were in trouble if you made him listen to another one. Even from the same era. Even with the same chords. Even by the same singer. Then he became furious. He wanted only "Be-Bop Baby." And nothing else. Here was his new obsession. The new method he'd come up with for keeping out everything else.

Well, all right, it's true, Leo said to himself, children are like that: obsessive and conservative. Stubborn reactionaries in miniature. But Filippo's obsession with that record seemed pathological. Just like the way he beat his head against the pillow for several hours in a row, stopping just to start the record again. Where did he get so much energy? And what was the sense of expending so much energy for nothing?

Filippo and Semi's nanny was called Carmen. She was a simple, proud Cape Verdian, whom the boys adored and whom Rachel, at least at the time (before Carmen gave signs of instability), trusted entirely. Carmen was the first to give a name to that bizarre behavior. As she said good night, a moment after turning off the light in "her" boys' room, she exhorted Filippo, "Don't *work* too hard." And then she warned his little brother, who was in the lower of the bunk beds, "And you, Semi, don't copy him."

Work. This was how Carmen had described Filippo's mania for beating his head against the pillow. And in fact some evenings, when Leo and Rachel came home from a dinner out, and, passing the boys' room before going to bed, heard that eerie squeaking sound, felt an odd tenderness for their little worker. Rachel thought of those factory assembly lines that operate all night. And Leo of Charlie Chaplin's *Modern Times.*

Once Leo had hypothesized, "Maybe it's a kind of Jewish atavism."

"In what sense?"

"Well, like the Hasidim at the Wailing Wall. Maybe at last we have a great rabbi in the family."

"Don't be a fool. The speech therapist says it might be a mild form of autism. She says it's not so alarming, but it could also explain his difficulties in relating to the world . . . "

Did there always have to be something? Was it possible that that blessed child every so often had to come out with a new peculiarity? Possible that all those doctors, groping in

324 · ALESSANDRO PIPERNO

the dark, always felt a need to give a name to his peculiari-
ties?

When Leo, after a nighttime call, came home at dawn, he
liked to go and see the children sleeping. Entering their room
he was invaded by the poignant odor of cookies just taken out
of the oven. He was very careful not to wake them. He sat first
on the lower bunk, where Samuel slept like a little angel,
caressed his hand, pulled up the blanket. Then he rose and
repeated the same gesture with Filippo. But merely touching
him set in motion that infernal machine. See how Filippo,
without even waking up, began to butt the pillow with his
head. This always produced a certain anguish in Leo, inducing
him to leave the room immediately, as if he didn't want to face
another demonstration that his son wasn't completely normal.
But mixed with that worry there was also a lot of pride. For the
character and the determination that Filippo put into things.
For his wisdom and his patience. Attributes that were far from
childish.

One thing that struck Leo was his son's endurance. His
extraordinary compunction in accepting everything his parents
forced him to do. Never once did he complain. He showed
such stoicism. As if by being subjected to those treatments he
had developed a passive acceptance of his own imperfection.
All that effort to learn to speak. All that effort to learn to write.
All that effort to try to go to sleep without rhythmically hitting
the pillow with his head because it upsets Mamma and Papa so
much. All that effort, in short. For what?

Maybe they were too apprehensive. Maybe it would have
been better to let Filippo give in to his harmless weaknesses.
But what could Leo do if, in certain things, both he and Rachel
had an interventionist spirit? And if Filippo's compliance
made things even easier? He wasn't the type of child to whom
you have to keep saying: we're doing it for your own good.
Something in his brain must have led him to believe that the

life of a child was a continuous, persistent process meant to correct you. He must have been sure that he was a creature full of factory defects.

But was it really so normal and so necessary to spend childhood afternoons with his mother in some waiting room, to then be greeted by yet another specialist? Was it really indispensable to subject him to all this? Or maybe little Fili was paying the price of having been born into a horribly perfectionist era, and of being the child of two doctors with a weakness for straightening what was crooked? Two tidy bourgeois parents incapable of accepting that their child expressed himself in a different way from the dreariest average and the most ordinary excellence?

Leo at times wondered if he himself wasn't a little too submissive to Rachel's will. He knew how proud she was of her son's stoicism. That was the way she was brought up. To consider personal sacrifice a kind of demonstration of humanity: people sacrifice themselves without a fuss. And certainly the fact that Filippo never complained must have been in her eyes truly admirable. Often at night Rachel would tell Leo about how impeccably the child had behaved at the speech therapist's or the psychologist's.

"He's so good, he sits there, without saying a word. Every so often he smiles at me. He pages through his comic books so politely. He looks at the other children in the waiting room with amazement. And he seems to be asking, 'What's wrong with these people that they complain so much?' Our Filippo's a little grownup."

"Where did you take him to eat?" Leo asked, to change the subject, because he knew that the pact agreed to by mother and son was the following: if he was a good boy when she took him out of school at noon to see one of his doctors, in exchange they would have lunch in a place of his choosing. Filippo loved to eat. He had a big appetite. And fiercely child-

326 · ALESSANDRO PIPERNO

ish tastes: sandwiches, French fries, Coca-Cola, steamed milk, chocolate cupcakes, cream puffs . . .

"We went to the Hungaria. He ate an entire hamburger and all the French fries. Then we went to the doctor. And on the way there he read me the newspaper. Or at least he tried to. Every so often he utters strange words, which don't exist, but then if you think for a moment you realize that it's an ordinary word where he's mangled a syllable and changed a vowel . . . "

These accounts, which Leo asked for almost every evening—not for the pleasure of hearing them but each time in the hope (inevitably frustrated) that Rachel would say to him, "Everything's fine, Filippo is finally reading with the composure, the style, and the diction of Vittorio Gassman"—had a terrible effect on him. Sometimes they made him furious, other times they made him feel insanely affectionate. Certainly they never left him indifferent. That his son should spend most of the afternoons of the only childhood he would get being tormented by doctors filled him with indignation and made him reconsider the whole interventionist choice that he and Rachel had made.

The compliance Rachel told him about, the greediness with which Filippo ate the hamburger, the blunders and frequent and ridiculous mistakes he made reading the newspaper irritated him. Surely, surely he should have had greater understanding. Didn't he treat gravely ill children? But the point is that without him those children wouldn't survive. Very often they didn't survive anyway. Filippo, on the other hand, without his speech therapists and his psychologists would manage very well, no question.

And then the children Leo treated were not his sons. Over time he had learned to tolerate the fact that his work consisted of seeing innocent beings suffer. It was also for that reason—in fact, for that very reason—that he couldn't bear to have a child suffering at home. No, he really didn't like Filippo's stoicism, as much as he didn't like Rachel's perseverance. Paradoxically he would have preferred from both some lessening of discipline. Indeed, laxity would have seemed to him a completely natural reaction.

Besides, Leo knew that if he hadn't been six feet tall, if he hadn't been the stylish man he was, if he hadn't over the years won such an eminent place in society, if he hadn't had the duty to keep up a certain comportment in front of his wife, probably, listening to Rachel's accounts of the daily activities of his son, composed of docility and resignation and such endless difficulties, he would have broken down in tears.

Dear God, his Fili sometimes seemed so defenseless, so incapable of fighting back against even the smallest obstacle!

One morning, in the house at the seaside in the Maremma where the Pontecorvos spent a month every summer, Rachel found Filippo on the bed in the maid's room, where the nanny—on vacation at the time—usually slept.

Rachel found him there, motionless, still wearing his sneakers, T-shirt, and soccer shorts, and exuding the salty, goat-like smell of someone who hasn't washed after sports. Rachel was astonished not only at finding him there but at the fact that he was so extremely happy to see her. Filippo was about to cry. The night before, Leo and Rachel, coming back from dinner at the house of friends, hadn't realized that Filippo wasn't sleeping in the room with Semi. Now Filippo explained to her that, returning from a soccer game on the beach, he had lain down for a moment on that bed, Carmen's bed. He had fallen asleep. Waking up a few hours later in absolute, terrible pitch-darkness.

"But, sweetheart, you couldn't go into the bedroom with your brother?"

"I thought I had gone blind."

"What do you mean, blind? Why blind?"

"Because it was all dark. I kept my eyes open all night to see if there was any light. But no."

"The shutters are closed. We're in the middle of the lagoon. It's normal that night is darker than in Rome. But couldn't you turn on the light?"

"Yes, I thought of that. I kept my hand on the switch all night."

"And why didn't you push it?"

"Because if the light didn't go on, then I really was blind."

"But look at you, my little silly."

Again the image of his son courting the light switch for an entire night, unable to make up his mind to push it, out of fear that he had gone blind, produced in Leo a feeling less cheerful than the one roused in his wife. Here was another demonstration of his fear and his inability to react. Poor Filippo, it must have been a real nightmare to think for all that time that he was blind. Why hadn't he called them? Why hadn't he shouted to summon them? Simple—because their arrival could have confirmed his blindness, just like pushing the light switch. Better to wait in anguish for the arrival of dawn! All that fear, what did it mean? What value did it have? What obstacles would it lead to? And, above all, was this the message that he and Rachel had given their son? The subliminal message that said, My boy, you are a defective child. A child who is coming apart, destined to fall ill and break into pieces.

"But do you know, sweetheart, how difficult it is to become blind?" Leo had explained later. "Do you know why many people, even if they want to, don't kill themselves?"

"What?"

"Because, in spite of what you think, dying is difficult. Getting sick is difficult. Our body is a structure that is marvelously designed to resist and adapt. Above all at your age."

And, after uttering these sensible words, Leo wondered if they were appropriate for a child of eight.

It also occurred to Leo to wonder what it could mean for a child like that to have a younger brother who seemed his exact opposite. Who had learned to speak precociously, who slept profoundly and quietly, who wrote and read effortlessly, whose preferred activity seemed to be to excel in school, in sports, and in pleasing others. What did it mean for such a complicated older brother to have a younger brother who enjoyed the birthday parties organized for him by his parents? A lighthearted child, whom life had spared the torture of speech therapists, psychologists, neurologists? Semi was the child everyone would like to have: cheerful, easygoing, funny. Maybe less handsome than Filippo: his looks were marred by a slight distortion of his features. But those imperceptible imperfections were what made him, if possible, even more likable.

It would be natural for them to hate each other. It would be natural for them to fight. When Semi was born someone always kept an eye on him. Rachel was afraid that Filippo, who had already shown signs of strangeness, might be violent toward his brother. Everything conspired to make the two competitive and envious.

Not at all. They were the closest, most solidly allied brothers that Leo had ever seen (and he knew something about children). In the morning they went to school together. In the afternoon they came home together. The older had infected the younger with his love for comic books, while the younger had introduced the older to collecting soccer jerseys. Over the years (and every year a little more) the two had elaborated a coded language all their own, which excluded others, it's true, but also made their fraternal solidarity something mystical, enigmatic.

And by now one could not be without the other. There was something unhealthy that made Leo uneasy but that Rachel was able to reduce to a reasonable and modest dimension. In the end life would separate them, making them autonomous, in a spirit of emancipation no less inevitable (and in a certain sense no less sad) than that which would one day drive both Filippo and Samuel to leave their parents. And to form, if fate offered them the chance, new nuclear families totally independent of the original one. Isn't this the great tragedy of life?

Some two years before finding himself at yet another moral crossroads—to emerge from his cave and go to the aid of his son who was writhing on the grass with a broken ankle or stand frozen at the window?—Leo had asked Rachel, along with the boys, to come with him to an oncology conference that was to be held in London in early December. His speech was scheduled for the Thursday evening, he had explained to Rachel, to lure her. Which meant that they would have a long weekend to enjoy themselves in a city where he—he loved to boast—knew "every puddle." Like all bourgeois families, the Pontecorvos were devoutly Anglophile. Like all bourgeois families (except English ones, I suppose) the Pontecorvos had a ridiculously conventional idea of the British world: rough as tweed, tough as Dunhill tobacco, soft as the whiskers of an admiral of the Royal Navy, and elegant as an aphorism of George Bernard Shaw . . .

For this reason Leo was particularly happy about his now ten-year friendship with Professor Alfred Hathaway, a smooth-spoken, genial oncologist who worked in a large hospital complex in the western part London. Every year Alfred organized, on behalf of the Royal Holloway University, a conference at which Leo always played the role of protagonist. Leo considered his colleague, Professor Hathaway, a kind of fellow-soldier in the great civil war that in those years pediatric oncology was waging to set up common strategies and protocols.

That year, with Christmas approaching, well . . . wouldn't it be magnificent to go with the boys? They could do the stupid things that tourists like, and the fashionable ones of frequent visitors. They would go shopping and eat strange, fatty things.

Everything was set when Rachel, because of a sudden flu, defaulted.

"Now what?"

"Now here I am in my funeral shroud."

"Come on, don't be stupid, what shall we do?"

"My plan for the weekend is to stay in bed, envying to death all the scones you'll be eating in spite of me!"

"How can I manage without you? Thursday I'm at the conference all day. At night I'll have to go to dinner with Alfred and the other participants. I can't take the boys with me. And then it would be so wonderful if you were there, too."

"You always complain that you don't see them enough. That you can never be together. That they're growing up before your eyes . . . Here, you have your chance. And it wouldn't be bad for me to have a few days without them around. And they're so eager to go. Samuel is all excited, I don't know which pair of pants or shoes I heard him babbling about the other day on the telephone. Filippo is happy because he'll be able to buy *Secret Love* or whatever the heck it's called."

It was typical of Rachel to mangle the names of books, films, comics. This habit played an important role in an iconoclastic strategy that was typical of Roman dialect and opposed by the philological rigor of her husband, who knew very little Roman. In the specific case the comic book that Rachel alluded to, and that Filippo had tormented her with in recent days, was *Secret Wars*, by Jim Shooter, a publishing event from Marvel. It had come out that year in England and the United States and fabulous tales were told about it (the Italian edition wouldn't appear until long after Leo's departure from this world).

"After all," Rachel resumed, "for several summers already we've sent them out on their own! Of course they can stay for

332 · ALESSANDRO PIPERNO

one day in a comfortable London hotel and take a nice walk around the neighborhood. Don't worry."

"Sweetheart, you don't know how sorry I am that you . . . " Leo had commented complainingly.

A few weeks before this conversation took place, Leo and Rachel, discussing the trip, had come to the subject of the airplane tickets. Filippo had flown once, with his father, on the short leg from Rome to Milan. Samuel had never flown: another reason for excitement.

Leo's ticket, bought by the conference, was in business class: as Alitalia, following other airline companies, now designated what at one time had been called, in a much more classist way, first class. But, apart from the designation, things were not so changed: green seats that were a little larger than those in economy class, better service and meals, prettier hostesses, and a price at least four times as high. Leo would have liked to take the whole family with him in business class. And Rachel naturally was opposed, indignant.

"It seems unnecessary."

"But really, doesn't it seem ridiculous to fly in different classes? You want us to play the great lord and his servants?"

"I don't want my sons, getting on an airplane for the first time, to do it like snobs. It seems revolting. Unseemly. Impolite."

"What nonsense! The same old story. Why do you never surprise me?"

"I could say the same to you."

"But for once let's do something all together. After all it's the *first* time Semi's been on an airplane. I'd like to share the experience with him."

"You can always do that."

"Yes, but after takeoff."

"Never mind. It means that your son will take off without you and will eat with plastic utensils."

"But takeoff is the moment most . . . "

He wasn't allowed to say "most" what.

"I'm not going to talk about it. If you buy first-class tickets you'll have to go to London without me."

"It's not first, it's business."

"Whatever it's called."

"All right. It means that I'll ask the secretary for the conference to get me an economy class ticket . . . "

"No, really, what does that have to do with it? They're paying for you. You're going for work. You have to arrive fresh and rested. You deserve some extra comfort. It's another matter. But to spend all that money for two and a half hours of flight seems to me contrary to every . . . "

Rachel was unable say to "every" what. Notion of logic? Morality? Sense of appropriateness? We'll never know.

One thing was certain: while Rachel had had the best of it on the question of tickets, and thus no longer had any reason not to go, it was the flu, in the end, that decided for her.

So Leo found himself at the airport, standing in line to check in, with his sons a little sulky because of their mother's absence and this problem of the airplane seats to resolve.

"If you promise me not to tell Mamma we'll make a last attempt."

"Signor Pontecorvo," the woman at the check-in counter said, "there is only one seat free in business class."

"So?"

"So I can only do the upgrade for one of your sons. Otherwise . . . "

Leo looked at the boys. Let them decide. Filippo, with a gesture habitual to him, had shrugged his shoulders as if to say: let him go, what do I care . . . While the face of Semi, who was so crazy about luxury, had lit up.

The only thing that Filippo asked for was a window seat. It wasn't hard to satisfy him. And now there he was, over his ears the headphones of a Sony walkman—a gadget obsolete today but avant-garde in those days, which Leo had bought some time ago in Hong Kong—his forehead resting on the window-pane, his gaze kept by only a sliver of wing from being lost in the immensity.

Semi, twenty seats forward, had no such contemplative attitude. Like a real parvenu, Leo thought fondly, he did not refuse a single option made available by Alitalia to VIP customers. Beginning with the glass of champagne offered by a pretty young hostess, which Semi accepted with a slight, polite nod.

Leo, winking at the girl in uniform and taking the glass from his son's hands, had said, "Champagne isn't strong enough for him, give him some Scotch. On the rocks, of course." And so the hostess, taking the hint, had brought a glass of Fanta, with three ice cubes.

Then Semi had taken such pleasure in the takeoff, his body contracting in a spasm of excitement and fear just at the heroic instant when the wheels left the runway. The December morning sky had a pitiless clarity. Leo, resting his chin on the shoulder of his son, whose face was turned to the west, had watched the line between sea and land sharpen. The fantastic patchwork created by yellow, beige, green, brown squares gave the earth a kind of pointillist shimmer. The slender white stripes of two boats fearlessly entering the open sea made him think of two wriggling spermatozoa in search of an opportunity. At that point Leo returned to his work. He took his notes out of his briefcase. He needed to concentrate.

Too bad Semi would not sit still for an instant. He had gone to the bathroom at least three times. He noisily unwrapped the earphones given to him by the same hostess. And he took on the job of unwrapping his father's as well. He had played with the buttons and controls. His excitement had reached a peak when the lunch tray arrived. Leo never ate on an airplane. But it was clear that his second-born would not imitate that paternal habit. On the contrary! Semi buttered the two rolls he had taken from the basket offered by the hostess and also the one on Leo's tray. He inhaled the lasagna, and then cut the roast beef into tiny pieces but didn't touch it. He had devoured the plum cake and demanded a double scoop of vanilla ice cream. Finally, the hostess, with a pewter coffeepot in her hand, had winked at Leo: "Coffee for everyone, sir?"

And Leo, "Yes, but if you could do me a favor, and dilute his with a little hot water."

Just when, more or less around the Riviera, Semi seemed to have calmed down and Leo had reached the right degree of concentration, again the little pest returned to the charge.

"What are you doing?"

"Going over my lecture. Tomorrow I have a test in class," Leo said, trying to be funny. "You know, papa will have to speak off the top of his head, and in English, and, well . . . it's always better to speak in your own language."

Leo had got in the habit of speaking about himself to his children in the third person, like his own father. It was the late Dr. Pontecorvo senior who had taught him that that is how one speaks to one's son. Papa does this, Papa does that . . . It was an expressive mode that in its impersonality and its pedagogic effect stopped just short of pomposity.

"But the notes are written in Italian," his son observed pedantically.

"The notes, yes. For Papa it's easier that way. But then I'll have to speak in English."

Samuel was always asking why. He hadn't stopped since he began to speak. "Why do birds fly?" "Why do cars move?" "Why are the ants eating that butterfly?" "Why does the television work?" "Why do we eat?" "Why does Mamma have blond hair and why is Papa's black . . . ?" These were the questions with which Semi bothered any adult within range.

Huge, not to say useless, questions, which should have deserved tautological answers—"Because," "Because that's how the universe works"—but which instead obliged Leo and Rachel to invent detailed and instructive answers. "Cars move because man invented something that's called the internal-combustion engine," "We eat and sleep because if we didn't we wouldn't survive," "Ants, just like us, need nourishment. For them, as for us, food is assured by the functioning of the food chain. Probably the butterfly crashed and happened to fall near the anthill: the accident made it the ideal meal for the ants . . . "

The fact is that Semi couldn't be satisfied. There was no answer that did not lead to another question, more metaphysical than the preceding, if possible. And although this was exasperating, still it gave evidence of a certain argumentative liveliness.

If for his older brother language had been a difficult and dramatic conquest, Semi had forged ahead: his precocity in appropriating expressions had appeared almost miraculous to his parents. From the first years of his life Semi had tormented them with two great passions: the desire to create a relationship between things and the taste for asking questions. Those two vocations combined made him a tireless interviewer and a frantic comparison maker. "Between me and Filippo who's a better swimmer?" "Between Mamma and Papa, who's been in an airplane more times?" "Who's stronger, me or my friend Giacomo?"

A kind of comparative delirium that also indicated a passion—very Pontecorvo—for competition. A passion that Filippo seemed totally immune to. A passion that, for different reasons, neither Leo nor Rachel minded.

"What's this?" Semi asked, pointing to a place on the page that his father was holding.

"The title of my paper."

And then Semi, with his nose stuck in his father's notes and uttering the words clearly, had read: "The Three Phases of Communicating the Diagnosis to Pediatric-Age Oncology Patients: Progress and Development."

After a moment's hesitation he asked, "What does it mean?"

"I told you. It's the title of my paper."

"Yes, but what does it mean?"

"Is there a particular word you don't understand? Or is it the entire formulation you don't get?"

"Both."

"For example, what word do you not understand?"

" 'Diagnosis.' "

And so our failed Hellenist began to pontificate: "It's a word of Greek origin. Like, in fact, almost all the words doctors use. It comes from *dia*, which means 'through,' and *gnosis*, a wonderful word that means 'knowledge.' It's the way doctors determine and classify the pathology the patient is suffering from after they've subjected him to a series of tests."

Seeing that Semi still looked perplexed Leo went on: "You know when you have a fever, when your bones ache and your mouth is hot and Mamma keeps you home from school?"

"Yes."

"Well, if you come to me and say, 'Papa, I have a fever, achy bones, a hot mouth,' first of all Papa will ask you for a lot of money. And then probably, given those symptoms, he'll tell you that you have the flu. That is a diagnosis, which you arrive at *through* the symptoms that the patient states. Flu is the diagnosis. The only difference is that the diagnoses that Papa has to make are more complicated and more, how can I put it . . . dramatic."

"Why dramatic?"

"Because they are more difficult and because they concern illnesses that are more serious and more insidious than the flu.

And because for the patient and the relatives of the patient they lead to some very unpleasant thoughts."

"What does 'oncology patients' mean?"

"Those are the patients afflicted by the diseases that Papa deals with."

"And 'pediatric age'?"

"That means it has to do with children."

The reason that Leo got lost in all that chat and took refuge in all those flowery euphemisms was the result of a peculiar and deep-rooted difficulty in speaking to his sons about his work. Not that he wanted to protect them from a profession that, to all intents and purposes, could be considered extreme. It would be more exact to say that he was superstitiously afraid that, if he talked to them about it, he might in some way infect them. Make them more vulnerable. Make them like all the other children on the planet, or all fragile creatures exposed to the caprices of chance, liable to get sick and die at any moment.

Leo—the son of hypochondriac parents—had chosen not to be, in turn, a hypochondriac father. Mindful of how unbearable it had been to carry that burden of shadowy parental fears, he had decided to relieve his sons and himself of it. But in order to stick fully to that decision he had had to convince himself that, unlike others, Filippo and Semi were not part of the cycle of life: invulnerable to any illness, they would remain that way as long as he lived. This was above all the reason that he had always been hesitant to talk about his work in their presence. The same reluctance that he had in speaking about them to anyone in the hospital. He didn't want to create any connection. He preferred to manage his life like that: in watertight compartments. His sons were not "pediatric age." His sons were his sons and that was all.

"So what are you going to say at the conference?" Samuel asked him, opening yet another can of Fanta. "I'm presenting the results that have been obtained in the past two years, thanks to innovations that, with the help of some enlightened colleagues, Papa has managed to introduce in his units. Results that have been really encouraging."

"Like?"

This time Leo hesitated a little more before answering. Not so much because he lacked the euphemisms but because with that question his son had forced him to think about all the battles he had had to fight in recent years, against a rigid system, in order, finally, to be able to work in what seemed to him the fairest and most decent way.

Innovation. There is a word hated by the bureaucrats of Santa Cristina. Innovation. There is the cause for which he had worn himself out, for which he had fought, argued, for which he had almost risked self-destructing, and ruining his career. There is the persistence that they might one day find a way to make him pay for, but that for now had produced extraordinary results, which Leo was eager to discuss with his colleagues in other nations.

The principal therapeutic innovation that, about five years earlier, Leo had introduced into his treatment protocol (with some years' delay with respect to other, more advanced European and American practices) was the central venous catheter: an instrument thanks to which he could easily inject his patients' bodies not only with the poison of the chemo but also with the so-called "comfort therapies," necessary to keep them alive and make them feel better. All this without having to torture the small, young veins, at risk of being damaged for good.

There had been an equally decisive revolution in, precisely, communication of the diagnosis to the patient. To introduce this Leo had had to challenge a more insidious enemy: the parents and their desperate wish. It was they, the parents, who couldn't accept the idea that the doctors should communicate the diagnosis to their children. What need was there to do so?

340 · ALESSANDRO PIPERNO

Wasn't it already shocking enough that they were sick? Wasn't it enough to subject them to those frighteningly destructive treatments? Now they also had to be informed of the illness that was trying to kill them, the risks they ran, the extreme therapies to which they would be subjected?

Well, yes, Leo believed. And with him an entire school of thought. Helped and supported in turn by a substantial and combative group of child psychologists.

If Leo merely thought back to all the nonsense he had told his patients in the early years; if he thought back to how difficult it was to keep all that nonsense in mind and exercise control over it; if he thought back to the distrust with which his patients, especially the adolescents, looked at him while he served up all that rubbish . . . If Leo merely thought back to it he felt sick to his stomach.

Leo still remembered the boy in whom he had diagnosed (or rather had pretended to diagnose) an abdominal infection that would be cleared up as quickly as possible with some medicine that was a *tiny bit* painful, administered intravenously. He was the same age as Semi today. Well, once during a visit, that child, seeing his parents a proper distance away, had whispered in Leo's ear, "Doctor, please, don't tell my mother I have cancer. She thinks I have an infection."

There: how long would such perverse hypocrisies still have been tolerated? The diagnosis was revealed to the patients. Although small, they had the right. Of course, along with the psychologists the doctor would learn how to treat each person as a separate case: between a child of six and an adolescent the differences are profound. The social background of the patients is a factor, as is the degree of culture. One can't treat them all the same way, it would be stupid even to presume it. Each patient is an individual. And each individual is a unique and inimitable treasure.

Leo had adhered to those principles, very Jewish, in truth,

when he declared war on the old directives and the old establishment. All in order to introduce this new practice into his department. And that was why, after doing so, he had made use of a team of psychologists, who guided him along that path designated "phases of communication of the diagnosis to pediatric-age oncology patients."

And, however ridiculous it might seem, perhaps because he had been caught unprepared or perhaps because he was flying ten kilometers above the cold and stormy sea of the Channel, Leo now found himself explaining the reasons for that battle, and the positive results of having won that battle, to his younger son. And that is, to one of the only two boys in the world to whom Leo had chosen not to tell things as they were. One of the only two boys whom Professor Pontecorvo had wanted to spare the weight of truth, taking refuge in the comfortable shell of a code of silence:

"Remember that the illness that Papa deals with is, thank goodness, very rare among children. There's no comparison with the number of adults who get sick. In my center there must be around sixty patients in all. In the center where Riccardo, Papa's friend, works, there must be at least a thousand patients. This gives me the opportunity, closed off to many of my colleagues, closed off to Riccardo, to deal with almost all my hospitalized patients personally and daily. I consider the opportunity to take care of them *personally and daily* an important fact. The secret of many remissions of the illness. This is what Papa is going to talk to his colleagues about tomorrow."

"Why?"

"To compare my results with results obtained by doctors all over the world is necessary for my work and for theirs. We call it 'cooperative study.' "

"What does 'cooperative' mean?"

"Well, 'cooperative' is the key word. It means that we are bound to cooperate, or rather, that it's right for us to do so."

"Yes, but what does it mean?"

"It means work together. I and my colleagues—Alfred, for example, and I—collaborate. It's impossible to do this work successfully without collaboration."

"And do your patients always want to know what they have?"

"That's a good question, Semi. Really a good question. Here, too, things are very complicated. Some patients want to know, some don't even understand what 'know' or 'not know' means. It depends on many things. But all in all that isn't so important."

"Then what is important?"

"It's important to set up a system—we call it a protocol—that helps us put ourselves, the parents of our patients, and, naturally, our patients in a situation to treat and be treated in the best possible way. And so we decided to separate the protocol into three phases. First of all we write down the diagnosis. We don't communicate it without first writing it down. Then we communicate it to the parents, and tell them what is the protocol that seems to us most appropriate in order to intervene in the most timely and effective manner."

"What does 'protocol' mean?"

"The treatments. The type of treatment that the patient will have to undergo. Then we tell the parents the probabilities of success of that type of therapy for that type of pathology. At the end of the talk with the parents we let them know that we are also going to communicate the diagnosis to their child. And this, I assure you, is one of the most difficult moments. It's almost worse than when you tell the parents that their child is sick. It's as if all the rage and despair that up to that point they have managed to control exploded at once. Sometimes with a terrible ferocity. Every so often it even happens that someone will tell you that you mustn't dare, you don't have the right, they call you a torturer, a Mengele."

"Who is Mengele?"

"Mengele was a Nazi."

"What's a Nazi?"

On the Nazi question, too, the Pontecorvo spouses had entered into a conspiracy of silence. After all, there was plenty of time to teach their children the risks run on this strange planet just owing to the fact of their being Jews.

"Too many irons in the fire. Who the Nazis are I'll tell you another time. I was talking about the reaction of some parents."

"Oh yes, the reaction of the parents."

"It can be truly violent. And that's where the psychologists come in. They get the job of making the parents understand why it's right, both on the ethical and on the therapeutic level, that their children be informed about what they have and what the risks are."

"And do they always manage to convince them?"

"I would say yes. They have great persuasive abilities. And at this point the third phase begins. When the small delegation—made up of me, the staff of psychologists, and the parents—goes to the child. And I can tell you that paradoxically that is the simplest phase, because the child is usually receptive. Because, unlike the parents, he wants to know. Because, in spite of the parents, he is still habituated to accepting the misfortunes that befall him. When the children are very small they don't understand precisely what you're saying, and after a while they're distracted and they stop listening. Adolescents on the other hand cry. For the most part they cry."

"And what do you tell them to make them cry?"

"I tell them that we've found some sick cells, let's say, in the abdomen. That there's the danger that these bad cells will persuade other cells to mutiny against the body. And that to ward off that possiblity it's necessary to do this, that, and the other. Of course, we don't do it so brutally, the way I'm telling you. We say it as we go along. The first time we tell them one thing.

The second another. And so on. We tell them that we are available, that they can ask us whatever they want, and we will answer all their questions."

"And then what happens?"

"It happens that the patient starts to trust you. He knows that you won't deceive him. Basically he expects that he has something serious. With all the tests we've done, all the worry that his parents, willy-nilly, have lavished on him in recent weeks . . . well, now they demand some sincerity. They have the right to sincerity."

"But why tell them no matter what?"

"Partly the fact that statistics show us that the treatment is much more effective in a patient who is aware than in a patient who isn't aware. And then, besides, there's a question of principles. Each of us has the right to know what might happen to us. Just to use a stupid example: if, after all you've just eaten, you had spinach in your teeth, would you want Papa to tell you or would you want everyone to see it and laugh at you without your knowing why they're laughing?"

"I'd want you to tell me."

"There, it's the same thing. Once you've told someone it sends the message that you don't talk a lot of rubbish. That he can trust you. That between you exists a relationship of collaboration. Even when we administer a certain drug we say what the effects are. We say, 'This might give you a stomach ache . . . this might give you some annoying blisters in your mouth . . . ' and so on."

With what eloquence Leo told these things to his son. And with what intensity. The eloquence and intensity of a man who put work above every other thing, even above a family so loved and so lovable. Maybe because the contentment Leo felt when he was working wasn't threatened by the unpleasant uncertainties that sometimes gripped him at home.

In his pediatric-oncology unit Professor Pontecorvo never hesitated, never missed the target, managed to be concise and effective. In any case, the expression "his department" should be taken literally. Not only because Leo, with the authoritative support of his teacher, Professor Meyer, had helped to found that department but because at only thirty-nine he had become its head. He had been a very young head doctor. An enterprising and strong-willed head doctor. A doctor who never delegated but preferred to get his hands dirty. Who didn't spare himself, didn't put up insuperable barriers: available to patients twenty-four hours out of twenty-four.

It should be said that this dedication to work had been fostered by Rachel's acquiescent attitude. She certainly wasn't the type of wife who sits around complaining about her absent husband, her husband who works too much and thinks only of his career. And not so much because she nourished specific ambitions regarding Leo's profession but because she was a disciple of the religion of work inculcated by her father: a man's work is sacred. The duty of a woman, a good wife, is to relieve her husband, as far as possible, from every responsibility not strictly tied to work. A husband is not supposed to change diapers, take the children to school, help them with their math homework. A husband shouldn't think of anything but work. And his family should behave in a way that guarantees him the right to that virtuous selfishness.

Rachel knew this very well, having learned it in the field, for, when her mother and sister died, she had become, so to speak, a kind of putative wife for her father. Then what she had been imbued with became law: her job as a daughter (made unexpectedly an "only daughter" by tragedy) was to relieve her father of any extra burden. There were days when, because of a pressing order for an important client, Signor Spizzichino remained in the factory until late. Well, in such circumstances he didn't even worry about telephoning his daughter. She, on the other hand, found nothing better than to sit in the kitchen and wait for him: the pasta water boiling, the sauce ready, the plates face down, and in the air an odor of loving fatalism.

The same that was breathed in the Pontecorvos' beautiful villa some years later, on the evenings when Rachel waited for Leo to come home from the hospital. She had fed the boys and put them to bed. Then, at a certain point, she sent the maid to bed, too. Refraining, in the meantime, from putting in her mouth even a single piece of bread (a matter of principle). So it happened, at least five or six times a month, that the Pontecorvos found themselves eating alone in the kitchen at one in the morning. Leo was silent, Rachel buzzed around, no less silent, fiddling with ladles and steaming soup bowls.

But not only: in the early years of marriage, Rachel had struggled to reform her husband's habit of waking up late in the morning. The rules of the perfect worker, in fact, obliged a man with Leo's responsibilities to arrive first in the hospital and leave last. That's how a boss behaves. That's how a chief exercises control over his underlings and, at the same time, serves as an example.

It was this attitude of Rachel's, in short, that had allowed Leo to devote maniacal attention to his unit, ever since its founding. And keep in mind the fact that for Leo the treatment of the sick person began the moment he crossed the threshold of the hospital: there was no decision, even the most apparently marginal, about which he did not feel authorized to have his say. Beginning with the furnishing of the interiors. The colors of the walls and the floor. No clowns. No bright colors. No parodically infantile wallpaper. We're not exactly in Disneyland.

What he wanted was a luminous, sober atmosphere. Orderly and hospitable. Where parents and children would feel calm. And which, besides, wouldn't encourage the deviant illusion that a pleasant trip to the country awaited them there.

Leo had fought to have the three big communicating rooms intended for chemotherapy face the hospital's only available bit of garden. Olives, weeping willows, magnolias: this was what the children had the right to contemplate while you were poisoning them.

Another of Leo's fixations was odors.

"Hospital smells are strictly forbidden here," he repeated endlessly to nurses, orderlies, cleaners. The stink of disinfectant, boiled chicken, cooked apple: that was what Leo meant by "hospital smells." There was trouble if, entering the unit in the morning, he caught in the air that depressing, deathly odor. The quietest man in the world flew off the handle. Losing his temper in a way that might seem incredible to those who were used to seeing him in another context. In his unit Leo was a despot. A Swiss. He gave in to the vice of nitpicking and made no allowances for anyone. He didn't tolerate meddling, imprecision, or any form of negligence. He had fought with the administration, with the union, with the entropy of the Roman hospital system in order to have control over the hiring of the paramedical staff, and to regulate the turnover (Leo knew that it's difficult to tolerate a job like this for long without going mad or growing cynical). The proverbial gentleness with which he habitually treated his underlings was redressed by the ferocity with which he addressed them when they got up to "one of their tricks." Leo would have liked to oblige the whole staff to have a military haircut, a crew cut. Not being able to impose that, he had managed to introduce coifs. And not for hygienic reasons but in a spirit of human solidarity. It was already a gigantic trauma, above all for girls, to lose their hair: all they needed was to be mocked by the pyrotechnic hairstyle of some inexperienced nurse.

In short, Leo's lack of interest in bureaucratic questions found no correspondence in the practical organization of his department, which was, to say the least, inflexible. As if there existed two Leo Pontecorvos in the world: one sloppy and indecisive, the other resolute and precise to the point of being pedantic.

And this was only one of the contradictions.

In spite of that organizational intransigence and adminis-trative negligence, in fact, Leo, in the practice of the medical arts (as he loved to call them), gave evidence of an unprece-dented flexibility and a wonderful eclecticism. Hostile to any therapeutic fundamentalism, he had no position to defend but adjusted to situations like a chameleon. He had assimilated well the lesson of his Parisian apprenticeship: cancer is a dis-ease different from all others; it's not an external agent that attacks the body but a part of the body itself—a rebellious, self-destructive part, a family member who has decided to kill himself. Cancer is not a part of us. Cancer is us. And that's why every single cancer of every single individual deserves a spe-cific treatment. Because there is one for every organism. For this reason it's up to the protocols of treatment to adapt to the patient and not vice versa.

When Leo saw that a boy could no longer tolerate a ther-apy, he did all he could to change it or to relieve it. When he saw a girl devastated by aplastic anemia, one of the most hor-rendous effects of the chemotherapy, he gave her a few weeks' respite. He waited for the bone marrow to start functioning normally, to produce the number of white cells that the immune system needed. Because Professor Pontecorvo never forgot even for a second that the most effective treatments devised by man against cancer—that is, chemotherapy and radiation—are, each in a different way, extremely harmful poi-sons. To be maneuvered with the mastery of an alchemist.

And it was precisely the form of humanism that Leo applied to the treatment of cancer that had made him so sensitive, before many of his colleagues, to the psychological aspects. His unit was the first in Italy to be provided with a staff of psychologists. Leo had formed a special alliance with the coordinator of the staff, Loredana Soffici: she had initiated him into the mysteries of child psychology.

Tell the patients the truth. Make them responsible. Don't feed illusions. Make them participate in the struggle. At the same time, however, urge them to go on in the most normal way possible. These were the watchwords of Dr. Soffici. Leo shared with that woman the wish for patients to have the best chance to continue to live, play, and study. Among the latest toys that Leo bought for Filippo and Semi when he went abroad, one of them always slipped into the playroom on the unit. Which, in fact, instead of seeming like a cemetery for discarded toys from an orphange had the luxurious aspect of the room of a spoiled child.

Leo had extraordinary faith in Loredana. He liked to participate in seminars she organized for teachers in the school that the unit housed. He liked to hear her speak. He observed how her concise explanations were corroborated by the many years of experience he had in the field. Loredana encouraged young, frightened teachers to pay attention to every behavioral detail and not to underestimate anything. And that encouragement, even in its generic nature, seemed to Leo very intelligent.

"You have to understand that if a child is essentially talkative, a child subjected to this stress twenty-four hours a day can show a devastating talkativeness. And don't underestimate bitterness. Resentment. Anger. Don't underestimate envy. Envy of the sick for the well. You are well, they are sick. You will agree with me that this is an almost unnatural thing. An imbalance that is utterly unjust. And don't think that they aren't aware of that injustice. They are absolutely aware. And for that reason they might hate you. There is nothing more terrible than the bitterness of a sick person toward a healthy one. And it's worse at an age when the emotional sphere has unchallenged dominion over the rational. And yet, in spite of this, in spite of the persistent risk that some statement or attitude of yours might offend them or make them suffer, they deserve the truth. If a classmate can't come to school anymore, because he's very ill or because he hasn't made it, well, it makes no sense for you to lie about his fate. Don't feed ambiguity, don't tell lies. Know that they are more prepared to die than you are."

It was listening to this type of discourse that Leo had formed his convictions. It was through contact with a personality like Loredana Soffici, who was at the same time compassionate and intransigent, lucid and visionary, that Leo had understood the indispensability of communicating the diagnosis to the patient. And it was in the name of a spirit no less honest and fair-minded that he was now, on the flight to London, trying to explain to his second son why hypocrisy is as harmful as the cancer.

Then something strange happened. Just as the plane was starting its approach to Heathrow airport, just as the loudspeaker voice of the hostess politely ordered the passengers to return to their seats, put the tray tables and seatbacks in the upright position, and buckle their seat belts. Just then Semi, with an agitation that struck Leo profoundly, because it so little fit the character of that usually so transparent child, had asked his father, "So if I had something, if suddenly something happened to me, you would tell me? Right, Papa, you'd tell me?"

Confronted by the anguish communicated by the tone, even more than by his son's words, Leo was at a loss, undecided whether to answer sincerely or shift the whole conversation to a less demanding register. In the end, he took refuge again in the spinach example, saying,

"I swear that you have nothing between your teeth."

But this wasn't enough for Semi. Semi wouldn't let go. Semi continued, frightened, "Promise me, Papa, will you promise me?"

"What?" Leo asked, exasperated, and regretful that he had let himself get out of hand, initiating his son into some of the cruel secrets of his profession.

"That you'll tell me. That if something happens to me you'll tell me. Promise me, Papa, promise me?"

Leo, irritated by Semi's insistence, unable to look at him—his gaze turned to the looming London suburbs—had promised.

And it's of that promise, that agitation, that Leo is thinking now as he looks at Semi, no less agitated than that other time, helping his older brother, whose ankle he has just broken. Leo wonders if the boy, now fourteen, still asks so many questions. He hopes not. He hopes he doesn't do it anymore. He hopes with all his heart not to have become in the eyes of his son the most important question. The most insidious and disturbing. The one that will never have an answer.

Leo can barely breathe. It's what happens to our body when it is invaded by pity and guilt simultaneously.

On a Wednesday afternoon in early December of 1984, the three freezing-cold Pontecorvo males went through the revolving door of the Brownstone Hotel, welcomed at the entrance with a bow from a strange fellow in a green velvet uniform with tassels and gilded frogs, a comical cylinder on his head.

A small plaque at the entrance (black background, gold lettering) informed the guest that that old limestone building, in Belgravia, had been transformed into a hotel by Lord Byron's butler in the mid-nineteenth century. Leo had stayed there for the first time with his father, some thirty years earlier, and since then had devoutly chosen it as his London refuge. He loved the small, quiet lobby, the smell of toast and roasting coffee, the way the thick mauve carpet, the dark-brown wainscoting, the shining brass knobs, and the crackling fire in the rose marble hearth muffled the noise of the traffic.

Leo was glad to have his sons see him in a place like this, at the peak of his worldly capacities. If there was one thing that gave him pleasure it was to be admired by them. And in that old hotel he could show off in front of the intimidated kids all his worldly savoir-faire. Which consisted, for example, of being recognized by the comical bellboy who had greeted them in the lobby. And of the servile "Welcome, Mr. Pontecorvo!" addressed to him by the receptionist, a thin man with mustard-colored hair and cheeks reddened by a network of nearly bursting capillaries.

Then it was Leo's turn, his English all but impeccable, to rattle off the two or three sentences he had prepared for effect, to remind the receptionist, in an almost irritated tone, that Mr. Pontecorvo would like a piping-hot American coffee at six-thirty in the morning, a muffin, the *Corriere della Sera*, and the *Times*. And then, maintaining that inflection of annoyance in his voice, he asked his sons (and who knows why he did it in English) what they wanted for breakfast.

So far, it's all fun. But Leo had barely put the key in the door of the minisuite on the fourth floor when, overwhelmed by anxiety at having the children there without Rachel's assistance, he felt suddenly inadequate. Like a virgin husband on his wedding night.

Quite a few years had passed since Filippo was the principal problem of the Pontecorvo parents. That was the period when Leo had been closest to his sons, especially to Filippo but, by osmosis, also to his brother. Once Filippo was no longer an emergency, their relationship definitely changed. Became increasingly formal. Leo, besides, was at that stage of life when successful men sacrifice the family on the altar of their profession. His days were a paroxysm of engagements: hospital, office, university, conferences, articles in dailies and specialized journals . . . Little time remained for his children. Who in the meantime had found nothing better than to change themselves radically from year to year, exhibiting a Dadaist tenacity.

And now there they were, suddenly entering, without knocking and unknown to their father, adolescence. And was he realizing it only now, in a London hotel room? Who were these two human beings? What did he know about them? Beyond some biographical data and some completely external qualities, what did he know of these boys with whom he shared a last name, some dead relatives, and a genetic heritage? Filippo was an angelic thirteen-year-old with a small weight problem, he was drugged by comic books and animated cartoons, he wasn't a great athlete but a center with magnificent ball handling, he had low grades in school. Semi was eleven. He was exuberant, had a lot of friends, was precociously hedonistic. He was a whiz in school. Life for him was light, as his slender body was light.

This was what Leo knew of his sons; there were a lot of people who must know much more about them. And now here they were, two aliens to rediscover all at once.

Also on the physical plane things had changed. Leo had been a very physical father, especially with Filippo. When he was an infant Leo had loved holding him. He liked to tease him, touch his cheeks, caress his smooth, shapely little legs, stick his cold nose in the warm sweet-smelling hollow between neck and cheek. He liked to wake him, when he came home in the middle of the night from the hospital, where he had been called for an emergency, and amuse himself with that beautiful, warm, slightly reserved infant. But over time, naturally, that physical promiscuity had vanished. Leo was not a father who was kissed or who, in turn, kissed. Not that he didn't at times feel the desire to hug one of his sons. He had, however, intuited that they, as a matter of manly modesty, didn't enjoy it. So he avoided it.

The impression he had now, upon entering the minisuite of the Brownstone Hotel, was that his sons were disgustingly different from his natural expectations. There was something prickly in them that Leo, attached to the mental image of a fragrant infant softness, was noticing for the first time. Semi's voice was low and grating, like the voices of all boys at that stage of development. On Filippo's chin and jaws a wooly down had sprouted. Both their bodies released the brackish odor of organisms in full hormonal revolt.

So Leo, to keep nervousness at bay, took refuge in hyperactivity. He began to unpack the suitcases, ordering his sons to do the same with an almost despotic attitude. He showed them didactically how to restore a crease to one's trousers after taking them out of the suitcase (door of the bathroom closed, rush of hot water, steam, trousers hung on a hanger). Then, to waste time, he ordered a fattening snack from room service.

Finally, in order not to share with them even the wait for the food, he took off his clothes and filled the tub, after pouring in a thick emerald-colored bath gel, supplied by the hotel. And immersed himself up to the neck. But not even that relaxing soak relieved him from the agonizing thought of having to take care of them. In order not to hear what they were doing on the other side of the wall, Leo had let the hot water run and he stuck his head under it. There he could enjoy the heavy muffled sound of a waterfall, which still couldn't dislodge the mental image of his sons on the other side of the wall, timidly, silently, waiting for him.

But now, coming out of the bath, heated by aromatic vapors and wrapped in a terrycloth bathrobe with the gold hotel crest on the pocket, he saw them sitting on the bed in their underwear, quarreling over the remote. Leo said to himself with relief that maybe the change in his sons might have some positive aspects: for example, making them more autonomous than he had imagined. They didn't need him to live or to entertain themselves.

Finally the bell sounded.

A svelte Korean woman dressed like a nineteenth-century housekeeper, in apron and cap, pushed a cart into the room. With a theatrical gesture she raised the pewter cover under which shone, like doubloons in a treasure chest, half a dozen bulging club sandwiches drowning in a sea of French fries and lettuce. The tiny Oriental woman opened the bottles of Coca-Cola. Finally she brought the man in the bathrobe a leather case containing the receipt, which he signed with a distracted scribble.

A postprandial languor, combined with the stupor produced by the hot bath, definitely finished Leo off. He had barely put his head on the pillow when he felt weak. But still he couldn't let go as he would have liked. That sense of agitation persisted.

"Papa, can we order some cake?"

The voice of Samuel.

Why not, Leo thought. Get what you like.

"Papa, can we order some cake?" Samuel repeated. Leo opened his eyes. He smiled. And made a gesture of assent.

In the end, he thought, finally relaxed, Rachel's absence also has its advantages: without that tight-fisted woman I can teach these kids how to live.

"You can do what you like," he heard himself say, like Willy Wonka, welcoming the children into his very exclusive factory of sweets. The factory of sweets that Leo had available was London: a cold, iridescent, and ironic London, full of wares and every sort of delight: a city at its best that knew what it meant to celebrate Christmas. In that way everything changed. Rachel's absence turned from a disaster into a blessing. Here's what we'll do, Leo thought, we'll do what we feel like. What joy! What fun!

He began to fantasize about the four magnificent days that awaited them. Days when Leo would be able to relive with his sons what he had enjoyed with his wife years before: the joy of initiating those amateurs into the pleasures of the consumer culture.

But yet again Leo had been a far too optimistic prophet. And the strange fact is that what kept that long weekend from being memorable was the lovely and disturbing spectacle of the passionate bond that inextricably linked his sons. Leo had a taste of it that first night. After Filippo had called room service to order the cake, Leo heard Semi asking if he would keep his promise.

"What promise?"

"You said you would take us to see a musical."

"I told you," Leo replied, increasingly satisfied, "that we can do what we want."

So he sent Filippo to the concierge to reserve tickets to *Gentlemen Prefer Blondes* for that night. And then he took some papers out of his briefcase and sat down in a big red leather armchair.

Leo was sitting there in his white bathrobe in the red armchair, making some changes with a pencil to the next day's speech, when Semi asked him, "What's happened to Filippo?" in a voice that attempted to conceal an unconcealable anguish. At first Leo attributed his distress to worry that there were no tickets. And he had reassured him: "Don't worry, *Gentlemen Prefer Blondes* is there every night. If it's sold out tonight we have plenty of time. I promise that we'll find tickets somehow, even if I have to ask Alfred." But then out of the corner of his eye he observed that his words had in no way soothed Samuel, who had started walking from one end of the room to the other, like a father-to-be in the waiting room, tormented as he awaits the birth of his first child. Until Semi, taking courage, asked his father again what had happened to Filippo.

"I said I don't know! There must have been a line. He might have gone to the bar to get something to drink. He might have met a friend, the woman of his life . . . He might have gone for a walk."

"And not tell us?"

"Why should he? Your brother is almost grown up."

"Mamma always wants us to tell her."

Then Leo remembered a conversation he'd had some time earlier with Rachel, which he hadn't attached much importance to. She had said she was anxious about Semi's excessive apprehensiveness: "He's always worried, especially about his brother. Filippo just goes out for a moment and he gets anxious. He starts thinking of the most terrible things. The other evening he even woke him up in the middle of the night because he thought he was dead."

Was this the weak point of his happier child? The invisible crack in the nobler, more polished vase in his collection? Apprehension, the fear that things that had started off so well could end badly, the far from glorious anticipation of the most devastating tragic event . . .

While Leo remembered that conversation he'd had with Rachel, Filippo came in with his usual lazy walk. And Semi threw himself at him, bombarding him with questions, like a jealous wife who has waited all night for her husband's return.

"Why did it take you all that time?"

"So? What the fuck, faggot?"

Although Samuel seemed upset, you could sense in him also a maddening contentedness. It wasn't as if his brother were the sole survivor of an airplane crash. When Filippo got on the bed, Semi curled up next to him with the catlike action of a geisha. The mini suite had two king-size beds. Leo had gone to lie down on one (papers and pencil in hand), the other was for the boys.

Filippo was absorbed in reading a guide to London and his brother had begun to bother him. In an irritating manner that seemed a way of both settling his fear about Filippo's delay and celebrating the happiness of his return.

Then another odd thing.

"Can I smell your stomach?" Semi asked Filippo. And Leo wondered if he had heard right. Filippo, as if he were answering the most natural and usual of questions: "If you get me some ice for my Coke I'll let you smell my arm for five seconds, faggot."

And now? What was this nonsense, Leo wondered. His sons sniffed each other? Why? It seemed to him somewhat strange, bestial, or worse: something for homosexuals. Something he didn't like at all and yet accounted for their relationship, which also might be called physically unhealthy. Otherwise, why would Samuel have reacted so violently to a few minutes' delay on the part of his brother? And why were they so attached to one another? And above all: why in the world did they sniff each other? How could one blackmail the other with his own body odor?

Now that Leo saw his sons in action, without Rachel, without the proverbial sarcasm she employed with the boys, without her capacity to play things down, they seemed to him truly strange. And it irritated him quite a lot. No, he didn't like the strangeness of his sons. Come to think of it, he didn't like strangeness in general. In any of its forms. He had always been afraid of it. Originality is a good thing, of course, provided that it doesn't pass the danger point, provided that it doesn't spill over into eccentricity. Leo had always calibrated his own behavior on the level of a norm that aspired to exuberance and even excellence, yes, but shunned bizarreness. There is something so reassuring about conformity! There is something so natural in being simply what everyone wants to be and what everyone expects you to be. What need is there to provoke your neighbor? Why be strange, except to cover up some defect? Except to hide some ridiculous flaw?

Sometimes, during the years when Filippo was showing the first signs of his troubles, the petty notion had crossed his mind that it was a high price that genetics asked of him for mixing his blood with that of a woman from another milieu.

So now, after all that time, the words that his mother had addressed to him when he told her he wanted to marry Rachel returned to his mind: "You'll see!" Yes, she had said that. *You'll see!* A kind of curse, which Leo had thought about later, when his older son had had problems, and he thought of it again now, confronted by his sons' bizarre behavior. Is that what his mother meant when she told him he would find out? You, my son, who so detest strangeness, are committing yourself to it. And for this you will be buried by strangeness, surrounded by it day and night.

Leo was startled by the silvery sound of Semi's laughter; he was on the bed writhing under his brother, who had started tickling him. Leo's repugnance toward that scene became so profound and unbearable that, contrary to his usual habits, he raised his voice belligerently: "Stop, God damn it! I'm not amused."

Right afterward he felt a little mortified. Leo didn't like to scold his sons. He didn't like to scold anyone. He found the effect produced by his own high voice unpleasant and was the victim of a deep-rooted guilt complex.

That was why for the rest of the evening, having taken them to the musical at the Queen's Theatre, and then to eat at the Bombay Brasserie, Leo, besides trying to expel from his mind the sight of his sons engaged in those strange activities, had done his best to win back their good will. He observed with pleasure the rapture with which Semi had enjoyed *Gentlemen Prefer Blondes*, not for an instant taking his eyes off Olivia Newton-John in the role of Lorelei Lee—in Leo's time played by Marilyn Monroe. He missed not a single word, a single note, a single step of those actors, singers, and dancers. Ecstatic. Tapping his foot in time with the music. At the end of the show he was the first to jump to his feet and the last to stop clapping, the palms of his hands red and his eyes sparkling. On the way to the restaurant he wouldn't stop humming "Bye Bye Baby", a truly irritating melody from the musical, and—with his head lowered to read and reread the list of songs on the cassette that he had made his father buy him—had been in danger of walking into a light pole.

If Filippo's reaction to the musical was much cooler than his brother's, his enthusiasm for tandoori chicken was not— it was so overwhelming that he ordered an extra portion, after polishing off of the first with a dozen solid forkfuls.

In short, everything seemed to have returned to normal. Leo had gone back to being the conscientious and brilliant parent who never shouts and they two privileged boys, on the threshold of adolescence, enjoying the advantages placed at their disposal by an adored and munificent father.

But at bedtime the atmosphere was again spoiled.

The older of his sons still had the habit of going to sleep every night with the headphones of his Walkman over his ears, listening to the same anachronistic music and running through his nighttime ritual. It was something he couldn't do without. For that reason Leo, after turning out the light and saying goodnight, had said nothing when he heard that bothersome sound, which meant that Filippo was beating his head against the pillow.

He began to get annoyed only when he realized that Samuel, driven by an incomprehensible spirit of imitation, was following him. There they were, his sons, who, instead of sleeping, were butting their heads in unison, making the bed squeak like two bloody fags going at it. One does it because he can't do without it. The other because of an insane instinct for imitation. And Leo couldn't really decide which was worse, all he knew was that he couldn't stand it. But he also knew that he had to control himself. He had no wish to reproach them again. So, in order not to hear it, first he put his hands on his ears. Then he put his head under the pillow, then he took refuge in the bathroom. Then he went back to bed. Until he realized that what irritated him was not the noise produced by his sons but what that noise implied. It wasn't enough not to hear them: he wanted them to stop being strange. This was what drove him to intervene. He turned on the lamp. He got up. And he shouted: "Will you stop it, God damn it! Anyone would think you were insane!"

While it couldn't have been so hard for Samuel to stop doing what he didn't do naturally, for Filippo it must have been torture. And yet, from then to the end of the vacation, not even once had he done it again. He lay there motionless. Surely he struggled to fall asleep. Without a doubt he was overwhelmed by his anxieties.

But he wasn't the only one who had a terrible night: Leo was tortured by a sense of guilt. All the things that psychologists, tutors, teachers, professors, speech therapists had told him not to do ever since Filippo was born he had done that night. He had prevented him from expressing himself. He had humiliated him. He had emphasized his strangeness. He had given it a name. And he had let him know how much he was repulsed by it.

But now it was too late to recover. If that first evening Leo had been so bothered by the fact that Filippo indulged in his grotesque rituals, on the following nights he was tormented by the idea that his son was doing everything possible not to give in to them. He would have liked to say to Filippo "Come, sweetie, it's not important. Start again where you broke off." But how could he? It would only make matters worse.

And so the weekend that Leo would have liked his boys to archive in the box of "memorable memories" was catalogued instead under large or small "missed opportunities." The rest of the little vacation was besieged by the dark sky of ill humor. Filippo's sleepless nights could be seen in his face, just like the mute rancor that took the form of a respectful demeanor and an ostentatious lack of enthusiasm. Maybe it was all that he had suffered, maybe his character, but that boy knew how to be hard and obstinate! O.K.—he seemed to say to his father— I will not act like a clown at night but during the day you will have beside you a statue of salt. And God knew that Leo was bitterly learning his lesson.

Since then many things had happened: Anzère, the first charges, Camilla's torture, the scandalous public disgrace, the definitive break with his family, prison, the trial, that cock-roach-like seclusion . . . Was it possible that only now did Leo think back to those days, to how he hadn't been able to seduce his sons as he would have liked, to how he had done everything wrong? Possible that only now he thought back to the irritation produced in him by the spectacle of their pathological behavior? Seeing them sniff each other, beat their heads against the pillows to fall asleep, how difficult it was to make them happy and how easy it was to upset them.

It must have been Filippo's accident that provoked the memory of London and all that it meant. Now that he saw his sons there, a few dozen meters from him, in the midst of yet another crisis, yet another trauma: the older with that leg dan-gling and the younger frightened by his brother's pain, not to mention, surely, full of guilt for having caused it.

The burning memory of those days in London—and of his indecisiveness then—was urging him to action. Finally some action, after so many months of ineptitude. He was ready, in short: about to go out. To go and save them. He had an absolute desire to. But, just as he was about to take the first step (the most difficult), Rachel emerged. The moment she knelt down, bending over Filippo's leg with the knowledge of one who has a degree in medicine, Leo finally saw her face. He realized that, between one thing and another, it was almost a year since he had seen her face. She appeared beautiful, just like his boys.

No, he would not spoil all that beauty (a mother rescuing her son) with the ugliness that he represented. No, he wouldn't do it. The last opportunity offered by the Heavenly Father to try to rejoin his family was destroyed in a few seconds. With Rachel lifting up Filippo, who was whimpering with pain, and Samuel asking with an insistence not unknown to Leo, "Right, Mamma, everything's all right?"

This was the last drawing to arrive. Exactly like all the others, it was slipped under the door. Imperceptibly.

By now we know Leo well enough to imagine how the sight of a drawing like this would upset and infuriate him. Whoever had conceived and executed it—after conceiving and executing all the others—had really screwed up. Dragging into that perverse game those whom Leo would have wished to leave out: it was the first time they had dared to depict his family. How to interpret that sudden involvement? A prelude to further developments? A change of perspective and ambition? A warning? An intimidation? Tired of killing him, were they now raising the stakes, threatening what Leo loved most?

Yes, what he loved most. Although at this point Leo had the right not to, it was nevertheless impossible for him not to love Rachel, Fili, and Semi, to damnation if necessary. Leo Pontecorvo wasn't a resentful or vengeful man. This particular nuance of his character leads me to say that, confronted by this drawing, he would react badly. Maybe he would be furious. Maybe he would even find the strength to leave his cover and take possession of his life. On the other hand I can only make hypotheses: through a concatenation of circumstances, in fact, the sight of this drawing was spared him; our recluse could not evaluate it with the care with which he had evaluated all the others.

Although I have been careful up to here to distribute these drawings in an illustrative way throughout the narrative, it has to be said that, with the sole exception of the last, the others reached Leo in no order and with no respect for chronology. The one of the panty liner abandoned in the bathroom in the mountains was the first, delivered a few days after he came out of prison. Followed, at a distance of a few weeks, by the one that showed him fleeing on the stairs, all out of breath. But this is not, I realize, the most disconcerting fact of the matter. What had begun to undermine Leo's faith in the sharpness of his own mental faculties was the impression that he had unknowingly posed as a model for an invisible cartoonist.

Was something or someone spying on him? Something or someone keeping an eye on him? A silent witness of the climactic moments in the course of his human degeneration, of his social decapitation? A presence that wished to make him understand that it was the only thing in his life now that would never fail?

From the start, the drawings and their mysterious maker had frightened Leo the way all things that don't make sense are frightening. But, with the passing of weeks and months, he had ended up accepting serenely the idea of that presence around him. Sometimes he had even tried to consult it. Other times he had had the temptation to strike a pose for it. Even though Leo immediately understood that drawing him in a pose did not interest it. The only subject that interested it was his model in a state of anxiety. There was no drawing that could not have been titled "Embarrassment."

Even though that presence might not be so mendacious and so derisory as he had naturally been led to believe. Maybe it was the only resource that remained to him. When the drawing that showed his mother and father's visit to the prison arrived, Leo had really reached the point of wondering—a little touched and a little anguished—if one of his parents was the cartoonist in the shadows.

Many times Leo wondered if he did not owe to that presence the evening meal that kept him alive. And, on the other hand, it was impossible not to wonder if it had been the one to trigger the alarm that had tortured him for a whole night. Was it that alarm? Was it calling for some attention? And what about the graffito of the hanged man on the wall that had greeted his return from jail? Could that, too, though the style was definitely different, be attributed to the same hand?

In any case, just as that last drawing was sliding silently under the door, Leo's nostrils, still possessed by a tormented half-sleep, had been tickled by the overwhelming smell of coffee.

And it was as if something inside him had exploded in a flash of incongruous welcome. Maybe because it was a long time since the fragrance of coffee had visited him. Probably because Rachel and the boys had been on vacation, as if it were any ordinary August. And now, at the end of that ordinary August, they had reappeared: returning to occupy the domestic spaces with a carelessness that bordered on impudence, without worrying about slamming the car door, calling Telma in a loud voice, walking or even running over the head of the reclusive and undesirable tenant, weakened (this they could not know, but, if nothing else, they might have imagined it) by weeks of a tropical heat that in the city had claimed a lot of victims.

In short, if the darkness had restored silence, the light of dawn had brought back the smell of coffee. Causing Leo's organism to rejoice in well-being. A delight that not even opening his eyes to the same anguishing ceiling could dissipate. Rather, in order not to let that small morning gift escape, Leo had closed them again, and, clutching the pillow with the passion of a teenager in love, went back to sleep.

The smell of coffee speaks to you so affectionately of your whole life. For years it heralded the end of nocturnal hostilities, the return of Mamma into your life after hours of insomnia. At that hour of the morning, perhaps because of her déshabillé or her lack of makeup, the angular wrinkled beauty of your mother had something Lebanese about it. That was your mother, the mother you loved, the mother who on June mornings, when you came into the kitchen, was already sitting at the table, in the middle of which sat enthroned, like an idol of antiquity, a large blackened coffeepot, resistant, having survived the siege of flames for years. From it, from that statue with its incomparable shape, from that masterpiece of Italian design, came the biting yet soft odor of the morning: life that opens up and starts hurrying along again. A streaming sensation, kindled by the drink that at the time was forbidden. And that the years would transform into the fuel needed for your every activity.

Getting up at an ungodly hour to be present at the anatomy lessons that Professor Antinori held at six in the morning.

"This is the time when medical examiners work. This is the hour of the pathologist. The hour when vampires and werewolves go to bed and we get going!" that madman said, sticking his hands into the thoracic cavity of Mickey. This was the name the third-year students gave the corpses they diligently dissected, as if it were always the same one. An old cadaver, the legend went, available to the institutes of pathology and forensic medicine from time immemorial. Dear old Mickey had a long history. It was said that he was one of the numerous legacies of the last war. Whatever had happened, now it was the property of that sadistic son of a bitch Professor Antinori, whose preferred sport seemed to consist in shocking the first-year students by confronting them with that viscous, repulsive mystery of life and death called Mickey. It seemed to have been an Italian-American student who saddled it with the affectionate nickname Mickey. Because it resembled an uncle of his in Queens. Uncle Mickey.

Now you recall the taste you had in your mouth before entering the kingdom of Antinori and Uncle Mickey. Coffee. From the university bar, in the entrance hall with its solemn Fascist architecture, almost completely empty at that hour of the morning. A dirty, oily coffee, with an aftertaste of shit, but effective precisely by virtue of its distastefulness.

Completely unlike the delicious coffee that characterized your married life. One of the demands of the young, fascinating, faithful husband had to do with the quality of the coffee. On that Rachel was not to skimp. The most precious Arabicas, the finest roasting. And especially the freshness. You had to buy it every week if you wanted it always fresh and fragrant.

That coffee, so aromatic, speaks to you of Sundays: yes, Sundays, when you don't go to work. You're in bed and you hear from a distance the squawking of the boys. Rachel is running their bath. And they can only give vent to childish protests. Filippo is five, Semi three. Rachel puts them in the tub together. It's the only day of the week when you let someone enter your bathroom. That imperial bath, which you had made in your image and likeness when the villa was built: white majolica, smell of lavender, large towels of rust-colored linen, and the tub in the middle, immense and round as if it belonged to a Roman proconsul. It's there, in that little pool, that Rachel sticks Filippo and Semi for their Sunday ablutions. They always make a fuss about getting in, but, once they're in, it's almost impossible to get them out. They wallow about in your tub while you wallow in a soft, savory half-sleep.

But now that odor pierces you, that odor gives you a charge. Rachel is approaching with the coffee tray. You feel your temples jolt, a slight shock between the shoulder blades, and your warm mouth flooded with saliva. It's like a Pavlovian reflex. The drug arrives: aromatic caffeine diluted in water. Here, too, the scene is repeated every time in a delightfully unchangeable way. Rachel arrives with the tray, accompanied by a frowning Filippo, his skin pink from the steam of the hot water he has just emerged from, in his blue junior-size terrycloth bathrobe.

"Leo, Semi wanted to come with us to bring you your coffee. But we can't find him. He must have disappeared . . . "

Rachel's words, always the same. Naturally Semi is right behind her. Perfectly visible: the only one who thinks he can't be seen. All that ingenuousness is a prerogative of his three years. That's why you stay in the game. With the scant breath you have in your throat you start calling his name as if you were really worried: "Semi, Semi, where are you? Where has that child gotten to?"

But he doesn't answer, even though you hear him laughing with joy. "Filippo, have you seen Semi?" Filippo gives you a complicit smile, as if to say, "You and I know where he is, but he likes to think he can't be seen, let's let him think . . . " And now Semi, overcoming the obstacle represented by his mother's legs, hurls himself onto the bed, still wet. And Filippo jumps up after him.

"Don't get Papa wet. Come, let him have his coffee in peace."

Your sons are in your bed, they don't dare embrace you or even touch you, they're exploding with energy, they're soaking Rachel's part of the bed. The room is still bathed in a blue-tinted yellow half-light. Rachel places the tray on the night table, lights the lamp. You know, she can't stand darkness. If it was up to her the house would always be lighted.

"No, sweetheart, please, the lamp, no. Open the blinds if you want, but not the lamp."

Finally the coffee. The children have climbed off the bed and gone around it, now they're at the night table. They quarrel over who puts the single spoonful of sugar you need. The quarrel is too noisy for your taste, you're about to lose patience. Thank heaven Rachel intervenes. "So: Filippo puts the sugar in and you, Semi, stir. All right?"

All right. That's what they do. Until Rachel speaks again.

"Come, Semi, that's fine. Don't stir it too much or it will get cold."

You have the cup in one hand and with the other you hold the saucer. You're about to bring the drink to your lips. Fili and Semi have again occupied Rachel's part of the bed and they are scuffling. Rachel with a gentle shove of her hip has let you know that she wants to sit next to you. You move enough so that she has room. Now the coffee, really. It's not very good. It's a little cold, a burned taste on the palate.

But it's your life. Like this bed. It's your life, your whole life.

Suddenly Leo discovers, without even giving it a name, what intensity nostalgia can reach. An infinite and primordial whiff of vitality. Leo wants everything, desires everything. He would like his children to be small again, even smaller. The scene changes: now it's not Sunday morning, now it's Friday night, it's very late, it's winter. The light has vanished, outside a storm is raging. The light from the lightning that pierces the large windows of the villa has transformed it into the set of some second-rate horror film. You're in bed and you know it's only a matter of time. Here they are, in fact. One behind the other, Filippo and Semi do their best to hide their fear. Without even asking they get into the bed, between you and Rachel. They are sweetly and irresistibly annoying. They fall asleep again almost immediately. And after a few minutes there they are, languid, gilded, their breath regular . . .

All of that is gone forever. To utter, if internally, in a semi-conscious state, that forbidden word, "forever," fills him with agitation. Something that has the taste of happiness and also of despair. Something he dares not give a name to. The strange sensation is that the big bed he is imagining—his marital bed, the one that from a spatial point of view is just a floor away from him, and from the temporal seems to him set in a different geological era—is widening.

On the bed now are not only his little sons but himself, too, as a child. Spoiled, coddled, beloved child of the forties. All his mother does is take care of him. She never leaves him when it's night. She watches over him, waiting until her Leo is asleep. That bed now is enormous. It holds his whole family, his whole history, his whole tragedy. Generations and generations of Pontecorvos. Leo's eyes are shining, he feels so congested he can hardly breathe. He would like to go upstairs to his sons and Rachel, ask them to make peace, to find understanding. He would like to shout at them, "This is happiness. You can't give happiness a slap in the face. Happiness is everything. I know. Now I know, I've learned. Too late, but I know it."

Now he also understands what that presence is that has obsessed him for days. That presence that never deserts him. It's God. Because there has to be a God. The last infernal year of his life is God. The abandonment in which he has lived. The progressive neglect. The crimes they have charged him with. The betrayal. Camilla. All this has a name. The name is God. All the terrible, frightening things that have happened sanction the hypothesis of God.

The coffee, the smell of coffee, is God.

See how Leo, who has never managed to be alone, who has always lived under a protector, see how he can't die alone. He doesn't have the guts. God is with him just as his mother was always with him, and as Rachel was. Now that the two women of his life have left him alone, to rot there, he needs something else. He can't believe that men can live in such silence. That men can live without being constantly thought of and cared for. This solitude is inconceivable. So it is that God slips into the cellar of the Pontecorvo house, with all his quiet porcelain light. God is a Great Mamma. God is a Great Wife.

And so it is that Leo dreams of dying. And while he dreams of dying he is pervaded by the smell of coffee. Wrapped up in the covers on a big imaginary bed. The most garish of shrouds.

Too bad that none of that can neutralize the painful embarrassment, which, to judge from its density, not even that dream of death and peace will totally dissipate. Too bad that not even in his dream has Leo learned the most important lesson: that there exists no lesson to learn.

A sound not unlike that of a distant alarm clock slipped into a stormy half-sleep that, for reasons of narrative coherence, our dream transforms into the sound of a bell or of dogs barking in response.

Immediately after he opened his eyes the sound became clearer and, so to speak, more imminent. It was the telephone. His private number. As far as Leo knew, it could be the tenth ring. Standing up, he felt an intense nausea: as if he had just gotten off a roller coaster. He stumbled to the desk. Incredulous that someone could still be looking for him, that someone could still be interested in speaking to him, he lifted the receiver and asked, "Who is it?," warily and in a voice that to his ears sounded grim, as if it were coming from beyond the tomb.

"Professor Pontecorvo, it's me! Luca. Little Luca. Luchino."

"Luchino?"

"Professor, don't tell me you don't remember? Luca, Luchino, I call you every year. Same day. The twenty-eighth of August. The day when . . . "

"Ah, yes, Luchino."

Ah, yes, Luchino. Luchino what? Luchino, enough. That Luchino. Who for years now, every August 28th, wherever he was, had telephoned Leo Pontecorvo to repeat his gratitude. Luchino was animated by the best intentions. He thought he was being polite by calling every year and extremely conscientious and frank in doing it at the same time. He thought it pleased Leo. Or maybe not: as with all persistent individuals the only pleasure that interested him was his own. And if there was something that made him happy it was to pick up the phone, every August 28th, at exactly eight-thirty, and call the doctor who had saved his life.

An osteosarcoma, if Leo remembered correctly, the most lethal kind, which had attacked Luchino's right leg, when he was barely older than fifteen. Leo's diagnosis was implacable: maybe we'll save the boy, certainly not the leg. At that time people were pretty blunt. At that time the surgeons blissfully amputated everything that came within reach.

Leo was wrong. The optimist Leo had committed the sin of pessimism. After exhaustive treatment, afer an extraordinarily conservative surgery performed by Professor Ricciardi, Luchino had emerged from the nightmare. Of course, he limped slightly, and was condemned to use a cane for the rest of his life—which had forced him to forget the idea of being a hundred-meter specialist—but anyway alive and kicking, recovered.

Luchino since then had not ceased to call every twenty-eighth of August: that was the day he had been released from Professor Pontecorvo's unit.

Not that Leo remembered it. Luchino took care of remembering it. He wished to show his Savior (as he liked to call him) how eternal his gratitude was and how happy he was to still be here. Among us. Ah, and, by the way, he wanted the Savior to know that since then his life had been wonderful. That he had learned to enjoy even the most insignificant moment. That he would so much like him to meet his two children. Also because in a certain sense those children were also yours. How his? Whose? Yours, professor. Yours, the Savior's. Luchino was bringing up the two kids in the cult of the Savior. "You know what they call you, professor? Uncle Savior. With respect, of course. With the greatest respect. Do you mind if they call you Uncle Savior?"

That obscene display of sentimentality, seasoned with revolting banalities, had been renewed every August 28th, at more or less eight-thirty in the morning, for almost fifteen years now, and, besides producing in Leo an annoyance that bordered on repugnance, put to an increasingly harder test his patience and the foundations on which rested the edifice of the impeccable upbringing he had had. Such that his treatment of Luchino—a cold compound of impatience and aversion—at every new recurrence became testier. But his rudeness, far from discouraging Luchino, seemed to have the effect of making him more irksome and insistent. Every year the same old story. Every year the same invitation repeated in almost the same words:

"Why don't you come see us, Professor? With your missus, of course. At our house. In the country. A small house. Very small. Nothing much. Nothing luxurious. But a happy house, full of honest folk. It's cool here, not like in the city, where you're still dying of heat. We have good wine, the real thing. My wife is an extraordinary cook. And she would so much like to meet you. Not to speak of my children. For my children, professor, you are God."

Leo, rather awkward in his refusals, always had trouble declining, inventing clumsy excuses. Unable to conceal the irritation that the mellifluous voice of Luchino provoked in him. It's that he was so antipathetic. His collection of pedestrian clichés and his bucolic little family were intolerable. The affectation of modesty. The rhetoric about simple things. The country culture. Holy God, Leo would have liked to shout. He hung up the phone every time breathless with anger. And every time he had to absorb Rachel's mockery, as she, naturally, had taken Luchino under her protective wing.

"You made it! You managed to say no yet again. What did you think up this time?"

"Forget it. This year he was more insistent than usual, he is refining his techniques of persuasion. He must have taken classes in rhetoric. Very likely by correspondence course."

"Yes, certainly, by correspondence course. Because he can't afford regular studies. Because he can't go and study at the Sorbonne, like our professor."

"What do you mean by that? I didn't study at the Sorbonne."

"You know perfectly well what I mean. It's your weak point. Anything that even seems pathetic disgusts you. You with your grand democratic airs, you fill your mouth with words like 'tolerance,' 'liberalism,' but you never stop being the same old snob. You're the son of your mother. A class snob. The only difference is that she at least didn't give a damn about hiding it."

"You're wrong. You're being unfair. I don't feel any perfunctory hatred, any class hatred toward anyone, least of all that slimy worm."

"Slimy worm? And that's not class prejudice?"

"No, it's not class prejudice. It's a judgment based on the merits, on the comparative study of at least a dozen conversations with that man. He's an impossible man. Not to mention his parents."

Luchino's parents, that is. Worthy of him: a concentrate of rudeness and invasiveness. Leo certainly hadn't forgotten their "little flowers for Padre Pio." How could he? All they did was talk about them.

"Just think," Luchino's mother had said to him once, "since our son has been sick my husband hasn't drunk a drop of wine. Not even at dinner. A little flower for Padre Pio."

How could all this not disgust our diehard scientist? Hardly class prejudice. Leo detested that type of person. No less than he detested saints and saintly offerings. Leo would have bet his entire fortune on the fact that Luchino's parents were anti-Semitic. They had all the requirements. That obsessive recourse to religion. The obscene devotion to certain solid superstitions. Such an opportunistic religious fervor. Was this really their idea of God? Is this really how they wished to bargain with him? By not drinking wine? Lord of Heaven, I swear to you, I'll give up my glass and in exchange you'll be merciful. Is that what they thought? If Leo had been God he would have happily responded, "I don't give a damn about your alcohol. Kill yourself with alcohol. Why should it matter to me?"

Unfortunately, God wasn't the only beneficiary of the offerings of Luchino's parents. There were also gifts from nature that they brought every day to the doctor of their only son to ingratiate themselves: sausages, milk and cheese, mushrooms, eggs, bottles of cheap wine. They had transformed his unit into a market, by God. Once, although politely, he had reproached them. This is not how to behave in a hospital. It makes no sense to show up in a place like this with so many provisions! For a while Leo had the illusion that they had assimilated his little lesson. At least until he began to receive all those good things at home. How the hell had they gotten his address? How could they have the nerve?

In recent years Rachel had intercepted those phone calls. It was characteristic of her to relieve Leo from the more irritating responsibilities. At the beginning of every year, when she did her so-called "change of datebook" (an important rite for her), one of the first appointments she entered was the one for Luchino and the momentous twenty-eighth of August. A pointless scruple: there was no need to consult the date book to know that when, at eight-thirty in the morning on the fateful day, she answered the telephone, on the line was Luchino. And who else if not? Rachel treated him with much more patience and politeness than her husband had ever managed. She let Luchino talk, vent all his enthusiasm in celebrating Leo's greatness. Then Rachel answered a few specific questions about the life of the Savior. And finally she asked Luchino how his children were—the boy and the girl—of whom naturally she remembered the names and ages. And, after declining the *nth* invitation on her husband's account (unfortunately he was away at a conference abroad or called to an emergency at the hospital), she got rid of the irritant with great style.

"Luchino? How did you get this number?" The only question Leo managed to articulate: the clumsy, convoluted tongue and palate of a Frenchman who has to express himself in English.

"Your missus gave it to me." Yes, Luchino was the type who used antiquated expressions like "your missus." But certainly it wasn't that obsolete lexical choice that punched Leo in the chest, so that it was all he could do not to retch.

"Yes, professor, two minutes ago."

Leo thus had proof that Rachel had returned. And that the aroma of coffee that had triggered his grandiose metaphysical delirium wasn't (that, at least) a dream.

"Two minutes ago," Luchino had said. Which meant that at least until two minutes earlier (what had happened after that Leo couldn't know) he had been present in Rachel's mind. Until a few minutes ago his wife had still had knowledge of the fact that Leo not only existed somewhere in the universe but that he was on the floor below, reachable by a single flight of stairs or by a phone call on his private line. A few moments earlier Rachel had spoken of him to Luchino. And probably she did it naturally. As if nothing had changed since the last time he spoke to Luchino. Then Leo tried to imagine his wife, enveloped in the casual summer bathrobe, a gift from him, just coming out of the shower, the taste of coffee still in her mouth, answering the telephone that stood on the night table in her room (in their room) on the floor above. Leo did his best to imagine that banal scene. But he couldn't. It's incredible how sometimes certain things that are completely natural can seem extraordinarily inconceivable.

Leo's incredulity wasn't much different from that of an adolescent who, while he's hanging around in the long corridor outside the classrooms during recess, is suddenly greeted by the school beauty, who, besides smiling at him, even has the sublime courtesy to remember his Christian name. That adolescent, at the height of joy and bewilderment, can't stop repeating: so she knows who I am, so she knows I exist, so I'm not a phantom to her.

That is, the same sort of astonished observations with which Leo was now wrestling.

"You don't know, Professor, what a great pleasure it is to talk to you. It's a long time since we've talked. Every year you're busy. Luckily this time I've reached you. Luckily you're back from the holidays, you're not at a conference, you haven't gone out, you weren't kept at the hospital because of an emergency . . . "

Leo wondered if by any chance Luchino was speaking with sarcasm. In which case it would have been a regrettable treachery. If Luchino knew what Leo was going through, what he had gone through in the past year (and how could he not know? who out there didn't know?), then that sarcasm was indeed unbearable: unctuous, gratuitous spite.

"This time you won't escape me, Professor."

"No, this time I'm here, Luchino." Leo's voice expressed a heavy resignation.

"This time in particular I'm pleased that you answered. And do you know why I'm pleased?"

"No, Luchino, I don't."

"Because I have a proposal for you. Something I want to ask you. Something for which if you, Professor, would honor us with your presence it would be a marvelous gift."

"What are you talking about, Luchino?"

"A magnificent idea, Professor. And also extremely original."

"Which is?"

"A prize, Professor."

"A prize?"

"Yes, a prize."

"What sort of prize?"

"A prize for arts and sciences."

"A prize for arts and sciences?"

"Yes, a prize for arts and sciences, Professor. And you know what we would like to call it?"

"When you use the plural, Luchino, to whom do you refer?"

"To me, to my family, to the citizens of the small town where I live. We still have to talk to the mayor, but it's a formality. We're sure he'll be enthusiastic . . . In short, Professor, do you know who we would like to name this prize for?"

"No, Luchino, I don't have the slightest idea. But I can guess. Garibaldi? Padre Pio? Mother Teresa of Calcutta?"

"No, Professor. But for a human being who is in no way inferior to the three you have just named."

"And that is?"

"You, Professor. 'Leo Pontecorvo Prize for Arts and Sciences.'"

This was the infamous absolute limit. Leo had only to determine if Luchino was touching the height of spiteful subtlety or, more banally, the apex of obtuseness. The fate of this phone call seemed to be playing with that dichotomy, and to Leo appeared no less surreal than anything else that had happened to him in recent times. For a moment he even wondered if Luchino's phone call was not the clever product of his own paranoia. The umpteenth trick played on him by the presence, which at that point would have crossed the line. For a second he saw himself from the outside: talking on the telephone with a nonexistent being created by an increasingly fervent persecutory imagination. Maybe this was the last act. The last act of persecution. Because after the tragic there is always the grotesque. After drama, there remains only parody.

"You must understand, professor, that at this point your presence is indispensable. This time you can't say no, you can't retreat. I've thought up a good way to invite you here. We've had the idea of putting up a committee of jurors, and we'd like you to preside over it. A respectable committee made up of judges, journalists, but also men of science like you, Professor. Not to mention that any advice you wish to give us would be welcome. Any."

Yes, perhaps it was all a joke. A committee made up of judges, journalists, and scientists? That couldn't be anything but a joke, a joke designed by a man who had never given evidence of that sort of subtlety.

Or no. Or it wasn't a joke. Maybe Luchino didn't watch the news on TV. Maybe he hadn't watched it during the time when it was running wild with the Pontecorvo affair. And maybe Luchino didn't even read the newspapers. Why should he? He already knew everything he needed to know. Why find out what was happening in the world if the only piece of the universe that interested him was right there, within the radius of his gaze? No, maybe Luchino knew nothing. And maybe his fellow-citizens also knew nothing. It could be that one of them, months ago, had heard something about some pervert doctor, but, in the meantime, he had forgotten the name of the protagonist of the ugly story. So that when Luchino, such an enterprising neighbor, an enthusiast, a true volcano of ideas, had decided to give luster to their lousy little town with a fine prize, and had thought of naming it for the doctor he talked about continuously, his savior, certainly it didn't even cross that fellow's mind that the identity of the eminent professor idolized by Luchino could be the same as that of the pervert doctor.

In short, was he making fun of him or was he speaking seriously? Leo didn't know what to hope. One thing was sure: whether Luchino knew and was making fun of him, or didn't know and was speaking seriously, there was nothing to be happy about. Luchino was depriving Leo of the satisfaction of considering his own story interesting. A crazy story, certainly, but at least emblematic, paradigmatic. The kind of story everyone knew about and no one would forget, a new Dreyfus affair, a new Tortora case. And instead Leo's story, or rather the absurd succession of events that had transformed his life into an unlivable nightmare, was to be considered, at most, a lively slice of life that concerned an individual in whom no one, apart from the people involved, felt any interest.

A news item: that is, the most insignificant thing in the universe. One of those experiences that plenty of people encounter. There was nothing tragic in his story. Nothing epic in his suffering. That's why, if Luchino carried out his project very likely, no one would oppose it. Because Leo's civic unworthiness wasn't famous enough to provoke contempt in anyone. Holy Christ, even the thing on account of which he lived as a recluse, on account of which he had now been fasting for days, and which was now killing him had no importance.

There: the perpetuation of his earthly memory would be entrusted not, certainly, to the posthumous devotion of his offspring but to a flea-bitten prize named in memory of a Signor No One. This really was dramatic. Maybe the most dramatic of all the things that had happened to him. And Leo felt it with such a precise intensity that all he could do, after looking for a few seconds at his wrist and observing that it was as thin and fragile as that of a skeleton, was to hang up on Luchino. And let the telephone ring uninterruptedly for the next two hours, while the rumbling countermelody of an electrical storm—the prelude to a tempest that every living thing outside seemed to invoke—sounded its final useless rounds.

It was Telma who, some years later, recounted to me—in bits and pieces, and not, to tell the truth, without Filipino reticence—what had driven her, that morning at the end of August, to open the forbidden door to the cellar. To violate the kingdom of Professor Pontecorvo.

"It was the water," she told me, "all that water." Probably the result of the summer storm that—heralded all afternoon the day before by violent thunder and lightning—had, around eight in the evening, noisily broken the siege of at least two months of suffocating heat.

There was nothing to be surprised about, really. The drain in the cellar had always caused problems. Especially in November, when it was always raining, the water would sometimes overflow onto the cellar floor. Ever since the Pontecorvos had lived there, ever since the house was built, that floor had been redone or repaired at least a dozen times.

And there, that was why Telma, opening the door of the kitchen that led to the cellar stairs, as she did almost every morning, and seeing all that food floating on a lake a couple of centimeters deep that had formed on the floor of the little hallway in front of the study door, was neither surprised nor particularly disturbed.

That also explains why, faithful to her domestic thoroughness, she had gone down with a bucket and a rag and cleaned up that disgusting mush.

But above all that explains why, after putting the rag back in the bucket and seeing more dirty water flowing sneakily in from under the door, she had finally asked herself why for several days she hadn't heard any noise coming from the secret room.

Telma told me that she was frightened, and she began to knock. First cautiously, then more and more vigorously. Finally she decided to embellish the dry, rhythmic pounding on the door with muted calls: "Sir . . . sir . . . " Nothing. And then: "Professor . . . professor . . . " Of course not: silence and a lakelike smell were all that came from inside.

She didn't feel she could try to enter. She didn't dare. If you think about it, there was nothing to prevent her. She hadn't received orders about it. In all that time no one had said to her, "Telma, you cannot go there"; the signora had never been that explicit about it. Even if that meant nothing, since Signora Rachel never told you to do things. She expected you to do them. That woman must possess a kind of telepathic power, or, so to speak, it was you who, to understand her, must have had it. Telepathy was the tool through which the signora was able to communicate to all the elements of the family (including Telma) what needed to be done and what didn't. And if there was an order that, since the summer before and through the course of the year, although it had never been given, appeared perfectly intelligible to everyone, it was that you weren't to go in there. The cellar was off-limits, enemy territory.

Telma liked to feel that she was one of the family. Although she hadn't worked for the Pontecorvos a very long time, and although she had replaced Carmen (the boys' famous nanny, whom, for some reason, no one ever mentioned), she had been welcomed to that house so naturally. And it wasn't something to take for granted, thought Telma, for a woman—a long way from girlhood—who had been catapulted into Italy without being able to utter a word of Italian and only a few in English; a woman of thirty-seven, not beautiful, too short, neurotically shy, born and brought up in a depressed town in the interior, a hundred kilometers from Manila, which owed its fame and its economy to the exorbitant density of chickens per square kilometer. A town where the women broke their backs in the farmyards and the men got drunk and smoked without stopping. The smell was terrible: the one that Telma had grown up with and so obediently got accustomed to.

How dreadful that smell was she had understood only by comparing it retrospectively with the intoxicating smell by which she was greeted on her arrival in Olgiata. A place that had the fragrance of paradise in every season of the year. In summer star jasmine, dust, chlorine, and newly cut grass. In the autumn, a damp aroma of moss and mushrooms was mixed with the crisp odor of dry leaves; in winter, the toasted odor of blasting furnaces and lighted fireplaces took over. And in spring, well, in spring, it was hard to figure out but so easy to be saturated: jasmine, heliotrope, lavender . . . It was a lovely place to live, to wake in the morning and go to bed in the evening, even if it was far away from everything.

Especially from the square at the other end of the city where, every Sunday, before Mass, a good part of the Filipino population gathered. Poor woman, it took her almost an hour and a quarter, on three buses, to reach that place of meeting. On the other hand, in exchanging opinions with all those fellow-countrymen, companions in work and misfortune, Telma understood how much, all in all, she liked working for the Pontecorvos. It was in talking to her friends and colleagues that Telma understood how deeply fortunate she was.

Of course, the Pontecorvos had plenty of flaws. They were strange, demanding, and they were Jews. She had never even supposed that individuals existed in the world who didn't believe in Christ, who didn't celebrate Christmas or Easter (or at least not the right one). And it wasn't without surprise that every year, during the days of religious observance, Telma helped Rachel prepare the house in the proper manner and cook those special dishes, which were not always appetizing. And yet even that business, Judaism, wasn't a big problem in the Pontecorvo household. Telma had a friend who worked for a family where the wife, a fervent Jew, had forbidden her to hang a crucifix in her own room. Now, never, ever would Signora Rachel take the liberty of such arrogance.

The Pontecorvos were never rude, they never had hysterical crises, they never displayed any excess. They didn't accuse you unjustly of sins you hadn't committed. Which was a stroke of luck. There were crazy people around. Especially the bored ladies, they were really unpredictable. Telma had been told about certain enterprises carried out by those ladies and especially by their children. Scenes, bullying insults . . . But not the Pontecorvo boys. They were polite, almost affectionate. Signora Rachel, that orchestra conductor, had brought them up well. She wouldn't let the boys play ball in the hot hours of early afternoon when Telma went to lie down. She reproached them if they gave her an order brusquely and without adding "thank you" or "please."

Lord, Signora Rachel. Telma adored that woman. At one time she had lent Telma money, a good sum, to send to the Philippines, because the roof of the house where her four good-for-nothing brothers lived had literally been ripped off by a typhoon. Not to mention the time when Jasmine, Telma's reckless young cousin, had been caught stealing from her boss's wallet. Well: not only had Rachel persuaded Jasmine's employer not to press charges, restoring to her, from her own pocket, the stolen money down to the last cent, but she had even let Jasmine move to the Pontecorvo house for a while.

No, Signora Rachel did not in any way resemble the other ladies who every so often visited the Pontecorvo house, or those Telma's friends and cousins worked for. Rachel was not a do-nothing, someone who woke up at ten in the morning with a headache and in a bad mood. When Telma got up she would find her already in the kitchen, sipping her coffee from a glass. She organized. She made a note of the things to do during the day. Rachel would say things like: "I think that today, too, I'll be wearing a taxi-driver's cap." Sibylline phrases whose meaning Telma struggled to guess at. So that she confined herself to smiling, wary of responding or commenting. Finally she relieved the signora from the task of the moment: a plate she was washing, a glass she was drying, a coffeepot she was refilling. Telma replaced her and the signora let her.

The comment on the taxi-driver's cap perhaps alluded to Rachel's day, which would be devoted entirely to ferrying people around the city. She had to take her children to school, pick them up, she had to take them to swimming, to tennis, to the dentist, to the eye doctor; there was the shopping at the market, there was the insurance, the bank, the notary. There were the shoes to take to the shoemaker. She had to go visit the old aunt afflicted by senile dementia, who always took Rachel for a thief and covered her with frightful insults. But, above all, that long pilgrimage through the city was in the service of a husband who, when he came home from work in the evening, had to be surrounded with pleasures. For example, when the professor returned to Rome from a journey, Rachel instructed Telma to make broth and boiled meat, so that he would be refreshed. The professor, further, wanted the sheets and towels to be changed almost every day. The professor, who didn't seem at all a severe man, was quite obsessive about food. At night he wanted to eat well. And if by chance that day the dried meat or the goose salami wasn't flavorful enough, or the tomatoes weren't tasty enough, or if the pasta was burned . . . well, he wouldn't let you know.

That's why in the past year the life of the signora had seemed to Telma so uncentered. Something terrible had happened to that family. Something everyone talked about. Something that Telma preferred to postpone knowing, not picking up the provocations of her informed friends. Something that had revolutionized in an unpredictable way the entire running of the household. One day, the professor had gone and hidden in the cellar. And Telma hadn't understood if he had done it of his own volition, spontaneously, or if he had been forced to. She remembered the time when an epidemic of meningitis had broken out in her town and suddenly the old people and children had disappeared from the streets, all confined to their houses.

A couple of times the police had arrived and searched every-thing, and Telma had been very frightened. One morning, straightening up the signora's room, Telma realized that the pro-fessor's clothes had disappeared. And not only the clothes: every banal reference to his existence had vanished. What had hap-pened? What had the professor done? Telma had trouble believing that that man, so handsome and so kind, who, for some reason, always addressed her in English, that man who dripped authority from all his pores, that man who had a way of life so simple and so elegant, had done something so terrible. Even though Telma was used to minding her own business, even though her Italian wasn't sophisticated enough to allow her to understand all the nuances of the conversations at the table between the mother and children, in spite of all this, by degrees, serving or clearing, she had understood that the professor had been banished not only from the life of his family but also from their conversation. And this had frightened her to death.

And that's why now, as the water continued to flow from under the door, Telma didn't know what to do. She was unde-cided whether to go in, to call the signora, or, as she had done at other times, ignore it. Not deal with it.

Finally she made up her mind. She went to look for some-one. The living room had a desolately bare look. At the begin-ning of summer, every year, it was orphaned of the carpets and curtains that adorned it during the other seasons. It was only a few days until September. After the monstrous storm of the day before, so similar to the ones that raged in her country, the air was refreshed. There were no longer many mosquitoes. Soon the house would be invaded by flies, but for now it was free of insects. And not only of insects. There was no one.

Telma glanced into the garden. The kitchen. The dining room. Then she plucked up courage and went into the sleep-ing area of the house, where the signora's room was, and the children's, and the guest room. If not for the wind that had scattered pages of the newspaper everywhere, the signora's room would have had, as usual, a marmoreal neatness.

Not the same could be said of the adjacent room, belonging to Filippo and Samuel. Telma had opened the door of their room, after knocking for a long time. She was always afraid of finding them naked. When she finally made up her mind to open the door, she was assailed by the usual odor and the usual mess. Filippo and Semi had just returned from a study vacation in England. The signora that year hadn't gone to the sea, she had moved for a few weeks to the house of the old aunt to take care of her. In any case Signora Rachel had arranged it so that her sons wouldn't lose the habit of the study vacation. They had returned the day before, as usual thinner and overexcited. Their suitcases were there, on the floor, carelessly unpacked, full of dirty T-shirts, unmatched socks, shapeless sneakers. There were three wet towels and a bathrobe thrown on a chair. A pile of records presumably bought in England. The condition of the bathroom was no less disastrous. It almost seemed as if the boys had decided that it was better to have a bath outside the tub rather than in it.

Then Telma felt truly desperate. She felt abandoned. She went back to the garden, deciding to call someone, but there was no one. Weeping to herself, she went back down the stairs that led to the cellar. The situation, if possible, had worsened, which led Telma to try again: she had knocked, knocked, knocked, louder and louder. At a certain point she had the sensation that something moved on the other side of the door, but maybe it was only a gust of wind.

Finally, disobeying the ban, pierced by anguish, continuing to call on Jesus as if only he could give her the strength and at the same time forgive her for this violation, she tried to open the door, certain that she would find it locked.

It was open.

The room was a real swamp. The smell must have been that

damp, rotting odor that Telma had come to know in the rice fields of her distant country. The body of the professor was there, on the floor, prone, face and chest sunk in the swamp from which emerged only a skinny spine, similar to that of an alligator in ambush.

Though I'm afraid that last simile should be attributed to me. Not to Telma, who, given the circumstances, found nothing better to do than emit the standard horrified scream that mystery books the whole world over have in abundance.

And while Telma can't stop screaming, I wonder if, now that Leo is no more, the world has not suddenly become a better place. Now that the error has been eliminated. And with it the vice, the corruption, the narcissism, the crime. Not to mention the carelessness, the foolishness, the irresponsible optimism, the irrefutable trust in the benevolence of fate. Well, surely now things will go better.

Yes, I know, I'm being sarcastic. And also tacky and cheap. I'm doing it so that those who should understand will understand. Because it's with you that I'm angry. *Toc, toc,* you hear me? With you: the three stainless and intransigent inhabitants of the floor above. The incorruptible guardians of public morality, who left him down here to rot. It's true, it's true, I agree, Leo took a little too long to die. But now that he has finally done it, well, it's up to you to clean up and pay the bill.

To be continued.

ACKNOWLEDGEMENTS

I would like to thank, above all, Marilena Rossi, for her extraordinary skill and her devotion to the cause.

Thanks to Professor Luca Cordero for the interview he granted me on the subject of pediatric oncology.

Thanks to Giovanna Ichino and Antonello Patanè for their advice on the judicial procedures in effect at the time of the novel's events.

And, finally, thanks to Simone, who provided the logistics for this novel and the next, and Saverio, who followed me step by step.

ABOUT THE AUTHOR

Alessandro Piperno was born in Rome in 1972. His 2005 novel, *The Worst Intentions*, won the Campiello Prize for First Novel and became an instant best-seller in Italy, where *Corriere della Sera* described its author as "a new Marcel Proust." *The New Yorker* wrote that *The Worst Intentions* was a "wickedly scathing début, a coruscating mixture of satire, family epic, Proustian meditation, and erotomaniacal farce." Piperno is the author of two works of nonfiction. *Persecution*, the first installment of a diptych entitled *The Friendly Fire of Memories*, is his long-awaited second novel.